I0574241

THE
ERROL FLYNN
CONSPIRACY

A NOVEL BY

DAVID PHILIPS

Black Rose Writing | Texas

ISBN: 978-1-68513-166-1
PUBLISHED BY BLACK ROSE WRITING
www.blackrosewriting.com

Printed in the United States of America
Suggested Retail Price (SRP) $22.95

The Errol Flynn Conspiracy is printed in EB Garamond

*As a planet-friendly publisher, Black Rose Writing does its best to eliminate unnecessary waste to reduce paper usage and energy costs, while never compromising the reading experience. As a result, the final word count vs. page count may not meet common expectations.

To Kirsten.
For all your continuing encouragement, support, and editing skills.

ACKNOWLEDGEMENTS

As all authors know, writing is a solitary occupation, our spells of seclusion broken only by the necessity to wash, eat, perform our bodily functions, and occasionally sleep. Our desire for other human contact comes secondary to our need to commit to paper those thoughts and ideas with which our imagination furnishes us.

Having written the above, however, most writers still need the approbation and help of our fellow scribes to convince us either that we are on the right track, and are bound for literary stardom, or, perhaps more often than not, to politely and delicately suggest that maybe we might want to find other means to augment our finances.

In this respect, my grateful thanks go to Kirsten Schuder of Apex Literary Management, and my A.L.M. writing buddies, Al Stoffel and Mark McQuown for their most helpful suggestions, remarks and continuing support, and for making this work infinitely better than it otherwise might have been.

I am also indebted to Johanna Hinkel of the Consulate General's Office of the Federal German Republic, Los Angeles, and Leah Taber from the U.S. Patent and Trademark Office, Virginia, for their invaluable assistance in providing me with the addresses for their particular offices during the period when this novel is set.

THE ERROL FLYNN
CONSPIRACY

INTRODUCTION

The film star Hedy Lamarr enjoyed a long career as a glamorous Hollywood actress, making over twenty-five movies during her time in California. Even before Hedy arrived in the United States from Europe 1938, she was infamous for her sex scene in the Czech picture *Extase*. Her final appearance was in *The Female Animal* which she made twenty years later. What is less well-known was her incredible intellect. When Hedy was not acting, she spent much of her time improving existing devices, as well as inventing new appliances. She developed her most famous invention during World War Two when, along with avant-garde composer George Antheil, Hedy devised an instrument which thwarted the Axis' ability to jam the Allied forces' signals to their radio-guided torpedoes. It is thanks to her and Antheil's pioneering work with radio frequency technology that we can all enjoy the convenience of mobile phones and internet communication. However, despite its obvious advantages, the U.S. Department of the Navy rejected this equipment, thus possibly lengthening the conflict by several months, if not longer.

Another celebrity who found fame in Hollywood at the same time as Miss Lamarr was the Australian actor, Errol Flynn, who was born in Tasmania in 1909. He arrived in Hollywood in 1934, and was known for his heroic and swashbuckling roles in such films as *The Adventures of Robin Hood* and *The Sea Hawk*. Despite portraying patriotic characters in many of his later movies, what was less evident at the time were the actor's anti-British and pro-Nazi sympathies. He was involved with an Austrian doctor named Hermann Erben, who was a Nazi agent and was reputed to be closely associated with Flynn.

Did Flynn and Erben have any part in the U.S. Navy's refusal to adopt the inventors' equipment? If so, how could they have influenced such an important decision? Did Hedy Lamarr and George Antheil know of Flynn's possible duplicity, and if Flynn and Erben were, indeed, responsible for this determination, why were neither never exposed?

Errol Flynn passed away in 1959 at the age of fifty, ostensibly from his hard-drinking and hedonistic lifestyle. Did he die naturally, however, or were more subtle influences at work in hastening his premature demise...?

CHAPTER 1

Northampton, Northants., and Teddington, Richmond, England
June 1934

His voice reverberated over the almost empty theater, its owner not caring who could hear it. "I don't give a flying fuck what you want, my dear; that is not how this scene should be played. If you were actually a director instead of some jumped-up stage-hand, you would understand this. If I stand to the character's left, half the audience won't see who I'm talking to. He could make obscene faces at me, and they would never know! I need to stand exactly where I am standing now, so the people who have paid their good, hard-earned money to watch this drivel can see his expression. That is, if he can show any emotion. The last time I acted with anyone as wooden as him, the idiot was playing *Pinocchio!*"

"But, Errol..."

"Don't you dare address me by my first name, you stupid cow. You haven't earned the right to wipe the snot off my handkerchief," he screamed at her, "let alone become so familiar as to call me Errol. When I want you to use my Christian name, I'll tell you, but it won't be anytime soon. Now, can we please get back to work, or am I going to stand rooted in this bloody spot until the floorboards rot?"

The young director stormed off-stage, tears cascading down her rouged cheeks. She had bought a new dress and stockings for this very occasion, hoping that she would make a good impression on the handsome

Australian actor. He might even find her pretty enough to ask her out after rehearsals. And now this; the screaming was terrible enough, taunting her as if she were an intransigent schoolgirl. However, it was the humiliation, being upbraided in front of the rest of the crew, that forced her to flee.

Acknowledging that he might have gone too far, the actor quickly followed her, intending somehow to mollify her, to entice her to return to trying to direct him. He would ease up on her, he decided. After all, she was only about the same age as him, with little experience in the world of the theater. He caught up with her at the top of the stairs, swinging her around by her shoulders, intending to plant a kiss on her cheeks by way of an apology.

As she turned, she lashed out at him, assuming he was going to continue ranting at her. Surprised by her actions, he pushed her away, inadvertently thrusting her down the steps. The sight of her tumbling down the wooden boards was awful enough, but it was the sounds of her body coming into contact with each tread as she fell that caused him to wince in empathetic pain.

He rushed down after her, knowing that he would not reach her before she hit the bottom rung. It was excruciating to watch her damaged body as she lay writhing and moaning. He kneeled beside her, cradling her head in his arms.

"I'm so sorry," he cried. "It was an accident. I never meant..."

Through her pain, she looked up at this tall, handsome, athletic and broad-shouldered Australian with his blond hair and jaunty mustache. Incredibly, she was trying to smile. "Such a beautiful man. What a shame you're such a bastard, too."

An inquiry was held into the incident in the office of the theater management. Flynn was summoned to appear along with the young director he had mistreated. "Look, I've already explained a thousand times," Flynn exclaimed. "It was a bloody accident. Ask her yourself, she'll tell you. Yes, I suppose I wasn't as nice to her as I should have been, and I was frustrated at her lack of experience. I admit that, but did I mean to push her down a flight of wooden steps? Of course not! Surely you must see that."

Dabbing at her red-rimmed eyes with a lace handkerchief, the victim nodded in support of the young actor. Sobbing in between breaths, she confirmed Flynn's contention. "If anything, it was my fault for pushing him away. I thought... I thought he was going to attack me again. I now realize he was trying to make it up with me, but at the time..."

"Yes, yes, quite," retorted the manager. "Be that as it may, this is a small provincial town, and word soon gets around. How would it look if we did not discipline the actor who caused the accident, as unintentional as it was? It would not look good for the theater or, may I say, for the repertory company that employs Mr. Flynn. We rely on our patrons' goodwill, and justice must not only be done, but it must also be seen to be done, to quote the Lord Chief Justice of England. I'm afraid we have no choice but to ask the repertory company to terminate Mr. Flynn's employment."

Flynn shot to his feet. "That's not fair. This is a bloody outrage. I've already apologized, and even she," he shouted, pointing to the injured director, "has acknowledged it was just a horrible accident. What am I supposed to do? You're leaving me without an income. How am I supposed to survive?"

"You'll be paid a months' wages in lieu. That should give you time to find some other acting position. Or any other job."

Flynn shook his head. "You fucking bastards. I hope you all rot. And as for you," he said, turning to the director of Northampton Rep, "You're nothing but a bloody coward. Why did you not stick up for me? After all I've done, and now this. What a bloody stab in the back. Just like Brutus betrayed Julius Caesar, and he was done to death in a theater as well, if my memory serves me correctly. How fucking appropriate." The repertory director at least had the good grace to cast his eyes down in embarrassment.

"Please, don't sack Mr. Flynn," the young director cried. "I... I don't want you to, and it was me he hurt. Please give him another chance."

"I'm sorry, my dear, our decision is final. This is not the first time he has been rude and abusive to the other cast members and the crew. He has already been warned about his conduct, a caution he seems not to have taken with the gravity he should have. Mr. Flynn must leave this theater and not return."

***

Flynn arrived in London a few days later, having made his way south from Northampton via Bedford, Luton and St. Albans. He had worked for Irving Asher, the movie producer, at Warner Brothers Studios in Teddington for a short while, as an extra in Asher's movie *I Adore You*, before joining the Northampton theater company. Perhaps Asher might use him again. There was only one way to find out.

He found a small hotel near the studios, and after settling into his temporary accommodation, the actor telephoned Asher. The producer was on-set when Flynn called, and the receptionist told him to try later. Finally, around six o'clock in the evening, he caught up with the studio executive. "Hello, Mr. Asher, it's Errol, Errol Flynn." The actor always wondered why he bothered to extend his greeting to include his surname. How many 'Errols' would Asher know?

"Hello, Errol," Asher replied, tiredness evident in his response. "What can I do for you?" As if he didn't know!

"I'm visiting London for a little while, and I was wondering if you might have anything coming up that you could use me for."

"What are you doing at the moment?"

"Nothing much. I've just finished a stint at the Royal Theater in Northampton."

"Yes, I heard all about it." the producer answered in his American West Coast accent. So, word had gotten around. It wasn't looking good for him. His reputation was tarnished enough without this latest episode hanging over him. Asher's next remarks, however, gave Flynn cause for hope. "Well, it so happens that I'm looking into a new project at the moment, and funnily enough, I thought of you. Are you interested?"

"You haven't told me what it is yet."

"No, I haven't." Then the line went dead.

CHAPTER 2

Vienna, Austria
May 1933

Spring rain lashed the cobbled streets of Vienna's ancient city, causing anyone who did not have to be out to stay indoors. Those poor souls who had no choice but to brave the elements found that even their most robust rainwear did not keep out the driving downpour. On such occasions, the man wished he smoked; anything to stave off the biting cold that the rain brought with it. He was in his late-thirties, above average height at just under six feet, clean-shaven, with a shock of black, wavy hair. He had dark, deep-set eyes, with bushy brows, which, although giving him a vaguely sinister appearance, belied a kind nature and quirky sense of humor.

It had been well over an hour that he had been standing in the shop doorway. His outer clothes, even his underwear, were now wet through. The store's clients and proprietor thought he was merely sheltering from the storm, but his purpose in holding his stance for such a long time was more than just to avoid the deluge. He couldn't even remember it being as bad as this in his home city of New York. It was as though the inclement weather was carrying out a singular vendetta, cascading down on him alone, punishing him for invading its beautiful city. The rain turned everything a misty, foggy gray as if almost daring the sun to come out.

Then, in his sodden despair, he saw her; at least, he was sure it was her. How many other beautiful eighteen-year-old girls would dare to be out on

5

a day like this? If his information were accurate, she would be making her way to the *Theatre an der Wien*. She was appearing in the title role of *Sissi*, based on the life of the nineteenth-century aristocrat, Empress Elisabeth of Austria. Running from the shop entrance's scant protection, his shoes splashed on the sidewalk beneath him as he approached her from behind. A few steps away, he shouted, *"Fraulein Kiesler, Fraulein Hedwig Kiesler."*

Instinctively, his quarry turned around to see who was hailing her. Her look of curiosity turned to one of alarm as she saw her pursuer holding something out in front of him. She gave a relieved smile when she saw it was only an umbrella.

"We can't have you going into the theater looking like a drowned rat, can we?" The man quickly erected the rain protector, holding it over the young actress's bare head.

She regarded him quizzically. "I'm sorry, do I know you?"

"Pralgovitch, Isidor Pralgovitch, *Fraulein* Kiesler. Please don't be alarmed; I mean you no harm. I saw you perform a couple of nights ago. I just wanted to express my admiration for your exceptional acting talents. You portray the part almost perfectly. If I didn't know any better, I would think I was watching the real Empress Elisabeth herself. It was uncanny how you managed to attain the character just right; the captured bird in the gilded cage. I could feel the whole audience crying out in empathy."

"You are American, *Herr*... Pralgovitch?"

"Yes, from New York; the Bronx."

"How exciting," she sighed. "Is New York far from Hollywood? That is my ambition. To act in Hollywood movies. I suspect, however, I may have to wait a little while to achieve my dreams."

"It's the other side of the country, nearly three thousand miles; I guess that's close to about four-and-a-half thousand kilometers."

"Oh my, so far away. I did not realize how big your country was."

"Yes, it's kind of vast, I suppose. I meant what I said, *Fraulein* Kiesler. I think you are a very talented actress. Talented and beautiful."

"That's very kind of you, *Herr*... Pralgovitch, but I must..."

"Doctor. It's Doctor Pralgovitch, *Fraulein* Kiesler."

"You're a doctor?"

"Why? Is something wrong with you?"

"No, not at all. It's just that I've never been accosted in the street by a doctor before. If you're trying to drum up business, I'm afraid you've stopped the wrong person. I am very healthy." the actress confirmed.

"I'm pleased to hear it, I'm sure. No, I did not approach you because I thought you looked ill, but I would like to have a few words with you, if you don't mind."

Hedwig stared at the handsome doctor. "I'm sorry, Doctor Pralgovitch, but I'm in a hurry. Maybe we can chat some other time. Perhaps…"

Pralgovitch cut across her, "I know you have to get to the theater, *Fraulein* Kiesler, but this won't take long, and it is a matter of some importance. Please. I will make sure that you are not late for your performance; in fact, I will escort you there myself. We cannot possibly keep your adoring public waiting," he smiled.

Hedwig wasn't sure if he uttered this last statement with irony or sincerity, but she opted for the latter by the look on his face. Looking at her wristwatch, she sighed resignedly. "Very well, Doctor. You seem so wet; wet, and sincere. Have you been waiting long for me to pass by?"

"I would have waited a great deal longer if I had to."

The young actress returned his smile. "I can spare you half-an-hour, no longer," she warned him.

"There's a nice café just a few streets away, and it's also on the way to the theater."

"Well, you were kind enough to offer me your umbrella, and you did say such nice things about my performance…." Linking her arm through his, she let him guide her towards the little restaurant. He would answer no more of her questions until they were out of the rain. What he had to say to her would be best discussed in a more relaxed atmosphere.

He led her to a quiet table where they ordered coffee. Now she was seated and out of the rain, he could properly take stock of the young girl sitting across from him. Small-to-average height, she was even prettier than she looked from the photograph of her he had been given. She had a small, elfin-like face with an upturned nose and an enquiring gaze, her raven-black hair cascading over her slim shoulders and resting freely around her shoulder blades. She declined his offer of a pastry, insisting that she needed to maintain her figure for her part.

Once the waitress had left, she asked, "Well, Doctor, to what do I owe the pleasure of your company on this dreadful day?"

Pralgovitch had rehearsed this meeting so often in his head. Now, in her presence, all he could think about was how he would ask her to do something that she would find abhorrent. He doubted if she would even wait for the coffee to arrive before storming out in anger. Exhaling, trying to clear his mind, he began hesitantly, "I understand you have been visited in your dressing-room by someone... a man."

"Many men seek my company, Doctor, and you wished to avoid the queue, so you importuned me in the street? I'm not sure whether to think that courteous or just highly impatient, if not improper."

"No, you misunderstand. I am not here for myself."

"Oh," she said, almost disappointedly. "I'm afraid I..."

"That's not to say that I would not like..." he stopped in mid-sentence, afraid of where his next words were going. Fingering his coffee cup, he continued, "I believe you are acquainted with a man by the name of Mandl, Friedrich Mandl."

"Yes," she replied. "he has been to see me in my dressing-room a few times and has showered me with bouquets of roses. He has even taken the liberty of coming to my home, my parents' home." she quickly corrected herself. "Quite frankly, I find his attentions unwarranted and tiresome. He has also said things I would rather not repeat. The man seems to think that because he is wealthy, he can speak to a mere actress however he pleases. I..." She stopped abruptly as an awkward realization dawned on her. "Oh, my goodness, he did not send you to...."

"No, *Fraulein* Kiesler, he did not. I have never met with *Herr* Mandl, nor do I ever expect to. In fact, it is probably best that we are never in each other's company."

"I'm afraid I don't understand, Doctor. Then why are you so interested in this frightful man and his unwanted advances toward me?"

"That is rather a long story, one which may take more time to explain than I had imagined."

"This is very curious, Doctor. You waylay me in the street, offer your umbrella like a gallant gentleman, and invite me to take coffee with you. Then bring up the name of someone I find quite repellent, but do not disclose your reason for mentioning him. I think that our meeting was not effected by chance. Would I be correct in that assumption?"

Isidor bowed his head. "This conversation has not gone the way I intended it to, and I apologize for any distress I might have caused you, *Fraulein*."

"It seems that you have caused more distress to yourself than you have to me, Isidor; I may call you Isidor?" The doctor nodded. This discussion was becoming far more difficult than he had anticipated. But she did ask him if she could address him by his first name. That was surely progress of a sort. She glanced at her watch. "I'm sorry, Doctor, I really have to go, or I will be late."

Hedy rose to leave, and he also got to his feet. "I promised you I would walk with you to the theater. Please let me pay the bill, and then I will gladly keep my word."

"On one condition."

"Don't worry. I promise I will not mention *Herr* Mandl's name again," he answered, anticipating her demand.

It took only a few minutes for them to arrive at the stage door. The rain had finally stopped, and Hedwig offered to return Isidor's umbrella. "No, keep it. It will give me an excuse to see you again, that is, if you would like to."

"As I told you earlier, many men want to be in my company. Why should I make an exception for you, Doctor?"

Isidor could think of no good reason she might single him out for preferential treatment. Clutching at his memory as a drowning man might grasp at a piece of driftwood, he stammered, "Well, you did ask if you could call me 'Isidor.' Have you ever asked Mandl the same question?"

Hedwig did not answer directly. "I usually finish by around eleven o'clock. I will instruct the doorman to permit you to come to my dressing-room—Isidor."

So, he would get a second chance. It was more than he could have expected, but he had to get it right the next time. There would be no third opportunity.

CHAPTER 3

Teddington and London, England – California, U.S.A.
December 1934–June 1935

Flynn had just finished making the motion picture *Murder at Monte Carlo* for Irving Asher. He had not proved so temperamental in this role. The actor realized that it would do his movie career no good by arguing with his fellow players, especially those who could make or break his acting ambitions. Asher had been so impressed by the young Australian that he called his studios in Hollywood, insisting that they put Flynn on contract.

The Tasmanian had become an ardent admirer of Adolf Hitler, mainly due to his antagonism towards the Jews for whom the actor had little regard. With the turmoil going on in Europe, Flynn was convinced that Britain would shortly be at war with Germany. He had listened to a radio broadcast a few weeks earlier, and if his instincts were correct, German bombs could soon be falling on British cities. The safest bet for the fledgling actor was to accept Asher's offer and move to the American west coast, the burgeoning magnet for all would-be film actors: Hollywood.

Two weeks before he sailed to the United States, a seemingly chance encounter occurred in London between Flynn and an Austrian national named Hermann Erben. Erben was a doctor who also spied for Germany and, like Flynn, was a virulent anti-Semite. He was in his late thirties, bespectacled, of medium height with a stocky build and a mass of brown-black hair. The two men had known each other sometime earlier when they traveled together, panning for gold in the South Pacific. It was a fruitless exercise for both men, neither seeing much return for their investment.

Flynn was dining alone in a restaurant just off Trafalgar Square. It was early evening, and the cafeteria had not yet filled up. His was still an unknown face in the acting industry, and most of his fellow diners did not recognize him. The waitress had just brought his meal when a familiar voice assailed him. The actor's back was facing the restaurant door, so he did not see his old friend as he came in.

"No, it can't be; it simply cannot be!" he heard the voice say. Flynn only knew one person with an accent like that. He froze as he was putting his fork to his mouth. "Even from behind, there is no mistaking the broad shoulders and the girth. My dear friend, how are you?"

The actor must have seemed quite a sight to Erben as he turned to face him with his fork still poised halfway to his face. "It is unusual to see you with an item of cutlery up against your mouth rather than a lady's lips. How long has it been?" the Austrian asked. "Why, it must be almost two years!" Flynn found his tongue and replied tartly, "Two years, three months, and five days. Not that I'm counting. How did you find me?"

"Find you? I didn't 'find' you at all. To find you would suggest that I was looking for you in the first place. No, I was strolling past and happened to glance in the window. I saw the outline of a form I thought I recognized and decided to follow my hunch. And there you have it. Pure happenstance, nothing more," Erben laughed. "Are you not going to ask me to join you? Surely you cannot be happy dining alone."

Flynn was quite content to eat by himself, but courtesy and etiquette forbade him to admit this. Reluctantly, he gestured with his fork for his former friend to sit across the table from him. "What are you doing in London? I thought you were in...." Flynn hesitated, realizing he did not know Erben's recent whereabouts. "Where have you been?"

The Austrian tapped his forefinger to the side of his nose. "Oh, here and there, you know, around and about."

Flynn knew Erben. The Nazi always tried to make himself out to be more inscrutable and enigmatic than he really was. He was giving the actor the impression that he was deliberately evasive to mask some hidden ulterior deception, but Flynn knew better. Despite his occasional forays into the world of espionage, the man was a nonentity trying to dress himself up as an 'international man of mystery.' But Erben's words belied his intentions. Flynn did not believe that this was a meeting of coincidence. He did not think for one second that the Austrian 'just happened to be passing.' That would take luck to a new level, which Flynn refused to accept. There had to be a reason for Erben's approach. The Tasmanian wondered what it was. He was about to find out.

"I understand congratulations are in order." Erben spoke. Flynn said nothing, but regarded his unwanted dining companion cautiously. The Austrian continued, "I heard you had landed a contract with Warner Brothers in Hollywood. You must be a better actor than I imagined."

Flynn sighed. He would not rise to the bait of Erben's insult. Why didn't the man just get to the point and leave to allow the actor to finish his meal in peace?

"I don't envy you, you know. Not that I would ever consider a career in acting myself, you understand. I don't think I would have the patience to learn all those lines, turn this way or that at the director's whim, have to show and endure artificial affection from women who do not interest me. I think that is where you and I differ, Errol. I need to have an honest affection for any lady I seek to romance. You, on the other hand..."

At that point, a waitress passed their table. To Flynn's chagrin, Erben stopped her and ordered a pot of tea. Flynn groaned inwardly. This man was becoming exceedingly tiresome. Erben continued, "The main reason I could not be an actor is that I would have to associate with all those Jews. Hollywood is overrun with them, don't you know?"

Flynn did know but was far more pragmatic than his unwanted guest. Despite his strong aversion to Jews, he recognized the influence and power wielded by all the studio heads, producers, directors, and many others from the Hebrew faith. He responded to Erben by declaring, "Well, you know what they say; 'if you sleep with dogs, you wake up with fleas.' But these dogs are very wealthy, and I want some of their *Judengelt*."

Erben laughed as he looked appreciatively at his host. "It seems some of my sympathies must have, how do you Irish put it, 'rubbed off' on you."

Flynn gave Erben a look of contempt. "How many times must I tell you? I am Tasmanian, not Irish. If you insist on labeling me as an Irishman, I will call you a Frenchman, and I cannot think of a worse insult than that. Do I make myself clear?"

"Very clear," the Nazi responded, chastened.

"And to answer your earlier point, no, Hermann, your sympathies have not 'rubbed off' on me. I don't need you, or anyone else for that matter, to tell me how and what to think. My opinions are my own; no one else's. Now," he continued with some asperity, "let's stop playing games. You no more bumped into me by accident than I would put a *mezuzah* on my doorpost. Why are you here? What do you want from me?"

"Excellent, Errol. Straight to the point. I like that. Very *Teutonic*." Erben smiled. "As I mentioned, I know you will shortly be sailing for the United States, courtesy of that Jew, Irving Asher. Once you are there, you will be under contract to Warner Brothers; a Jewish-owned studio. Is there not a certain whiff of hypocrisy about this?" Before Flynn could respond, Erben waved his hand. "It is of no importance. You may be as duplicitous to these people as you like. I care nothing for them. That is the very reason for my imposing on you, as I have done. You are quite correct, of course. Our meeting was not a haphazard one. Let me get to the point."

At last, thought Flynn. As the Austrian was about to continue, the waitress returned to their table with his beverage. After pouring himself a cup of tea, Erben went on, "There are many of us on both sides of the Atlantic who are concerned by the disproportional Jewish influence in American life and its commerce. Some Jews are now even getting into the American military. In our opinion, this perfidious infiltration has to stop before the world is overrun with these *Yids*. We are looking for like-minded people who might help us diminish their insidious domination of such institutions. Does this prospect appeal to you? Do you think you would like to help us?"

"And who, exactly, is this 'us' you keep referring to?"

Erben shook his head slowly. "My dear Errol, the less you know, the better. Suffice it to say that you would have the thanks of some of the most powerful men in Europe if you decide to assist us. These people could greatly benefit you should you wish to pursue a career outside the make-believe or when you finally decide that taking *Judengelt* is more than you can stomach. What do you say? Will you join us?"

"What exactly do you want me to do?"

"Nothing too onerous, I assure you."

"That doesn't answer my question."

Erben smiled. "First, let's get you settled in your new home. Once you've got your feet under the table, so to speak, and have established yourself, someone will contact you and let you know what we want from you." Erben drained the last dregs of his tea, patting Flynn's arm as he rose to leave. "Bon voyage, Errol. Try not to seduce too many women on the journey over. Oh, and by the way, if you must indulge yourself, make sure that their age is at least into double digits." He said, knowing Flynn's propensity for young girls.

Flynn could not think of a suitable retort and could only watch in silence as the Austrian swaggered out of the restaurant as if he owned the place. It never ceased to amaze the actor how an insignificant individual like Erben could have such a huge ego. Maybe it was his supposed proximity to those who had real influence that caused some of their arrogance to rub off on him. As for Erben's suggestion that he should subvert Jewish enterprises; as much as he felt no affinity towards the 'Isaacs,' did he want to bite the hand that fed him? He would have to give this notion some considerable thought.

***

Flynn sailed to the United States on the *S.S. Paris*. While he was on board, he met a young French-American woman called Lili Damita, whose real name was Liliane Carre. Lili Damita was an actress who had started her career in the silent era. She had a sultry complexion and had just finished filming *Brewster's Millions* in the U.K. before returning to Hollywood to appear in the western, *The Frisco Kid* with James Cagney. She had been married for a short while to the Hungarian-born director Michael Curtiz. Although Flynn's senior by eight years, the couple were instantly attracted to each other. For the first time in his life, he was the one being seduced and not the other way around.

Before the ship had left British coastal waters, he found himself in her cabin, with her adroitly undoing the buttons of his pants while shoving him gently onto the bed. Almost without him realizing it, she had undressed him, caressing his face with her moist lips and her tongue while expertly exploring and arousing him with her fingertips. She worked her way slowly down his body, her face coming ever tantalizingly closer to his enlarged manhood. Just as he thought she was about to engulf his organ with her mouth, she pulled away. She was teasing him, raising her head to nibble at his pubic hairs before lowering her face once more and biting him playfully on his inner thigh. Again, she angled her mouth close to his groin, her tongue darting quickly onto his hardness before removing it to continue her foreplay. It was clear that she enjoyed sex as much as he did. He tried to turn his body around to reciprocate the pleasure she was giving him, but she held him pinned on his back. Keeping one hand on Flynn's manhood, she lifted the hem of her dress with the other, undoing her stocking suspenders before pulling down her underwear. She then climbed up his body before straddling him, but keeping her mound just out of reach of his erection.

Flynn was now uncontrollable with lust, writhing spasmodically on the bed. Finally, the actor could endure his carnal torment no longer. He grabbed her around the waist and hoisted her onto him, entering her almost without being aware of his actions. Lili undulated in time to Flynn's movements, but the actor was too far gone in his sexual excitement to wait for her. He climaxed quickly, spent beyond salvage. She was content to satisfy him for now, aware that this would not be a onetime-only interlude. He owed her an orgasm. They would be at sea for six days, and she would have plenty of time to call in his debt before the journey was over.

The trip across the Atlantic passed in idyllic bliss for both of them. By the time they landed in New York, each knew that neither wanted the affair to end. They arrived in California by way of Yuma, Arizona, where they got married. Reaching Los Angeles, they made their way to Hollywood, where she would start rehearsals for her latest role, and he presented himself at Warner Brothers, the find of Irving Asher, and ready to begin his film career in earnest.

Their relationship had gotten off to a fairy-tale, if exhausting start, but it was time to get into the film business for real. After all, he was now in a foreign country with a living to earn.

CHAPTER 4

Vienna, Austria
May 1933

He had not expected her to be so mature for her years but for all her adult-like persona, there was a certain degree of youthfulness about her. Isidor was old enough to be her father, but this did not stop him from having feelings for her, emotions that he had no right to entertain. This was not supposed to happen. He was in Vienna for one singular purpose, and that was to persuade a young, not-so-impressionable girl to marry a man almost as old as he, Isidor, was himself. A man who already had one disastrous relationship behind him that had ended almost before the ink was dry on the marriage certificate.

No matter his own desires, he had to take himself out of the equation. If their plans bore fruit, the young lady would be in an extraordinary position. He knew his task would be next to impossible, especially now he had met her and realized how headstrong she was and how much she despised this man. But these were extraordinary times, and the dangers were mounting. She had replied favorably to his letter and agreed to meet him after her evening performance three days hence. It was good that she had preferred to see him sooner rather than later. Time was of the essence, not least because his funds were running low, and he was afraid that he might run out of money before he had the chance to achieve his objective. He could have borrowed some funds from the local Jewish agency, but his plans were to be kept secret, known only to the men in the house on Rothschild Boulevard. The fewer people who knew the real reason for his presence in the city, the better.

As he arrived at the stage door, a smartly dressed man brushed past him, seemingly oblivious to his presence. The man was attired in a black formal evening jacket and matching pants, his shirt cuffs shot with diamond cufflinks, and he was wearing an expensive silk cravat, fastened tightly at the neck with an emerald pin. His expensive black patent shoes were highly glossed. The elegantly dressed man was well-built and of average height. He had an angular face with a jutting jaw and a prominent nose. Despite his face being creased in a troubled frown, he would have been considered handsome by women. He did not seem in the best of humor and barely acknowledged the doctor as he stormed by him.

Isidor entered her dressing room as she was finishing getting changed into her street clothes, and if anything, she looked even prettier than she had at their first encounter. He was almost lost for words as he mumbled some embarrassed greeting. Replying airily, she said, "You've just missed him."

"Missed him? missed who?"

"Fritz. Fritz Mandl. You must have passed each other. He's only just left."

"Yes, someone did rush past me just now. So that was Friedrich Mandl?"

"Good looking, isn't he?"

"I...I didn't notice," Pralgovitch stammered.

"Oh, don't worry," she teased him. "You're far nicer than he is. To tell you the truth, I find him quite obnoxious. He keeps asking me to step out with him, but I have no wish to do so. Despite making my feelings plain, he keeps persevering. He seems to think his wealth can buy him anything, even me. Maybe that's what makes him such a successful businessman, don't you think?"

The doctor sighed inwardly. This was not going to be easy; in fact, after the revelations she had just confessed, he wondered if he should even try.

He forced himself to smile, hoping it would appear natural and relaxed. "Where would you like to go?" he asked the young actress.

"I'm absolutely famished. There's a restaurant around the corner that caters for us stage folk and stays open later. Perhaps we could go there. I just hope *Herr* Mandl has not had the same idea."

The restaurant was packed with her fellow actors and theater-goers, who also felt like a late-night meal. Fortunately, a couple was just vacating a table, and Isidor quickly strode over to claim it before it could be taken. "They do a wonderful baked fish," she said. "I understand the proprietor has his own special arrangement with a local wholesaler who gets the fish fresh every day. He once told me that the sea bass is flown in especially overnight from Marseilles in the South of France."

"That's nice," he said distractedly. He hadn't really been paying attention to her, trying to formulate his opening gambit in his mind. The attendant came over, and Isidor allowed his companion to order for both of them. Once she had left, he looked at her, holding her attention with his eyes. "*Fraulein* Kiesler, I..."

"*Hedwig*, my name is *Hedwig*, but I would prefer if you called me *Hedy*. I think we know each other well enough by now to forego the formalities."

"Very well, *Hedy*, I need you to listen to me very carefully..."

"Oh dear, when someone says something like that, it means they are going to announce something awful. Are you going to tell me something dreadful? Are you married?"

Despite himself, Isidor smiled. "No, Hedy, I'm not married. I don't even have a girlfriend."

"Would you like to have a girlfriend?" she asked coyly. Once again, the conversation was slipping out of his control.

"Yes... no... I mean... I...," he stuttered, and he could feel himself reddening from the neck up. She may have been half his age, but she had certainly found a knack to get under his skin in more ways than one. "Please," he begged her, "I must speak with you about something vitally important. It concerns... it concerns *Herr* Mandl."

"You promised you would not mention that foul man again," she pouted.

"I know, and I am sorry that I have broken my word, but hear me out, please."

She regarded him impatiently. "What about him?"

"What do you know about him?"

She took a few seconds to consider his unusual question. "Well, he runs some sort of business and is very wealthy. I believe I said as much to you earlier."

"Yes, you did. Can you think of anything else, for example, what kind of business he controls?"

She grimaced, trying to recall what else she could tell her inquisitor. "I believe he runs a munitions factory, but that's all I know, oh, and that he is very determined to get his own way, and gets angry when he does not, although he tries very hard to hide that side of his nature from me. He is not as good an actor as I, and I can see through his veneer of respectability. What else can I say?"

"I think you've told me enough."

"You sound as if you already know all this. Am I correct?" He hesitated for a second or two before confirming her suspicions. "Yes, I did."

"Then why...?" Before he could reply, the waitress brought their supper. She had ordered the baked fish for them both. After they were again alone, he said, "*Fraulein* Kiesler, Hedy, I am going to ask you another question which you may think is very forward of me, but I need to ask it all the same."

This time, it was the young girl's turn to blush. She smiled shyly, expecting the obvious inquiry. Signaling him to continue, he began, "Do you... do you think you might be able to... ah... to change your feelings about *Herr* Mandl? I mean, surely he cannot be as bad as you make him out to be."

Hedy struggled to regain her composure, flustered by Isidor's unexpected outburst. "I find your questioning very impertinent. I have already expressed my opinion about that gentleman, and I use that term in its broadest possible sense. That should be the end of the matter. Are you quite positive he did not ask you to intercede on his behalf?"

"Yes, Hedy; as I have already explained, I do not know Friedrich Mandl, nor have I ever met him, but he may hold the key to something incredibly important, and you may be just the person to prise that key from him."

"I am not sure what you mean, nor do I like the way this conversation is being directed. Doctor Pralgovitch, what is this all about, and please do not treat me like a child?"

Isidor closed his eyes briefly before opening them again, to concentrate his thoughts. *"Fraulein* Kiesler, you were quite correct when you stated that *Herr* Mandl was in charge of an armaments factory. It belonged to his father, who has handed over the day-to-day running of the company to his son."

"And what has any of this got to do with me?"

"Please let me finish. As I said, the firm is now being run by Alexander Mandl's son. *Herr* Mandl sells these weapons to many customers. He does not care how these weapons are to be used, nor does he wish to know. All that matters to him are the profits he makes from his clients."

"Are you a pacifist, Isidor?" So, it was back to 'Isidor' again.

"No, Hedy, I do not have the luxury of being a pacifist. Please do not misunderstand me," he added quickly. "I would like nothing more than to see the prophecy foretold in the bible, the Old Testament, I believe, about beating swords into plowshares, and spears into pruning hooks coming true. Regretfully, however, I think that time is still some way off."

"Then what...?"

"If you let me continue without further interruption, I will explain." He was now becoming irritated by her, but trying to keep his impatience in check. "We know that Mandl sells his 'equipment' to regimes that do not care as much for the rights of their citizens as other, more enlightened nations."

"Like the United States, you mean?"

"Well, yes, like my own country."

"And does your government not also use weapons in its police forces and its armed services?"

He was now becoming exasperated by her seeming unwillingness to allow him to get to the point he was trying so hard to reach. "Yes, but we only use our arms when it is absolutely necessary, as a last resort, not as a first and only response to any civil unrest, or peaceful protest. That is the difference, and it is a significant distinction between our form of government and those of other countries."

"So, in all those American gangster movies like *Little Caesar* and *The Public Enemy*, the police do not use firearms?" she mocked him.

"Please, Hedy," he pleaded. "Let me continue." He took her silence for acquiescence. "Mandl is supplying arms to rulers like Mussolini and intends to arm Hitler as well. You cannot be blind to what is happening across the border; how Hitler is treating the Jews there. People like me; people like you. Where do you think he is getting the hardware from to carry out his criminal actions? He's getting what he needs from people like Friedrich Mandl!" He was now becoming animated and had to remember to lower his voice. Who knew who might be sitting at the next table? "At least Mussolini has shown no animosity towards the Jews, so far. But Hitler is another story. Now he is in total command of Germany, there is no one to stop him, and he has surrounded himself with sycophants who think the same as he does. If we cannot curtail him now, it will soon be too late, and I fear for the future of the Jewish people in that country."

"You are quite right, of course. I have seen this dreadful little man myself. I acted in Germany a couple of years ago, and even then, things were not so good for the Jews. My parents and family are also worried about what is happening in Germany, but I do not see how I can be of any help. Also, what does any of this have to do with you? You are an American."

"Yes, Hedy, I am an American, but I am also a Jew; first and foremost, a Jew. Your parents are right to be concerned. All Jews should be concerned, but some of us are more than just concerned. We want to do something about it."

Although Jewish, Hedy's parents were far from observant, and paid scant recognition of their religious heritage. "You still haven't answered my question. How can I possibly be of help? I am an eighteen-year-old actress, for goodness' sake, not *Mata Hari*!"

"An eighteen-year-old actress who has taken the eye of someone who may help to perpetuate what is going on in Germany." He looked down at the table. Neither of them had touched a mouthful of their meal. "Do you not feel that you could foster some feelings of affection for this man?"

"Feelings of affection? What on earth are you talking about? I believe I've made my sentiments quite plain. I want nothing to do with Fritz Mandl, no matter how wealthy and influential he is. I'm sorry, Isidor, but what you are asking me to do is quite preposterous."

"You may not have much choice in the matter, I'm afraid," he responded quietly.

"I beg your pardon. What did you say?" Hedy demanded.

"I said that you may not have much choice in the matter."

"So now you are threatening me?" she asked in disbelief.

"No, Hedy, it is not I who is threatening you, God forbid."

"Then what are you saying?"

"Mandl has been to your house, yes?"

"I've already said as much."

"Then I'm afraid whether or not you like it, you will be Mandl's. I don't think even you realize just how powerful that man is, or who he is connected to. Quite simply, what *Herr* Mandl wants, *Herr* Mandle gets."

"But my parents, my father... would never permit this. It is just too awful." Isidor could see the apprehension in her eyes. "They would never permit that man to..."

"They will probably have no choice. Either by personal financial inducement, or commercial enticements, he would persuade your father to allow you to see him. If these strategies fail, he may even threaten them somehow. I am not exaggerating, Hedy. I wish I was. One way or another, you will belong to him. It is only a matter of time."

"Are you asking me to do what I think you are asking me to do, because if you are, then I am sorry, Isidor, but I cannot help you. I will not prostitute myself for anyone, do you understand me? I cannot believe my father would... would capitulate to that man and compromise my happiness for monetary or material consideration. It is unthinkable. He loves me. My father adores me!"

"As I said, he may not have a choice." He had to get her to agree to his suggestion, but how? She was slipping away from him, and he was alienating her every time he opened his mouth. "We did not take lightly the decision to ask you to help us. Trust me, Hedy, we discussed, debated and argued for many hours before we concluded that you, and you alone, will be in such a unique position. If there was any other way, I assure you, we would not ask this of you. Hedy, you are an actress, yes?"

"You know I am, so..."

"You have to use your imagination to get into the part you are playing, do you not? How did you prepare for your role as *Sissi*? Did you not read up on her, what she was like, what her life was like at court, am I correct?"

"Of course I did, but..."

"So, you had to use your imagination, yes?"

"Please, Doctor, don't..."

"You had to use your imagination," he insisted.

"Yes," she shouted across the table, causing those nearby to turn their heads in bemusement.

"Well, I want you to use your imagination now, right now. I want you to imagine that your family is not living safely in Austria, but living in Hitler's Germany. How do you think they would be feeling right now, this minute?"

"I don't have to use my imagination for that," she blurted out. "I do have family there. My father's sister lives not far from Munich. We hear all about Hitler and what he is doing!"

"My God, Hedy, so you already know, and from your own *mishpochah*, *noch*!" He had inadvertently struck a raw nerve, a very raw nerve, if Hedy's reaction was anything to go by.

The girl was now in tears as she sobbed, "What you are asking me to do... I don't know if... I mean... I don't even like this man, let alone want to marry him. He is so... so full of himself." She stopped as a thought occurred to her. "What you want me to do... it will be dangerous, won't it? I mean, if he finds out whatever it is I am supposed to do, I could be in trouble, couldn't I?"

"Earlier on, you asked me not to treat you like a child, so I will not do that. Yes, there is a certain risk in what I am asking you to do, but if you hold your nerve, there is no reason this mission should not work. You will not be alone, but that is all I can tell you until I know if you will help us."

"You keep mentioning 'we' and 'us.' Who are you working for, and why me? Why do you think it is only I who can do what you want done?"

"You are quite right, of course. I am not working by myself. I belong to a certain organization who are very concerned about the events that are happening here and in Germany. You wish to know why you were singled out. Well, that's quite a story and it may take a little while to explain. I hope you're not in a hurry..."

CHAPTER 5

The United States, France, Spain
January-April 1937

The year after Flynn settled in California was a momentous one for Europe. Civil war broke out in Spain in July 1936 between the Fascists led by Hitler-influenced General Francisco Franco and the mainly left-wing Republicans supported by the Soviet Union. Although he did not realize it at the time, Flynn would play his own disreputable part in the conflict.

The actor's marriage to Lili Damita was not going well. Being wed did not diminish Flynn's roving eye; his affairs with women and his hard-drinking lifestyle were becoming legendary in Hollywood. It did not take long for the rumors and gossip to get to the ears of Mrs. Flynn.

"How many women is it now?" Lili screamed at him in her Parisienne-English accent during one of their not infrequent shouting matches. "It can't be because you're not getting it at home, God knows. The mattress is almost worn through, not to mention the sofa, the carpet, two armchairs, and the back seat of the car. I don't know where you get all the energy from, I really don't, yet it seems you still want more? Am I not enough for you? What more do you want from me?"

"It's not like that, Lili. We're actors. We have to get into the part. We..."

"Don't give me that crock of *merde*. I don't drop my panties for every man I play a love scene with, although there are a few I would like to. There's getting into the act, and then there's getting into the actress. And I know which one you prefer. It had better stop, Errol, so help me. If you don't, or can't, don't expect me to stick around. How do you think I feel knowing that when you're inside me, you've probably been doing it with God-knows-who an hour before. I will not be your whore. Do you hear me, Errol? I will not be your cheap little streetwalker!"

"Lili, darling, it's not like that, I promise you. I don't know what you've heard, but you're the only one I've got feelings for, I promise you. No one else comes close."

"I might be the only one you have 'feelings' for, but not the only one you have desires for. The trouble is, Errol, you don't seem to understand the difference. You should be giving me all your business, not some two-bit wannabe actress. This is a final warning. It stops, or this gal walks."

"O.K., Lili, I'll keep it in my pants, I promise. Please give me one more chance. I do love you. You know that."

"I used to, but now I'm not so sure."

"Oh Lili, please..."

"And another thing," she interrupted him, "why am I not getting offers anymore? I can't remember the last time I got a script. Is this anything to do with you, you bastard?"

"No," Flynn screamed, outraged at the suggestion that he would sabotage her career. He could not bear to tell her the truth, the real reason parts were now becoming so infrequent for her. Despite her stunning looks, she was not the beauty she was, and new, prettier actresses were now coming to the fore. Her time had come and gone, while his star was on the rise. It was a sad reality, but that was how it was. One day, she would realize that. If he was truly honest with himself, he would admit that this was one reason why he had an eye for other women. Yes, they still had an active sex life, and he still enjoyed their lovemaking, but it was true. He did need more than she could give him. And he was a man, after all; a man with needs.

One day in January 1937, on a break while filming his latest movie, *Another Dawn*, in Yuma, Arizona, the Australian actor found himself face-to-face with Hermann Erben again.

"Hermann, how the hell did you get in here? This area is a closed set!" were the first words that greeted the Austrian. Erben tapped the side of his nose in his customary manner. "It's not what you know, *et cetera, et cetera,*" was the only explanation the Nazi agent would give. "I thought you might have invited your wife along, returning to the scene of the crime and all that," Erben smiled, referring to where Flynn and Lili married eighteen months earlier.

Ignoring Erben's remark, Flynn asked testily, "What do you want, Hermann? I'm rather busy at the moment if you haven't noticed."

"Yes, yes, I, too, have other places to be, so my visit here will not take long. I will get straight to the point."

"Please do."

"Very well. It is like this. You will be aware, of course, what is happening in Spain right now, with their internecine war." He paused to allow Flynn to take in the import of his words.

"Yes, everyone is. So what? What has this got to do with me?" Flynn retorted, looking at his watch.

"Nothing... yet."

"Hermann, will you stop being so bloody obtuse? What exactly are you driving at?"

"You are a man of adventure, a man of daring, are you not?"

"What the hell are you getting at?"

"How would you like to get involved in the greatest adventure of the age? How would you like to be able to tell your children and your grandchildren that you fought in the Spanish war?" Erben enthused.

"Get the fuck off this lot before I have you thrown out. Have you taken leave of your senses? And in case you didn't know, I don't have any fucking children, and the way my marriage is going, I doubt I ever will, at least to this woman. Go away and leave me alone. Now!"

"Such a pity. You would have had such a promising career, as well..."

"What's that remark supposed to mean?"

"Oh, nothing," Erben replied lightly. "It's just that when your antipathy towards your employers becomes known, I doubt there will be a studio in Hollywood that would care to take on such a trouble-making Jew-hater. Not with most of them being controlled by these people. Of course, it's entirely up to you. You may wish to take that chance. I doubt I would, though."

"So, it's blackmail now, is it? Is that how low you've come, you Austrian prick? And I would remind you that it was you who encouraged me to work against them back in London, remember?"

"Oh, come on, Errol, get off your high horse. Look, I happen to know that you've arranged to take some time off after you've finished this movie. Something to do with making a documentary about that British imperialist James Brooke, or some such nonsense."

"You're remarkably well-informed," Flynn conceded. "Do you know what? I think I'd rather take my chances with the Jews than get involved in one of your hare-brained schemes."

Erben raised his eyebrows comically. "Really? Would you? And there was I thinking you actually enjoyed this acting game. Ah, well, I'm sure you can always go back to..."

"Alright, stop!" commanded Flynn. "What do you want me to do?"

"That's better, Errol. Cheer up; you'll like it, I promise you. Now, to the best of my knowledge, which is usually quite accurate—I make a point of getting my facts right—this movie winds up filming early next month, as long as it does not overrun. That would mean you would be available to travel to Spain with me, let's say, sometime around the middle to late February. How does that sound? It might even give you some time to reconcile with the lovely Lili. In fact, why not bring her with us? It will allow you some distractions on the ocean voyage."

"Leave Lili out of this, you miserable bastard. She has got nothing to do with you or any of this. If I find out you've spoken to her or even gone near her, I'll kill you with my own bare hands. *Verstehen sie*?"

"Very good. Perhaps I should say, '*Sehr gut.*' I did not realize you were familiar with our tongue, the language of Goethe and Mozart. We might make a scholar out of you yet, my dear Errol."

"Don't you be so bloody patronizing, or I'll show you what an English private boarding school education can accomplish."

"Don't take on so, my dear Errol. I was only having a little fun at your expense."

"And one other thing..."

"Yes?"

"Stop calling me 'my dear Errol.' It makes you sound like a queer. I think there's something you may have forgotten in your haste to get me to Spain."

"Oh, and what is that, my dear... er... Errol?"

"As soon as word gets out that I'm there to support Franco, I might as well take out a front-page banner in the Los Angeles Times proclaiming my admiration for Hitler. Everyone knows he's behind all the mayhem over there. How long do you think my career will last then?"

"Oh, no," smiled Erben enigmatically. We're not going over to support the Fascists; quite the opposite. You and I will travel to *España* for the Leftist cause. We're going to aid the Communists!"

***

Flynn and Erben sailed from New York at the end of February, arriving in France a few days later. Flynn had taken Erben's advice and invited Lili to go along with him. She jumped at the chance to travel with her husband and return to the country of her birth. His wife was unaware of her fellow traveler and was content to stroll about the different decks and spend money in the onboard shops. In her absence, Flynn questioned Erben over how they would be allowed to enter the war-torn country. Erben replied by saying, "I will need a visa to get into Spain, and I doubt the French U.S. consul will provide me with one if I state my true intentions. Better to say that we are on a humanitarian mission to supply assistance to those poor people resisting Franco's iron-fisted persecution of those freedom-loving resistance fighters. These sentiments always play well with your foolish but well-meaning statesmen. How easy it is to hoodwink them."

"Be that as it may, I still don't understand what it is you want me to do once we get there."

All in good time, Errol; all in good time." Erben would not be drawn further. Flynn's justified curiosity would have to wait a little longer to be satisfied.

Arriving at Le Havre, they all made their way to Paris, where Flynn suggested Lili should remain until his return.

"But why, Errol," she pouted. Madrid is such a lovely city, and as for Barcelona..."

"Look, darling, I'm not going to Spain for pleasure. There's a war going on there. It will be just too dangerous for you. I won't be able to concentrate on my... work if I have to look out for you, too. Don't worry; I'll make sure I'm not in the thick of it too much," he assured her.

Before the onset of their trip, Erben had arranged with Hearst newspapers to give Flynn a commission to write about the situation. It would be good for the American public to get an objective view of what was going on in Spain. The Austrian Nazi now revealed to the actor that as well as going for humane reasons, he was as also going to be a non-partisan reporter gathering information for the American authorities. With his eminence already known even in Spain, it would not be too difficult for both sides to respect him as an impartial observer.

"Are you mad? I'm not a journalist. Why didn't you tell me this earlier, you cunning bastard? What else have you got in mind for me? Are you going to get me to eat a can of spinach and pretend to be Popeye so I can bop all those fascists out of the park?"

"Don't take on so, Errol. You're an actor; it's what you do. Just pretend you're a newspaper reporter. It will all work out just fine, you'll see," he assured Flynn, patting him avuncularly on the shoulder.

Both men made their way south through France, arriving at Perpignan, thirty kilometers from the Spanish border, on March 27th. With his popularity, it was not difficult for Flynn to obtain the necessary permit. Despite Erben's earlier optimism, his application was refused. Unbeknownst to the Austrian, he was on an F.B.I. watch list, and they had circulated his details to all embassies and consulates, should such a situation arise.

"Do not worry, Errol. I did not attain my present level as an asset for our cause without being adept at a little subterfuge. I have friends locally I can call on. They are based around Corbières, which is about fifty kilometers from the border. I will meet up with you there tomorrow."

"This is all getting a bit too much, Hermann. I don't enjoy playing all these cloak-and-dagger schoolboy games. And I've already signed up to do my next movie. It's due to start shooting in May. That's only a few weeks away. There'll be hell to pay if I'm not there when production starts."

"Oh, I wouldn't worry too much. You'll most likely be there, or..."

"Or...?"

"Or you'll be dead!"

* * *

With the help of friendly agents from the International Brigade, Flynn and Erben journeyed to Barcelona by a train crowded with Leftist fighters, bristling with all kinds of weapons, on their way to do battle for the Socialist cause. The Republicans still held the city, and on his arrival, they asked Flynn to give a speech. The actor was reluctant but was persuaded by Erben to do so. After a few words of encouragement, Flynn ended his address by saying, "God bless you all." and raising his right fist clenched in salute. Although all the fighters cheered at this spontaneous expression of solidarity, Erben quickly pulled him down from the platform. "It was such a rousing oration you gave. Pity you had to spoil it by asking God to bless them all."

"Why? Surely..."

"Don't you understand? They are Communists. They don't believe in God or religion. Lucky most of them couldn't understand you. You could have got us killed!"

"Well, I didn't, and that's the main thing."

You may be as blasé about your own life as you wish, but please do not include me in your desire for self-annihilation."

For the next few days, both men traveled together around Barcelona, meeting the Leftist rebels and offering words of encouragement. Erben occasionally went off on his own for short periods, which were gradually becoming longer absences. Finally, he said, "Now, listen to me, Errol. I need to disappear for a while. Some things have arisen that it is better for you not to know about. I may be gone for some time. If I don't return in, say, a week, go back to Paris without me."

"A week here in Barcelona on my own? In the middle of a bloody civil war? You have got to be kidding me. I don't even speak the lingo. What the hell am I going to do here by myself?"

"You're the great Errol Flynn. I'm sure you'll think of something. If it's any comfort, I think the bordellos are still running."

Flynn stayed in Barcelona for a few days, constantly telling anyone who would listen that American help was on its way. This aid never arrived. Neither did Flynn ever file any reports about his experiences. Either because he never intended to do so or because of Franco's warning that he would kill any journalists caught behind enemy lines, reporting the Republican's cause. Even the celebrated actor might not be immune to the general's threat. However, he did endure some gunfire and was shot at several times, receiving minor wounds. Flynn eventually made his way back to Paris to be re-united with Lili.

Erben did not return. He had fulfilled his mission using Flynn as his unwitting decoy. It was now inevitable that Franco would win this war. Erben had made sure of it.

CHAPTER 6

Tel Aviv, Palestine
April 1933

The dying rays of the late afternoon sun spilled into an orange glow as they streamed through the open windows, casting long shadows on the cramped and crowded upstairs room in the house on Rothschild Boulevard. Its light reflected off the dust-covered glass doors of the dark mahogany bookshelves, which lined the whitewashed walls. Most of the tomes were printed in Hebrew or Yiddish. Many were biblical tractates; others were political and philosophical works mainly written by Jewish intellectuals, but others, published in English and German, were authored by gentiles. The aging motor of the overhead electric fan labored noisily. It added little cool air to the oppressive heat of the room as it slowly turned the blades in their desultory rotation.

Almost all the individuals present smoked, and the room was fuggy with cigarette fumes. Empty coffee cups littered the wooden table, which, together with the chairs, took up most of the available floor space. The six men, all shirt-sleeved, seated around the table, had been debating the one topic during most of the day. The issue they were discussing was involved, with many facets. The men were equally divided as to what action they should take to resolve the situation.

Eli Golomb, whose house it was, and who was in charge of the small cadre, sat at the end. Although he was the leader of this group, it had been made clear to him that he would have no more influence on the outcome than any of the other five. If nothing else, this was a democratic organization, with its ideals rooted in Leftist principles despite one of the members being a 'far-right Socialist.'

The subject which divided them was not a what, but a who. Vladimir Jabotinsky was all for devoting some of the organization's scarce funds to execute the operation. What was the life of one individual when compared to those of so many others? Especially when that one life would be spent in opulent luxury?

"Yes, Ze'ev, I understand what you are saying, but this is someone's emotions we are talking about here. Such sensitivities can run considerably deeper than any physical attractions. What if they are not compatibly suited? What if the subjects are not agreeable to each other? Then all our plans, not to mention our resources, would have gone up in smoke. All that effort, all the calculating, would be for nothing. Right now, we cannot afford to waste any of our time or our funds on such a... a speculative venture. I'm sorry, that has to be my final word." said Eliyahu Golomb.

Dov Isaacs, Israel Gadder, and Ephraim Ben-Pinchas nodded their heads in silent agreement with Golomb, as Isaacs and Gadder were finally convinced by Golomb's fiscal logic. The last member displayed no partiality, being lost in his private thoughts, seemingly oblivious to the arguments raging around him. This man was Doctor Isidor Pralgovitch, considered to be the most analytical of the company present.

Golomb was born in Eastern Europe, and Jabotinsky hailed from Odessa. The other three occupants of the room were native to Palestine. Pralgovitch's origins, however, were in New York. His parents had immigrated to the United States with his older sisters in 1895, traveling from Lvov in Ukraine. They eventually settled in the Bronx, and Isidor was born fifteen months after their arrival. The family that Isidor grew up in was deeply religious, and much of their life revolved around their Jewish roots and traditions. His parents and sisters were safe in America, a country that welcomed them, and many other Jews from the pogroms of Russia and Eastern Europe. There, in their adopted homeland, they were able to practice their religion without fear of persecution. They could walk the streets free from the threat of some Cossack's whip lashing them, merely for being Jews. The Pralgovitch family owed a lot to America, and what better way to repay the country's kindness and hospitality than to give it their children. Ruth and Naomi had graduated as nurses and worked in the local hospital. Isidor had just come out of medical school as a doctor, his parents scrimping and saving to see their only son achieve his ambition.

But the Jerusalem riots triggered something in the young man, something indefinable. He could not begin to understand what his parents had endured back in Ukraine, and now it was happening again. Not in Eastern Europe, but the birthplace of Judaism. The local Muslim population was attacking Jews simply for what they were: Jews. The rights and wrongs did not enter into the equation. It was enough to know that his estranged brothers and sisters were being killed. He could not let this go on. He was only one man, but if many people like him thought as he did, maybe, just maybe, they could stop the murders and reach some sort of accord with the Arabs.

His father, Avraham, and his mother, Minke, had mixed emotions over their son's intentions. On the one hand, they were anxious for him, fearful that he would come to harm, maybe worse. They could not bring themselves to voice their most profound fears, worried that even saying them might bring about the *ayin hora*, the evil eye. And yet, despite their concerns, they knew that he had to go. As his father had said to him, "The Cossacks had whips and swords and guns; we had prayer books, and *talleisim*, and *tefillin*. Maybe if it were the other way round, we would be the rulers, and they would have been on the boats."

Jews in Palestine still carried the accouterments of their faith, but now, they also carried guns and rifles. Avraham believed firmly that the Lord had covenanted the Holy Land to his people, the Jewish people. Didn't it say so in the Bible? If God had chosen his son to play a small part in carrying out His ordinance, so be it. How could any father not let their child fulfill his destiny? It would be like an offense against the Almighty Himself.

By the time Isidor had arrived in Palestine in September 1929, the riots were all but over. A peace of sorts had been restored, but there was still an underlying tension. Most of the trouble had been over who had rightful control of the Temple Mount and the Wailing Wall. Both Jews and Arabs had claimed the ancient properties, and the British, fearful not to offend either side, had tried to stay neutral, but in the end, had only succeeded in upsetting each faction. There were many casualties in both the Jewish and Arab camps. Pralgovitch was reluctant to treat those he held responsible for the unprovoked attacks on his people. His Hippocratic obligation and his medical conscience, however, forbade him to be partisan. Eventually, he found himself aiding as many Moslems as Jews.

It did not take long for his involvement with the local Arab population to come to the Haganah's attention, the underground Jewish defense organization. Having a Jewish doctor who was trusted freely to enter Arab homes and help local Muslims was a godsend to the secret group. With a man on the inside, who knew what information he might 'accidentally' overhear? When Ben-Pinchas originally proposed the idea, Pralgovitch thought he was joking. He was a doctor, not a spy. He had not been trained in the arcane world of espionage. Even had he been, Ben-Pinchas had forgotten one other tiny detail; he did not speak Arabic. Only through his fluency in Yiddish could he converse with the three native Palestine Jews seated beside him. What Ben-Pinchas suggested was an anathema to the young doctor. His medical training made it clear that anything he heard from patients or their families had to be treated in the strictest confidence.

Despite his earlier intentions, he realized that the best way to help his people was to minister to their physical needs and their Arab neighbors. Nothing more, nothing less. While he respected the Haganah and their necessity to prevent more Jewish bloodshed, he was in Palestine for one reason and one reason only. He was there to treat those who needed the help of a physician. Pralgovitch underestimated the persuasiveness of his newfound companion. "Isidor, you told me a minute ago that you came here primarily to help Jews who were injured in our disputes with our Arab neighbors. Is this not correct?"

The doctor conceded that this was the reason he had traveled almost six thousand miles. "So, tell me, my young friend, which do you think is better? Treating those who have already been hurt or preventing the injuries from occurring in the first place? If you saw a small child about to put his hand into an open fire, would you permit him to do this, then treat the burns, or would you slap his hand away?"

"You surely don't expect me to answer that, do you?"

"No, I don't. It was a rhetorical question. I was only using that example as a metaphor, but I'm sure you will see the equation." Ben-Pinchas waited. The art of selling was brinkmanship. He who spoke first lost. The Haganah man watched as Isidor looked into the middle distance, his eyes scanning for an invisible object just beyond his horizon.

It was the young doctor who eventually broke the silence as his resolve finally weakened. "As I told you already, I don't speak their language. They usually have to get an interpreter in so we can converse. Yes, I've picked up the odd word here and there, but..."

"They must not know you comprehend even a little of their tongue; otherwise, this whole exercise will be futile. Do you understand?"

"How many New Yorkers do you think can converse in Arabic?"

Ben-Pinchas grinned an answer. "We only need you to understand some keywords, expressions, and phrases which someone might use if they were planning an attack. *Alqanabil, albanadiq,* and *alrasas.* That's bombs, guns, and bullets. Another word to listen out for is *aemal alshaghab.*"

Pralgovitch regarded Ben-Pinchas questioningly. "It means riots," the Haganah agent explained.

"Even if I did pick up on these words, how could I put them into context? They may be said innocuously or in jest. When I was growing up in the Bronx, my mother would sometimes call me up from the street by shouting, 'Issy, take a *misah meshinah* and get up these stairs right away.' Now, we both know she did not wish me to take a fit and die. It's just how she spoke, how they all spoke. Do you see what I'm driving at? I might hear these words, but -"

Ben-Pinchas smiled. Hadn't his late mother used the same expression many times, and Isidor was right. His mother certainly was not literally cursing her son, but this wasn't about Jewish mothers summoning their errant children. "This is going to sound awful, but it needs to be said. If any Arabs talk about guns, or bombs, or bullets, you can be pretty sure they're not using those words as analogies. We have to take them at their face value.

Look, come with me; I want to introduce you to some people. We'll take it from there. If you are agreeable, we'll teach you some Arabic phrases which you might hear in the context of aggression. All you have to do while you're mending their wounds is to listen out for them. You may never come across such words, and I pray to Hashem that you do not, but if you do..."

"If I do..."

"All you need do is contact us, and we'll do the rest. Whatever you do, do not try to be a hero. We have said *Kaddish* for too many of those already."

And so, Doctor Isidor Pralgovitch, late of New York, met with some of the other clandestine group's members and allowed them to persuade him into acting as a covert agent. They taught him the words that he would need to listen out for, and as his Arabic improved, he was able to discern more Arab vocabulary. He ensured that he never revealed his understanding of their alien tongue. Only once in the intervening years he helped the Arab population did he glean any hostile intelligence and prevent an attack on a local Jewish business. He later discovered that this intended assault was not mired in terrorism. It was provoked by a personal grudge against the proprietor, who the assailant believed had been overcharging his customer for several months.

Now, as a fully-fledged member of the team, he was debating the matter, which was currently under discussion. He looked up slowly, his sepulchral features taking in the expectant expressions of all those waiting for him to speak. Looking straight at Golomb, he began, "I came to this country a few years ago to try to help stop the attacks on Jews. I don't know if I've contributed a lot to bring about peace, but this much is clear to me. The attacks that my family went through back in *der Heim* still go on, as they do here. It seems to me that there has been anti-Semitism as long as there have been Jews. We have to fight it, to confront it wherever it raises its insidious head. If we do not, it will engulf us, and eventually, it will destroy us. If history has taught us anything, it is this; we cannot rely on anyone but ourselves for our survival. Right now, in Germany, their new Chancellor has made his feelings about Jews abundantly clear. Years ago, we could write him off as an ill-educated lunatic, an ignorant boor, and nothing more than a minor irritation, but that time has passed. He is now the leader of his country, well, his adopted country, and he has mitigated nothing he has said about us. We can no longer ignore his rants, and I sincerely believe that our people face dangers that they have never experienced. I do not know how these dangers will manifest themselves. I only know that if we do nothing, their current plight will only get worse. For the first time in modern history, we have the head of a modern country, a European country, answerable to no one but himself, openly hostile towards Jews. How long will it be before he institutionalizes anti-Semitism as government policy? But we are in a unique position here. We have an opportunity that will most likely never come again. If we do not grasp this opportunity now, we may live to regret it. My even worse fear is that we might die regretting it. This idea either will work, or it will not. If we cannot persuade the subject to go along with our objectives, we will have lost little, except a few lire, well maybe more than a few, and a week or two in time." Pralgovitch nodded his head before continuing, "But if we succeed, imagine the benefits that might accrue. Maybe we can even stop the violence in Germany that our people were never able to do in Russia. 'Forewarned is forearmed' gentlemen, and we will never be more forewarned again."

There was a silence, an almost audible void in the room's close atmosphere, and they could hear the afternoon traffic sounds in the street below. No one spoke for almost a minute, each man considering the powerful speech they had just heard. Eli Golomb stroked his chin, his forefinger covering his lips. Behind his finger, a smile was forming from the corners of his mouth. "That was a very eloquent discourse, Isidor. You have certainly given the situation a new perspective; one, I must admit, I had not considered. In the light of what you have just shared with us, I am prepared to forego my previous opposition to the plan." Even the two other dissenters, Isaacs and Gadder, finally applauded the doctor's words. "So, it is settled, then. It only remains to discuss who will carry out this enterprise." said the leader.

"After the forceful way that this man turned around the previous stalemate, surely there is only one of us who can do what needs to be done."

Ben-Pinchas grinned at his doctor colleague. They all turned to face Pralgovitch.

"Well, Isidor," prompted Golomb. "Do you feel up to the task? After all, it was you who drove the argument."

"Yes, Eli. I've never been more focused on anything in my life. Of course, I'll do it."

"Very well, Isidor, you had better get ready. You've got a *shiddach* to organize!"

CHAPTER 7

Los Angeles, California, U.S.A.
September 2nd. 1939

It was now inevitable that there was going to be another European conflict. Despite signing a peace agreement with the British prime minister, Neville Chamberlain, the year before, the Nazi dictator showed no sign of lessening his bellicose stance against those governments who defied his wishes to extend his German empire. German troops had invaded Poland, and Hitler had ignored Chamberlain's demand to withdraw his forces immediately under the threat of war. Britain was mobilizing, and civil defense measures were being set up in London and across the Home Counties. Air defense barrage dirigibles flew over Whitehall and Buckingham Palace. Britain was in a somber mood, and those who were old enough to remember thought back to the previous conflict. It was starting again, and once more, Germany was the instigator.

At last, thought Hermann Erben. He had been frustrated that Hitler had taken so long to finally flex his military might. The Rhineland in 1936, The *Anschluss* in 1938, and the annexation of The Sudetenland a few months later were only the preludes to the main event. It was Hitler testing the waters. The Allies had capitulated each time he had made an aggressive move, desperate to avoid at all costs another European conflagration. There was no reason to believe they would not react in the same craven, cowardly way over Hitler's move into Poland.

But it seemed that on this occasion, the Allies could not just close their eyes. Hitler had broken every treaty he had signed, and Britain and France looked like laughing stocks to the rest of the world, and their policy of appeasement was in tatters. Poland was the line in the sand, and Hitler had crossed it, figuratively and literally. Let battle commence, thought Erben. Nazi troops would be marching through London's streets within the year. It was now time to put his plan into action. He had duped Flynn once before over his foray into Spain. He would now use him again, but in a much different way.

***

Flynn had just finished filming *The Private Lives of Elizabeth and Essex* and was glad the movie was over. His constant arguments with his co-star, Bette Davis, left him physically drained, reminding him of his increasingly unhappy marriage to Lili. He was spending less and less time at home and more time looking for young women and welcoming bars, hopefully finding one within the other. It was in one of these bars just off Sunset Boulevard that Erben came back into Flynn's life. "You seem to have a canny knack of always knowing where I am. Do you spend your whole life following me around everywhere? Can't you see I'm busy?" the actor slurred, with his forehead barely an inch from the bar counter.

"Yes, Errol, I noticed you were giving the drink in front of you quite a lot of attention. As for knowing how to find you, you're quite a creature of habit. It only took me six watering holes to track you down. If you do not want my company, I suggest you change your routine. Why not become a monk and take holy orders? I'm sure you would still find a way to smuggle girls into the cloisters." the Austrian joked.

Flynn did not look up. "Piss off, Hermann. I'm not in the mood for your charmless wit."

"What's wrong, Errol? I hope I haven't offended you. That certainly was not my intention, and if I have done so, I humbly apologize."

"No, it's not you, not this time. It's Lili. She's becoming even more erratic. She still thinks it's my fault she's not getting film scripts."

"And is it?"

"Of course it's bloody not, you idiot. She's past it, but she doesn't see it, and I don't have the heart to tell her. Now go away and leave me alone. Find someone else to trouble."

"I wish I could, my old friend. I truly wish I could, but on this occasion, I'm afraid it's you I must come to." There was something in Erben's voice, something Flynn had never heard. There was none of the usual brashness, the misplaced jocularity. No, this was a different Erben. Then, through his drunken haze, he spotted it. This was a serious Erben that Flynn had not seen before. The Austrian shook his friend gently by the shoulder. "Errol, my friend, we have things to discuss. Come, walk with me outside. You must listen very carefully to what I have to say." The Austrian lifted his much heavier friend from off the barstool and supported his weight as he helped to ease his friend into the night air.

The change in temperature caused Flynn to look up in confusion. He was now coming round and was almost coherent.

"What do you want?" the actor asked wearily. "Why can't you just leave me alone?"

"Errol, listen to me. Within the next twenty-four to forty-eight hours, Britain will be at war with Germany. Can you understand what I'm saying to you?"

"Yes, but we've been through this already."

"What are you talking about? Been through what?"

"The war. Nineteen-fourteen to nineteen-eighteen. Don't you remember? It wasn't that long ago."

"No, you imbecile. This is a different war; a new war. Same people, different war, and I need you to hear me."

"But we won, didn't we? I think we won that one."

"Well, your side did. My side didn't do so well. We came second."

"What is it this time? A rematch? Do we change sides at half-time?"

"Oh, for God's sake, Errol. Do you remember the conversation we had in London a few years ago? Do you recall that I said the time would come when we would want your help in ridding this country of those parasites? Come on, Errol, think! Do you remember?"

Flynn shook his head, trying to clear it of the alcoholic fug that enveloped it. "Hermann, right now, I can't remember my last drink, never mind a conversation you say we had years ago. Perhaps you might care to refresh my memory a little."

As if patiently explaining an adult issue to a child, Erben spoke slowly and concisely to his friend. "It's the Jews. They're the ones that have started it this time. They fooled Hitler into invading Poland. He didn't want to, you know. He likes Poland. Nice little country; harmless, inoffensive, doing no harm to anyone. But they whispered in his ear. You know how they can be, persuasive and manipulative. They told Hitler that there were many natural resources there, which he could use against his real enemy— Stalin. The Jews want Hitler and Stalin at each other's throats. Then they can mop up after the whole thing is over."

"I'm not sure I know what you're saying. Can you be a bit more specific? My head's not thinking straight. What has any of this got to do with me?"

"Where do you think the European Jews are getting their money to beguile Hitler? It's from here, the United States, from the wealthy Jews like your employers in the movie industry. Sam Goldwyn, Jack Warner, all of them. They're sending money, huge truckloads of it, to their fellow kikes in Germany. What do you think they're doing with it? They're using it to promote their own agenda. They've pushed Hitler into a war he didn't want, and now they're rubbing their filthy hands with glee, waiting to pick the bones out of what's left after it's all over. We've got to stop that money and other resources from getting to them. Anything that can help their aim, we have to prevent. I need you to start whispering in ears, just casually, if you see what I mean, and begin to cast doubt on what they're saying."

"What are they saying, exactly?"

"You know, that Hitler is persecuting them, that he is making life intolerable for them and rot like that. It simply isn't true. The only Jews he's against are those who he sees trying to run Germany down, to betray it to the Communists. Wouldn't you do the same thing if they tried to do it here or in Australia?"

"Well, yes, I suppose I would. We don't want them to take everything over, do we? Not if they're all a bunch of Communists. No, I see what you mean. But..."

"But what, Errol?" There were things that Erben said that made sense, but somehow they didn't. He wished he could get things clearer in his mind and formulate Erben's words into a logical sequence, but right now, he didn't even know his way home. Erben interrupted Flynn's confused train of thought. "If you don't believe me, let me take you to somebody who'll convince you I'm right." Without giving the actor time to gather his wits, the Austrian Nazi guided Flynn to his car.

"Where are we going at this time of night? I can't be home late. Lili will think I've been out on the prowl, and I can't face another row with her."

"This won't take long, Errol, I promise. There's a couple of people I want you to meet. You need to know that you won't be alone in this endeavor. We can be there in a few minutes. After our short discussion, I will drive you home myself. How does that sound?"

"It sounds like you won't take no for an answer."

Erben smiled. No, he would not. The Austrian drove to the German consulate in the Garland Building on West 9th. Street. He was waved straight through the usual security formalities. It was obvious that this meeting had already been arranged, and he was ushered along with Erben into a formal and well-furnished oak-paneled office. The first thing that struck the actor was the large portrait of Hitler on the wall facing him as he entered. His intimidating stare glared down at the actor, as if by its very presence commanding him to do as he was bidden. Flynn had no time to study his surroundings more closely. In a far corner of the room, two men were whispering. In the spill of the light from the wall lamps, Flynn thought he vaguely recognized one of the new attendees. He had seen him before somewhere but could not place him for the moment.

The Austrian doctor led him over and introduced him to his fellow conspirators. Deferring to the first of the two men, he said, "Errol, this is Georg Gyssling. Georg is the German consul here in Los Angeles." Turning his gaze slightly, he continued, "And this is Joseph Breen, who I believe you may have heard of."

Joe Breen. Of course, he had heard of him. There was not a studio executive or actor in Hollywood who had not heard of him. Breen practically ran Hollywood and was responsible for sanctioning every movie the studios produced. He was the moral conscience of the movie studios and scrutinized every film script for obscenities, language, and any other material he found controversial, offensive, or immoral. No movie could be produced or released without his organization's approval, the Motion Picture Producers and Distributors of America, or MPPDA. He was also anti-Semitic and once wrote to an associate that he thought Jews were 'the scum of the scum of the earth.' "It's a pleasure to finally meet you, Errol. I've been a fan of yours for some time. I hope we can work together on our little project, eh?"

"What project is this, Mr. Breen?"

"Joe. Call me Joe, please," Breen said affably. The movie executive reached into the inside pocket of his jacket and produced a sheet of paper. When he unfolded it, Flynn saw it was a typed list. When Breen handed the folio over, the actor saw that it contained a menu of names, some twenty in all. He was familiar with a few of the people on it, others he did not know. He looked up at Breen, waiting for him to enlighten the actor what this document signified. "These folks are, ah, how can I put it, like-minded souls. Like us, they are appalled at the entrenched influence these Jews have in the Hollywood system. We need to get a more positive message out there, as to what's really going on in Germany. Hitler is only giving the Jews there what they've had coming for a long time. They want this war to give Stalin the excuse he needs to send his troops in to put down the German government and install a puppet regime answerable to Moscow."

"But didn't Germany and Russia sign some sort of agreement, promising not to attack each other?"

"Yes, they did, but the treaty isn't worth the paper it's written on. Stalin has no more intention of abiding by that agreement than I have of marrying the Chief Rabbi's daughter. He'll break it as soon as he thinks it's politically expedient for him to do so. And who do you think will tell him when the time is right, eh? Who do you think is fomenting all the trouble over there? Do I need to spell it out? We need to stop all this nonsense about persecution, and how the Jews are being discriminated against and attacked without reason. The only ones who are being assaulted are the Communist ones, the ones who are in Stalin's pocket."

"Yes," responded Flynn tiredly. "Hermann has already explained all this to me."

"Ah, but now we have to put our plans into action. The list I have given you, as I said, is of those individuals we know, or believe, to be disposed towards us. Errol, we need you to marshal these people together to give them a sense of focus, a sense of purpose, and pride in their country. To help us rid ourselves of these parasites who are sucking us dry. If you can persuade these names to join us, and each of these names reaches out to twenty more, and each of those twenty does the same, you can see what will happen. It will not take long to build up such an irresistible force that not only will it force the Jews to leave, they will be crying to do so as their ancestors did in Egypt. Only this time, there will be no plagues. And when the glorious history of this period is written, whose name do you think will be on everyone's lips?"

Flynn had no love for Jews, but this was too much. Maybe they were behind Hitler's aggression or maybe they weren't, but he was also minded of an old Chinese saying—'be careful of that for which you wish, for you may attain it.' He would go through the motions, and do as they asked, but not with the ardor they would have liked. After all, if all the Jews left, who would employ all these out-of-work actors, actors like him?

It was now Gyssling's turn to enter into the discussion. Flynn assumed they were meeting in the consulate simply for convenience and discretion; somewhere where they would not be seen together, but Gyssling, too, had a part to play. The consul looked like the archetypal Nazi with his wire-rimmed spectacles and penetrative stare, and his urbane, but coldly arrogant voice. In his German-accented English, he said, "It is my country's hope that despite the unpleasantness currently happening across the Atlantic, our two nations can remain on friendly terms. My government has no quarrel with your country, nor do we wish to have. As long as you do not interfere with our geographical and political aspirations, there is no reason why we cannot exist in a mutually respectful relationship. Having said that, we have noticed that there is a certain element of anti-German sentiment slowly creeping into your movies, portraying our leader in a less-than-favorable light. We cannot tolerate this, of course, and have already made representations to your movie producers and Herr Breen's company. In this regard, they have invited me to peruse various manuscripts and pre-release movie prints to ensure that there is equanimity in your production values and that my country is not depicted unfairly. This must include, unfortunately, even films in which you, yourself appear. I felt it was only right to let you know how things stand, so there can be no bad feelings later."

This is nothing but censorship, thought an outraged Flynn. They are trying to stifle what the American people see, and feel, and think. And they want me to be a part of it. These people are bringing Nazi-ism right into the heart of Hollywood! Do I want to get this involved? It seems I already am. He nodded in feigned agreement with Breen's and Gyssling's strategies, telling them what they wanted to hear. That he would start implementing their instructions as soon as he could. What else could he do? He shook their hand and allowed Erben to escort him out of the room, but not before he gazed once more on the oil painting of the Führer. In his mind, Hitler was staring down at him, warning him not to betray them. The penalty for doing so would be swift and merciless.

CHAPTER 8

Vienna, Austria
May 1933

After Isidor had finished his narrative, Hedwig said, "And so, you are a... a spy for these people?"

"I wouldn't put it quite like that," he grinned modestly.

"What would you call someone who uses his talents and abilities for an entirely different purpose than he professes to? Who lulls people into accepting him as a benefactor, a healer, but who has an entirely different agenda for helping them?" Hedy interrogated him mildly.

"Well, if you put it like that...."

"That is exactly how I would put it, and you wish me to do a similar thing with *Herr* Mandl. To engage in some sort of subterfuge while pretending to show love for this man? Do you realize what you are asking me to do? You are asking me to marry someone I do not care for, to show affection for him, to allow him to share my bed, to have... relations with him. I find this whole suggestion quite appalling."

"I'm sorry, Hedy, that I had to be so frank with you about Mandl's intentions. The one thing you must not do is mention this conversation to your parents. If word gets back to him, we, you, your parents, could all be in jeopardy. Knowing his attraction to you, we felt that this was the one chance we had. I know it was an audacious idea, but we had to try. I apologize for putting you in this position. Perhaps it's better if I should go now. Please forgive me..." and he made to rise to his feet.

Hedy stayed his arm on the dining table. Looking straight into his eyes, she asked, "This is really important to your organization, isn't it? Important to you?"

"Yes, Hedy, it is, but this is not about the Haganah or me. It is about the fate of all the Jews in Germany, maybe even beyond Germany, your own family included. I believe as bad as things are right now, we have still only seen the tip of the iceberg. We have to do something...."

"Please sit down. Tell me, what exactly is it that you would want me to do...?"

And so, sensing a softening in Hedy's vehement reluctance, Isidor explained some of what his group would require of her. After hearing him out without interruption, she asked in astonishment, "And you honestly think this will work?"

"Quite frankly, Hedy, I don't know. We think it will, we hope it will, but truthfully..." he shook his head thoughtfully, "we just can't be certain."

"And so, you are asking me to gamble my future, not to mention the lives of hundreds of thousands of Jews, on an uncertainty?" she asked incredulously.

"I'm afraid those are the best odds I can give you, in all sincerity. To say otherwise would be false and the least I can do is tell you candidly how things stand." He could see her weighing up her options before answering.

"You have been honest with me, I think, throughout this appointment, so please let me be as open with you. I find what you are asking me to do, deplorable. But you have made it abundantly clear to me the perils our people are facing, including, as I mentioned, my own father's sister, her husband, and my cousins. You have brought home to me that which I suppose I already knew but would not face. Despite my serious misgivings, I do not see how I can do anything else but to... to agree to your request." Sobbing, but smiling as she agreed to help him, tears coursed down her cheeks, and Isidor wished they had been tears of joy; however, he knew they were anything but. "If you ever decide to stop being a doctor, a whole new career might be available to you," she suggested.

"I have no plans to give up medicine any time soon, and if you meant my other occupation as an occasional espionage agent, that is unpaid, I assure you."

"No, I did not mean that."

"Well, what...?"

"A *shadchan*; you would make a wonderful matchmaker."

"Aren't they usually women?" he asked humorously.

"There's a first time for everything," she countered, squeezing his hand, wishing it was him and not Mandl to whom she was to be betrothed.

CHAPTER 9

Vienna & Schwarzenau, Austria
June 1933-January 1934

It was shortly after her dialogue with Isidor, that her father, Emil, and her mother, Gertrude, called Hedy into the parlor. She could tell by their expressions that whatever it was, it was not good. She had rarely seen her parents in such a serious mood, and thought for a minute she had done something to displease them, to make them angry with her. Then she realized. It was nothing like that at all. It was Mandl. He had finally made his move and whatever he had said or done to make it happen, it was now clear that she was to be married to him. She knew this day would eventually come, and had tried to prepare for it, but now it had, she was still taken aback. She dare not tell her parents that she had been forewarned about him, that an American doctor, now a spy for the Haganah in Palestine, had already prepared her for this very occasion.

Emil closed the parlor door behind her. It felt as if she were being imprisoned. "Sit down, please, Hedy. Your mother and I have something to discuss with you."

Hedy had to feign ignorance, to pretend she did not know what was coming. Well, she was an actress. She would now have to put all her training into practice, to perform her role so well, it would even fool her parents. Once she was seated with her back tensed straight and her hands clasped on her knees, her father cleared his throat. She could see he was finding it hard to know how to broach the subject, but knew it would have to come from him. She could not second guess what he was about to say.

"Hedy," he began slowly, "I, that is, your mother, and I have been giving a great deal of thought to your future. Although you are still young, we believe it is time you should think about settling down."

"I'm sorry, Papa, I don't understand what you mean."

"Let me continue; please. I... oh, it's no use. I can't do it. She's my daughter, my only child. How can I offer her up like a sacrificial lamb?" He began to sob until the tears were running down his cheeks.

"What is it, Papa? What have I done to make you so unhappy?" Now Hedy, too, began to get upset. Gertrude sat quietly, not knowing what to say that could make the situation any better. "You've done nothing, my darling, nothing at all. Your mother and I couldn't ask for a more perfect daughter, and now..."

"Hedy, the time has come for you to get married," her mother said. It was clear Emil could not continue. Someone had to take charge of the situation. "As you may know, a certain gentleman has been to the house with a view to, ah, getting to know you. We, that is, your father and I, think you should arrange to meet with him. He is very nice, and also, he can provide you with a standard of living even far above that which we have been able to give you. You know, of course, to whom I refer. It is Friedrich Mandl, the armaments manufacturer."

Hedy believed that feeling a cold chill going up your spine was only an old wife's tale. But now she felt it. Her skin crawled, and the fine hairs on her arms stood up as if they had been rubbed with a wire brush. So Isidor was right. What he said had now come to pass. She was to be sold off like a piece of livestock to the highest, no, the only bidder. It was time to get into her role. She must make herself believe this was the first time she was being presented with this situation. "There is one thing you have not mentioned, Mama."

"What is that, Hedy?"

"Love, Mama. You have not mentioned love. You have explained that he is a nice man and that he is presumably wealthy. But I did not hear you say it, Mama. I did not hear you say that he loves me." Hedy was now pretending to get angry with her mother. "Say it, Mother. Say the words. Say that he loves me!"

Gertrude looked to her husband, Hedy's father. His head was bowed. He could not bear to look at his daughter, such was his shame. "I do not know this man, and he barely knows me. How on earth do you expect me to marry someone for whom I have no feelings? It is wrong to ask this of me. You must know that."

Emil slowly raised his head. He had finally summoned the courage to face his only child. "You must understand, my love, this situation was not of our choosing. We never dreamt that anything like this would ever happen. *Herr* Mandl is a powerful man and very well connected. It was..."

"What did he offer you?" Hedy asked softly, hating herself for the words she was about to utter. "How much was I worth to you, to see me sold off like a sultan's harem woman?"

"It wasn't like that," Emil cried. "Do you honestly think we could put a price on our only daughter, our only child that we would die for? Do you think we had any choice? Do you? You've known me since the day you were born. I, we've, smothered you with love and affection. If there was any other way, don't you think I would have taken it? I would have put a gun to my head and gladly pulled the trigger if it would save you from this. But it would not. Mandl means to have you and have you he will."

"Did he threaten you? Is that what it was? Did he threaten to hurt you? You and Mama? Is that it? We can go to the police, to the authorities. They can stop it. They must stop it!"

Her father shook his head. "Hedy, you don't understand. It is men like Friedrich Mandl who owns the police, who consorts with the authorities. If I did what you say, that would only make things worse. I promise you. His friends are some of the most powerful men in Austria."

"But you have a position of influence as well. You are a bank director. Surely that must count for something."

"Perhaps once it might have. But we live in troubled times, Hedy. You know what is going on across the border, and it will not be too long before the same thing happens here, if *Herr* Hitler has his way. We may not be practicing Jews, but that will make no difference to people like the new

German chancellor. Now maybe you will understand. That is why you must marry Friedrich Mandl. It will be his position in Austrian society that will save you. Despite his Jewish heritage, even Hitler would not dream of harming him. He is too powerful, and besides, Hitler needs men like Mandl to furnish him with the weapons he requires to wage war on those around him. And wage war, he surely will. He cannot help himself. It is in his blood, his lust for absolute power. Please, Hedy, go to this man. He is your only chance to survive if... if anything happens to your mother and me."

Hedy could stand it no longer. She rushed to her father and threw her arms around him. He was still trying to protect her in the best way he could, even if it meant giving up the possibility of ever seeing her again. She released her grip on her father and went over to her mother. Holding Gertrude's hands in hers, she bent forward and kissed her on the cheek. "I'm sorry, Mama, so sorry, Papa, for the things I said just now. I didn't know; I had no idea..." she lied.

"Of course you didn't. We have always tried to shelter you from the worst of things, but even we have our limits. Unfortunately, on this occasion, there is nothing else we can do. Our main purpose, our whole reason for doing what we're doing, is to try and keep you safe." Emil smiled sadly.

"It will work out for the best, you'll see," Gertrude said with a confidence she did not feel. Hedy knew she was only trying to make the best of what they had, but it was hard for her. And just what would life be like to be the wife of a multi-millionaire like Friedrich Mandl? She would soon find out.

* * *

It was a brief courtship, and Mandl proposed to her after their fourth date. In their intervening trysts, her feelings for the man had changed. Yes, he was overbearing and arrogant, but there was also another side to his nature. He could be sweet and caring and kind, and he was obviously very much in love with her despite her earlier misgivings. Maybe things would turn out right after all, but she never forgot the other reason why she agreed to be his wife.

In a further meeting with Isidor, he briefed her on how she should apply herself once she came to live in his palatial home. Sitting beside him was a woman of indeterminate age, whom Isidor introduced as Magda. "Magda is already employed in the Mandl household as a maid. She will be your conduit for any information you glean from your husband," here he smiled, "she will pass on anything she thinks is relevant. You must keep your eyes and ears open at all times. If Mandl even suspects for a minute that you are scheming behind his back, God knows what he'll do. Be careful, that's all I'm saying."

Hedy took Magda's hand in hers. She estimated the maid to be in her forties, but she could have been anywhere between her late thirties and mid-fifties. The woman was woefully thin with straggly mousey-brown hair, which was showing signs of greying at the roots. Her appearance was non-descriptive, save for her eyes, which were the saddest Hedy had ever seen. They were prematurely 'baggy,' and Hedy could only guess at the misery which the woman had seen or had endured. Her mouth was down-turned at the tips as if she were in a constant state of unhappiness. Despite only just meeting her, the actress had never felt so sorry for anyone in her life.

The Haganah had anticipated that this domestic help, Magda, would get close enough to her employer to do what they were now asking of Hedy. Unfortunately, this had not been possible, as he was too careful not to leave any important documents or papers lying out where they could be seen. They were about to write off the exercise when Magda told them about Mandl's infatuation with the actress. By amending their strategy, they could see how this arrangement might even improve on their initial plan. Magda made frequent trips to the village and would relay any intelligence Hedy found to a Haganah agent. It was all going to work out just fine...

And now, here she was, on August 10th., inside this vast cathedral, the *Karlskirche*, attired in her black and white wedding gown, carrying a posy of white orchids, waiting to become *Frau* Mandl. Despite bowing to the inevitable, her parents, Gertrud and Emil, had mixed emotions when they saw their only daughter walk down the aisle; saddened that she should be coerced into to marrying a man she did not love, but content that, at least, she would be safe. It was a trade-off they would have preferred not to have made, but it was what it was. Renouncing her religion was not such an important issue for them. After all, they had both become 'assimilated' Austrians, and despite living in a predominantly Jewish area, they did not have much interest in their religious heritage. But she was only eighteen and was marrying a man fifteen years her senior. Hedy longed to confide in them, to reveal the other reasons for agreeing to this union. She understood, however, that in doing so, it might not only endanger her. It could also put her parents' lives in peril, not to mention the maid, Magda.

It was only through Emil's deep love for his daughter that he agreed to be at her wedding. He would not give her away, however; no one in her family would. That honor would go to one of Mandl's close friends. It was a lavish affair attended by the cream of Austrian society with no expense spared. Mandl even catered for his new wife's family by having part of the meal prepared in the kosher tradition. Mandl himself was half-Jewish on his father's side, but did not acknowledge any part of that religion's culture. With Fascism on the rise and Hitler's public hatred of Jews, it was not a good idea, especially as he wanted to do business with the German dictator.

He had planned an extraordinary honeymoon for them, which would take them to several European countries. The Haganah had already assumed that she would not be able to start her clandestine role within the Mandl household for a short period after the nuptials. It would be almost six months, however, before the newly-weds returned from their extended vacation. Mandl had kept in touch with his business while he and his new bride were away, but now it was time to get back into harness properly.

In January 1934, he stepped into his Austrian factory for the first time since his wedding. He had considered taking his new bride with him, but his jealousy and paranoia forbade him. What if she caught the eye of one of his employees? She was so stunning that it would not be surprising if any of his workforce might consider... who knew what? No, she was his, and his alone. He would not permit any other man the temptation of longing for his wife: something they could never have.

Hedy was also eager to get back to work and spent some of her time perusing stage plays and movie scripts. One evening, her husband looked over at her. "What are you reading, my dear?"

"It's a movie script that Jacques Koerpel sent me. He thinks I might be quite suitable for the part of Diana. It looks interesting."

"I trust it's not another pornographic movie. I will not have you acting in a film like that again. Do you understand me?"

"Yes, Fritz, of course, but I've already explained to you countless times that I was not aware of what Machaty was planning. The script mentioned nothing about performing naked, nor about simulating an... er...well, you know."

"Yes, I know very well, and I will have no more of it. You made me a laughingstock, and I will not abide being ridiculed. That is an end to it. Am I making myself clear?"

"That was totally uncalled for. I made that movie long before I met you. I had no idea it was going to turn out the way it did."

"Be that as it may, I must insist that from now on, you will show me all the manuscripts you are sent. I will decide which ones are suitable and appropriate for you to consider. I will not have my guests, my male guests, looking at you and wondering what you are like beneath your clothing. That is for me, and me alone to know. Do you understand?"

It soon became clear that Mandl was not keen for her to resume her career under any circumstances and would not permit her to audition for any parts. At first, he told her it was because the roles she was being offered would do little to enhance her ambition or show her acting talents. However, as time went by, it became clear that he would never allow her to go back to either the stage or the screen. Despite her arguing that it was her occupation, Mandl forbade her to read any manuscripts at all. It eventually became apparent that he was intensely jealous of her and would not tolerate her speaking to another man out of his presence, even a fellow on-stage, or on-screen actor. He would not even allow her to see any of her theater friends.

After one of their increasingly frequent arguments on the subject, Mandl shouted at her, "You will do only four things in this house. You will appear at my side when I have important guests over. You will look glamorous, dress appropriately, and keep your mouth shut. These are not requests; do I make myself clear?" to which there could be only one response.

Mandl's growing antagonism towards his wife's ambitions helped to harden Hedy's resolve. While she had no qualms about performing the tasks Isidor had asked of her, there was still a pang of conscience within her that she was betraying her husband. This sentiment was diminished by his overbearing attitude and his refusal to listen to her pleas to perform. Although he kept most of his company's files in the factory office, he occasionally brought papers back to study at home. With Magda acting as a lookout, Hedy stole into his private sanctum and copied out any information which might be of use to the Haganah. Production schedules, raw material purchases, new capital equipment requirements were all meticulously recorded. So were any weapon orders to Mandl's clients. Using Magda as her conduit, all the documents she transcribed were delivered to the Haganah agent, who was staying in nearby Schwarzenau.

One evening on his return from the factory, Mandl called Hedy into his office. On her entry into his private study, she was horrified when she saw that some papers she had copied earlier were in disarray. Mandl was meticulous about his paperwork and always stacked each bundle of documents neatly in regimented piles within wire filing trays. He seemed not to notice the disruption as he walked behind his desk and called Hedy to sit in front of him. There was a hardness in his voice that she had not noticed before, despite their frequent heated discussions. "I intend to hold a dinner party in two weeks, with some very important guests. I am telling you this now so you can go and buy a new gown for the occasion. I want you to look lovelier than you have ever been. This occasion is extremely important to me. Do you understand?"

"Yes, Friedrich," she answered meekly, still unsure if he had seen the disordered papers. "Who is coming to the dinner party? Will it be anyone I know?"

"It is none of your business who I invite into my home. Is that clear?"

"Yes, I only..."

"You will know only when I am ready to tell you. Now please leave me. I have some work to do." As Hedy got to the door, Mandl called to her.

"Hedy..." She turned around to face him. "My papers. Do you know how they came to be so untidy? It looks as though someone has been through them. Have you been snooping among my documents?" he asked suspiciously.

"Me?" she asked feigning indignation. "Me? I don't even have a key to this room," she reminded him. This statement was, of course, untrue. Magda had had a copy made of the office key, which she had given to Hedy earlier. "You have made it quite clear on previous occasions that this office is out-of-bounds, and I have respected your wishes. I have only ever been in here when you have... invited me." She refrained from using the word 'summoned.'

"Very well, my dear. I accept your denial." To Hedy, the very fact that he used 'denial' rather than 'explanation' implied to her that he did not believe her. However, believing she was lying and confirming she had secretly invaded his domain were two different things. She would have to be much more careful in the future.

Mandl's dinner party guests included his friend Prince Ernst Rudiger Camillo von Starhemberg. Starhemberg was a fascist and the head of the *Heimwehr*, the militia-style organization set up after World War I to defend Austria from external military threats. He was also heavily involved in Austrian politics and had been Minister of the Interior a few years earlier. Mandl had offered to support his friend for two reasons: firstly, he was himself, an austrofascist, and an admirer of the Italian dictator Benito Mussolini. Secondly, he saw Starhemberg's fascist group as a bulwark against the growing tide of Nazi-ism and Hitler's anti-Semitism, which was also gaining support in Austria. His other guests were distinguished businessmen and their wives and senior members of the Prince's political party, the *Heimatblock*.

Despite all the prominent guests at his table, Mandl spent most of the evening in conversation with Starhemberg. At almost two meters tall, the Count struck an imposing presence. With a beautiful Hedy at Mandl's side, it was no hardship for the Prince to allow himself to be singled out for his host's attention. Even the Countess was impressed by Hedy's allure and engaged her in witless discussion about her former career. This meaningless chatter was frustrating to the actress. She was trying to listen in to the exchange between her husband and Starhemberg. Hedy could hear them talking about weapons but could not overtly eavesdrop, so she could only pick up part of what they were saying. "...new generation of Light Machine Guns...", "...developed from Browning automatic rifles...", "...FN Type D capable of firing six hundred and fifty rounds per minute..."

The double conversation between Mandl and Starhemberg, and Hedy and the Countess went on for a few minutes with Hedy trying to listen in on the men without seeming to disregard her guest. Whether because she knew her hostess was ignoring her or due to a genuine need, the Countess graciously excused herself to find the restroom. Hedy took advantage of her absence to devote herself entirely to her husband and his friend and client. "I have been told that the Českà Zbrojovka vz30 has a rate of fire of six hundred rounds per minute and is chambered to take the seven-point nine-two cartridge. This version seems to be a more effective delivery than the Type D surely," observed Starhemberg. "This weapon only produces five hundred and seventy rounds per minute. If our men are outnumbered or outgunned in the field, we will need to take advantage of every bullet we have."

"Quite right, my dear Prince, but what one loses in one area, one generally gains in another."

"Please be more specific..."

Mandl smiled benevolently, as though explaining the more abstruse parts of some complex algebraic equation to an eager but not very academic student. "I think you are getting the FN M1930 confused with its more current model, the FN Mle D. This has a rate of fire a little greater than its predecessor and even better than the vz30. However, as you so rightly stated, one needs to make the most of every opportunity. The vz30 has an effective range of over nine hundred and twenty meters compared to the FN D, which only has a range of eight hundred and seventy meters. Also, the vz30 is slightly heavier than its Belgian rival. We are only talking about a half-a-kilo; however, in battle, especially if your troops are in a boggy field, every gram counts, does it not? I believe I am also correct in saying that the FN D's overall length is slightly greater than the vz30. As I noted, what one gains in one area, one loses in another. 'Swings and roundabouts,' as the British might say. One must also not forget our indigenous weapons manufacturer, Steyr. They have also recently produced their own version of the LMG, which has a firepower even higher than the FN D. It can release over seven hundred rounds per minute. Its only real issue is its weight, which is significantly heavier than the other two guns. However, it does compensate for its increased mass with higher accuracy, and it also takes the seven-point nine-two cartridges. We can acquire as many as you need."

"...and as to the cost...?"

"I'm sure we can come to some arrangement, my dear Ernst. You will find my prices not unreasonable, especially to my friends." Both men smiled warmly. It had been a done deal even before this dinner party that Mandl would get the contract to supply the *Heimwehr* with their ballistics. It only remained to determine which weapons the Prince and his paramilitary force would prefer.

Hedy was disgusted that the price of a man's life could be reduced to and negotiated over the cost of a bullet and the merits of its lethal means of delivery at an innocuous dinner party. They were discussing the most effective ways of killing their fellow human beings as casually as they might discuss the qualities of a new motor vehicle. Into what sort of world had she got herself involved? Hedy had been included in many of Mandl's discussions with his clients, mainly arms dealers and the defense ministers of various European countries. This involvement was mainly at their insistence due to Hedy's striking looks. Her consuming intellect allowed her to retain much of what she heard. The more she listened in on these discussions, the more appalled she became.

Damn Isidor and damn the Haganah for introducing her to this obscene nightmare. She decided that this would be the last time she would consciously note any matters of this kind. It was not how her parents had raised her. Her father had been the kindest, sweetest parent any child could hope for. In her younger years, it was he who had introduced her to the wonders around her. Her thirst for knowledge had stemmed from his enthusiasm for science and the wonderful scientific advances being made in Europe and around the world. He could not possibly have foreseen that his daughter would get mixed up in other technological inventions, so horrifying that no sane man or woman would wish to have anything to do with them. No, this was it. The Haganah would need to find another way to curb the excesses of that putrid little corporal now running Germany. She was done with weapons of war.

CHAPTER 10

Schwarzenau & Vienna, Austria, and The Bronx, New York
January 1934

The morning after the party, Hedy spoke to Magda. "I can't do this anymore. You do not know what it was like, listening to these people, my own husband, casually discussing the different ways to take the lives of their fellow men. It was obscene. I honestly do not know how I kept from gagging. I'm sorry, Magda. I am not the person you need. You will have to tell them I can't go through this again."

"I understand, *Frau* Mandl, but I do not think you realize the importance of what we are asking you to do. Count von Starhemberg does not concern us much at the moment. He is a blowhard of little consequence despite his grand titles and exalted position. It is not him about whom we worry. It is other men of far greater importance that we seek to gain information from. Believe me; the time will come when you will gather..."

"No, Magda. It's over. I've made up my mind. Nothing I find out will help you. Do you think they will reveal their innermost ambitions in front of anyone who is not part of their closed circle? Even the wife of one of its members? After last night, I realized that nothing I say or do or tell you will make any difference. I'm afraid it has been a wasted exercise. Please tell Isidor I'm sorry. I can't help you anymore."

"Is that your final word?"

"Yes, it is."

"Very well. I will relay your message, but I beg you to reconsider. Please."

"Don't you understand? Even if I did discover any information which might be of use, it would not stop Hitler in his relentless persecution of the Jews. And besides, there are many other purveyors of death than my husband. These businesses would be more than happy to furnish the Germans with weapons of war. That's why I feel this is all so pointless."

The Haganah wanted to reply by a note sent through Magda, but they still needed Hedy, now more than ever. They had to make her see that she could make a vital contribution to their cause despite her misgivings, and they would not achieve this by mailing letters back and forth. They would need to meet her in person; it was the only way to convince her. The only one who could accomplish this was the individual who had recruited her in the first place – Isidor Pralgovitch.

***

The American doctor was spending time at his parents' home in the Bronx. His sixty-eight-year-old father had suffered a heart attack, and the prognosis was not good. The doctors were doing their best, but Avraham was getting weaker, and it was now only a matter of time. How ironic, he felt, that between himself as a medic, and his sisters who were nurses, they could not prolong the life of their beloved father, the man who had given them so much. The man who had given them everything.

Avraham was pronounced as life extinct on a cold, dry January morning by Dr. Donald Mowbray, one of Isidor's colleagues and friend, someone he had gone through medical school with. Although the doctor was not himself Jewish, he had many clients of that faith. He knew the laws and traditions which the religion demanded. As the death was simply due to natural causes, the *Chevra Kadisha* would bury his father as swiftly as possible, and they quickly arranged the funeral for the following day. There would be no problem in organizing a *minyan* at such short notice. This was the required quorum of ten Jewish men who they would need to lay his father to rest under the rites of Judaism.

On the evening of his father's death, Isidor took a phone call. As the family was in mourning, he should not have answered, but it may have been a family member or a friend wishing to know the time of the burial service. It was neither; it was Chaim Goldstein, a member of one of the many local Jewish charities. Unbeknownst to most other members of the community, Goldstein was also a conduit to the Haganah. Goldstein began by issuing the traditional Jewish greeting after a bereavement. "I wish you a long life, Isidor, and to your family as well." He then discussed the purpose of his message. "I'm sorry to telephone you at such a terrible time, but I've just had a message from one of our overseas friends." 'Overseas friends' was a cryptic reference to Golomb's band. "They need you to go back to Austria now. There's a problem with an acquaintance in Vienna that needs to be dealt with immediately."

Isidor was shocked. How dare they contact him on such an occasion? His father had just died, for God's sake. Whatever it was, would have to wait. Nothing could be more critical at this minute than burying him. No matter how important, nothing, absolutely nothing, took precedence over this. The reference to his 'acquaintance' could only mean one person: Hedwig, Hedy Kiesler. Whatever trouble the actress was in, there was nothing he could do for her right now. Apart from the funeral, there was also the traditional ritual of sitting *Shiva* for seven days. It was abominable. It was outrageous, and Isidor would have plenty to say to Golomb on his eventual return to Tel Aviv. Surely there had to be someone else the Haganah could send over to assist with whatever problem she had caused for herself.

"I'm sorry, Isidor, I'm only passing on the instructions. There is a vessel sailing from New York to Bremen tomorrow. You need to be on it."

"I need...? Who does Golomb think he is to order me to sail on a ship on the day of my father's funeral?" he spat. "To hell with you! To hell with you all! You can tell Golomb that I have resigned from the Haganah, and if you've got the balls, you can also tell him I said he could go fuck himself!"

"Please, Isidor, you don't understand..."

"Oh, I understand, alright. Nothing is more important than his precious Haganah. Well, some things are more important, and this is one of them. Surely you can see that."

"It is not a question of what I can or cannot see. I am only relaying the instructions I have been given. I will certainly pass on your... suggestions. I am sorry, truly sorry for your loss. Your late father, may he rest in peace, was an exceptional man."

Isidor was calming down, reluctantly recognizing that Goldstein was, indeed, only a go-between with no authority himself. "Yes, he was, but even if he had been a low-life *gonif*, he was still my father."

"I'll let them know. Maybe they can make other arrangements." Isidor could hear Goldstein's empathy and regretted his earlier language. It was unwarranted and was certainly not directed at him personally. "I'll see you at the cemetery, Isidor. Good night." and with those parting words, the phone went dead.

It had stayed dry, and mourners packed the cemetery. Avraham had been well-liked in the community, and many people, even some non-Jews, had come to pay their last respects. Isidor's mother was distraught with grief, as were his sisters, so none of them noticed a swarthy, well-dressed man appear from out of the crowd. He gently pulled Isidor aside and whispered in his ear. As the man continued speaking, and without turning to look directly at him, Isidor responded by shaking his head. It was only when the stranger persisted that the grieving son and brother looked up. Their eyes locked, and disbelief was evident in Isidor's expression. He showed at first bewilderment, then such a sense of purpose, it was almost as if, for the moment, he had forgotten his surroundings. He nodded to the dark-skinned mourner who bent his head down once before raising it again almost imperceptibly. The arrangement, unspoken and only barely acknowledged, had been made.

Isidor put a protective arm around Minke, his mother, as he said the final Mourner's *Kaddish*, the *Yisgadal*. He knew this was probably contrary to Jewish tradition, but he did it anyway. He needed to comfort his mother, and Isidor knew his time with her and his sisters would be cut short. He would barely have time to return to the *Taharah* House to wash his hands in the customary manner and announce where they would be holding the *Shiva* before being driven to the harbor. He had a ship to catch.

CHAPTER 11

Schwarzenau & Vienna, Austria
January 1934

The Haganah agent in Vienna who had been sent to monitor Mandl and his business clients received a message from Magda. This news was an astonishing revelation, if it were true. Mandl had organized another dinner party; only this time, the guests would not be local Austrian warlords. There would only be one visitor at this social event, a personality Mandl had tried to cultivate in the past and whose endeavors were now bearing fruit. The individual coming to Mandl's stately home was none other than the German chancellor, Adolf Hitler. This was the break they had been waiting for, and with Hedy's help, they might be able to deliver a crippling blow to the Jew-hating leader.

Western governments had long suspected that Hitler was breaking the Versailles Treaty's terms faster than it had been written. Believing and proving, however, were not the same. If the Haganah could get evidence of Germany's rearmament program, it might be enough to warn the Allies of German intent. It would undoubtedly help their cause if they could show unequivocally that Hitler was breaching the conditions of the armistice document. It should give Britain, France, and the United States all the reason they needed to declare a new war on Germany to get rid of the despicable tyrant once-and-for-all. Everyone, not least the Haganah, understood the grave risks involved. However, surely it was better to send

71

troops in now while Germany was still relatively militarily weak, rather than wait for them to re-arm fully. Under the terms of the Treaty, Germany was limited to the types of military hardware it could deploy and the number of armaments and ballistics it could stockpile. Many rumors were circulating that since attaining power, the Chancellor had ignored or intended to defy much of these embargoes. Governments could not act on hearsay alone, but maybe they would take action if that hearsay could be confirmed.

And now, when they were on the brink of achieving their real goal, the one person who could do more than anyone else was refusing to help them. That was why it was so important to get Isidor back to Vienna quickly. If anyone could persuade Hedy to recant on her earlier decision, it was him. The urgency lay in the fact that, according to Magda, the function was scheduled in less than two weeks. This event alone showed how powerful Mandl was. Getting the German head of state to attend a dinner party at such short notice was a feat even other government leaders could not achieve.

Taking advantage of Mandl's absence, the maid approached Hedy. "There is someone who wants to meet with you, *Frau* Mandl. It is a person you know well and who I believe, going by our previous discussion on the subject, is someone for whom you have feelings. You must see him." Hedy knew at once about whom Magda was talking. There was only one man that matched this description.

"Why should I condescend to meet him? He is no longer anything to me. I have made my bed, and I must lie in it. It is bad enough that thanks to him and my husband, I no longer have a career. Because of them, I am kept a virtual prisoner in my own home, only to be taken out and presented when my husband sees fit. Isidor Pralgovitch is no longer a part of my life, nor do I wish to resume any relationship with him."

"Please, *Frau* Mandl, Hedy. It is not for his sake or mine that he wishes to see you. Much larger issues are at stake, things even I do not know or comprehend. But it was made clear to me that it was of paramount importance that you should forgive him for what he has put you through."

"Can you tell me anything about why he is so insistent?"

"Only that it concerns an upcoming dinner party that you should attend."

"I don't understand. Why does Isidor want me to do something that Fritz will no doubt insist upon, anyway?"

An exasperated Magda breathed in through her nose before exhaling. "Very well. It is about who will be at this affair."

"Do I need to drag it out of you? Who is coming to this party, and why has Fritz not already told me himself?"

"He cannot tell you yet. He has been sworn to secrecy."

"This is all becoming very mysterious, and if I don't know, how did you find out?"

"It was by accident. You were out riding in the grounds, and the master took a telephone call. I just happened to be nearby and heard the conversation, or at least *Herr* Mandl's side of it."

"Yes...?"

"It seems that whoever was phoning him was returning a previous call made by *Herr* Mandl. It appears it was to confirm a dinner party to which he had sent an invitation but had not received a reply. *Herr* Mandl had telephoned the guest to ascertain if they were coming."

"And these guests are...?"

Magda hesitated before responding. Despite looking furtively round to confirm no one else was within earshot, she whispered her reply. "Hitler - Adolf Hitler," she revealed breathlessly.

"But why is it so important for me to see Isidor? What can they possibly want from me?"

"It would probably be best if Isidor tells you himself. Can I confirm that you will see him? It will not take long."

Hedy closed her eyes, raising her face upward to hold back the tears. She had wanted so much more from the American doctor, more than he could give her. She had even married a man she loathed because he had asked it of her. Since her marriage to Mandl, he had been out of her life, which had probably been for the best, for both their sakes.

Even now, if he asked her to run off with him and leave her opulent life behind, she would find it hard to resist. Could she trust herself to be with him? Instinctively, she wanted to refuse; her head said so. Her heart, however, was another matter. She longed to see him again and, allowing her emotions to overrule her logical mind, told Magda that she would agree. It was done.

The following evening on his return from the factory, Mandl summoned Hedy into his study. "I am hosting another dinner party in two weeks' time. I am reluctant to tell you so far in advance who the guest will be, but on this occasion, it is probably for the best if I forewarn you.

Hedy feigned ignorance of who the invitee was to be. "Guest, you said guest. Is there only to be one person coming?"

"Yes, but this person could be very beneficial to me, so I want you to look lovelier than you have ever done. Do you hear me?"

"Of course. Who is it? Who's coming?" she asked, pretending to be excited.

Mandl hesitated a second before revealing who would be his guest of honor. "It is to be the German chancellor, Adolf Hitler," he replied without emotion.

"Adolf Hitler is coming here? To our house?"

"Isn't that what I just said? I want you to go into town and order a new dress for the occasion. You will spare no expense. Even a good impression may not be enough. I want you to look better than perfect."

As the beautiful hostess, Hedy would be the center-pin of his auspicious evening. Mandl was still covetous of his young wife, and his selfish pride would not permit him to allow her to travel alone. He had grown used to other men looking at her, admiring her; she was stunning, after all. But what if their admiration developed into something more... physical? She was his. She belonged to him, and he would not permit her the opportunity of even speaking with anyone else, especially a man, any man. The exceptions would be his manservant and those dignitaries he invited to his home.

"Heinrich will accompany you to purchase your gown and any other items of apparel you need. Perhaps a piece of jewelry to complement the outfit might be nice," he suggested. "Maybe a tiara to show of your lustrous dark hair, eh?"

Hedy had to think quickly. This would be the ideal opportunity to meet with Isidor, but not if she was with Heinrich. If she suddenly 'disappeared,' it would look suspicious and would give Mandl all the excuses he needed to sequester her even more closely. "If I am to go with one of the staff, it would be better with a female. Men know nothing about clothes and even less about jewelry. If it were up to your manservant, I would probably come home looking like a cheap streetwalker. I will take..." she pretended to consider her choices for a few seconds, "I will take Magda with me. She is an older woman and looks as if she might know the difference between a tiara and a strudel." she laughed.

"Very well," conceded her husband. "You may take the maid. I will instruct Heinrich to have one of the cars ready for you. There will be much to arrange, so do not take too long."

"If you wish me to look attractive for your guest, you must allow me the time I need to pick the correct dress and whatever else I think I will require. You men simply do not understand, do you?" she shook her head sadly.

Mandl gave one of his rare unforced smiles. "Of course, my dear. Just try to take your time quickly." Hedy knew he meant this remark as a witticism, but behind the flippant retort, he was sending a serious message – 'I will not tolerate you being away from my sight, or that of my staff I can trust, for too long.'

"It is unlikely I will be able to purchase anything locally. Schwarzenau has no suitable dress shops, much less any stores I can buy a decent piece of jewelry. I shall have to go to Vienna. With your permission, of course. I realize it is some distance away, but if we leave early, I should be back by late afternoon."

"Very well. Just don't make a habit of it."

"No, Fritz, I won't. Only when you have nasty little dictators coming to tea." She left him before he could think of a suitable reply.

The actress did not take long to pick out a suitable dinner frock. Thanks to Magda's keen eye and Hedy's sense of haute couture, they quickly finished their shopping. Picking out a suitable jeweled headdress also did not tax her too much, not when she had Mandl's inexhaustible resources at her disposal. She had arranged to meet with Isidor at the same coffee shop they went to on their first encounter. As Magda stood, or rather sat furtive lookout near the door, Hedy took a table further into the room. Less than five minutes later, Isidor joined her. Almost unconsciously, he embraced her hands with his across the white linen table cover.

Before her arrival, she had been determined not to give in to his demands, but now she was sitting in front of him, all of her resolve seemed to melt away. "I... I hardly know where to start, Hedy. Marriage has made you blossom, and you are even more pretty now than you were before, if that's possible."

Hedy blushed at Isidor's comments, unsure how to respond. "It's been a while, Isidor. How are you?"

He told her all about his father and how he came to be back in Vienna. "We don't have much time. My husband keeps me under continual scrutiny, if that's the proper word. What do you want from me?"

"Then I won't waste our valuable time with small talk. Thanks to Magda, we know who is coming to Castle Schwarzenau. Hitler is shortly to be Mandl's dinner guest. We will never have a better opportunity to –"

"To what?"

"Let me explain. Even Krupps cannot produce enough armaments to satisfy Hitler's war aims if our assumptions are correct. We knew that eventually, Hitler would find his way to your husband and his armaments factory. This is the exact opportunity we've been waiting for. It could not have worked out better. With the right person in place, any discussions regarding the Führer's military plans that could find their way to the Haganah might see Germany stopped in its tracks." He almost added 'its tank tracks,' but under the terms of the Versailles Treaty, this was another field weapon forbidden to the German army, not that this prohibition would stop Hitler from acquiring them.

"But how can the Haganah benefit from knowing about Hitler's plans?"

Isidor shook his head slowly. "There are two main reasons I cannot go into too much detail. Firstly, even I do not know all there is to know about this mission. Secondly..." he hesitated, "...secondly, the less you know, the better. I won't lie to you, Hedy. We are dealing with not very nice people here. These men are ruthless, and even your sex might not save you if they catch you doing things that they find, ah, inappropriate. As it is, you already know too much about us, about me. I can tell you this much. There are people out there," he gestured with his hand as he raised his arm, pointing to the outside, "who are as afraid as we are of what Hitler will do. These are very important and powerful people, Hedy; powerful enough to stop this lunatic before he destroys the world. But to take these steps, they must have proof of his intentions. If we can get this information to these men, there might be a chance to prevent bloodshed on such a scale the world has never seen. That was the real purpose of your recruitment in the first place. There, I've said it. You may choose to hate me for this massive deception, and it would be your right to do so. But in all honesty, if I had to do this all over again, I would. Events are happening not just in Germany and in Europe, but even in my adopted home, in Palestine, that I cannot disclose to you. It would be too dangerous for you to know about them, but this Nazi menace is growing, and if we do not stop it now, it will soon be too late."

"I have heard Fritz talk of such things also, but he does not discuss them with me. I think he is trying to shelter me from them, and I love him for it. He can be cruel, it is true, but he can also be caring when he has a mind to. It does not disguise the fact, however, that the things you have just mentioned are happening. I know Fritz detests Hitler as much as you do. He is half-Jewish on his father's side. Why do you not approach him yourself? I am positive he would be more than happy to help to depose this awful man, despite wanting to do business with him."

"No, Hedy, we cannot do that."

"Why, for God's sake?"

"Mandl is no Nazi. We know this, but he is a Fascist and a supporter of Mussolini as well as his friend Prince Starhemberg. Quite frankly, although your husband is a big blustering fellow, I, we, think that at heart, he is a coward. He would not have the stomach to go through with any underhand deception that needs to be played. If it meant the difference between helping the cause of peace and righteousness and serving his own selfish interests, I honestly cannot be sure which side he would choose. It is you, Hedy, for all your youth and your fragile beauty that we believe we can trust. The very fact that you are here now, with Magda keeping watch by the door, proves this, especially when you say that Mandl has you under constant surveillance. Your courage is there for all to see, and I am only sorry that it has to be tested under such trying circumstances."

"If I help you, and you can get such intelligence to these people you mention, how would it enable them to stop Hitler's madness?"

"I think I know what is in your mind, and I won't disabuse you. Yes, if you can get us the proof we need, it will mean a new war with Germany, and yes, there will be much bloodshed on both sides. But Hitler is not the kind of person with whom you can reason. If this were the case, it would be much simpler. The only language he and his kind understand is the language of violence. Make no mistake, Hedy, this *miturof*, this *meshuggener*, is intent on war. To him, the end does justify the means, and if it entails him being the last man standing, so be it. He needs to be stopped, not just for the sake of the Jews, but for the sake of the world!"

After taking a few seconds to absorb her companion's profound words, Hedy smiled ruefully, "Don't you see the delicious irony, Isidor?"

The doctor was confused by her question, the look on his face confirming his bewilderment. "Well," she explained, "if what you seek comes to pass, my husband will not only be the third richest man in Austria, he will be the third richest man in Europe. Where do you think Hitler will get his ammunition to fight such a war, eh? It will be from people like Fritz Mandl. I sincerely hope that he will make a sizeable contribution to Haganah's funds."

Isidor couldn't help it. He had to contain his laughter for fear of drawing attention to himself. "My God, Hedy, you're right. I hadn't thought of that. We might even raise a statue to him in the Clock Square," he pondered on the statement he had just made. "well, perhaps not, eh?" He returned to the discussion in a more somber mood. "Will you do it, Hedy? Will you help us this one last time? I honestly don't think we'll ever get such a chance again."

"No, you're probably right," she agreed.

"So...?"

"What is it you want me to do?"

"As I've already said, we need any tidbits of information you overhear concerning Hitler's warmongering policies. Any intelligence you can furnish us with, no matter how insignificant, will help us. Anything you overhear, which points to his plans, his aggressive ambitions, will be of immense importance. We need to pass these to those who will put an end to him."

"Very well, Isidor, I will do it, but this is positively the last time. I am an actress, not a spy."

"I know, Hedy, and thank you. Just please be careful. I..."

"Yes, Isidor?"

"I...nothing; it's nothing."

Hedy knew what he was thinking, what he was longing to say, but could not. Neither could she.

Across the road, sitting in one of Mandl's many automobiles, was Heinrich. Despite Hedy's instructions to leave her and Magda, he drove away only to return a few minutes later. Leaning forward in his employer's Daimler, he sported a pair of Zeiss binoculars strapped about his neck. As efficient as always, he had noted the name and address of the coffee house, the time Hedy entered, the duration of her stay, and when she left. He also wrote, as best he could, a description of Hedy's coffee companion.

At dinner that evening, Hedy and Fritz were discussing the details of the forthcoming dinner engagement. As calmly as if he were deliberating what to choose for the fish course, Mandl suddenly turned to Hedy. "Did you meet anyone when you were in town earlier?"

"When I was in town earlier...?"

"Yes, when you were in town buying your dinner gown. Did you see anyone you knew—a friend, perhaps...?"

Hedy could tell by his tone that he was toying with her, waiting for her to refute any such assignment. He must have somehow discovered her meeting with Isidor, but how? It certainly was not from Magda, that was for sure. Who else...? With blinding clarity, she accepted the obvious. Hedy had dismissed her chauffeur once he had dropped her and Magda in the town center, with instructions when to return. He must have secretly kept them in sight and followed them to the coffee shop. There would be no use in denying it. Heinrich would have jotted it all down. She had to think quickly and not appear nonplussed. "Well, actually, I did meet someone. I've just been waiting for the right moment to broach it with you."

Mandl cocked an eyebrow, believing he had caught out his young wife. "And who is this mysterious person whom you've been waiting for the right moment to tell me about? If you've been seeing someone..." and his affable exterior suddenly turned dark and menacing.

"No, no, Fritz, it is nothing like that. Good heavens, no. Surely you should know me better than that. No, it is something else entirely, I assure you. Something that will benefit you, I think."

"This is becoming curiouser and curiouser, and I cannot wait to hear it."

She could see he was doing his best to keep his temper in check. Hedy was playing for time. An idea had found root inside her fertile imagination, and it was just a matter of how to nourish it so it would appear to be credible.

"Was it someone I know?"

"No," she admitted quietly.

"Hmm. This is most strange. So, if I am to believe you, it was not a romantic assignation, but this person is unknown to me, as well. If I were a patient or a trusting man, I would allow you the benefit of the doubt, but I am neither, so you will tell me now who this man is. Do you understand, my dear?" He spat out the word 'dear' with a sneer.

She was ready. She had to be prepared. So much depended on what she was about to say, not just its content, but its delivery as well. "He knows about your guest, that is, who you have invited to dinner next week..."

"And...?" his face darkened. "This is supposed to be a secret, only known to a select few. Any member of my staff found to have breached this confidence will suffer instant dismissal. And now a stranger, a complete stranger, has gotten wind of my plans. Did you tell him?"

"No, I swear I didn't. He already knew, how I don't know."

"What is his name?"

"I don't know. He wouldn't say."

"What did he want? Money to keep quiet?"

"No, it was nothing like that."

"Then what?" he demanded.

"I doubt you would believe me if I told you."

"Yes, you are probably right. I doubt I would believe anything you tell me, but tell me anyway."

"He told me to tell you that you must sell weapons to Hitler, and munitions, of course. Anything Hitler wants, he must get. It was of the greatest import that Germany should be armed as much and as soon as possible. He said that by doing this, you would become incredibly wealthy."

He opened his arms expansively, and Hedy's eyes followed his gaze almost unwillingly around the large dining room. "Look around you, my dear. I am not exactly penniless now."

"Yes, I know, but if you furnish Hitler with what he needs, you will not only have more wealth than even you could dream of. You would have the thanks of one of, no, the most powerful man in Europe." Appeal to his greed and his arrogance, she thought. They would be his weaknesses.

"Did this man say why it was so necessary for me to provide Hitler with his armaments?"

"No, only that you needed to do so."

"Did Hitler send him?"

"I don't know. I don't think so, but that's only speculation. It seemed as if he wanted this to happen, but I got the feeling that he was acting alone."

"Probably a local Nazi. Unfortunately, there are quite a few of them around, but it still does not answer my question? How did he know about the dinner? I think Hitler probably did have a hand in this, but that then begs another question...."

Hedy could feel herself getting out of her depth. It was an old truism, never more apposite than now. One lie begets another until one can no longer distinguish truth from falsehood. "What is that?" she asked.

"Why did this un-named man not come directly to me? Why did he think it necessary to approach my wife instead?"

"Well, if I may say so without seeming to appear arrogant, were I a young man, to whom do you think I would rather speak? A pretty young woman or a bombastic, truculent businessman? Maybe he was just frightened of your reputation. You can be rather... brusque, you know."

"Even so, it all sounds somewhat implausible. How can I be sure any of this is true?"

"Do you honestly think I could concoct such a story? I am, I was an actress." she corrected herself. "Please credit me with some imagination. You know how much I detest that horrid man as much as you do. Would I relate such a discourse unless it was what actually transpired?"

"As you say, it is doubtful you would encourage me to sell arms to such a despicable character, although I probably will anyway. Did he say anything else?"

"No. I believe he thought he was being watched and wanted to get his request over as quickly as possible. He did seem very nervous, I am sure."

Mandl was in two minds, whether or not to believe her story. It was so incredible; it might just be real. On the other hand, there was one element Mandl had not disclosed to his wife. Going by Heinrich's report, they seemed to be clasping hands more like lovers than two people meeting for the first time. These did not seem to be the actions of a desperate or frightened man. He would do nothing now, but later, after the dinner party, there would be a reckoning.

CHAPTER 12

Schwarzenau, Austria
January 1934

Hedy looked resplendent in a blue chiffon and taffeta gown and wore the tiara she had purchased with Magda. Before dinner, Mandl ushered the German leader into his sumptuous library, where, with Hedy beside him, he engaged in small talk with the Führer. The more serious discussions and the main reason for Hitler's visit would come later.

Mandl had already played host to Benito Mussolini, Italy's Fascist leader, sometime earlier, so was no stranger to entertaining important personalities. Unlike Mussolini, however, who exuded a sense of humor despite his bellicose nature, Mandl found conversation with Hitler stilted and strained. He expected the Nazi leader to behave the same way in private discussion as he gave his bombastic public speeches, loud, brash, and passionate. But the Hitler who was occupying a blue brocaded chair in Mandl's library was diametrically different from the industrialist's expectations. He spoke so softly that both Mandl and Hedy had to strain to hear what their guest was saying. It was almost as if he did not wish to be heard.

"Our meal will be ready shortly," Mandl offered, trying to break the awkward silence that had descended after their earlier discourse. "Can I perhaps get you a drink in the meantime...? A soft drink," he added hastily, remembering Hitler's well-known temperance and abstention from alcohol.

"No, that is quite alright, *Danke*." The hiatus in the room could be cut with a knife; it was so palpable. It was obvious that Hitler did not want to be here anymore than the Mandl's wanted this dreadful man in their home, but this gathering was far from being a social occasion. So much depended on the outcome of the discussions that would take place later. Turning to Hedy, Hitler said, "I believe you used to be an actress, *Frau* Mandl."

"Yes, that's correct. I was, in fact, playing on stage in Vienna when I met Fritz," she responded, glancing lovingly at her husband.

"Quite so. I understand you have also acted in talking pictures as well. I do not attend the cinema often; pressures of state, you understand." Hedy nodded in agreement, glancing worryingly at Fritz. "Have you been in anything I may have heard of?"

The former actress hesitated. "Well," she began, "I have had some small parts in minor movies which I doubt you will have seen..."

"Yes...?"

Remembering her previous roles, Hedy continued, "I acted in only a few films. My first small speaking role was as a secretary in '*Storm in a Water Glass*,' then I played 'Helene' in '*Building and Marrying*' although it was originally entitled '*The Trunks of Mr.O.F.*' and my other part was in '*No Money Needed*.' All very unmemorable," she answered modestly.

"Hardly that," Hitler smiled. "I believe you were the main character in this film, is this not so?"

"One of them," she admitted. He was obviously playing games with her, with both of them. He had either done his own researches into her background or had been made aware by an aide. Mandl could only sit and listen in horror as he knew what his guest would allude to next. Hitler sat in silence for a few seconds before bringing up the subject they both feared.

"I believe you have also taken part in another movie, is this not correct?" Mandl made to interrupt, but Hitler held up a hand to silence him before he could speak. "Is this not correct?" he repeated more forcefully. This was hardly a rhetorical question. *Hitler knew exactly the part she had played in Extase.* The bastard was enjoying her discomfiture and that of his host.

Hedy knew it was useless to deny her role and what it entailed. She decided to meet this man's disrespect head-on and suffer the consequences later. "Yes, I really would have preferred not to discuss this picture. I am sure you know all about it, despite your earlier professed ignorance. After all, you have banned it from being shown in German cinemas."

Fritz shot her a terrified and angry look, but before he could interject, Hedy continued, "I only have one question for you, *Herr* Chancellor. Did you ban it because of its subject or because the leading lady is of Jewish descent?"

From the time he became the leader of the Nazi party, and especially since his election to the Chancellery, Hitler was not used to anyone, even his closest friends and advisers, speaking to him like this. The woman was deliberately trying to provoke him, and his bodyguards who were standing silently by the doors looked uncertainly to their Führer for guidance. Had these words been uttered in Berlin, no doubt Hitler would have taken some action. He would not be able to afford for his authority to be undermined, especially by a woman. No, not just a woman, but a Jew! But he was not in Berlin now; he was in the home of a man (and his wife) who could help him achieve his ultimate aim. He smiled affably at Hedy while motioning his entourage to stand down.

"You must excuse my wife, *Herr* Chancellor. She can be a little headstrong but she means no harm."

"No offense taken, *Herr* Mandl. It is quite... refreshing to meet a woman who is not afraid of speaking her mind so openly on such intimate subjects. It must be her association with the acting fraternity which causes her to be so unconstrained."

Hedy looked around herself to be sure she was still in the same room. Both her husband and their guest were talking about her as if she were not present. To ensure to herself that she had not turned into a wraith, Hedy asked, "Have you seen the movie?"

Hitler appeared to be confused by the simple question, as if unsure how to respond. By acknowledging that he had viewed her performance, it would make him look weak and almost voyeuristic; by admitting he had not seen it, he would appear to be ignorant and nothing more than a mouthpiece, listening to the opinions of others, and who could do little more than repeat their own disapproval. As Hitler was about to respond, Mandl quickly interceded. "I do not think the Chancellor would wish to discuss a production with so questionable a subject. Perhaps we might move onto other topics more suited to a respectable household than some sordid celluloid trash."

Before either Hedy or Hitler could reply, there was a knock on the library doors. The butler did not usually wait for a reply before entering, but having been briefed who the guest-of-honor was, he waited discretely until he heard Mandl's voice.

"Come in," boomed the host, as if trying desperately to re-establish his authority in his own domain. The guards moved away from the doors, allowing the butler to enter. Trying not to look at the German leader, he announced, "Dinner is ready, sir."

"Very well," replied Mandl, relieved at the interruption. "We will be along in a minute." After dismissing his servant, Mandl said, "Perhaps the Chancellor would care to escort my wife to the table."

Hedy shot her husband a disapproving glance but could do nothing except allow their guest to take her by the arm and walk with his hostess sedately into the large dining room. As they approached the table, Hitler pulled out her seat. Over the musical strains of Wagner's *Lohengrin* being played by the five-piece orchestra Mandl had arranged for the occasion, the German leader leaned forward, his lips almost caressing Hedy's neck. "This is the first and only time I have ever held a chair for a Jewess. Make the most of this moment, *Frau* Mandl. It will never happen again," he hissed into her ear. Hedy felt her whole body suddenly run cold as if she had come into contact with an ice block. At that precise moment, it seemed as if all Hitler's venom and spite against Jews was directed solely at her.

There had been some discussion earlier regarding Hitler's favorite foods and his aversion to most meats. The German leader wanted to bring his personal chef, but Mandl persuaded him that his cook would not tolerate another professional in 'his' kitchen. Mandl repeatedly assured

Hitler's staff that the house chef was just as inventive as his own, and nothing would be served up, which would irritate Hitler's stomach or cause culinary offense. Mandl's chef was told that although Hitler was not a vegetarian, he ate meat only sparingly, and his favorite and possibly the only animal-based dish to which he was partial, was liver dumplings.

Out of respect for their guest, Mandl did not smoke his customary Cuban cigars, and neither Hedy nor Fritz touched alcohol during the meal, although Hedy was longing for a glass of wine, anything to dull her senses at having to sit at the same table as Hitler. The five-course dinner passed almost uneventfully. They stayed well away from the subject of politics. However, Fritz could sense that Hitler would have liked nothing more than to expound his intolerable racial purity theories, judging by the hints he was making about his hostess's background.

Seated on her chair, Hitler's words came back to haunt her, and she realized as if for the first time that this man despised her, not for being in the acting profession, or for her salacious part in *Extase*, but for the simple fact that she was a Jew. Isidor was right. She could almost smell the evil emanating from him and his unfathomable, illogical, pathological hatred for her race. Whatever it took, no matter the cost to her, she would do all she could to see this man humbled and defeated.

Hedy knew she was treading on very thin ice but could not bear to listen to this man's odious diatribe any longer. "Both my parents are indeed from Jewish backgrounds, but neither my mother nor my father is observant in any way. In fact, my mother has converted to Catholicism. In your eyes, I suppose that does not make me any less a Jew, but although I do not practice my religion, wear a *sheitel*, or light Shabbos candles, I am still proud of my heritage, and I always will be. I would be grateful if you would desist from disparaging Jews while you are at this table and in my home," she finished icily.

Mandl did not believe what he was hearing and could only gape with an open mouth and a latent fear such as he had never experienced. This man had the power through those Austrian Nazis that were themselves gaining strength and influence in Austria to make his life very difficult. It would be of no matter his substantial influence as one of the country's leading arms dealers and industrialists, as well as his connections to political leaders. Now his wife, his own wife, was putting everything in jeopardy, not only his businesses and fortune, but their very lives.

He tried to admonish Hedy for her outburst, but before he could open his mouth, Hitler sneered, "To the best of my knowledge, *Frau* Mandl, this is not your home. You live here, in some palatial splendor, only because you happen to be married to the man who does own this magnificent castle. If, or I should say, when he finally tires of your insolence, it will not be your home any longer. Out of deference to *Herr* Mandl, I will speak no more of these matters." Addressing his host, he continued, "Perhaps it is time for us to conduct our business."

Mandl turned to his wife, glaring at her in almost uncontrolled malevolence, "Hedy, I must insist that you apologize to *Herr* Hitler for your unseemly outburst, and then I would be obliged if you would leave us. The Chancellor and I have some affairs to attend to."

Hedy hesitated as she rose from the chair. She had gone too far. In irritating Hitler, she had spoiled any opportunity she may have had to sit in on their discussions and report back to the Haganah what was said. To her astonishment, their guest smirked, "No, I would like *Frau* Mandl to join us. It might be... instructive for her to see how real leaders comport themselves in each other's company. What do you say, *Herr* Mandl?"

Mandl did not understand Hitler's purpose in having his wife present at such a sensitive meeting. He knew it could not be for the reason his guest stated. Hedy knew all too well. This was Hitler's way of punishing her. To have to sit through hours of grueling negotiations and counter-negotiations, listening to the two men discuss various weapons and ballistics, their particular benefits and drawbacks, the costs, the lead times, the logistics. How boring this would all be to a woman with no knowledge or interest in such matters. Unable to read a book, much less listen to a radio, or become absorbed in her knitting or sewing. Just having to sit and listen patiently, quietly, and reluctantly while her husband and his potential client hammer out a mutually acceptable contract.

Hedy could see that Fritz was not happy about this, but she had caused enough damage already, and he did not wish to compound her recalcitrance with further reluctance.

"Very well, she may sit in on our meeting; much good may it do her. Before we go any further, however, I must insist on one thing. Hedy, you will apologize to Chancellor Hitler for your earlier outburst. Such behavior was uncalled for."

Hedy glowered at her contrite husband. Her instincts told her not to compromise her beliefs, but if she did not acquiesce to Fritz's demand, she would lose any chance she had of harvesting Hitler's ambitions. Through clenched teeth, she barely glanced at her nemesis as she said the words, "I am very sorry, *Herr* Hitler, to have caused you any distress, and I trust you will forgive my earlier tantrum." she smiled wanly.

"That's quite alright, my dear. Your apology is accepted, and we can consider this unpleasantness over." However, Hedy knew it was anything but over.

They repaired to Mandl's conference room. Mandl took his usual place at the top of the table with Hedy sitting to his right side. Seating himself to his host's left, Hitler took a chair, finding that he could look directly across at his hostess with his intimidating gaze.

The German leader began the discussion, but not in the way Hedy or Fritz expected. "It has long been my belief that we, that is Germany and Austria, have much in common, our language, of course, being the main uniting factor. I know your own chancellor is very much against this idea, but even he will see that this has to be the way forward eventually. You will understand, I expect, that I now consider myself a German although I was born in Austria. I and I alone will bring my country back from the brink of economic ruin, and I intend to make it the powerhouse of Europe. But I cannot do this without persuading the population that it would be in all our interests to bring this aim to fruition. There are many people in both our countries who already see the benefits of such co-operation. Sadly, however, there is still a sizeable number who have yet to be convinced. Your friend, Prince Starhemberg, is one such stumbling block. He believes that if Germany were planning to take Austria by force of arms, which I assure you, we have no intention of doing, his friend Mussolini would step in. I regret to disabuse him, but the Italian and I have come to an... arrangement. I cannot divulge to you what this is, but what I can tell you is that he may not be as staunch a friend as you believe him to be." Warming to his theme, Hitler continued, "Whatever Dollfuss hopes or thinks, our two countries will be united with or without his approval. I will remember those who help us achieve this ambition, just as I will not forget those who hamper our plans. Thanks to that despicable Treaty, it has officially limited us in our military capabilities, and this is where manufacturers like you can come in."

Mandl knew instantly the treaty to which Hitler was referring. It was the Treaty of Versailles, specifically *Part V, Military, Naval and Air Clauses, Article 159 through Article 210.*

"But if you mean what I believe you to be saying, you are asking me to betray my own country. You must also know that both the Treaty of Versailles and the Treaty of Saint Germain absolutely prevent our two countries from amalgamating. The Allied nations would never stand for such a flagrant disregard of these terms. Are you really willing to provoke another European war?"

"The so-called 'Allied nations' do not want nor seek another conflict. Their populations would rise up in revolt at the very suggestion. The last conflict is still too fresh in their minds to contemplate a second conflagration. They are complacent and fearful of such carnage. We, on the other hand, have much to prove. If such a conflict were to occur, they would discover that this time, Germany was led by a government that would not bend the knee so obsequiously. Other arms dealers and distributors have already agreed to help us. The rewards for doing so, both politically and financially, will be enormous. The alternative may not be so good for you and your businesses. Before we go any further, let me show you something," and in so saying, Hitler undid the buckles of his brown leather case and brought out some papers. "This excrement is part of the Treaty that the Allied powers made our cowardly politicians accept. Look," and Hitler threw the documents in Mandl's direction. "Maximum of seven infantry divisions, three cavalry divisions, and two army corps headquarters staffs," he recited without even looking at them. Maximum number of rifles, eighty-four thousand, carbines – eighteen thousand, heavy machine guns – seven-hundred-and-ninety-two; seven-hundred-and-ninety-two," he repeated, as if not believing the figures he was quoting. "Less than eight hundred heavy machine guns for the whole of the German army? I still cannot believe that the German government so meekly capitulated to these outrageous terms. See for yourself; it gets even worse. Eighty-four, yes, eighty-four howitzers. What am I supposed to do with eighty-four howitzers? How can I be expected to protect Germany when I am not given the adequate means to do so? And the list goes on. We are a population of sixty-five million people, yet they want to limit our military capability to that of a small backwater nation. My country was not a signatory to their London Naval Treaty; we were not even invited as an observer nation." He raved on as if unaware he was in company, "I am sure they want to eventually demilitarize us totally. I am convinced that this is not the final tally. It is merely the first step in emasculating the German people as a permanent punishment for losing the war. It will not stand!" he ranted. "The Allied nations wanted their pound of flesh; well, they have got it, but not for long."

It was then that Hedy noticed that on the margins, figures had been over-written in ink, with other numbers. She looked in astonishment as she saw what had been scribbled. Instead of eighteen thousand, she saw sixty thousand. Hitler had scored through the number of heavy machine guns and had replaced it with a higher figure of ten thousand. And so it went on, all down the list of armaments permitted to Germany. Even Hedy knew that these numbers could not be for defense measures only. When Mandl, too, saw the dramatic increases in weapons, munitions, and other ballistics which had been annotated, his loyalty to the country of his birth was sorely tried.

Hedy's contact was quite correct after all, and this would be just the start. It would propel him, Fritz Mandl, into being one of the wealthiest men in Europe, many times richer than he even was now. He, too, would show the Allies that they had chosen badly when they did not accept his company as the only official arms manufacturer allowed to exist within Austria. With the money from Hitler's coffers rolling in, Mandl could extend his business empire beyond anything he could have ever contemplated. But at what cost? Would his conscience and his sense of duty permit him to re-arm this warmonger? Mandl, too, realized that the number of extra weapons Hitler was seeking was far more than would be required solely for the protection of Germany. The arms dealer was in no doubt that Hitler was speaking the truth when he asserted that other arms dealers would be falling over themselves to do business with him, either because of the profits to be made from such a venture or the justifiable fear of what would happen to them if they refused. Why should Mandl's own company, *Hirtenberger Patronen-Fabrik*, miss out on the lucrative deals which were sure to be available? And Mandl had an ace up his sleeve no other munitions supplier could hope to match. Before then, however, they had to get down to the business at hand. Smiling affably, the industrialist agreed that he could meet Hitler's military materiel requirements, and more. All that was needed was to thrash out a price that was mutually acceptable to them both.

The negotiations and discussions went on well into the early hours, and Hedy was finding it difficult to stay awake and focused. Although she had been used to late nights during her acting career, her eyes felt as if leaden weights had been attached to them. Believing he had secured an armaments deal with Hitler, Mandl waited expectantly, remembering his secret asset which he had still to play. The German leader showed no signs of tiring despite the lateness of the hour.

Eventually, he turned to face his host full-on, and said, "I expect you wish me to decide as to the types and quantities of weaponry I would want to purchase from you. Well, first of all, *Herr* Mandl, I do not make my mind up so easily. There are various factors for me to consider." He paused, watching for any reaction from the arms dealer. Mandl sat immobile, quietly seething under his bland, non-committal countenance. "The one subject we have not yet discussed is our ability, or should I say, our inability to protect ourselves in the event of a naval incursion by our enemies. I am sure you will be aware of the restrictions placed on our navy in terms of our capability to fend off any attack by sea. We have been forbidden, *forbidden*, to build or buy submarines. How dare they? How dare those... those political pygmies dictate to us what we can and cannot use to protect our shores? Twelve small torpedo boats, twelve torpedo boats for a navy the size that our navy should be." If Hitler was looking for an audience to project his wrath on to, he could have found no better a listener than Mandl. With what the arms manufacturer had in mind, he would have this despot eating out of his hand.

He allowed Hitler to rave about the perceived injustices meted out to Germany and her allies, the Central Powers, in the aftermath of the previous conflict. Mandl was very well aware of the limitations imposed by the victorious nations.

"They have allowed us to have torpedo boats, but the torpedoes we may use are almost obsolete with the advancements in naval warfare. Wire-guided projectiles will soon be a thing of the past. Did you know that there are now torpedoes that are radio controlled? Imagine being able to manage the guidance system remotely using nothing but radio waves. It is almost unimaginable. This is the type of weapon I am talking about." Mandl did know of such things; it was his job to know of the latest developments in all kinds of armaments and munitions. He remained silent.

"I must have up-to-date military equipment if I am to..." and then he stopped. Mandl held his breath, positive that Hitler was just about to betray himself and his objectives. Hedy also, while appearing to be indifferent to Hitler's ambitions, listened in rapt attention. Was he about to reveal why he really needed so many weapons? This was exactly what the Haganah wanted. But then Hitler seemed to remember where he was. "Well, maybe I will come back to that another time. You have been very hospitable, *Herr* Mandl, but I have to ask myself a couple of questions before I agree to do business with you."

Mandl smiled inwardly, assuaged by the thought that there was nothing Hitler could ask of him that he, Fritz Mandl with his wealth and resources, could not accommodate.

"Firstly, do I want to become involved with an arms supplier who is already so closely aligned with someone who has diametrically different political philosophies from my own? As I believe I have already mentioned, it is well-known that your friend Starhemberg is not well-disposed towards me or my territorial ambitions. If such decisions had to be made, I wonder where your loyalties would truly lie, eh?"

"Chancellor, I am first and foremost a businessman. Neither politics, military aspirations nor religion interest me. I am only interested in the politics of profit. Guns, tanks, bullets have no conscience. They are only guided by the patriotism, the dedication and the professionalism of those who use them. I am merely a facilitator. Would it really be so hypocritical if I were to arm you as well as the Prince? If it came to a war, at least you would both be evenly matched."

"I do not want to be evenly matched!" screamed Hitler. "I want..." Again, the dictator stopped himself from saying any more. "You may have to choose between us. I cannot have you furnishing weapons to my enemies, surely you must understand that. I suppose it all really depends on what you value more—your ephemeral friendships or your long-term sustainability." There was a non-too-veiled threat there which Mandl was not slow to recognize. "But there are other considerations as well. I have already offended your wife, *Herr* Mandl, and now it is my turn to offend you." Before Mandl could even open his mouth, Hitler continued unabashed, "Do I want to give a Jew my business? Just because I do not see any *mezuzahs* on your doorposts, and your well-known conversion to Catholicism, in my mind you are still a Jew, granted a very wealthy and successful one. Do I want to see you become even wealthier at my country's expense? That is another question I have to consider. Should I compromise my principles, even to gain military superiority? We shall see, *Herr* Mandl, we shall see." Hitler clamped both hands on the armrests of his chair, using his elbows to lever himself off the seat, bending over as he rose. "It is very late, or perhaps I should say very early, but I must return to Berlin at once. I prefer not to fly, so have come by road. I trust my driver has been well taken care of, and has rested. It is almost six hundred kilometers, so you will excuse me." and without waiting for any formalities, the Führer made to depart, his two guards marching either side and two steps behind their leader.

As Hitler made for the conference room doors, with a subdued Mandl at his back, neither man nor Hitler's protective entourage noticed Hedy lift one of the pages and secrete it down the front of her dress. She did not accompany her husband as he bade Hitler a desultory farewell. Had she done so, she would have noticed something very telling; the German dictator did not glance backward to bid his host well, or to thank him again for his hospitality. It was still dark as the limousine drew away. Hedy would never see Hitler again, but their relationship was far from over.

Hedy was well aware of the temper her husband could demonstrate when he did not get his way, and she was sure Mandl would blame her, at least in part, for the evening's failure. She decided that it would be better for her to withdraw to her room than face his wrath. Before she could go upstairs, however, Mandl came storming back into the conference room. He was indeed angry, but he did not vent his frustration at Hedy. Quite the opposite. Looking at nothing in particular, he said, "I wish I had done what you did, Hedy. Tonight, you have shown me what real courage is. You stood up to that mountebank and gave him, or at least tried to give him a dose of his own medicine. That took guts, and I wish I could have been as forthright, even if I reprimanded you for doing so. If he had not been so objectionable, I could have given him so much. I rarely involve you in my business affairs, and what I am about to tell you must not leave these four walls; is that understood?" Hedy nodded in acquiescence, slightly ashamed that she had purloined Hitler's discarded document. "You will probably not be aware of the conditions of the treaty Hitler mentioned, but it prohibits Germany from having a military air force. I am just about to enter into negotiations to purchase a small aircraft company called Hopfner. Had that bastard not been so obnoxious, I would have been able to supply him with planes, ostensibly civilian but easily convertible into military use. I had intended to use this as a bargaining chip, but now..."

"Do you still intend to buy this company?"

"Yes, probably. Many of the aircraft this company makes are seaplanes. I'm sure I'll find a market for them."

As they walked out of the conference room together, with his arm around her waist, Hedy put her hand to her chest, to stop the document from rustling against her brassiere. She would soon have to undress in front of her husband and hoped she could secrete the paper just long enough to place it where he would not see it. If Hedy were right, this piece of paper would stop Hitler. All she had to do was to hide it long enough to get it to Magda. After that, it would be out of her hands in every sense of the word. God only knew where it would end up, or who would see it. But whoever it was, Hedy prayed that it would give them what they needed to put the little corporal firmly in his place.

CHAPTER 13

Schwarzenau, Austria
January-February 1934

A couple of days later, Mandl asked Hedy to come into his office. He wished to discuss something with her in private and not to be overheard by any staff. Once they were both seated, Mandl said, "I am more confused than ever over your meeting with that stranger in the coffeehouse. On the one hand, you say that he all but implored you to tell me to supply weapons to Hitler, and yet, you were witness to what happened here two nights ago. These two events do not come together. I'm sure you can see what I'm getting at..."

"Of course, I can, Fritz. The obvious conclusion is that the man who accosted me was not aware of Hitler's profound hatred of Jews, which I agree is unlikely. Even if he were, how could he know that you or I, for that matter, were of Jewish heritage? I certainly did not tell him. I think you are over-imagining things here. Please let it go. I'm sure you have more important problems to worry about at the moment."

"Yes, you may be right, but all the same, I'm afraid it has left something of a bad taste. Whether or not it is as you say, your staff are under my employ, and any issues surrounding you should have been brought to my attention. The fact that the maid did not do this means that I can no longer trust this woman who was with you; therefore, I have asked her to leave immediately."

"Magda?" she asked incredulously. "You have dismissed Magda? What right did you have? I..."

"I have already explained to you. Why do you not listen? You do not live with your doting parents anymore, who gave in to your every whim. You live with me now and are subject to the rules of this house, to my rules. Do I make myself clear?"

"Yes," Hedy replied, chastened. "Is... is she still here? I would at least like to say goodbye to her."

"I believe she is packing at the moment. Do not be long; there are things to be done. More important things than saying goodbye to a servant."

"She is... was... not just a servant. She was my friend."

"Your friend? Your friends will be the ones I choose for you, not the hired help."

Making her way to the servants' quarters, Hedy found a tear-stained Magda, suitcase in hand, getting ready to leave Castle Schwarzenau for the last time. "I'm so sorry, Magda. This was all because of me. I should never..."

"Please don't fret yourself, *Frau* Mandl."

"Hedy; please call me Hedy."

"Very well, Hedy. Please don't concern yourself over me. It is you who needs to watch out. I know Mandl, sorry, *Herr* Mandl distrusts you because of what we asked you to do. I do not know how to thank you for what you did for us. It is more than we could have hoped for."

"All I did was to purloin a sheet of paper..."

"This 'sheet of paper,' as you call it, may well change the course of history. Between that and the intelligence you were able to furnish us with, we might yet see that arch anti-Semite put in his place."

"What about you, Magda? What will you do now?"

"I've been thinking for some time that it is getting less safe for us Jews here in Austria and Germany. Even if, with your help, we can get rid of this Jew-hater, the damage, unfortunately, has been done. He has put into the minds of otherwise reasonable men and women that we Jews are somehow less than human, *Untermenschen*. We Jews who, through *Moishe Rabbeinu*, gave the world His commandments by which all peoples should live, who worshipped the One True God when his ancestors prayed to rocks and stones and trees. It is so ironic that I can hardly speak of it. He has opened a Pandora's Box and has got into the very soul of the German people. He has held a mirror up so they can see themselves, see what they truly are, and the awful thing is, Hedy, that they seem to like it. To answer your question, I have been thinking of going to live in Palestine. Perhaps there, I might find..." she shrugged her shoulders. "Who knows what I might find? Perhaps even a husband, eh?"

"I'm sorry, Magda. It never even occurred to me that you were Jewish. Does Fritz know?"

"I don't know. I don't think it would trouble him; after all, he married a Jew!"

"Yes, you're probably right. What will you do with the information I've given you?"

"I'll pass it along, but where it will eventually end up, who knows? Probably in Tel Aviv, I shouldn't wonder. What they will do with it, I don't know, nor do I wish to. I must go now, *Frau* Mandl, Hedy. I do not want the master to become any more suspicious of you than he already is."

"Before you go, there are one or two more things I need to tell you. They may mean nothing, or... I don't know." She shrugged her shoulders. "It just sounded like he..." and Hedy recounted the conversation she had heard between her husband and the German Chancellor. Clasping Magda's hands, Hedy said tearfully, "I hope you find what you are looking for, Magda. Maybe one day, I might come to Palestine and visit with you."

"Yes," agreed Magda warmly, "that would be very nice and something for me to look forward to." But both women knew this would never happen.

***

A few weeks passed, during which Mandl had not heard from Hitler or his representatives. Any arrangement between the German dictator and the Austrian arms dealer now appeared to be over. It was almost as if the meeting had never happened. Then on Monday, February 12th., Mandl arrived home from the *Hirtenberger Patronen-Fabrik* in a state of alarm. He rushed into his office, where he switched on the wireless. On his way back, as he listened to his newly installed Blaupunkt car radio, reports were coming in of an incident in Linz, a major Austrian city about one hundred-and-twenty-kilometers south-west of Schwarzenau. It appeared that Emil Fey, the Vice-Chancellor, had kept his word to clamp down on Hitler supporters and Austro-Nazis. He had instructed a twenty-man squad of police officers to raid the Hotel Schiff to search for hidden weapons belonging to the *Socialist Schutzbund*. This group was a proscribed Nazi-supporting paramilitary organization and bitter opponents of Fey's and Starhemberg's *Heimwehr*.

In a moment of blinding clarity, he believed he had reasoned out the purpose of Hedy's café visitor the previous month. Of course, he wanted Mandl to furnish arms to Hitler. Not so the dictator could use them to suppress his people further, but to furnish his Nazi supporters in Austria. That was it. Just like the Nazis to be so devious and underhand. They must have foreseen this eventuality and wished to prepare for it. But now, in the light of the confrontation that was taking place, why had Hitler not purchased weapons from Mandl? Because he had a Jewish background? Then why agree to the meeting in the first place if he had already made his mind up not to do business with his company? None of this made any sense.

The operation had started around six a.m., and by late afternoon, similar skirmishes were happening across Austria, even in Vienna itself. It was also being claimed, although unconfirmed, that army brigades were shelling working-class complexes, *Gemeindebauten*, occupied by German-supporting families. One of these apartment blocks, the *Karl-Marx Hof*, more a fortress than a social housing compound, was less than five kilometers from Hedy's parents' home in *Peter-Jordan Strasse*. The Linz *Socialist Schutzbund* was not going to go down without a fight. Under the command of their leader, Richard Bernaschek, they retaliated in kind. It was only with the regular Austrian army's help, so the report said, that Government forces finally took the hotel around twelve midday, some six hours after the initial attack.

Mandl knew that the outlawed group was no match for the combined forces of the *Heimwehr*, the police, and the federal army, but if Hitler were to send re-enforcements, what then? Would he risk a war with the country he wanted to 'peacefully' absorb into his Nazi Germany? He had already promised not to take over the country by force of arms, that is, with a regular German army. Not least because the Allies would surely not allow this to happen and would find a means to warn him off. But would they care one way or the other? After all, both countries had been allies in the previous conflict, and there were already a sizeable minority of Austrians who would welcome unity with their larger neighbor.

Mandl, however, was not one of them. Although he, or rather his company, stood to benefit from any armed hostility between the opposing factions, the arms dealer realized, perhaps for the first time, that this might impact on him personally. He was not supplying munitions to some far-flung regime or militia in another God-forsaken part of the world. The armaments his company were producing at this moment did have consequences right on his very doorstep. He was providing weapons that were being used in what was, in reality, a civil war. He reluctantly gave a rueful smile when he considered that he might literally be a victim of his own success.

When he had finished listening to the news bulletin and had changed for dinner, Hedy could see the concern in his eyes. At first, she thought she had done something to displease him, although she could not think what this might be. It soon became apparent that it was not her about whom he was anxious. He seemed even more distracted than usual and barely acknowledged her presence. When she tried to engage him in conversation, his answers were curt and monosyllabic, as if he was reluctant to speak. "Please, Fritz, what's wrong? What is troubling you so? You can confide in me; you know that."

"Not now, Hedy. I have much to think about, but nothing that concerns you. It's just..." he sighed in exasperation. He knew the *Socialist Schutzbund* were vastly outnumbered and outgunned, and would undoubtedly pay the price for their resistance. Still, Dollfuss was becoming more unpopular daily, with his autocratic form of government. He had taken advantage of a hiatus in Parliament over voting procedures and had assumed total control of the legislature. How long would it be before the people rose up against him, egged on, no doubt, by the National Socialists? How would that situation affect his business interests? Did he even have the loyalty of his own workforce? These were troubled times indeed.

Winston Churchill had made a speech to the British parliament a few days earlier. He had referred to Hitler's military ambitions and warned the government not to cut back on defense spending, especially air defenses. He cited a hypothetical situation based on an actual event that occurred just before the start of the previous European conflict.

The German ambassador to France, Wilhelm Eduard Freiherr von Schon, demanded a meeting with René Viviani, the French premier. During the conversation, von Schon divulged to Viviani that his country might be forced to take up arms against Russia, an ally of the French. The ambassador asked Viviani what the French position would be in the event of a war. Viviani responded by saying that Paris would act in its own best interests, which would probably mean upholding its treaty with Moscow. With these few words, what might have been a more localized struggle engulfed the whole of Europe and beyond.

Germany had not changed much in the last twenty years. It was still, even more so now, under Hitler, a belligerent nation, hell-bent on territorial conquest. Churchill then asked the question: What if a European leader or his ambassador (by which he meant Germany) gave Britain a similar ultimatum? Would the Prime Minister allow the United Kingdom to form an alliance with such a war-mongering leader as Hitler? Would failure to ally this country into such an agreement see bombs falling from enemy warplanes onto British cities? If a pompous ass like Churchill could see that, why did other European and world leaders also not heed the warning?

Mandl thought through yet another frightening scenario. Would Paris agree this time to side with Berlin? If so, what would the consequences be for Austria and the rest of the continent? Would Mussolini agree to a trilateral alliance? Likely, this would embolden Hitler even more. Dinner in the Mandl household that evening was not a joyous affair. Throughout the meal, Hedy tried to converse with Mandle, but his only responses were a series of ill-tempered grunts and bellicose replies.

Hedy slowly realized that she would eventually have to leave this tyrannical man before he broke her spirit, her soul completely. She had begun to devise the beginnings of a strategy that would eventually see her leaving her controlling husband for good. This would be on her terms, not his. In the meantime, she would play the role of the subservient wife, but, God willing, not for much longer. Not for much longer.

CHAPTER 14

Civitavecchia, Italy and Tel Aviv, Palestine
February-July 1934

Magda had been disingenuous with Hedy at their final conversation. She was not just 'considering' emigrating to Palestine; she had already resolved to do so. The document and information she had in her possession were too important to be left in the hands of other intermediaries. The only way she could be sure it would get to its intended destination was to deliver it herself. Through her contact, she had heard that a Jewish naval academy had been built at a town called Civitavecchia on the northwest coast of Italy. If she could travel the twelve hundred or so kilometers there, she might get a vessel that would take her to the newly opened port in Haifa.

Betar Naval Academy was built with the blessing of Benito Mussolini. He saw an emerging Palestinian Jewish state as a buffer against an attack from the east. In gratitude for his approval and assistance in its construction, those naval cadets and other Italian Jews supported Mussolini in his east Africa ambitions.

Because of all the unrest, it was several weeks before she felt safe enough to move freely, and with the money she had saved, made her way south via Graz into Italy. Stopping briefly in Rome, Magda caught the train to her destination. Indeed, she was a strange sight for the Jewish trainee sailors and their Italian military hosts as she walked up to the security barrier. She looked like a refugee with her slightly greying matted chestnut-auburn hair, shabby blue overcoat, torn stockings, and battered leather suitcase with its frayed stitching, the lid secured by a cheap hempen rope. As she approached the barrier, she asked to see the 'person in charge.' Her Italian was almost non-existent, and the guard did not speak German. It was unlikely she was a spy; very few spies walked in so brazenly through the front gate, but if not that, then what exactly was she?

At first, the security guard tried to tell her that she had come to the wrong place and that she should turn around and leave. He attempted to make her understand with dismissive motions from his free hand, his other hand still holding his carbine. Magda stood her ground and repeated in German her request to meet with someone in authority. Both were becoming exasperated with the other's stubbornness, but eventually, it was the guard who capitulated. The soldier phoned the compound office from his hut, explaining the situation.

The titular head of the naval facility was an Italian naval scientist called Nicola Fusco. In actuality, it was run by Jeremiah Halpern, a certified ship's captain and experienced seaman. It was not Halpern, however, who came out to speak to Magda. Angrily striding towards her was Ze'ev Jabotinsky, former senior member of the Haganah. They had briefly met when Ze'ev was in Austria, setting up the operation to discredit the German leader.

After escorting her into his office, Jabotinsky sat behind his desk before starting his interrogation. "What on earth are you doing here, Miss...?"

"Magda will do, Mister Jabotinsky. I have some information which..."

"Never mind that. What are you doing here, at Betar?"

"I was hoping to get a berth to Palestine with my intelligence, to hand it over to the men in Rothschild Boulevard. I felt it was too important to leave it to anyone else."

"This is merely a training facility. No ships actually sail from here, and certainly, none that would go to Haifa. There may be one that leaves from a different part of the port, but I wouldn't recommend taking it. Some of the local Fascists are not as predisposed toward us as their leader. They might cause some trouble if they see me, us, getting on a boat. I'm afraid you've given yourself something of a wasted trip."

"But I have to get to Palestine. What I have to hand over is very important, and I need to see it gets to Tel Aviv safely. I cannot afford for this document to fall into the wrong hands."

"Do you not think that was rather arrogant of you, Magda? Are you saying that there are people in our organization who cannot be trusted? Do you think we have been compromised?"

"Not at all. Please, God, I hope not."

"Then why did you not hand over what you have to Michael, as we arranged? He has the conduits to get your details to the right people. Why did you go against protocol?"

"If you will stop interrupting me for a minute, I'll tell you. I do not just have oral intelligence. I have a document..."

"May I see this document, or do you not trust even me?" he asked without humor.

Magda asked him to turn around. "I have hidden it somewhere... intimate," she explained.

Jabotinsky swiveled round in his chair while his agent extracted the paper from the top of her thigh, tucked between her stocking top and suspender. The Haganah man read the missive curiously. "I don't understand. What's so special about this piece of paper?" he asked her, waving it in the air.

"Can't you see what this is?"

"All I can see are numbers of ballistics. I still don't see the significance..."

"The penned notations are in Hitler's own handwriting. In other words..."

"You don't have to explain any more. I understand now. He wants to massively increase Germany's armaments in flagrant defiance of the Versailles Treaty. My God, Magda, this is almost as good as hearing his aspirations from his own lips."

"There were other similar papers, but *Frau* Mandl could not risk taking any more in case her husband noticed their absence."

"I'm due to return to Palestine next month. If you don't mind, I'll hold on to this, and you can tell me what else you know. You have done excellent work."

"No."

"No? No, what?"

"No, Mr. Jabotinsky."

"Do not try my patience, Magda. I asked you a question. What do you mean, 'no?'"

"No, I cannot let you keep that document. I must deliver it myself."

"Are you out of your mind, woman? Do you know who I am? You work for the Haganah, and I am your superior officer. You will not disrespect me in this manner. You will apologize to me, and that will be the end of it. Are we clear?"

"I have just spent the last year working for the most bombastic and overbearing man I have ever met. I had to put up with his tirades and ill-humor for the sake of our mission and at great personal risk, but I have now fulfilled my assignment. If you dislike the way I am comporting myself, then you may dismiss me. If you do not hand over that paper right now, I will leave this office and stop the first Italian officer I find and tell him what I have just given you. I doubt even you, with your closeness to *Il Duce*, will be allowed to leave this facility." She held out her hand, her arm extended in front of her. "Now, you will please return the document to me." she said frigidly.

In a more conciliatory tone, Jabotinsky replied, "Don't worry. I'll make sure you get the credit for this if that's what's troubling you. You deserve..."

"You self-righteous bastard. Do you think this is about me? I would give my final breath to get this paper to Palestine and die a happy death if my last action was to transfer what you have in your fist to our men there. Don't you understand? The Arabs know who you are and what you are connected to. If they even suspect you have such a paper, they would slit your throat rather than let it remain with us. Some of their people have already been to see Hitler. I don't know what this means, but I do know that it will not augur well for us Jews. They might watch you, but who would suspect a poor emigrant Jewess straight off a boat from Italy? Now, do you see?"

"Well, you have certainly made your case forcefully, if somewhat discourteously. You have a good point, of course. And I must remember you have already carried it over one thousand kilometers to get this far. You must be tired and hungry. Why don't I get you something to eat while you rest up? After that..."

"After that...?"

"After that, I'm going to Genoa, and you're coming with me."

"But why Genoa?"

"Because that's where the boat leaves to get to Palestine."

* * *

The short civil war in February only lasted four days, but the hostilities were far from over. By the time Jabotinsky and Magda arrived at Haifa towards the end of July, conflict was flaring up again in Austria. A *coup d'état* orchestrated by Austrian Nazis, German soldiers, and Nazi sympathizers tried once more to de-stabilize the Austrian parliament. This act came to be known as *The July Putsch*, but the attempt to take over the country was unsuccessful. Failure to succeed was mainly due to two factors.

Firstly, the vast majority of Austrians stayed loyal to the Dollfuss government, despite Dollfuss being killed and replaced by Kurt Schuschnigg. The other reason why the Nazi incursion did not make much headway was more encouraging. It was something the Haganah men discussed with Jabotinsky and Magda on their first visit to Rothschild Boulevard after they arrived in Tel Aviv. Hedy would not have recognized her former maid. In the short time that Magda had been in Palestine, she had transformed herself. Gone was the humble, dowdy, and downtrodden servant; in her place was an attractive and assertive woman, her pale skin grown darker in the Mediterranean sun. She had cut her hair short into a fashionable bob, and although her eyes still retained some of their puffiness, she had lost the look of perpetual sadness Hedy had seen on their first acquaintance. Confident in her newfound appearance, she sat as an equal member of the Haganah team.

"Mrs. Mandl was party to the conversation between her husband and Hitler," Magda revealed to her Haganah colleagues. "I cannot think why he would discuss such things in front of her, or even Mandl himself for that matter, but he did. One of the pieces of intelligence that she heard was that he and Mussolini had reached an agreement over their territorial ambitions. She heard Hitler say that he would not intervene in Mussolini's East African pretensions, especially concerning Ethiopia. In return, *Il Duce* would turn a blind eye to Hitler's desire for *Anschluss* with Austria. He did allude to something like this earlier in their meeting, but would not disclose what it was. Perhaps he did not even realize he had blurted it out. Maybe he thinks he is so unassailable, he can afford to boast of his militaristic intentions. With a *meshuggener* like that, who knows? But if it is true, it does not bode well for Austria."

Eliyahu Golomb spoke up. "You have been traveling for a while, so perhaps you have not heard the news. Whatever Hitler believes, it seems that the Italian dictator is prepared to betray him. He has instead decided to uphold his accord with the Dollfuss/Schuschnigg government and has offered military and diplomatic assistance in the event of a full German invasion. If this act of reneging by the Italians isolates Germany all the more, it can only help our cause. Hitler would be furious with his Italian counterpart and might even declare war on his erstwhile ally. This is unlikely at the moment, as Germany is not yet in a position to wage war against such a well-armed adversary, but it would sow the seeds of discord. Perhaps we may even be able to use such disharmony to our advantage. This is something else for us to consider."

When Magda disclosed the document she had been guarding so jealously, there were cries of disbelief from around the room. Having Hitler's own notated handwriting on a copy of the Versailles Treaty, clearly demonstrating his desire for massive rearmament, was astonishing. The question now was what to do with this paper. They debated several options.

"Perhaps we should deliver it to the Jewish Agency. Surely this is the most logical solution. They will know what to do with it," suggested Ben-Pinchas. "After all, they are the main institution for world Jewish affairs and would have more authority than a bunch of raggle-taggle, poorly equipped, haphazardly coordinated vigilantes like us."

"Unfortunately, it is their very size that works against this idea. The problem is that they are just too big. To whom would they give it? What control would we have once it was out of our hands? No, this organization is too amorphous. We cannot take the risk of someone disclosing its contents prematurely, even albeit accidentally. Like most Jewish groups, dare I say, even within our own organization, everybody wants to be the *gantse macher*, the Big Cheese, even those who have no right to claim to be so. Present company excepted, of course," he added smiling, before anyone could take offense. "If we give this document to them, each member will want to be the one who discloses to the world Germany's warlike intentions. Such in-fighting will get no one anywhere, and these delays would only give the Nazi leader even more time to amass greater numbers of weapons. No, I'm afraid the Jewish Agency is out of the question."

"What about the League of Nations?" asked Magda.

"Same problem, but with an added dimension. Not every country in that august body is well disposed towards the Jews, and some might even wish to see it suppressed. Not only that, but the United States is not even a member of this organization. Without them, this intelligence will lose much of its impact. There is so much riding on the information we have in front of us; we will only get one chance, and we have to get it right."

There was a heavy silence in the room while each man (and woman) contemplated what might be the best option. Without looking up, Golomb addressed the others. "Do you remember," he began slowly, "some years ago—I think it was nineteen twenty-one or nineteen twenty-two, a British delegation came here and convened a meeting at Government House in Jerusalem?" Several of them nodded, trying to recall the exact circumstances of that event. "There were some prominent members from the British parliament at this summit, including Winston Churchill, who was Colonial Secretary at the time. We all know, and I am sure we appreciate, his predisposition towards us and our aspirations for a national homeland here in Palestine. He is also a very outspoken critic, probably one of the few members of his government to be so, of the cruel Nazi regime and its despicable leader. What if he somehow got hold of this document? With his influence, there is no telling what he might be able to achieve? After all, he has the prime minister's ear, and..."

"A prime minister who does not raise his head out of the sand and refuses to see what is in front of his eyes. MacDonald is a craven coward who opposed his country's participation in the earlier European conflict. Why should we think he would behave any differently now?" spat out Gadder.

"Israel, no one, not you, not me, no one, could have foreseen the carnage and destruction that war caused. It was unprecedented in the realms of human history, with so much suffering and bloodshed. But now we do know. We know what can happen when one country's unbridled ambitions go unchallenged. And do not forget this. Not only can countries be attacked and invaded by land and sea, but now they can also be assailed by air. I do not believe the world will ever allow a conflict to happen again on such a scale. Even pacifists like MacDonald must see that it is in all our interests to stop Hitler now before he truly becomes militarily invincible. One other thing to remember. Although Ramsay MacDonald is the leader of the Unity Government, his Labour party is in the minority. It is politicians from Churchill's party, the Conservatives, who form most of his administration. Them and a few from the Liberal..." his voice trailed off as he slowly looked around the room at each one of their expectant faces. He forgot what he was going to say as a new thought flashed into his head. Raising his right index finger, he said, "Gentlemen, and lady," deferring to Magda, "an idea has just struck me. There is someone else who may be able to do something, someone even more influential than Winston Churchill. Also, I happen to know this individual personally," he concluded as a smile spread across his face.

CHAPTER 15

London & Westerham, Kent, England
October-November 1934

Herbert Louis Samuel was born in Toxteth, Liverpool in November 1870, the youngest of three children, to Clara and Edwin Samuel, an orthodox Jewish family. The family was originally from Poland, and Samuel's paternal great-grandfather had come to Britain in the latter half of the eighteenth century. Although Samuel himself did not claim to be a devout Jew, he was a committed Zionist and pushed to establish a Jewish state as far back as 1915. However, in a later article, he had diluted these aspirations to incorporate other non-Jews into a Jewish homeland. As President of the Local Government Board in Asquith's Liberal administration, he met with Chaim Weizmann.

Weizmann was a member of the Zionist Organization and was another strong proponent of Jewish statehood. In 1924, when Samuel was High Commissioner for Palestine, he dedicated a plaque on King George Street in Jerusalem. Also, at that ceremony were some members of the young, fledgling organization known as the Haganah. They provided unofficial additional security for the visiting dignitaries, including Samuel. Also present at the plaque ceremony were the Jaffa district governor, Sir Ronald Storrs, and the mayor of Jerusalem, Ragheb Bey El Nashashibi. Both declined the offer of a Haganah security detail despite warnings of violence.

Golomb met Sir Herbert Samuel at this commemoration, and the two men stayed in contact through the years.

At this point in his illustrious career, Samuel was the member of parliament for Darwen in Lancashire, and leader of the British Liberal Party, with considerable influence in the House of Commons. If the Haganah could get the Hitler paper to Samuel, there would be no doubt to whom Samuel, in turn, would show the document. With Samuel and Churchill's combined forces, they could steer Parliament into threatening Hitler to desist from his warlike objectives. Even more critical to the Haganah team, it would be an essential part of any discussions that his persecution of the Jews had to stop immediately. Failure to comply with either demand would lead to a resumption of hostilities. Hitler would have no choice. He was not yet in a position to prosecute another war, much less one he was sure to lose.

* * *

Samuel received the letter at his parliamentary office some weeks later. Its arrival coincided with a visit to his Darwen constituency, so he did not take possession of it until his next visit to the Houses of Parliament in early October after the summer recess. Even as a non-observant member of his faith, Samuel was well aware of Hitler's hostility towards his fellow Jews. If this document was authentic, it provided all the evidence that anyone needed of the German Chancellor's belligerent intentions towards his geographical neighbors. All those armaments could not possibly be for defensive purposes only. If this document read as Samuel believed it did, steps would have to be taken as quickly as possible before Hitler achieved his objectives.

As if working from a prepared script written by the Haganah, Herbert Samuel took the action Eli Golomb had predicted. He telephoned Churchill at his country estate at Chartwell in Kent. Winston's wife, Clementine, took the call. "Hello Mrs. Churchill, it's Herbert Samuel here. I wonder if I could speak to Winston, please."

"He's rather busy at the moment. Would it be possible...?"

Samuel cut across her abruptly. "I'm sorry, but it's a matter of grave importance. I must speak with him now. It's imperative."

Clementine Churchill sighed wearily. It was always imperative. Why else would they phone? "Hold on, Sir Herbert, I'll go and see if I can find him."

After what seemed an interminably long time but was only a couple of minutes, Churchill's gruff voice came on the line. "My dear Herbert, to what do I owe the pleasure of your phone call? Whatever the panic is, you know you are always welcome here at Chartwell. Why did you not come yourself?"

Samuel lost no time in responding, his impatience apparent in his reply. "Winston, I've just had a communication from a friend in Palestine. The letter contained a document that I'm sure you'll want to know about."

"Well, if it's so damn' important, why didn't you just come down in person?"

"Before I say another word, I need to know if this is a secure line. Could anyone be listening in to this discussion?"

"Listening in? They better not be, dear boy. This is a free democracy, not Stalin's Soviet Union. I will have plenty to say if I find that anyone has tampered with my phone. On that score, you may be sure. Now, what's this all about?"

"As I said a minute ago, I've received a letter from a contact in Palestine. A Jewish contact. I'll show you the paper when I see you, but this is so serious, I felt I had to let you know...."

"Let me know what?"

"It's the document I mentioned. It's part of the Versailles Treaty limiting..."

"Yes, yes, I know what the damn Versailles Treaty is," Churchill interrupted testily. "What about it?"

"This is a page torn from a copy of that document which contains Hitler's own handwriting. He has over-scored what armaments he has been allowed and superimposed much higher quantities. In my opinion, far more ballistics than he could need purely for defense."

Churchill was speechless. Indeed, this was the intelligence he needed to persuade parliament to take a much tougher line with the German dictator. But the politician had a few questions of his own. "Are you sure this document is genuine? It couldn't be a forgery, could it?"

"No, Winston, I can guarantee it's the real thing. My source is unimpeachable. That I can promise you."

"May I be permitted to know how your contact came by this momentous information?"

"I'm sorry, Winston, I can't tell you. It has come at a high cost and could mean a death sentence if the bearer's identity was discovered—the fewer people who know the origin of this document, the better. At least, for the time being. I trust you understand."

Churchill did not respond directly. "Have you shown this paper to anyone else? Anyone in the intelligence services, or armed forces, perhaps?"

"No, Winston. Not yet. You and I are the only ones outside a handful of people in Palestine who know of this document's existence."

"I must see this pernicious paper for myself, not that I doubt it's provenance, you understand. It's just so... remarkable."

"How soon can you get to Westminster?"

"I'll be there within the hour."

* * *

Churchill was dumbfounded to read the super scripted additions to the Versailles Treaty in Hitler's own handwriting. This was, indeed, the evidence he wanted. Now he could talk from a position of confidence about the wretched dictator's plans. This time, Parliament and the government would have to listen. It would be a folly of the highest order if they did not take this document seriously. As he considered his next strategies, he suddenly stopped. In his mind, he saw the consequences of his actions if he declared to the House what he knew. They would ask questions, questions to which he did not have the answers and could not divulge what he did know. This would make life even more difficult for him in Parliament than it already was.

Despite his constant warnings both within and outside the Palace of Westminster about the threat of Hitler, very few people were taking him seriously. If anything, much of the London aristocracy was either closet or overt supporters of the German dictator and his odious anti-Semitic regime. As several people of his acquaintance put it, 'Hitler was just the man to put the Jews in their place.' No, maybe another address to the House of Commons was not the best way on this occasion to alert the British people of the threat posed by this man. No doubt, he would meet with the same resistance as in his previous speeches. This time, Churchill decided to go around the protocols and the closed minds of his political colleagues. The member of parliament for Epping would broadcast to the British people directly through the medium of radio.

On November 11th. 1934, appropriately on Armistice Day, Winston Churchill made a speech on the BBC Home Service. He did not mention the Hitler document. Neither did he mention the German leader, or even the country, by name, but no listener could have been in any doubt about whom he was discussing. After speaking on other topics for a few minutes, Churchill continued, '...*only a few hours away by air, there dwells a nation of nearly seventy million of the most educated, industrious, scientific, diligent people in the world who are being taught from childhood to think of war as a glorious exercise, and death in battle as the noblest fate for man. There is a nation which has abandoned all its liberties in order to augment its collective strength. There is a nation which, with all its strength and virtue, is in the grip of a group of ruthless men preaching a gospel of intolerance and racial pride unrestrained by law, by parliament, or by public opinion. In that country, all pacifist speeches, all morbid war books, are forbidden or suppressed, and their authors rigorously imprisoned. From their new table of commandments, they have omitted, 'Thou shalt not kill.' It is but twenty years since these neighbors of ours fought almost the whole world and almost defeated them. Now they are re-arming with the utmost speed and ready to their hand is this new lamentable weapon of the air against which our navy has no defense, and before which, women and children, the weak and frail, the pacifist and the jingo, the warrior and the civilian, the frontline trenches and the cottage home, all lie in equal and impartial peril. Nay, worse still for with the new weapon has come a new method... of compelling the submission of races by terrorizing and torturing their civil population, and worst of all, the more civilized a country is... the more it is vulnerable; the more it is at the mercy of those who may make it their prey... these are the facts..."*

After his speech, once the broadcast was over, Churchill removed his eyeglasses and glanced thoughtfully around the enclosed studio. The technical staff saw his wistful look, but could not understand what he was thinking about. He was recalling the time two years earlier when he and his family stayed at the Hotel Continental in Munich. Another guest who was there at the same time was Adolf Hitler. Churchill sent a message through Hitler's aide, Ernst Hanfstaengl, who was dining with the Churchills, if he would bring Hitler to dinner with them. The Nazi leader refused, first stating that he was too busy, then suggesting that he would have nothing to discuss with the British politician. Churchill later discovered that Hitler refused to meet with him because his other dinner guest was his scientific adviser, Frederick Lindemann, who was reputed to be Jewish.

How different the world might be today, Churchill thought, if Hitler had accepted his invitation. Maybe I could have found the words to assuage Hitler's anger over the Versailles Treaty. Perhaps we might have reached an accord. Possibly his bitterness might have been tempered so that he did not feel the need to assert German might to compensate for his country's humiliating defeat. But it was not to be.

And now, he had just told the nation that Britain was no longer safe. Not only could the country be invaded by sea, but it could also be attacked from the air. What made this situation even worse was that there would be no defense against such an offensive, no way to stop an aerial onslaught of British cities by German bombers. The politician had circumvented the protocols of speaking to the people through Parliament. Instead, he had appealed directly to their patriotism – and their fear. If his colleagues would do nothing to address German aggression, perhaps the populace would demand that the government took some action before enemy aircraft flew over the streets of London.

The producer and technical staff looked quizzically at each other. Did Churchill just say that Britain was about to be bombarded by German missiles? What was the government doing about it? According to Churchill, the answer was—nothing. If this oration did not galvanize the authorities into action, nothing would.

Sadly, for Churchill and the world, even his striking rhetoric did not move enough people, both within government and the public, to want to put Hitler's ambitions to an end. For reasons best known only to himself, Churchill made no mention of the Hitler document. It may have been his reasoning that although he wanted to warn the British public of the threat posed by Germany, he did not wish to alarm them. Or worse still, to panic the population by detailing just how much weaponry the Nazi dictator wanted to acquire.

All of the schemes laid by Eli Golomb and the rest of the Haganah team had come to nothing. It would take the world another five years to realize the mistake it had made in not listening more carefully to that wireless broadcast on Armistice Day 1934.

CHAPTER 16

London, England, the Mid-Atlantic Ocean, L.A., California.
August 1937-July 1940.

It was now July 1940, and Hedy was living and working in California. After Hitler's visit to Castle Schwarzenau, her subsequent theft of his handwritten superscription of the Versailles Treaty, and especially Magda's dismissal, Hedy broke off all contact with the Haganah. She had managed to endure living with Mandl for a further three years, but could take no more of his bullying. In August 1937, finally making good on the promise she had made to herself earlier, Hedy fled from him, with a considerable amount of his jewelry concealed in her valise. Recompense, perhaps, for the four years of misery to which he had subjected her. She had already mailed other valuables for safekeeping to trusted friends in Paris, where she arrived before making her way to Britain.

She divorced Fritz Mandl while she was in London, expecting the arms magnate to exact some post-marital revenge. However, it seemed that he was just as glad to be out of the relationship as Hedy. She had instructed her lawyer not to reveal her address, so perhaps this was the reason Mandl had not vented his wrath on her for absconding.

Bob Ritchie, a theatrical agent, heard that Hedy was in London and wasted no time contacting her at her hotel. "Mrs. Mandl, how do you...?"

"It is Miss Kiesler, Hedwig Kiesler. I no longer use my married name since my divorce. Who is this, please, and what do you want?"

"Miss Kiesler, I'm sorry, my name is Robert Ritchie. I'm what you might call an actor facilitator. I wonder if you might spare me a few minutes."

"An actor what?" asked a bemused Hedy. "What do you want?"

"I guess that does sound a bit highfalutin'. I'm a theatrical agent. I find work...."

"I know what a theatrical agent does, Mr. Ritchie. What can I do for you?"

"Well, it's rather what I can do for you, Miss Kiesler. One of my clients is looking to sign up young actresses with a view to offering them a contract. Are you interested?"

"How did you find me? I mean, how do you know who I am and where I am staying?"

Ritchie laughed. "Miss Kiesler, I make my living, a good living, I might add, by finding out these things. That's all you need to know. Now, are you interested? I don't have much time."

"Who is your client?"

"No, Miss Kiesler, it doesn't work that way. First, you tell me if you're interested in my question. If you say 'yes,' we can talk. If you say 'no,' I thank you for your time and hang up. That's how this goes. Now, I'll ask you one more time, are you interested in meeting with my client?"

"I suppose so," she sighed. "Where is his office? Give me a time, and I will arrange to be there."

"He... ah, he doesn't have an office here in London. He's based in the United States."

"The United States? Do you mean Hollywood?"

"Yes, Miss Kiesler, I mean Hollywood."

Ritchie arranged an introduction to Louis B. Mayer, who was in the capital to sign up all those movie actors fleeing Hitler's encroaching presence. The head of M.G.M. Studios was impressed with her beauty and wasted no time in offering her a contract.

"One hundred and twenty-five dollars a week?" she asked him. "Oh, no, Mister Mayer, you'll have to do better than that; much better."

Mayer smiled at her. "Do you know who I am?" he asked her.

"Yes, of course I do. But I also know how much I am worth, Mister Mayer, and it is a lot more than that."

"How much more?" he asked her, more out of curiosity than anger.

"Oh, no, you tell me, and then we'll see if I agree with your estimation."

"I think our negotiations have now ended, Miss Kiesler," Mayer answered her abruptly. "It has been nice talking with you, and I wish you well. You might yet have a future in movie acting, but it will not be with my studio. Goodbye."

Hedy realized that she had overplayed her hand. She felt instinctively that he might have paid her more but could not be seen to lose face in front of his subordinates or Bob Ritchie. Her father had always instilled into her never to undersell whatever talents she may possess. Still, Hedy had also learned another lesson that day—'he who pays the piper calls the tune.' But she was not done with Louis B. Mayer quite just yet.

The movie mogul had arranged to sail back to the United States on the passenger liner, the *S.S. Normandie*, and Hedy had booked herself a berth on the same ship. She felt if she could speak to Mayer alone, she might convince him to raise his offer. Once onboard, Hedy lost no time in 'accidentally' bumping into the studio head. She knew he had a penchant for young starlets despite being married and flirted shamelessly with him. Mayer's wife Margaret found them in discussions in the first-class smoking room. A short while later, she said to him, "This had better be about contract business and not 'monkey business.' If I find out that you've given her anything more than an offer, I will become the ex-Mrs. Mayer, and you will become a lot poorer."

To stop the aspiring young actress from pestering him and placate his suspicious wife, Mayer agreed to Hedy's terms, but not without some conditions of his own. "You are very pretty, Hedwig, but I'm afraid you are going to need to be even more glamorous if you are to succeed in Hollywood. There are already more beautiful women there per square mile than anywhere else in the world."

"What do you suggest?"

"Perhaps a little weight redistribution, my dear. Nothing we can't sort out with the correct diet and some good, old-fashioned exercise." Hedy studied herself. Her figure and her features looked just fine. She did not think she needed to diet or engage in a harsh fitness regime. Still, it would be a small price to pay for movie stardom. There was one other issue that they had to address.

"It's your name. 'Hedwig Kiesler' is just too German and too Jewish." Mayer shook his head sadly. "Unfortunately, some people, maybe even more than 'some,' might not take too kindly to your background, especially in times like these. Even I," he continued, thumbing his chest, "sometimes come across fellows not too disposed towards people like us." by which he meant Jews. "Alas, it would be better all-round if you buried your Jewishness entirely. Does that suggestion trouble you?"

"Not really. My parents were Jews in name only. They paid scant regard to their religion, so it is of no concern to me to do as you ask."

Mayer beamed at his new signing. "Excellent. I also have another reason for insisting you change your name. It was how they billed you in your role in '*Extase.*' It might be as well if we can erase the memory of that movie from their minds, eh? I don't think the American movie theater-going public is quite ready yet for an actress with such an avant-garde reputation. We make wholesome family movies here. A woman's ass is for her husband's eyes only. I trust you understand what I mean."

Hedy thought for a moment. This move was a big step for her and one she had not considered. To change her name? Again? After her divorce from Fritz Mandl, she had reverted to her maiden name. And yet, it might not be a bad thing to erase her European past. Start again, fresh; yes, it might not be a bad idea at that. "Did you have a name in mind?"

"No, but Margaret may have."

"I didn't think your wife was so interested in my career."

Ignoring this remark, Mayer revealed, "We, that is, Margaret, and I have been discussing your future with the studio. It was actually Margaret who suggested coming up with the name we've been considering."

"Oh, and what name is that?"

"Margaret was a fan of a movie actress called Barbara LaMarr, who passed away a few years ago. She was a very talented girl and wrote scripts as well as being an accomplished and beautiful actress."

"She died?"

"Sadly, she burned the candle at both ends, to quote a popular saying. I can't remember all the details, but I believe excessive alcohol consumption was part of the problem. I trust I don't have to worry about you on that score, Miss Lamarr?"

Hedy smiled inscrutably. Her silent acquiescence said one thing, but her actions and body language implied something else. "So, I'm to be known as Hedwig LaMarr?"

"Well, not quite. Hedwig is still too European, too German. Tell me, when you were young, did your parents have a pet name for you, perhaps?"

Hedy thought back to her childhood. "When my father was pleased with something I had done, and even sometimes when he was angry with me, he would shout, 'Well done, Hedy,' or 'You naughty girl, Hedy.'" She smiled fondly at the memory of her now-dead father. "How does that sound, Mister Mayer?"

The studio head nodded his head in approval. Yes, it was still a faintly foreign-sounding name, but it also evoked an air of exotic mystery. Coupled with her exquisite beauty, 'Hedy' would do very nicely, very nicely indeed.

And so it was that a young Austrian actress by the name of Hedwig Kiesler boarded a trans-Atlantic vessel in Southampton, England, to disembark a few days later in New York as Louis B. Mayer's newest find, Hedy Lamarr. She had negotiated a seven-year contract with him at five hundred dollars a week, a sum unheard of for someone yet to make a Hollywood movie. Since that time, she had starred in five movies for Mayer and had just completed her latest role, playing opposite Clark Gable in 'Comrade X.'

* * *

War was raging across Europe, and Germany had invaded and conquered Poland, Norway, Denmark, Czechoslovakia, France, Belgium, and the Low Countries. Hitler showed no signs of stopping, and the whole continent now seemed his for the taking, including the United Kingdom. Newsreels showed jackbooted German troops goose-stepping down occupied streets. Austria, Hedy's own country, had been annexed by Germany in the *Anschluss* in March 1938, not long after her departure. From the letters she was receiving, things were not going so well for the remaining Jewish population.

Hedy had never felt the emotion of hatred, even for Fritz Mandl, not like this. It was not in her nature, but this situation was something else, something very dark and disturbing. She cast her mind back to her meetings in Vienna with Isidor Pralgovitch. Hadn't he mentioned even then his worry over Hitler's treatment of the Jews? And what had become of the document she and Magda had smuggled out? Had that all been for nothing? It would appear so as Britain, almost alone, was left to face the might of the encroaching Nazi *Wehrmacht*. She had heard the BBC news broadcasts and had seen the newsreels at the movie theaters. Although the authorities had heavily censored both briefings and newspaper accounts, anyone with Hedy's intellect could tell by what the announcers were not reporting that the war was not going well.

The British Expeditionary Force had been out-maneuvered by Germany and had been cut off at Dunkirk. It was only by a miracle that so many Allied servicemen had escaped back across the English Channel. And now London was being bombarded by the Luftwaffe. Night after night, German bombers dropped their lethal cargo of incendiary missiles over innocent civilians. This was not war; it was barbarism. What made it even more unfair in her eyes was that since the fall of France, the German pilots had clear aerial passage from their bases to directly above the heart of the British capital. The British pilots did not fare so well and came under constant attack as soon as their warplanes reached the French coast.

Although the Royal Navy was still vastly superior to the *Kriegsmarine*, German U-boats patrolled the seas and seemed unstoppable. It appeared that the British navy was having trouble locating, much less sinking this underwater menace. They would have to think of some way to thwart this threat. Britain was an island, heavily dependent on imports for its food and other important supplies. If the German submarines could stop friendly ships from reaching their ports, it would not be too long before they starved

Britain into surrendering. How would that bode for British Jews, not to mention her own mother, who had fled to London to stay with relatives? Feelings of frustration and impotence began to rage within her. It was now not only her beloved Austria and its Jewish population, which was in peril. Jews all over the continent were in danger, including, of course, her own family.

As Hedy had confided to Louis B. Mayer, she had not considered her Jewishness for many years. However this did not make her blind or unsympathetic to the illogical persecution, violence, and destruction perpetrated on them by this evil regime. One train of thought led to another, and Hedy cast her mind back to some of the conversations she had heard around the Mandl dining table. The subject of submarines re-entered her head, which inevitably led to the weapons most feared by modern navies – the torpedo. If only there were some way to stymie those attacks and block the Germans' ability to sink so easily the vital lifeline Britain desperately needed.

Since her early childhood, Hedy had always had a curious and inventive mind, encouraged by her late father to marvel at the world around her. He was never too busy to satisfy his daughter's enquiring brain and loved to teach her all he knew about science, mechanics, and engineering. Mandl, who saw in Hedy nothing more than an attractive, but not-too-bright marriage companion, stifled these ambitions.

In March 1939, she had married Gene Markey, a Hollywood movie producer, and screenwriter. Although they had been wed for barely a year, the marriage was not going well. Despite becoming the adoptive parents of a baby son, James, Hedy was considering whether or not to leave her husband. She had had a brief affair with fellow actor John Loder after being introduced to him by Bette Davis at The Hollywood Canteen. She could not bring herself to tell Markey that the baby they had 'adopted' was not some unfortunate's infant but was hers and Loder's.

Markey saw no reason to inhibit Hedy's desire to indulge in her hobby. She even had an inventing table with scientific apparatus set up in their marital home. Now, in her spare time, Hedy considered the dilemma of the Nazi U-boats, but it was no use. Whatever solutions she came up with would not be enough to stop the Nazis. It was then that she had her brainwave. She could not accomplish this issue on her own. The task was just too great for one person, but with someone else, especially the individual she had in mind, maybe, just maybe, together, they would find the answer.

CHAPTER 17

Glendale & Los Angeles, California, U.S.A.
July–September 1940

Hedy consulted her watch. It was almost four o'clock in the morning. Had she really been awake all these hours contemplating the torpedo problem? It seemed as if she had. She had to catch some sleep. She was due to be on-set in a few hours to continue shooting her latest movie, *Come Live with Me*. But this was too important to wait. Even a few hours might make a difference. She dialed the number which rang several times before a heavily somnolent voice answered. "Hello?"

"Howard, it's Hedy. I need to speak to you. It's very important."

"Hedy...? Hedy...?" the voice answered sleepily. There was a few seconds delay, while Hedy guessed her contact was squinting at his bedside clock. "Do you know what time it is?"

"Yes, but this is too urgent to wait until the morning."

"Hedy, nothing is that urgent it can't wait until a more respectable time."

"No, Howard, it's terribly..."

"Nothing is that terribly..." He stopped talking as a sudden thought came to him. "You're not going to tell me at this Godforsaken hour that you've just discovered you've got a little Howard growing inside you, are you?"

"Don't be so vulgar. No, it's nothing like that. It's far more serious."
The actress heard Hughes exhale an audible sigh of relief. That was all he
needed. He tried to remember if he had started seeing her before or after
her divorce from Gene Markey but could not be sure which it was.

"I'm heading to the factory tomorrow morning, this morning, I should
say, if that's any good."

Hedy thought for a moment. "Damn, I'm back on set all day
tomorrow. I know I said it was urgent, but tomorrow just won't work for
me. Listen, it's Thursday now. Could we maybe say Saturday?"

"Sure. I'll pick you up around ten o'clock, and we'll head to the plant.
I need to be there in any case. We can use my office. That'll give you all the
privacy you need. How does that sound?"

"Perfect, Howard. I'll see you then." She hung up, settling herself down
to rest, grateful that she could start to get her project underway. With
Howard's innate intelligence and his engineering skills, between them, they
might be able to come up with a plan to sabotage Hitler's war aims.

* * *

It had been a long forty-eight hours, but Howard Hughes finally arrived at
her door only slightly later than they had arranged. He quizzed her the
entire journey, but Hedy would not be drawn, not until they had entered
his airplane factory at Glendale. She immediately wanted to go to his office,
but Hughes insisted on showing her around his plant.

"Howard, I didn't come here to look at some moldy old aircraft. I'm
sure they are fascinating, but we have more important things to discuss.
Can we please go to your office?" Hughes was hurt by Hedy's comments,
replying, "My airplanes are neither moldy nor old. Just the opposite, in fact.
We're looking at new, innovative ways to make planes go faster and farther
than ever before. I thought with your inventive mind, you might be
impressed by what we're doing here."

"Yes, Howard, I'm sorry I was so mean. It's just that..."

"Obviously, flight technology is not something you're interested in. I'm sorry I brought you out here now. I can see I was wasting both our time."

"No, it's not that. It's just this war in Europe. It's dreadful, don't you think?"

"What I think, or don't think doesn't matter, Hedy. There are always going to be wars somewhere. I'm just thankful that this time, we can sit this one out. O.K. I'm all yours now. What's got you so fired up you couldn't discuss it on the phone?"

"Before you scream at me, please just listen. It's the war. I know we're not affected, not yet, anyway, but as sure as night follows day, eventually we will get involved. Hitler isn't going to be satisfied just with Europe. Eventually, he is going to come calling. We need to find a way to stop him before he can cross the Atlantic; before he can sink our ships not out in the ocean, but here, in our ports, American ports."

"Yes, and when that time comes, we'll do something about it. If it happens."

"Don't you understand? By that time, it will be too late. Winston Churchill was warning the British about this years ago, and their government did nothing. Now, Britain is fighting for its life. I don't want this country to copy Britain's mistakes."

"So, what do you want me to do about it? I'm not a politician or a general. I'm a businessman." They were still on the shop floor.

"Not here. Let's go somewhere more discrete, then I'll explain." Hughes took Hedy's hand indulgently and led her to his office complex. They went into Hughes' inner sanctum after the aviator gave instructions he was not to be disturbed. Seating himself behind his lavish walnut and teak desk, and motioning his guest to take the chair in front of him, he asked, "Very well, Hedy, now what is it you want?"

The Austrian actress considered using the chalkboard in the room, but Hughes was smart enough to understand what Hedy would discuss without the use of diagrams. "I'll get right down to it. As I see it, the gravest threat the British face is from the German submarines, U-boats, I believe they call them. Not so much from the submarines themselves, but from their torpedoes. They are sinking shipping like nobody's business, and if this goes on much longer, Britain will be driven to the wall. We have to find a way to stop them, stop the Germans before it's too late."

Hughes allowed himself a wry smile. "So the best British military planners, naval scientists, and academics can't find a way to deter the Nazis, but you think an actress and a businessman can? How very noble and imaginative, not to mention impossible. How do you propose to do it? Send Hitler a strongly worded letter? Let's face it, Hedy. The British are doomed. Let Hitler finish what he started, and then our politicos can work out a deal with the Third Reich. Why should we be getting involved in matters that have nothing to do with us?"

"Nothing to do with us?" Hedy spluttered. "Don't you see how he's behaving towards the Jews over there? They're being driven out of their homes, their shops and factories are being burned and looted, synagogues are being ransacked. How would you feel if it was your home, your factories, your loved ones who were being treated like that?"

"Well, all I know is that there ain't much Jewish being spoken around the parts I come from, and if it is, it's spoken with a Texan twang. What are you getting so all fired up for, anyhow? You aren't one of them, are you?"

It was now or never. This was her seminal moment. Should she reveal her birth religion to this man or stay silent? The pros and cons of doing or not doing went fleeting through her mind. Finally, inevitably, there was only one thing she could say. "Of course not. Whatever gave you that idea?"

"Nothing. It's just the way you spoke so passionately about them. I thought perhaps..."

"Well, you thought wrong, then. No, it's just the injustice and unfairness of it all. I would feel the same way about any oppressed people who were being treated like they are. Now, are you going to help me or not?"

"I'd like to, Hedy; really I would. But I've got problems of my own at the moment. Much more serious than helping a few Jews, even..."

"You utterly selfish and contemptible man. I turned to you because I thought you might have some compassion as well as brains. It seems I was wrong. On both counts."

"Please don't be like that. I'm doing some damn important work at the moment, work that will help this country a great deal if we do get sucked into this blasted war. I need to devote all my time and energy to these projects. Surely you can understand. You do understand, don't you?"

"No, I don't, and I'll tell you why. As you rightly say, so far, we aren't involved in what's happening over there. I hope and pray we might never be. But they are involved, the British, I mean. They are involved right up to their necks. They need our help now! Not at some indeterminate time in the future. If Britain falls, I don't know what will happen next. The one thing I do know is that by conquering Britain, Hitler will be just that bit closer to America. To us!"

This last remark stopped Hughes in his tracks. "You know, Hedy, I hadn't thought of it like that. I always knew you had brains, but you've just made the whole thing crystal clear to a foolish man. I'm sorry. Of course, I'll help you, but I must finish my current project first. It is vital to any future war effort, I assure you. In fact, maybe you can help me."

"If I do help you, if I can, do you promise to work with me?"

"Hedy, I've never welshed on a deal or a promise in my life, and I don't intend to start now. Especially not with you."

"But Howard, this is so important..."

"So are the projects I'm working on. Come with me. Let me show you." Hughes took Hedy by the hand and led her once more onto the factory floor. She saw many aircraft in various stages of construction. "The problem we have, Hedy, is that although we are building faster and better-equipped planes, we're just not getting the speeds we're aiming for. We've redesigned whole sections of the airplanes, the fuselage, fuel capacities, propellers, you name it, we've done it, but we're still limited. Somehow, we're missing something. I just can't put my finger on it."

Hedy slowly walked around the factory, closely studying the machines, those still in the manufacturing stage and other, completed units. Looking puzzled, she glanced at Hughes, returned her gaze to the airplanes, then back to her host. "You mean you haven't worked it out? How to make the planes fly faster, I mean."

"Isn't that what I've just said?"

"Yes, but..."

"But what?"

Almost to herself, Hedy muttered, "No, it can't be that simple, surely. If I can see it, then why can't they?"

"See what?"

"No, I can't say what I think for now. You'll just laugh at me."

"Hedy, I promise I won't make a fool of you. This is too important to my company and me. Now, for Heaven's sake, what is going through your mind?"

"No, Howard, I need a little more time. Just give me a few days, and I'll get back to you. I will keep my word, just as I expect you to keep yours."

Hedy had a grueling film schedule and could not accomplish what she had in mind for almost two weeks. Eventually, she managed to find the time to do what she had promised Howard Hughes. Driving into the center of Hollywood, she found what she was looking for—a bookstore. It had come to her in a flash of pure inspiration while she had been in Hughes' factory. How do you make something go faster, fly faster? Simple. You look at someone, something which is already doing what you are trying to achieve. In this case, birds. By studying their body shape and wing formation, if you can make an 'artificial' bird in the shape and form of the real thing, it will surely have the same effect. The same principle would also apply to fish. If you combined those two attributes, it must emulate the original. But could it really be that simple? There was only one way to find out.

After she returned home with her purchases, Hedy quickly leafed through the books. She found what she was looking for, then opened a sketch pad and artist's pencil and began to draw. It took her several attempts to achieve the design she wanted, but finally she had come up with something approaching her desired effect. She had found that the fastest bird was the Peregrine falcon. The fastest fish was the black marlin and the sailfish. By combining the properties of all these creatures, it might provide the solution to the Hughes conundrum. She called Hughes and told him she was ready to unveil her ideas.

"O.K. Do you want to give me a clue, or are you going to keep me guessing?" he laughed.

"Only for a little while longer. Do me a favor, Howard. Can you get your chief designer to meet us at the plant? I think..."

"He'd better be there already. He's getting paid damn well for not producing what I want him to. Don't you worry, Hedy darling, he'll be there. I'll pick you up in an hour."

Hedy had wrapped the books with her sketches so as not to reveal their contents before arriving at the factory. If Hughes was curious about the package, he did not show it. When they arrived, Hughes summoned his head of design, Glenn Odekirk, and all three went into Hughes' private office. "Very well, Hedy. You have center stage. Let's see your big idea." Slowly, confidently, Hedy took out her purchases. She seemed to make even unwrapping a couple of books a sensual experience. Hughes and his designer looked at each other bemused. This was it? This was what all the hoo-hah was about? A book on birds and a book on fish? She had to be joking, hadn't she? But when Hedy explained her rationale, both men stopped carping. "I saw it straight away, but I couldn't believe I was the only one who had noticed what you couldn't see. It's the airplane's wings. They're too 'boxy', too 'square.' Think about it for a minute. We've only been airborne for less than forty years. Birds have been flying in the sky for over forty million years. To have lasted this long, they must be doing something right, mustn't they? The same goes for fish. They have developed their fins and their streamlined shape to adapt to their environment. Now, if we, or you, could somehow couple, or incorporate the best features of both designs into your airplanes, I think you'll find the answer to your problem. Faster, smoother, sleeker, more cost effective and efficient models."

"Good God!" exclaimed the draughtsman.

"I don't believe it." Hughes said. He leaned over and kissed the actress. "I've said it before and I don't mind saying it again. Hedy, you're a genius."

Caught up in the moment, even the designer made to embrace the movie star, then remembered his place. "It's O.K. I'm sure your employer won't mind just this once, will he?"

Hughes shook his head. "It's not me he should be worried about. It's his wife, Esther. I don't think she's the forgiving type," he laughed.

"It would be worth it, just to be able to tell my grandchildren I've kissed Hedy Lamarr."

"Well, just make sure you don't tell them when Esther's around," cautioned Hughes.

Odekirk leaned forward hesitantly, unsure if Hedy would allow him to embrace her. She smiled, holding out her arms. She expected Hughes to show some displeasure at this flagrant, if humorous display of appreciation by Odekirk. But nothing could dampen his mood at the moment. And it would give the designer something to tell his grandchildren. The day he got to kiss the screen idol, Hedy Lamarr. And he wouldn't bother even if Esther was within earshot when he told them. After all, his wife was also a fan of the screen actress.

* * *

A few weeks later, Hedy arrived at her movie trailer to find a large truck at the door. The driver and his mate were unloading crate after crate. "Stop!" shouted Hedy in alarm. "What are you doing? I never ordered any of this stuff. There has to be a mistake. Will you please reload this stuff on to your truck? You need to take it away."

The delivery driver rechecked the details on his manifest. "No, ma'am, it says right here," and he pointed to the top of the paper, "Addressee – Miss Hedy Lamarr. That's you, ain't it? I seen ya in that movie, wotchacallit, 'Algerians,' with the Frenchie."

"Algiers," she corrected him. "But I don't understand. I..."

The deliveryman handed her an envelope. "They said at the depot we were to leave this letter once we'd dropped everything off, but I guess you'd better see it now. Might shed some light, eh?"

"You're too clever to be doing this job," she answered sardonically. Mistaking her meaning, the man preened himself. "Gee, thanks, Miss Lamarr. That's real kind of you."

Hedy ignored him as she tore open the envelope, reading out loud, *"Dear Hedy, I don't think you'll ever know just how much your brilliant suggestions have contributed to improving our designs. Please accept these gifts* as a "thank you" for your help. I hope you get some practical use from the equipment. I also want you to know that any of my engineers, designers and technical staff are at your disposal, should you need them. Best regards, Howard."

Giving the men a few dollars, Hedy got them to unpack the contents of the cases and carry them into her trailer. The boxes contained a near-duplicate set of the apparatus she used at home. The actress was overawed by his generous expression of gratitude. Despite his solemn promise, however, Howard Hughes never collaborated with Hedy in her quest to find an answer to the perplexing issue of German U-boats and their devastating effect on the Allies' war effort.

Just when Hedy thought things could not get any worse, an event happened that galvanized her more than anything she had experienced in Austria or had witnessed in the newsreels, and it shocked her to the core. On September 18th., a civilian ship, the *S.S. City of Benares*, was sunk by a German U-boat en route from Liverpool to Quebec. What made this destruction even more despicable was that the ship was carrying a group of children being evacuated from war-torn Britain to safety in Canada. Reports said that at least fifty schoolkids had perished in the freezing waters of the North Atlantic. Hedy was horrified. What were these cruel monsters thinking? How could any civilized person, anyone with an ounce of humanity, consider an unarmed vessel carrying non-combatants, youngsters, for God's sake, be a threat to their navy? It was unforgivable. Now, more than ever, she would have to consider the problem which was gnawing away at her. But who could she turn to? Despite his generous expression of gratitude and his solemn promises, Howard Hughes had proven himself to be selfish and useless.

Hedy knew she could not solve this problem by herself, but who would help her, now that Howard Hughes was no longer interested? She needed to find someone before it was too late; before Nazi jackboots marched down London streets; before her mother was taken, along with the rest of the Jewish population to a fate that could only be guessed at.

CHAPTER 18

Los Angeles, California
July-September 1941

Hedy was tired. She had been working non-stop and was about to start on her next movie, *H.M. Pulham, Esq.*, playing opposite Robert Young. But the constant work was taking its toll; it meant she was spending little time with her son James, something her maternal conscience was not prepared to accept. That, and her recent separation from Gene Markey, not to mention her concerns over what was happening across the Atlantic, were engulfing her.

She had still not come up with an answer to the German U-boat menace, nor found anyone who could help her. Even sitting at her science table, tinkering with her experiments, did little to calm her. Hedy could not let her mind coast into a layby and quietly park. She always needed to be driving at full speed down the cerebral highway.

Despite outwardly being a confident woman, Hedy was self-conscious about her anatomy, specifically, her breasts. She had even asked Howard Hughes, with his engineering and mechanical expertise, if he could come up with an answer to her problem. Hedy had envisioned some kind of cantilevered arrangement but did not have the technical background to formalize her design. Hughes dismissed her request telling her she looked fine as she was.

In a telephone call with her good friend and fellow actress, Janet Gaynor, Hedy had confided her perceived lack of ampleness. Gaynor's husband, Adrian Greenburg, known in Hollywood as simply 'Adrian,' was a well-known costume designer and had made the gowns she was wearing in her current role, playing opposite James Stewart. Perhaps he might be able to offer a solution.

"No, Hedy. Adrian is a wonderful couturier but an engineer he isn't. I'm sorry. I don't think he could help you. Quite frankly, honey, woman to woman, if you don't mind my saying so, I think your breasts are just fine. When someone is as beautiful as you are, believe me, it's not so important."

"That's so nice of you, Janet, but I still think I could do with some, er, enhancement up top. I suppose I'll just have to find a doctor..."

"No, wait," her friend interjected. "if you're determined to go through with this nonsense, there's maybe someone you should meet. He's a friend of ours. He might be able to help you."

"I didn't realize you and Adrian moved in such exalted circles. Who is this marvelous surgeon?"

"He's, ah, he's not a doctor. He's a composer, a musician."

Hedy laughed. "I'm sorry, for a moment, I thought you said he was a musician."

"You heard right. Yes, he's a musician, but he also dabbles—sorry, that's not the word I meant to use. That is, he has interests in other areas, too. He's actually written quite extensively on the subject. For *Esquire* magazine, no less."

"He's written about women's breasts? What is he? Some kind of pervert?"

"No, silly. Not about women's breasts, as such..."

"As such," mocked Hedy.

"Listen, he's also quite an expert in endocrinology, among other things. You know, glands, and things; 'women's things.'" Janet said suggestively. "Why don't you have a word with him? What harm can it do? If you think he's a charlatan just out to cop a feel, fine. Send him on his way." Janet shrugged her shoulders. All she could do was make the suggestion. The rest was up to Hedy.

The Austrian actress thought for a few seconds before answering her friend. "Oh, why not? What harm can it do, I suppose? Besides, I've not been out much lately. Nobody's tried to cop a feel from me in ages."

"Don't you dare get carried away with yourself, young lady," Janet warned. "I was only joshing about that. George is happily married. Very happily married."

"George...?"

"George Antheil. He's a...."

"Yes, I know who he is. He's a bit... strange, isn't he?"

"Well, some of his music certainly is, but honestly, Hedy, he's one of the smartest people I know, present company included."

"O.K. How do I get to meet this wunderkind?"

"Tell you what? Why don't Adrian and I throw a party next week? I'll invite him and his wife along. George can play some of his marvelous compositions. It'll be fun."

"I'm sorry, Janet, you'll have to explain that word to me."

"What word?"

"Fun. It's been so long since I've had any, I've forgotten what it means."

* * *

It was a strangely apprehensive Hedy who sat at her friends' green onyx dining table awaiting their other guests. "They're late," she fumed, consulting her wristwatch. "Oh, you know these musical types," Janet replied airily. "They always have to make an entrance, even when they're not on stage. I'm sure they'll be here soon."

"My mother was a concert pianist back in Hungary," Hedy retorted. "I do not think she was late, even once, for a performance. It is the height of discourtesy to one's guests. A time is a time; that's all I'm saying."

"Oh, get off your Austrian keister, Hedy. We're not in Europe now. It'll be worth it when you hear him play. He's magnificent."

"So is my mother. If I wanted to listen to music, I could have turned the radio on or played a recording on the phonograph. That's not why I'm here," she blurted out. Adrian turned and looked questioningly at his wife.

"Janet, what's going on? What haven't you told me?"

"Nothing, darling. I..." Hedy's hostess looked flustered, her face reddening, as she searched for a discrete reply.

"Oh, Janet, I'm sorry. I assumed you would have told Adrian. It's a... woman's problem," Hedy said, turning to Greenburg. "I believe Mister Antheil has experience in these areas. I just wished to consult him about something."

As if on cue, Antheil was ushered into the dining room by the maid. They all rose together to greet the new arrival. The composer waved them to resume their seats, saying, "Sit down, for goodness' sake. I'm not the President." His hosts did not fail to notice that although his remarks were directed at them, he could not take his eyes from his fellow guest. The first thing that struck Hedy was Antheil's lack of stature. She had imagined that someone with his formidable reputation would be, well, 'bigger.' Antheil was just over five feet tall, but his personality dominated the room.

"Where's Boski?" asked Adrian. "Isn't she with you?"

"No, she's gone back to Trenton. She needs to help my parents deal with Henry's estate."

"Your brother's estate? Your brother died? He must have been young." offered Hedy, compassion evident in her voice.

"Unfortunately, if that's the right word, it wasn't due to natural causes. Henry was a diplomatic courier based in Finland. He was on a flight that was shot down. It must be over a year ago, now. I can't tell you very much more about it, I'm afraid. The State Department has asked us, well, told us might be a better way of putting it, not to discuss the circumstances with anyone."

"I'm truly sorry for your loss, George. This damn war has affected so many people..."

Dinner was served with the usual small talk, mainly concerning who was doing what with or to whom within their own world, the world of the film studio. As all four were connected with the industry, no one felt the need or the desire to change the subject out of respect to an outsider. It was an environment in which they all felt comfortable.

After the meal was over, Janet suggested that it might be nice if Adrian and her left their guests alone to get better acquainted. This euphemistic expression did not fool her husband. Once their hosts withdrew, George got straight to the point. "Janet tells me that you're rather concerned about the shape and size of your, er, breasts. Is that correct?"

"Tell me, George, do you have any European blood in you?"

"Yes. My family is originally from Germany, although I wouldn't shout that too loud at the moment, if you get my meaning. Why do you ask?"

"I don't think Americans, I mean those whose ancestry goes back generations, would have been so forthright. After all, it's not usual for a relative stranger to just come out and discuss the intimate areas of a woman they hardly know, is it?"

"No, I guess not," Antheil agreed, "But Janet did say, in absolute confidence, I might add, that you had some concerns about them. I have to tell you that from where I'm sitting, your breasts look absolutely fine to me, just perfect, in fact. What do you think is wrong with them?"

"Well, they... sag, for a start. And I really would like a fuller bust. Can you do anything for me, George?" Hedy thrust out her bosom to Antheil's alacrity. It wasn't every day a famous and beautiful actress pushed her chest in your face. After composing himself, the musician leaned back on the sofa they were both on, the better to examine her figure. "Well, Hedy, it's all about the pituitary gland and how we can improve the axons that store and release hormones into your upper torso."

Hedy took a small notebook and pencil from her purse and began to write. "You're taking this seriously, aren't you? Why are you taking notes? Do you intend to get a second opinion?"

"No, not at all," Hedy smiled, "but this is all beyond my comprehension. It just helps me to retain whatever information we discuss."

"Very well," the composer conceded.

And so, for the next half-hour or so, Antheil went through the various treatments that were available to enhance Hedy's bust. Finally, the talk turned to other issues, and, inevitably, the war in Europe eventually entered the conversation. "It's not going too well for the Brits," Antheil observed.

"The Germans are flying over, night after night, dropping bombs on London and many other cities. You have to wonder just how long they can hold out."

"Yes, I know. I'm sick with worry. My mother is over there. She managed to get out of Austria just before Hitler arrived, but it looks as if she's gone from out of the frying pan and into the fire."

"I'm so sorry, Hedy. I hope she'll be alright."

"They don't seem to be issuing passports now. She's managed to get identity papers, which will be valid for a year. I've asked Mister Mayer if he can help me to get her over here, or at least to Canada. You know, with his contacts and everything. He keeps promising to do something, but so far, he doesn't seem to have done very much."

"I wouldn't rely on L.B.," Antheil cautioned. "He does what's good for him. If he can't see a buck in it, I'm afraid he might just be stringing you along. I hope I'm wrong, though."

"Oh, please don't say that, George. Surely he'll do something."

"Yes, I'm sure he will," smiled the musician, with a confidence neither of them truly believed.

"I know you can't talk about your brother, but surely, if he was shot down, that's tantamount to an act of war. I don't understand why the government is so reluctant to voice its anger with the Germans. We should have..."

"It wasn't the Germans who shot the plane down. It was the Russians." Antheil explained quietly. "You mustn't say anything to anybody about this. I shouldn't have told you even that much."

"The Russians? Why on earth would the Russians...? No, you're right. I suppose the fewer people who know about this, the better. I promise you; I won't say a word to anyone. I know how to keep secrets. My first husband was a munitions manufacturer in Austria. You should hear some of the conversations I've been privy to around our elegant dining table. We once had Hitler himself – but that's a story for another day."

"It's one I'd like to hear if you're allowed to discuss it."

"Maybe another time." Hedy looked at her watch. "Gosh, it's getting late. I really must be going; I've got to be at the studio first thing. Maybe we can meet again soon."

"Yes, I'd like that," the composer replied.

Hedy bade her hosts farewell. Nothing was said about what was discussed between her and George. Discretion sometimes really was the better part of valor.

Antheil left the Greenburgs shortly after Hedy's departure. As he approached his car in the darkness, with only his hosts' exterior house lights for illumination, he noticed something scrawled on his windshield. It took him a few seconds to discern its message. It was a telephone number, written in lipstick. Hedy Lamarr had left her number for him to contact. The most beautiful woman in Hollywood wanted to see him—again! Whatever would Boski think? It was probably best for all concerned if she didn't know. Not until he chose to tell her—if he ever did.

CHAPTER 19

Los Angeles, California
October–November 1941

The City of Benares incident still troubled Hedy. If an answer to the submarines, and more importantly, the torpedo question, could not be found soon, Great Britain faced certain annihilation. In her previous conversation with Antheil, the germ of an idea had come to Hedy. She could not even find a way to formulate it in her earlier discussion, but she somehow knew it might be worth investigating—if she could define her vague notion into words. She had seen a newspaper advertisement for a Philco radio, the *Philco Magic Box*, which could be operated wirelessly. The remote-control instrument resembled a wedge-shaped casing with a larger version of a telephone dialer mounted on its top and connected remotely to the radio. It did not use wires or cables. By dialing a pre-set number built into the unit, you could alter the radio's frequency to change the station.

U-boats were operating largely unchallenged. Their speed and agility easily out-maneuvered the older and slower British vessels, and the Royal Navy's outmoded marine ballistics were no match for their enemy's newer equipment. The Germans had discovered ways to intercept the frequency on which the Allies were launching their radio-guided underwater missiles. By interfering with these signals, the torpedoes were sent wildly off course, most exploding harmlessly well away from their targets. If they could only somehow find a way to modify the frequency of the torpedo's signal being sent from the British warships, it would hamper the *Kriegsmarine's* efforts to affect its trajectory. The Philco advertisement gave her the concept.

If you could remotely alter the frequency of a domestic radio, why couldn't the same application be used to change the frequency of the signal being sent from the ship to the torpedo? The Nazis could jam the frequency of one radio command. Could they interfere if those commands changed; or kept changing? Perhaps Antheil might find a solution. His intellect was almost on a par with hers. He had displayed some of his brilliance in their earlier encounter. Maybe the answer to her conundrum was there, inside his mind. All it might take was the right stimulation. She would soon find out.

* * *

Antheil wasted little time responding to Hedy's unusual message and called her a few nights later. He was glad his wife was still in Trenton. She might jump to the wrong conclusion if she discovered he had the private telephone number of one of the most glamorous women in Hollywood. Hedy invited the composer for dinner at her Benedict Canyon home but did not mention her ulterior motive. After the meal was over, with the remaining detritus still littering the dinner table, they got around to the subject of the current situation in Europe. "I feel so utterly useless sitting here, George, in my nice home when there is so much trouble going on over there. I sometimes think my fellow actors don't realize how lucky they are, not to be where I came from. It frustrates me that I can't do more to help their war effort."

"Between you and me, Hedy, I wouldn't be surprised if it wasn't too much longer before we get roped into this. I know all about our stance of neutrality and Roosevelt's outward display of isolationism, but he's no fan of Hitler or Stalin. I think eventually, one of them is going to set their sights on us."

"Oh, George, I hope not. They couldn't anyway, could they? Their airplanes couldn't reach America, could they? Not yet, at any rate."

"Maybe not yet, but it might come sooner than any of us thinks."

"You know, I've half a mind to postpone my career and go to Washington. They've just set up an organization called the *National Inventors Council*. I'm bursting with ideas I think could be useful. I still remember many of the conversations my first husband had in our house. I'm sure if I told them what..."

Antheil interrupted her. "Hedy, I get the impression you didn't invite me around just for dinner. You know I'm married, and I think you're honorable enough not to take advantage of my wife's absence to take advantage of little old me."

"No, George. Whatever gave you such an idea? I do like you, of course, but not in that way. But you are right. I did have another reason for asking you to come over."

Antheil arched an eyebrow. "Come on, Hedy, spit it out. What have you inveigled me into?"

"Nothing. It's just... I've been thinking about the havoc the German submarines are causing in the English Channel and out in the Atlantic. We need to try to find a way to stop them. Otherwise, God knows what will happen."

"And when you say,'we,' you mean..."

"Well, anybody, really. It's an amorphous 'we,' but I guess, specifically, I mean me, us." She pointed her index finger firstly at her dinner guest before turning it into herself. "I've had a thought..." saying which she outlined her ideas to Antheil.

After she had finished, Antheil blew out his cheeks. "Whew. That's quite a tall order. To keep changing the frequencies connecting the ship to the torpedo while the missile is in motion—I don't see a way to... wait a minute." Antheil stroked his chin, sending some dinner crumbs falling onto the table. Staring at Hedy but seeing no one in front of him, he began to postulate, more to himself than his host. "So, the issue is, the torpedo is launched from the boat, or the submarine, maybe the aircraft, directed on to its target by radio wave. Once the Nazis home in on the signal, they intercept the device by sending another signal on the identical frequency, confusing, subverting, and re-guiding it away from its intended objective. So, if it was possible to change the frequency mid-course...."

"Yes, that's it exactly!" Hedy enthused. "I knew I'd found the right person."

"Wait a minute," he wagged his finger in warning. "It's all very well to know what the problem is. It's another thing to find the solution."

"But you sounded so positive a minute ago."

"Did I? I don't remember, ah, yes, now I recall."

"Recall what?" The actress asked impatiently.

"Well," he hesitated, "when I wrote the 'Ballet Mecanique' back in 1923, I originally composed it for sixteen Pianolas, among some other esoteric apparatus. All the Pianolas were meant to play in synchronicity, but I couldn't find a way to achieve this satisfactorily. Maybe..."

"Yes...?"

Antheil shook his head. "No, I don't see how, but then again..."

"George, you really are infuriating me. What are you trying not to say?"

"Listen, can I come back in a couple of days or so? I need to try something out, an experiment if you like. I don't want to build up your hopes in case it doesn't work, but if it does, we might be on to something."

"Can you not at least give me a hint?"

"Yes, I could, but no, I won't."

"Oh, George, you are an impossible man. I don't know how your wife puts up with you."

"Sometimes I don't either."

* * *

It was almost two weeks later when Antheil called Hedy. "I've changed my mind," were the words with which he opened the conversation.

"Changed your mind, what?"

"Can you come over to my studio instead? I've got something interesting to show you."

"Yes, of course. What is it?"

"If I told you now, it would spoil the surprise."

"Oh, you..." But she knew it would be no use to argue. If George wanted to keep whatever it was a surprise, then that's what it would be.

"O.K. Give me a couple of hours." Hedy ended the call and got herself ready. The composer sounded excited on the phone, almost as if it was taking all his effort to contain himself. She hoped his summons was worth it.

When she arrived at his studio, he welcomed her inside hurriedly. "Close your eyes," he commanded her.

"George, I've got no time for these childish and theatrical tricks. Now, what have you got to show me?"

"Very well," he answered peevishly, "come and look at this." He led her into his workroom, where Hedy immediately saw two identical Pianolas sitting silently side by side, barely six inches apart, in a corner of the large room. As she drew closer, she could see each one had a perforated piano roll, both wound to the starting position.

"Both instruments are switched on and ready to play," Antheil said. "Go and stand at the instrument on the left. When I say, 'now,' press the start key. You must press it immediately I give the word; do you understand?"

"I don't like the way you are ordering me around. I had enough of that with my first husband, and Mister Mayer isn't much better. Now, please moderate your language, if you don't mind."

"I'm sorry, Hedy. It's just that, if this works, we could be onto something big. Now, you'll notice that although the instruments are close to each other, they are not attached in any physical way."

"Yes, I can see that. So what...?"

"When I give the word, press the button on the Pianola where you are standing. Do you see it?"

"Yes, I see it." Hedy stood beside the Pianola, awaiting Antheil's command.

"O.K. I'll count down from three, and when I nod my head, that will be your cue. On the count of one, he signaled his guest as he started his own Pianola, and both instruments began to play together. It was ragtime music, not dissimilar to Scott Joplin's pieces, ubiquitous in bars and saloons at the turn of the century. The pieces were not only identical, but they were playing simultaneously. They were not even a beat out. "Something I rigged up," he replied modestly.

"I'm sorry, George. It is quite a clever contraption, but how does it help us?"

"I'm surprised you don't see the significance." he chided her gently. "Both piano rolls have identical perforations in exactly the same places. I've set them up to start and end at precisely the same time. So they are playing in complete..."

"Synchronicity," Hedy echoed.

"Indeed. It's what I tried to do seventeen years ago, but with sixteen pieces. I couldn't get it to work then, but I have now, at least with two units."

"That's amazing."

"If we can get two piano rolls to play a whole series of different notes together, why not a series of radio frequencies?"

"So instead of one frequency guiding the torpedo, there will be, oh, maybe hundreds, changed every couple of seconds. It will be impossible for the German navy to block the signals!"

"Well, that's the theory, anyway. I don't know about hundreds of frequencies, though. There are eighty-eight keys on a standard piano. If we could modify this system to alternate the radio frequencies, this number will be more than sufficient. It would mean installing a piano roll inside the torpedo. All it would need is to ensure that it was synchronized with the same equipment onboard the vessel. The Germans can never crack the signals. All we have to do now is to work on the project to make it a viable proposition. If it works."

"If it works? Of course, it will work. George, it's brilliant. Thank you, thank you so much."

"I'm not doing this just for you, Hedy. I despise Hitler every bit as much as you do. If we can develop this idea between us, who knows, it may even shorten the war. Maybe our boys won't be needed, after all."

"I hope you're right, George; I honestly do. Have you told your wife about what you're doing?"

"Not yet. I want to wait until I see if we can practically apply my theory. Otherwise, it will be a complete waste of time."

"As I said already, I've got a good feeling about this. Who knows, by this time next year, the war in Europe might be over, thanks to an Austrian actress and an American musician.

CHAPTER 20

Los Angeles, California
January–August 1942

It was now the beginning of 1942. Thanks to the Japanese attack on Pearl Harbor, America found itself embroiled in the war, which had now stretched beyond Europe and North Africa. Hedy and Antheil worked on their project whenever time permitted. Both artists were still contractually obliged to meet their respective employers' commitments, Hedy for M.G.M. and her partner for the movie producer Ben Hecht. Antheil had just written the musical score for Hecht's movie, *Angels Over Broadway*, and was hoping for more work from him. Antheil was the more technically experienced member of their collaboration, but even he was having some difficulty implementing their theoretical work into a practical application.

"It's no use, Hedy. I've tried everything I know to make this thing work. I didn't know there were so many matchsticks in California," he quipped, referring to the little pieces of wood they used to simulate the perforations in the piano rolls.

"What's the matter, George?"

Antheil shook his head. "It's the electronics. I know something about this, but we need someone who is far more knowledgeable than me. I hate to admit it, Hedy, but I'm way out of my depth here, if you'll pardon the pun. We have to find someone far more sophisticated."

"I'm an actress, George, not a technician. I don't know anyone in that line of work, let alone anyone who could keep his mouth shut. I suppose I could call Howard Hughes. I helped him out with a little problem he had, and he promised me the use of his technical staff, his way of showing appreciation for what I did."

"Oh?" asked Antheil. "You helped Howard Hughes on a technical project? Wow, I'm mightily impressed. May I ask...?"

"I'll tell you another time. What do you think? Maybe one of his electricians could help us."

"No," Antheil cautioned. "I wouldn't do that. Hughes is a businessman, first and foremost. Although I assume he's a loyal American, if he sees merit in what we're doing, he'll find a way to hold the government over a barrel to get the price he thinks our invention is worth. While everyone is haggling, more lives will be lost. Sure, it would be nice to make some dough out of this, but that's not the main reason I agreed to help you."

"Yes, I suppose you're right. But apart from Howard, I don't know anyone else."

"No, maybe you don't, Hedy, but I might. I met a guy a few years ago at a symposium in New York. His name is Sam Mackeown. He's an electronics lecturer at Caltech. We've kept in touch occasionally. There's only one thing...."

"What?"

"He's very reclusive; keeps himself very much to himself. I got the impression he doesn't have many friends, doesn't mingle much with the rest of the faculty. I could contact him to see if he can help us. The only thing is, if I tell him I'm working with you, the famous actress Hedy Lamarr, it might put him off. He will equate your stardom with popularity, and I'm sure he won't want to be anywhere near the public spotlight. Would it trouble you if I called him without mentioning your involvement at this stage?"

"Right now, George, I wouldn't care if you contacted the devil himself. This thing is bigger than me or you or anyone else, including the President.

If my anonymity is the price we have to pay to get this project finished, so be it."

"Thank you. I'll contact him tomorrow."

"If he agrees to help us, will you go to the campus?"

"No. This thing is better kept away from prying eyes or ears. I'll invite him over for dinner. Boski won't mind, I'm sure."

"If he's so reclusive, can you be sure he will want to come over?"

"Yes. He met Boski once and always asks after her. If he comes, it will be for no other reason than to see her again."

* * *

The talk at dinner was the usual mix of family, work, and, of course, the war against Japan and the situation in Europe. Antheil's wife was not overly surprised when the composer told her about his friendship with Hedy, assuring her their association was purely platonic and no more. Being in show business, he had already made friends with several female movie stars and other industry figures. Why should one more celebrity be any different? His wife was somewhat taken aback when Hedy agreed to conceal herself until they were ready to discuss the true reason why George had invited the professor over.

After Boski had removed the empty plates and stayed inconspicuously in the kitchen, the composer cleared his throat before announcing Hedy's presence. "Sam, I have a confession to make. I'm afraid I've invited you over here under false pretenses," he began. The academic cocked his head to one side, his bottom lip protruding in a slight pout, as his eyes questioned his host. "You may leave now if you wish to do so, but I beg you to listen to me before you make up your mind."

"Well, it would be very discourteous of me to go home before I know the reason you've brought me over to your lovely home. You haven't arranged for me to meet a woman, have you?" he asked nervously.

Antheil laughed out loud. "However did you guess?" he asked once his mirth had subsided. Before his guest could get up, Antheil held up both hands placatingly. "No, it's not what you think, I promise. You're more prescient than I would give you credit for, but, no, it's not an unwanted romantic assignation. I would not do that to you." Antheil explained the motive for his invitation, who his mystery guest was, and why she had remained hidden. "I must impress on you, even if you wish to leave, you must not discuss with anyone what I've told you. Is that clear?"

"It may come as a surprise to you, but you are not the first person who has wished to consult with me. These are parlous times, and my field of expertise is much in demand. Just as I would not dream of revealing to you who has been at my office door, so I will respect your wish for secrecy and discretion. Now, are you going to introduce me to Miss Lamarr or not?" Antheil's smile spread across his diminutive face, his sunken eyes beaming with delight.

After the introductions, the trio got down to work. Antheil explained again what their problem was and his failure to overcome the electronics. The lecturer read their notes and examined their diagrams and schematics. Finally, he looked up from his deliberations, glancing at both of them over the rims of his spectacles. "This is one of the most innovative pieces of electrical science I can ever remember reading. What makes it even more remarkable is that the two people who achieved it did it with very little electronics training."

"Thank you," they chorused.

"But can you help us? Can you see what we're missing?" Hedy asked earnestly.

"Yes, I believe I can. Do you trust me enough to make some notes? You have my word that I will show these to no one without asking you first. Give me a few days, and I think I'll have a solution for you. I only have one condition."

"Anything," Antheil responded. "What is it?"

"I assume you will eventually wish to patent this. It will be a prerequisite anyway if you want to present it to the War Department. They will have to have some sort of verification that it is a viable project."

"What is your condition?"

"That my name does not appear anywhere on any document you submit in support of your patent application. I am more than happy to help you, but it must be done anonymously."

"But why? If this works…"

"It will work," the academic insisted.

"If this works," Antheil repeated forcefully, "it will not have been done without your assistance. You have every right to be included in our application. This collaboration will have been a three-way effort."

"You're not listening, George. Either of you. Believe me; it will be enough for me to know that I've played my part, a tiny one, perhaps, but important nonetheless. If your invention can help in any way to rid the world of those foul monsters, that will be all the recognition I need – or want." he finished pointedly.

* * *

It only took the electronics lecturer a few days to call Antheil. "I've done it, George. It's finished. I've drafted my own sketches, done the calculations, and it works; well, at least on paper."

"But will it work in practice?"

"Oh, yes, George. It'll work all right. I can guarantee it. All done. I'll bring all the results and the documentation later. But remember what I said. This is all your work; yours and Hedy's alone."

It had taken them almost six months, but eventually, on June 10th. 1942, Hedy and George filed their application at the Patent Office in the Herbert C. Hoover Building in Washington, D.C.

It was an anxious few weeks for both amateur inventors as they waited for their designs to be examined by scientists and engineers from the Patent

Office. Finally, on August 11th. they got the news. Patent number 2,292,387 had been granted to Hedy Kiesler Markey of Long Beach, California, and George Antheil, Manhattan Beach, California. They had done it! They were on their way.

CHAPTER 21

Los Angeles, California and Washington D.C.
August 1942

Since his meeting with Georg Gyssling and Joseph Breen just at the onset of the war, Flynn had done as he was bidden. He had contacted the names on the document to galvanize them to subtly influence their like-minded friends to subvert and undermine Jewish influence and authority in the Hollywood movie industry. He had been surprised by some of the identities they gave him. They were well-known movie stars but, to his knowledge, had never made their anti-Semitic tendencies known. He would never have believed they were like him, but he was sure Breen had not chosen those stars randomly. They must have done their research to ensure word of what he was doing would not get to the ears of the movie moguls themselves.

Flynn could not be sure how far he had reached into the psyche of Hollywood's Jew-haters. He knew he was not the only one with antipathy towards these people, but little of what he had instigated got back to him. He always felt an undercurrent of animosity on set and around the studios but could never discern anything tangible. He had either done his job too well, or not well enough.

* * *

After receiving their patent, Hedy and George flew to Washington D.C., where they arranged an appointment to see Charles Kettering, Chairman of the *National Inventors Council*. Kettering was well used to meeting innovators, both novice and professional, but had never expected to get a call from a famous Hollywood actress with a new device to peddle.

"So, Miss Lamarr, Mr. Antheil, what can I do for you?" he asked, trying not to sound too patronizing. He had been intrigued by her phone call, but she had kept her words vague, not wishing to give too much away before their visit. Hedy unclipped the clasps of the document case she had purchased. She extracted the schematics with their patent number embossed on the pages and handed them over to Kettering. The Chairman of the N.I.C. read the drawings for a few seconds before glancing up at the couple. "What exactly am I looking at here?"

"Well, I thought that would be rather obvious, Mr. Kettering. It's all there in front of you." Hedy said tartly.

"Humor me, Miss Lamarr. I'm not as young as I used to be, and my eyesight isn't what it was."

So Hedy and George took it in turns to explain the nature and purpose of their invention. After they had finished, Kettering said, "Well, that's quite an interesting piece of equipment you have there. Just so I have it clear in my mind, let me see if I've understood you properly. The ship's operator fires the torpedo and directs it to his target using the existing radio-guided apparatus. An enemy patrol in the area locates the torpedo, maybe the vessel at which it has been directed. The hostile ship's operator homes in on the signal directing the torpedo and emits a signal on the same frequency, effectively jamming the signal being sent to the torpedo. This maneuver confuses the projectile, sending it wildly off-course, exploding harmlessly well away from its intended location. So far, so good?"

"Yes, you've understood the problem," Hedy smiled. "Now, let's see if you can explain our solution."

"And there was I trying not to be condescending," Kettering smiled. "Well, as I read it, your device works on a multiple signal system. Therefore, if an enemy operator does lock onto the signal, by the time he tries to jam it, the signal has been changed, rendering his attempt to block it useless."

"Yes, we call it 'frequency hopping.'"

"And this interruption to their jamming device is achieved by two piano rolls?"

"Yes," Antheil answered. "That was my minor contribution." Hedy nudged him reprovingly with her elbow.

"Oh, George, don't be so modest. Without your brilliant suggestion, this would still be gathering dust in the attic I call my brain."

"So, getting back to your brainchild, we have these two piano rolls. One is fitted into the ship's radio guidance system and the other is embedded into the torpedo. Instead of playing music, they marry up to the frequency changes, which are constantly being emitted while the torpedo travels towards its target. The enemy operator does not have the time to track each change as they happen so frequently, thereby being unable to prevent the missile from detonating on its target. How did I do?"

"With a bit of coaching from us, I think you'll do well in the inventor's industry." George quipped.

"This is remarkable. Do you mind if I copy these schematics? I want to discuss them with someone. You've certainly got my appreciation, but when you get his approval, there will be no doubt the Navy will fall over themselves to use it."

"Who do you intend to show it to?"

"I suppose it won't do any harm to tell you. I can't call him a friend, exactly, but he's a very distinguished colleague. His name is Vannevar Bush. He's the director of the *Office of Scientific Research and Development* and a brilliant intellectual. Give me two or three days, depending on how busy he is, but I will get back to you both; that's a promise."

So they now had a positive response from the head of the *National Inventors Council* and likely approval from the O.S.R.D. With the backing of two such illustrious men, it was virtually certain that the Navy would adopt their invention. What could go wrong?

CHAPTER 22

Los Angeles, California
August–September 1942

After her divorce from Gene Markey, Hedy dated several men, but eventually went back to the lover by whom she had borne a child – John Loder. Born William John Muir Lowe in 1898, Loder was originally from England, and had enjoyed an upper-middle-class upbringing. During World War I, he was taken prisoner and transported to Germany, where he stayed after hostilities were over. He eventually arrived in the United States at the start of the 'talkies,' making his way to Hollywood, where he gained some fame as a leading man in the early to mid-1930s.

Hedy had been secretive about the work she was doing with George Antheil. Loder was aware of their friendship, but knew that the composer was happily married and saw no cause to feel jealous of her association with him. Now that she and Antheil had acquired their patent, Hedy felt she could be more open about what they had been working on.

"You'll never guess, darling, what I've just been given," she announced.

Loder sounded disinterested as he replied, "Oh, I expect it's some award or other. They tend to dole them out like candy these days. What's it for? Not that awful *Come Live with Me*, is it? You were delightful, of course, but Stewart – ugh! as wooden as a tent-pole."

"Now, don't be bitchy, darling. James is a lovely fellow and so easy to work with. Far less demanding than me, I'm sure. But no, it's not that kind of prize. It's something far more valuable, in fact."

"More valuable than an acting award?" he asked distractedly. With his pipe clamped between his teeth, he was barely listening to her and did not raise his head above the manuscript he was reading.

"Oh, way more valuable. It could help win the war and also make me very rich," she retorted. It was probably the word 'rich' that made Loder look up at her.

"What do you mean?" Hedy disclosed all she and Antheil had been working on. Loder removed his reading glasses and stared at her, not believing what she was telling him. "You... you've been awarded a patent? A scientific patent?" he asked in disbelief.

Hedy smiled self-consciously. "Yes. George and I. Both names are on the document."

"And it's a... what?" Although she had already explained it to him, Loder had scarcely been paying any attention.

"It's a device that stops the Germans from interfering with the signals of radio-controlled torpedoes. It means they won't be able to jam our signals and stop the torpedoes from hitting their targets."

"Yes, I understand that but how...?"

"Oh, it will take too long to explain, but it works, John. That's the main thing. Our invention works!"

"Hedy, that's marvelous; anything that can stop the Bosch. I don't just mean Hitler. They're a cruel race of bastards, all of them." He suddenly remembered Hedy's place of birth and stopped, embarrassed by his outburst. "Hedy, I'm so sorry. I..." he stammered.

"That's quite alright. I'm not German; I'm Austrian. We might speak the same language, but believe me, we're poles apart, at least, we were, before Hitler. I cannot believe that horrid little man comes from the same country as me. Austrians, especially the Viennese, were always far more polite, more cultured than those Hun barbarians. And you're quite right. They are bastards. As far as our invention goes, George and I intend to take our plans to the Navy Department, see if we can get them to adopt our designs and fit the equipment onto their warships and dirigibles."

"Aren't dirigibles things that fly in the air?"

"Oh, no, John. Well, yes, they are, but they can also mean machines that glide through the water. That's something I learned when we were doing our research."

"I know it's an old cliché, but in this case, it's perfectly true."

"What's that?"

"You never cease to amaze me."

Hedy had just finished making her latest movie, *White Cargo*. She had no more projects in the pipeline, and with no movie scripts to distract her, she was waiting not-so-patiently for Kettering or Vannevar Bush to get back to them. The suspense was intolerable, and every day they waited was a day lost. How long did it take them to discuss her and George's idea? Kettering had said only a couple of days or so, and it was now over a week. What was keeping them? Loder had suggested that she should take her 'contraption,' as he called it, to the Navy herself, with George Antheil. After all, they would probably be the ones who would sign off on it. Why wait for the heavy hand of bureaucracy? By the time they came to a decision, the war could be over.

Loder himself was currently working on a Flynn vehicle, *Gentleman Jim*, where he was playing Carlton De Witt. Despite Flynn's dislike of the English, Loder and he became friends while on-set, often going for meals and drinks after work. The usually calm, quiet, and unflappable Loder was the perfect foil for Flynn's brash and outspoken manner. Loder's association with Hedy was no secret, and the two were often seen out together. So it came as no surprise when the Tasmanian asked after the Austrian actress. "And how is the beautiful Miss Lamarr these days? We don't see nearly enough of her."

"After her appearance in that foreign film, I'd think most other people might say the opposite," Loder quipped, referring to Hedy's nude role in *Extase*.

"Yes, I'd rather forgotten about that one. Well, you don't have to worry on that score, old son. You can see her naked whenever you like. Lucky old you, eh?"

"That's quite enough, Errol. You can take things far too far. Especially when you have an attractive piece of flesh, yourself," Loder scolded.

"Not any more. It's looking like the parting of the ways for Lili and I. Our marriage has run its course, I'm afraid. But in any case, you're right. Those remarks I made weren't called for." But in his mind, Flynn had other ideas.

"Besides," continued Loder, "she's been busy."

"Oh?" queried Flynn. "I didn't think she was doing anything at present. Except keeping you warm at night," Flynn said with a knowing leer.

Ignoring his charmless remark, Loder went on, "She's just back from Washington, you know."

"Oh, what was she doing there?" Fynn asked casually. "Family there, is it?"

"Oh, no, something far more important." Loder leaned across the table, theatrically looking around to ensure no one was eavesdropping. "She's gone to the War Department. The Navy, actually. She..."

"She's not thinking of enlisting, is she?" Flynn said. "She'd look quite fetching in a navy uniform, I bet."

"No. She's invented a new device. It's all to do with ships and submarines and torpedoes. Very hush-hush," The Englishman added, pointing his forefinger to his closed lips. Loder now had the Tasmanian actor's attention.

"What do you mean?" he asked, acting indifferently.

"I'm not sure how much I can tell you, old chap. It's a bit top-secret, you know?"

"It can't be that important, surely? What? An actress, a movie actress with national secrets? Come on, pull the other one. It's got bells on," Flynn scoffed.

"No, seriously," insisted Loder. "This thing could shorten the war. I wish I could tell you, but..."

"No, that's quite alright. I understand." But Loder was keen to divulge what he knew despite his protestations. "She's even been to see Charles Kettering himself." Loder said breathlessly.

"And who's Charles Kettering when he's at home?"

"Why, he's the chief of the *National Inventors Council*." Loder replied, apparently surprised that Flynn didn't know.

"And what did this Kettering have to say for himself?"

"He wants to go with her when she goes to see the people at the Navy. He thinks this invention could tip the scales in favor of the Allies; it's that important. Kettering is even going to discuss the thing with someone called Vannevar Bush. I'm not sure who he is, but I suspect he's someone with quite a lot of clout in government circles. This invention of hers could really take legs."

Now Flynn was really listening. He had no love for the British and would not have been too disappointed to see a Nazi victory. This machine, or whatever it was, could put paid to all that. She had to be stopped. As nonchalantly as he could, Flynn asked when Hedy was going to see the Department of the Navy.

"I don't know," Loder admitted. "She's waiting to hear from Kettering. A few days, perhaps. Maybe a week."

"That soon, eh?"

"Oh, yes. It seems they want to get Navy approval as soon as possible. Once we fit this device into our ships and get it to the British, the war will be as good as over," Loder crowed, "And it's all thanks to Hedy. Can you believe it?"

No, Flynn couldn't believe it, but if Loder wasn't playing some sick, demented game with him, Flynn would need to do something immediately. Not wishing to incur Loder's suspicion, the Australian actor turned the conversation away from the war. He stayed with his friend a while longer, before making his excuses. He had places to go, things to do, and people to see, people far more important than an English upper-class twit of an actor who didn't know when to keep his big mouth shut.

* * *

Flynn was committed to being at the studio to continue filming his movie. There was no way he could suddenly disappear, not if he wanted to keep his job. He already had a bad reputation for his drunken behavior and his unreliability. He could not risk taking French leave without jeopardizing his career. He still received the occasional call from Hermann Erben, reminding him of his promise to suborn Jewish influence in Hollywood. This situation was a bit different from what Erben had in mind; very different, indeed. If anyone could prevent La Lamarr's device from being utilized, it was him. The Austrian spy was as slimy as they came, but this war was not being fought and would certainly not be won playing by Marquis of Queensbury Rules. Flynn had not seen much of Erben since their return from Spain, apart from their visit to the German consulate.

After the episode in Barcelona, the Australian wasn't even sure which side Erben was on. There was only one way to find out. Flynn did not have an address for him. All he had was a contact number, but there was no guarantee that Erben would be there when he called. His movements were erratic and uncertain. Flynn would just have to keep trying until he found him and hope he would not have to wait too long. It was only by good fortune that Erben picked up the phone on Flynn's second try. "Errol, how are things going with you? I'm surprised a famous movie star such as you would still care to bother with a journeyman worker like myself. What can I do for you?"

"Well, you can cut the fake modesty for a start," Flynn said, before continuing, "I need to talk to you, and it's rather important."

"I'm all ears."

"Yes, and there might be more ears listening in. Let's meet somewhere more discrete."

"Where did you have in mind."

"Do you remember the restaurant we ate in just before our last trip down Mexico way?"

"Yes, I think so."

"O.K. One hour from now."

"My goodness, it must be urgent. Very well, I'll be there." But Erben was talking to an empty phone. Flynn had already hung up.

They met in the car lot, Flynn opting to sit in Erben's vehicle. "What, are we not even going to have something to eat?" Erben asked plaintively.

"Forget your stomach for a minute. I've got some news to tell you, but I'm not sure I can trust you."

"Then why are we even here?"

"Ever since Spain, I'm not sure where your loyalties lie in this bloody war. You seem to be rather ambiguous in your support. One minute, you behave as if you're best buddies with the Nazis; next minute, you look as if you're rooting for Comrade Stalin. Which is it, Hermann? Whose side are you really on? And don't lie to me. I can smell bullshit a mile away."

"I assume you're talking about our little visit to Barcelona some time ago?"

"Among other things, yes."

"Oh, Errol, Errol, for someone so worldly, you can be awfully naïve."

"You haven't answered my question."

"I'm not sure you will like the answer."

"What? Are you playing one side off against the other? Is that it?"

"Oh no, not at all. I am very loyal to my paymasters. I have to be. If they even thought for one minute I was duplicitous as you say, a very sharp blade would be drawn across my neck."

"You still haven't..."

Erben held up his hands. "I assume you won't divulge what you know until I tell you."

"And I believe you."

"I am, and always have been faithful to Germany. Anything else you may have seen, or thought you saw, was, as the Americans say, merely window dressing."

"But Spain..." Flynn exclaimed. "When you got me to rouse the Leftists..."

"Oh, that?" Erben said with a dismissive wave of the hand. "How easy it was to fool them – and you. Why do you think I asked you to accompany me? I had this all planned, well before we left the United States. By using your celebrity status, and getting you to believe I'd switched sides, it granted me access to places I would never have got to otherwise. Places where I could see their troop displacements, weapons, ballistics; why, I even discussed some of their strategies with them, which, of course, I passed on to my friends in Berlin. I'm sorry if my subterfuge offends you, but it was necessary, I assure you. I do not think I am being immodest when I say that if it wasn't for me, General Franco would still be fighting the guerrillas in Catalonia instead of leading his country."

"You used me! You exploited our friendship, you bastard!"

"If our positions were reversed, would you have done any different?"

"Well, at least I know which dictator you want to win; if I believe you."

"Oh, I am being honest, I assure you."

"Does a liar ever admit to being a liar?"

Erben laughed. "I suppose not."

"Well, let's say I think you're telling the truth; you're going to want to hear this," and Flynn told the Austrian all he could remember about his discussion with Loder. "This will earn you some kudos with the OKW."

"No, I think this one I will handle by myself. Do you know the one thing more important than alerting one's superiors to a crisis?"

"No, what is it?"

"Telling them that there was a crisis, but you have prevented it!"

"You're going up in my estimation all the time, Hermann." Flynn smiled his trademark lopsided grin. "So, what are you going to do to prevent this crisis?"

"Well, you've only just mentioned this problem, so you must give me time to consider it. I can think of a few strategies, but one must not act in haste. That is the sure way to fail."

"You're quite a philosopher, aren't you?"

"I have my moments," Erben replied smugly.

CHAPTER 23

Washington, D.C. and Gaithersburg, MD U.S.A.
September 1942

It wasn't difficult to locate Charles Kettering. A few discrete telephone calls uncovered the details Erben wanted. He was a scholar with a doctorate, business entrepreneur, engineer, and an inventor in his own right, currently employed as head of research at General Motors. He was also chairman of the newly created *National Inventors Council*. Happily married with one son. No known vices. Likewise, his investigation into Vannevar Bush threw up some even more extraordinary facts. Not only was he the director of the *O.S.R.D.*, but he had also been on the board of two other government bodies, dealing with defense matters. A gifted scientist with a probing and investigative mind. An intellectually brilliant man, very loyal to his government and his country. Not someone to be dismissed lightly.

A few more inquiries told him that Hedy Lamarr and her composer friend, George Antheil, had already approached the *National Inventors Council* with their patent. When Kettering heard about what they had done, he wasted no time contacting Bush at the *Office of Scientific Research and Development*. This was an amazing achievement and had to be acted on quickly. Time was of the essence as the German war fleet was fast gaining parity with the Royal Navy, especially as so many Allied ships were being sunk. Funding for such an important project would not be a problem. All it would then require was the formality of the Navy's rubber stamp before production could begin.

It seemed that Erben had received this intelligence too late to stop it. There had to be something he could do. He just did not know what it was – yet. The Nazi had discovered who the procurement officials were within the Department of the Navy. Having nothing better to do, he sat in his car outside their offices, hoping inspiration would somehow come and provide an answer.

It was the middle of the afternoon, around three p.m., when a figure Erben recognized left the Navy Department building. He was attired in a Naval uniform and appeared to be in his late forties, tall, a good few inches over six feet, and muscular, with a prominently angular jaw. Although appearing to stride confidently away from the entrance, Erben noticed that the officer was walking with his face angled toward the sidewalk as if looking for something on the ground. He occasionally stole furtive glances behind him. Was anyone following him? Erben didn't think so. The street was almost deserted, and no one else seemed to be in the vicinity. The Austrian Nazi also saw that the officer had pulled down his peaked cap slightly over his eyes. It would not impede his sight, but might help to hide his identity from any casual passer-by. This action may not have been suspicious in itself, but it was out of the normal. Maybe there was nothing in it, but then again, maybe...

Erben decided to follow the officer he recognized as Vice-Admiral Bernard Lavering, deputy head of Naval Procurement. He might have been wasting his time, but it was his time to waste. He watched as Lavering stole into a bar a few hundred yards along the road. Was the Vice-Admiral a secret drinker, even, perhaps, an alcoholic, dependent on liquor to get him through the day? His was undoubtedly a very stressful job, so it would be no surprise if this were the case. If this was his weakness, it was one which Erben could use to his advantage. Sure enough, in the time it took the Nazi to enter the bar, Lavering already had a drink sitting in front of him.

The bar was dark, with a pall of tobacco smoke hanging in the air. There was a faint smell of urine and disinfectant around him as well as the familiar stench of stale beer. Not the most salubrious place he had ever been in. All it would take would be for him to see how many glasses he consumed in how short a time. Erben wondered why Lavering would choose such a dingy haunt, then understood. It was the last place anyone would suspect such a high-ranking officer to frequent. The Austrian observed his quarry, perturbed that he appeared to be nursing the drink, taking his time, seemingly in no hurry to order a refill. Was he starting slowly to build up momentum? His question was answered a few minutes later when another man entered the establishment.

This individual was not in uniform but was smartly dressed in a dark double-breasted worsted suit, white shirt adorned with a plain red tie. His black brogues were highly polished, almost matching the sheen from his slicked-back hair. Erben judged him to be in his late thirties. He was clean-shaven but with a slight stubble suggesting he had forgotten or had chosen not to shave that morning.

Although trying to appear as strangers, it was obvious to Erben that both men knew each other. The newcomer made for a stool a few feet away before making eye contact with the Navy man. A cursory nod by both men was all the proof the Nazi needed. The only question now was what their connection to each other was. After their informal greeting, the newcomer ordered a drink. Five minutes later, Lavering finished his drink, rose from his seat, and left the pub. It did not take much imagination to deduce that 'stubble-man' would not be far behind, and sure enough, he quickly drained his glass before following Lavering outside. Erben waited two minutes before he, too, exited. He looked to his right and, seeing neither man, quickly turned his gaze in the other direction. He glimpsed the newcomer's unmistakable form from the back as he walked at a measured stride, keeping a constant pace behind the Navy officer. The Nazi waited until the well-dressed man was about one hundred yards ahead before he, too, kept a safe distance while furtively pursuing both men.

Was Lavering working against his own government, and this was a clandestine meeting with a foreign agent? Could it be that he was already betraying his country? Lavering turned a corner two blocks ahead, with the other man closing behind. Erben increased his pace, reaching the same corner in time to see the second man climbing into the front passenger seat of a black sedan. The car then drove off, leaving the Austrian standing alone. The car was a Pontiac Streamliner, meaning whoever it belonged to was not short of the odd dollar or two.

This was an unfortunate setback, but not entirely unexpected. Erben slowly retraced his steps, thinking as he walked back to his car. It was unlikely that this was the first time both men had rendezvoused this way. They had surely met like this before. The trick now was to work out when they might do it again. The times and the frequencies. He was unprepared on this occasion, but would be ready the next time. He took out his little notepad and a pencil and noted all the details of their meeting.

Erben considered the situation. He knew nothing about the plainclothes man. He was an unknown quantity. His only information was what he had gathered from his sources about Lavering. Surely if he were to leave at the same time every day, or even once a week, someone might spot his regular absences. Were their assignations pre-planned, or did one telephone the other just before their meetings? How often did these appointments occur? And why during the day? Why not meet after hours? Why take the risk of a colleague happening upon them, although this was unlikely given the venue they used? There were just too many variables and unanswered questions for Erben to formulate any sort of timetable. His only option would be to keep as much surveillance on Lavering as he could. He just hoped he would not be spotted spending so much time outside a government building, especially one dealing with matters of defense.

A few days later, his patience was rewarded when he witnessed Lavering leaving his office again, this time slightly earlier, just before two p.m. At least he had the sense to stagger his trysts, Erben thought. That was if, indeed, what he was up to. Erben drove slowly behind the Vice-Admiral, watching as he entered the same bar as before. He drove past, directing his car toward the street where the Pontiac had parked. His patience was rewarded twenty minutes later when the same scene played out as he had witnessed before. This time, they would not get away so easily.

The Streamliner drove through the streets of Washington, D.C. Eventually, the car turned north until it was out of the city. As the houses began to thin out and the landscape changed to a more rural setting, the two men pulled into the car lot of a small motor hotel standing in its own ground. The neon signed flickered, advertising that rooms were to let. There was only one other car in the unpaved lot, presumably belonging to the manager or owner.

Erben drove past, parking his car at the side of the road, a hundred yards further on. He got out of his vehicle and walked back towards the hotel, rays from the afternoon sun streaming into his eyes. He already had a story in mind if anyone challenged him. His car had broken down, and he needed to find a telephone to call a garage. He crept around the outside of the building, passing some of the hotel's bedrooms. He did not like any nasty surprises unless he was the one who was springing the surprise. It was a small establishment. Erben estimated there could be no more than a dozen chalet-style rooms, all on one level. The doors to all the rooms faced onto the car lot, each having its own parking spot. The rear of the hotel was clear, so Erben walked back round to the front. As he did so, he spotted the Pontiac outside the chalet bearing the number six. Both men had obviously made their way to a guestroom. They could not have driven to the hotel room door, parked up, and one of them (for it would surely only have been one of them) enter the reception area, book and pay for the room, and return to it all in the time it took him to get from his car to the hotel. So, had the room been pre-booked and paid for? If so, by whom?

The Austrian stole quietly to the door. The room's curtains were closed as Erben stood silently listening. From inside, he could hear noises, guttural and gasping, with what sounded like bedsprings creaking in rhythm. So that was it. This would be all the leverage he needed. The actress's invention would never see the light of day. Of that, Erben was absolutely confident.

CHAPTER 24

Los Angeles, California, Washington, D.C., Gaithersburg, MD
September 1942

Having no movie projects to occupy her, Hedy kept phoning George to see if he had been contacted by anyone.

"Hedy, I promise, if I hear anything, you'll be the first to know," he said.

"Yes, I realize that, George, but it's so frustrating, you know? Here we are twiddling our fingers when so much badness is happening everywhere."

"It's 'thumbs,' Hedy."

"What is?"

"The saying you just used. It's twiddling your thumbs, not fingers."

"George, if I want elocution lessons, I shall get someone myself. I do not need you to tell me how to speak English."

"Hedy, calm down, for goodness' sake. I was just trying to..."

"No, I'm sorry. That wasn't called for. Forgive me."

"There's nothing to forgive. Listen, it's just a formality. You know how these things are. The wheels of bureaucracy, especially military bureaucracy, grind very slowly. We already know how keen everyone is on what we did. Didn't Charles Kettering himself say how important what we've done is? Just give it a little more time. It'll all come good, I assure you."

"Yes, I know, but don't they understand? Our invention could shorten the war and save so many lives. Can't they see that? What on earth is keeping them? I am getting so frustrated with them all. This is not some child's game. Why are they taking so long? It's so infuriating, I could scream!"

"Please, just try to be a little more patient, Hedy. It can't be too much longer now."

"I don't know how much more patient I can be, George. It is not in my nature to be so sanguine."

"I know how you feel, but just try to calm down. We need to see this thing through together. You and I, Hedy. You and I."

* * *

Thirty-five minutes after Hedy and George's conversation, a phone call of quite a different nature was made. From a public telephone box not far from the Department of the Navy building, Erben dialed Lavering's offices. After being transferred by the telephonist, the Vice-Admiral picked up the receiver. "Hello, Vice-Admiral. I will make this call quick. I know all about the motor hotel in Gaithersburg, and more importantly, I know what you do there. If you want to keep your position and your standing in the naval community, you will listen to me very carefully..."

Lavering began to bluster down the line. "Who the hell is this? I...I don't know what..."

Erben cut him off. "Vice-Admiral, you have little time, and the clock is ticking. In precisely five minutes, you will leave your office and walk to the bar along the street you use to start your little assignations. You will order your usual drink and wait until someone approaches you. You will be given further instructions then. Needless to say, if you are not there or attempt to contact anyone else, this situation will be out of my hands. Do you understand?"

"Yes," Lavering hissed down the line, "but you don't understand. I'm about to go into an important briefing. I can't just..." Lavering hissed into the mouthpiece.

"Three minutes, Vice-Admiral." Then the line went dead.

Erben was satisfied that his plans were in place as he watched Lavering leaving the building. The Vice-Admiral would do as he was told, or he knew what the consequences would be. He stayed where he was for the next few minutes to be sure Lavering wasn't doing anything foolish. When he was satisfied that the Vice-Admiral was not being followed, he started his car and drove away. As the Austrian was leaving, a taxi driver entered the bar, immediately spotting his fare. "Hi, sir. I believe you ordered a cab. It's outside if you'd care to follow me."

"I didn't order any taxi. There's been some mistake."

The cabbie reached into his pants pocket, pulling out a grubby piece of paper. "You're Vice-Admiral Lavering?"

Lavering was the only man in the bar in uniform. The navy man nodded slowly in reply. "Then it's definitely for you. You want to go to..." and the driver peered at the scrawl, unable to read his own writing. Eventually, he read out the name of the Gaithersburg motel, which might now be the scene of his undoing.

"Yes, yes, of course," Lavering spluttered. "I, uh, I forgot." Saying this, Lavering left the bar, with the cabman quickly overtaking him to open the rear passenger door. The driver tried to make small talk but soon gave up when Lavering barely answered his questions and only with grunts. His mind was elsewhere. Had he been more alert, he would have noticed that the taxi driver was driving slightly slower than he could have done. Erben had insisted on this when he booked the fare to allow himself time to prepare for the next phase of his plan.

Erben had already parked his car at the same spot as he had on the previous occasion. He walked back to the motel, entering a room a few doors along to the one used by Lavering and the other man. He had just settled himself down when he heard the wheels of the taxicab driving into the graveled lot and parking outside Lavering's room. As he had arranged, the cab driver had been ordered to stay but switch off his engine.

Lavering entered his already unlocked room where he saw what appeared to be a Bakelite box on the bedside table, twelve inches high and four inches in width and depth, with some dials on one face and a mouthpiece protruding from one side at the bottom. A very thin metallic rod protruded from the top, and a small plate with basic usage instructions was riveted onto the face. He had heard of these devices, but had not seen one before. He believed they were called 'walkie-talkies.'

Erben waited for a few seconds for Lavering to familiarize himself with the equipment. Then, speaking into the mouthpiece, he said, "Thank you for coming so promptly, Vice-Admiral. I will say what I have to say very quickly without interruption. Is that clear?"

Lavering pressed the talk button and replied simply, "Yes."

"Good. Now, very shortly, you will be asked to give your approval for the production of a piece of equipment that will prevent the signals to radio-guided torpedoes from being impeded by opposing vessels. Under no circumstances must you authorize this device's use. Do you understand?"

"Yes, but…"

"No 'buts,' Vice-Admiral."

"Listen, please, you have to listen. From what I understand, this equipment has already been designated as 'red hot.' I cannot refuse to authorize this. People will wonder why I…"

Erben rebuked Lavering sharply. "Vice-Admiral, you will not facilitate in this equipment's manufacture or use aboard Allied ships. If you do, you know what will happen."

"But that's treason! I would be court-martialed and sent to prison if I agree to your suggestion. I could even be shot!"

"Oh, come, come, Vice-Admiral, do not be so melodramatic. I doubt if your government would show its disapproval so vehemently. After all, the publicity alone would be counter-productive at a time like this. The public might say, 'if they've found one, how many more are there we don't know about? What do you think that would do for public morale, eh, Vice-Admiral? No, the worst thing that would happen would be that you would be dismissed very quietly, court-martialed behind closed doors, as you say, then spend several years in an out-of-the-way prison at the American taxpayers' expense. But just think of all the opportunities that would be open to you to indulge in your sordid little escapades." Erben laughed into the mouthpiece.

"You filthy bastard," Lavering spat back. "It's not like that between Jack and I. We... we love each other. It's just..."

"Oh, come, Vice-Admiral, spare me the sanctimonious hypocrisy. Whatever you call it, this little affair would finish your career. Not to say what it would do to your marriage."

"Leave my wife out of this, you evil son-of-a-bitch. She knows nothing about..."

"Exactly my point, Vice-Admiral. What do you think would happen if she found out that you were betraying her not with another woman but with a man? That she was sharing a bed, was being intimate, with a sodomite? That she allowed herself to be entered by someone who..."

"But you don't understand. These things are decided by a committee of which I am only one member. Matters are considered by my colleagues as well as me. I..."

"Then you will just have to use your powers of persuasion to convince them to take your line."

"But how on earth am I going to do that?"

"Oh, I'm sure you'll think of something, Vice-Admiral. I am sure you did not attain your current rank without having some degree of imagination."

"Alright, alright," Lavering screamed. "I'll do it. I'll do as you say. But how do I know you won't still..."

"Won't still expose you? Now, why ever would I do that? Who knows, you might be useful to us again in the future. Why would I jeopardize my, ah, influence over you, Vice-Admiral? That would be rather short-sighted of me, would it not? No, your secret will be safe with me for the time being, as long as you do as I say. I should also make it clear that if you relieve yourself of your position, I will take that as if you had disobeyed me, do you understand?"

"Yes."

"Very well. I believe our conversation is now concluded. You may return to your briefing if you wish. Be so kind as to leave the communication device in the room. Just before you go, look inside the bedside cabinet drawer. You will see a piece of paper with a telephone number on it. It is the only number you will be able to reach me on to confirm that you have done what I have asked of you. I am not always at the address where the number is located, but you will reach me eventually. Do not waste your time trying to trace it. I will know if you do." And with that, Erben closed down his walkie-talkie. He watched with jubilant satisfaction as a dejected Lavering left the chalet and returned to the taxicab.

As he, too, left his room after the cab had driven away, Erben made a mental note to buy Flynn drinks and dinner. It was a small price to pay for the service he had rendered. Besides, the Austrian could reclaim the cost from his paymasters. With a bit extra added for his own time and effort.

CHAPTER 25

Washington, D.C. and Gaithersburg, MD
September–October 1942

Eventually, George and Hedy decided to take matters into their own hands and flew to Washington to lobby the Navy Department themselves. Why was it taking so long to authorize their invention? Didn't they realize that with every hour's delay, more lives were being needlessly lost? They finally arranged to meet with some senior officials, unaware of the heated discussions which had gone on before their arrival. Mindful of Erben's threat, Lavering reluctantly objected to the device's installation in Allied warships. "I think we need to look at this in broader terms. I'm not satisfied that this equipment is the best way to husband our finite resources," he stated.

"I'm not sure what you mean, Vice-Admiral," objected Commander Fred Lansing. "We've investigated its principles, analyzed its schematics, and studied its mechanics. It's a sound piece of machinery as far as I'm concerned. I don't see any problem with it." Choruses of approval came from the other officials seated around the conference table.

Lavering continued unabashed. "It's not so much the product itself, perhaps, as it's provenance."

"What do you mean?" Lansing asked.

Lavering framed his next words carefully. "Let's look at where this idea came from. An erratic composer of music, who uses a gun, *a gun*," he repeated emphatically, "to quieten his audiences and make them pay attention to his performances. A musician who, although a native of these shores himself, traces his immediate ancestry back to Germany! Germany; the very country with which we are currently at war. Then there is the movie actress, Hedy Lamarr, who is, I believe, of Austrian extraction. Austria; another country which we are currently fighting. She might even be construed to be called an enemy alien. How can we trust anything these people offer us? Maybe it's some other kind of gadget than the one they claim it to be. How do we know?"

"Firstly, Vice-Admiral, Miss Lamarr fled her native country because of the Nazis..."

"So she says."

"And secondly," Lansing continued, unfazed by Lavering's interruption, "didn't Antheil start his own anti-Nazi organization? Hasn't he spoken out against them? Why would he do this if he was collaborating with them? Your arguments, if you don't mind me saying so, are ludicrous, if not preposterous."

"Surely starting an anti-Nazi party is the best way to convince us of his sincerity, when, in fact, he may be using it as a way to introduce a 'Trojan horse' into our armed fleet?"

"But we've examined their technology in-depth," interjected another panel member, "and we can't find anything that would even suggest what you're implying."

"That's the beauty of Nazi science, gentlemen. These people are very cunning and are masters of deception."

"And I think you're in danger of becoming paranoid, Lavering. We've just had our budget increased to over twenty-one billion dollars. Surely we can find a tiny part of this sum to produce equipment which will help us defeat this Nazi menace sooner, especially when neither of the two inventors want a cent for all their hard work. They're giving us this technology for free, for God's sake!"

"May I remind you, Commander Lansing, that the increase in our budget is to be spent on troop carriers, warships, aircraft carriers, submarines, ballistics, and extra navy personnel. It was not raised to its current level to be used for mumbo-jumbo, science-fiction, fantastical devices, which for all we know might blow up in our faces."

"Stop acting so stupid. Even Donald Nelson at the War Production Board thinks it's a good, sound device. Why, anyone sitting around this table might think you were the subversive one here. It's a good, solid invention, and I'm right behind it. I say we begin manufacture as soon as possible."

Another committee member spoke up. "You know, as daft as it sounds, maybe the Vice-Admiral has a point. Has anyone done any sort of background check on either of these two? I mean, we all know who they are, of course, but maybe he's got onto something. Are they who we think they are? Could they be some kind of fifth column, as the Spanish say, secretly working for our enemies? For all we know," the naval officer continued, now warming to his theme, "maybe these devices have some kind of built-in, hidden mechanism which directs our torpedoes back to our own ships. With no way of us being able to stop them," he added.

"This is all nonsense. Have you two taken leave of your senses? We found no trace or evidence of any such mechanism when we studied the plans, did we?" Lansing insisted.

"No, we didn't," agreed the officer, "but that doesn't mean that they're not there. As Lavering said, these people are very smart. Look at Einstein. He's German."

"You're not suggesting Albert Einstein is a Nazi agent, surely?" scoffed Lansing.

"No, not at all. I'm merely saying that if they had installed such a device, they would hardly indicate it with an arrow saying, 'booby-trap here,' that's all."

"But we're the ones who'll be manufacturing it. We're not going to sabotage our own ballistics, are we?"

"Of course not, but maybe it is somehow an integral part of the whole arrangement. Don't forget, each of these torpedoes is fitted with an explosive device. Maybe they've rigged it so that we don't see it on the plans or even during the production process. Have we actually test-tried one of these units yet?"

"No," admitted Lansing. "We haven't. There's been no time. We are at war, in case you've forgotten."

"So," Lavering asked, incredulous, "you propose to start manufacturing these things without even trying them to see if they work? Isn't that a bit presumptuous, if I may say so?"

"Of course, they damn well work," exploded Lansing. "We've all read the reports and the recommendations by the *National Inventors Council* as well as the O.S.R.D. Do you think they're all a bunch of half-wits? If they think that this is fit for purpose, that's good enough for me! And it should damn well be good enough for you, too," he thundered at Lavering.

"So, let me get this straight. Are you suggesting we put a piano player inside a torpedo? Is that what you're proposing? Do you know how large and heavy that would make it, not to mention the extra fuel our ships and torpedoes would need to carry to compensate for the extra weight?"

Lansing sighed loudly in exasperation. "Have you actually studied the schematics, Lavering? Because, if you have, you'll see that the torpedoes don't need to include the piano player itself, merely the player rolls. What the hell is wrong with you? Why are you so all-fired up against this? Why in God's name are you being so obstructive? This machine is one of the best pieces of equipment we've looked at since this blasted war started. Can't you see that?"

"All I can see, Lansing, is that we're being offered some dubious contraption which we haven't yet test-fired, by two people of doubtful origin who have still to undergo investigation by the F.B.I. or anyone else to be sure they're not working for the Germans, the Italians or the Japanese, even. I'm not prepared to risk the security of this country, even if you are!"

"Why, you blasted incompetent! No one is more loyal to their country than I am. How dare you accuse me of putting the United States in peril? Despite all your blustering, Vice-Admiral, you've not given me one good reason why we should not proceed with putting this device inside our warships."

"On the contrary, Commander Lansing, I've given you several. You're just too blind by your own self-assurance to see them."

"My own self-assurance? Why, you fucking prick, you…"

The committee chairman and oldest member of the group, Admiral Walter Mackenzie-Walker, intervened. "Gentlemen, gentlemen, this isn't getting us anywhere. You have both made compelling and serious arguments for and against the use of this equipment. After listening to both sides, I must agree with the Vice-Admiral. Had we been offered this invention from an American citizen, then perhaps..."

"Antheil is American!" Lansing cut in.

"Well, with American antecedents, then," answered Mackenzie-Walker, "I might have taken a different approach, but..."

"So how far back does a person have to go to be a true American, Admiral? Two generations? Three? Four? Ten? You, yourself, must originally come from non-American stock. We all did! We all came from immigrant families at some time in the past. The only true Americans are the ones we've consigned to reservations!"

"That remark was uncalled for, Commander. I must ask you to apologize." the Admiral rebuked Lansing.

"Like hell I will!" Lansing shot back, rising to his feet in anger. "So now, I have to apologize for speaking the truth? Is that what you're saying?"

"Sit down, Commander. This is getting us nowhere. My decision is final. As much as I would have liked to use this equipment, I believe we should err on the side of caution. Especially when we have not yet trialed it in any test situation. We will not use this equipment on any United States naval vessels."

Quivering with emotion, Lansing stormed out of the room and into the hallway. He took out a packet of cigarettes and had just lit up when Hedy and George approached him, unsure of the directions they had been given downstairs. The actress approached the Commander, who instantly recognized her. "Miss Lamarr, it's a pleasure to meet you. What can I do for you?" Lansing knew all too well what they had come for, but he was damn sure that he would not be the one to break the bad news to them. It was Lavering who had been so insistent on not using their wonderful device. Let him be the one to tell them.

"We were just wondering when the Navy was going to start using our radio frequency alternator," Hedy replied.

"'Radio frequency alternator?'" Antheil queried. "When did you come up with that name?"

"As we were climbing the stairs just now. Why? What's wrong with it?"

"Nothing's wrong with it. It's just that I haven't heard that terminology before, is all," smiled Antheil.

Lansing directed them to a room a few doors down the hallway. "Someone will be there to see you shortly."

A couple of minutes after the inventors walked in through the office door, Lavering appeared. After the formalities were over, Hedy asked about their submission.

"Well, Miss Lamarr, Mr. Antheil, we've given very careful consideration to your designs and were extremely impressed by your professionalism. For two people with so little experience, you've both done a remarkable job."

"You've already discussed it? Why weren't we told. We could…"

"It's not usually customary to tell the submitter beforehand. There is the risk that he or she could try to influence our decision, even if the invention is not suitable or appropriate to our needs. We must be able to come to a decision without undue outside interference." Even as the words were escaping from his mouth, Lavering felt like the biggest hypocrite who ever lived. Wasn't that what he had just done? Allowed himself to be influenced by much more sinister forces. Forces that were not interested in financial gain, but something far more valuable.

"Yes, but what about…?" began Hedy, impatient to hear what the outcome was.

Lavering held up his hand. "I'm coming to that. As I said, the committee was overawed by your skill and inventiveness, but unfortunately…"

"Unfortunately, what?" asked George, anger rising in his voice.

"We won't be using your device, I'm afraid." said Lavering, truly sad that he had to be so duplicitous to save his career and his marriage.

"Why ever not?" they chorused. They were all still standing at this point, and Lavering directed them towards some chairs. "Please sit down, and I'll explain."

"I don't want to sit down," objected Antheil, getting animated. "Why aren't you going to manufacture it? If it's about money, neither Hedy nor I want a penny, at least, not now. Maybe that's something we can discuss later. Right now, all we want to do is to contribute something towards the war effort."

"Well, I'm afraid it won't be with your invention. Maybe, Mr. Antheil, you could compose some stirring music to boost morale, and you, Miss Lamarr..."

"Yes, Vice-Admiral?"

"Maybe you could follow your fellow actresses and go on tour selling war bonds?"

"Selling war bonds? Is that all you think I'm good for? Selling war bonds? Do you know how much hard work George and I put into this project? The nights we spent, the calculations, everything. George and I have put our lives on hold for the past eight months for this, and all you can say is that he should write some more music, and I should travel around the country like an itinerant woman selling war bonds? Do you know how patronizing that sounds, Vice-Admiral?"

Lavering had never felt more ashamed in his life. Here were two outstanding people offering their services and their intellect free for their country's benefit, and he was rejecting them like a bad steak.

They both saw the hesitation in Lavering's manner as he wrestled with his conscience in front of them. Should he tell them the truth? It would see the end of his career and his marriage. But his country was at war with implacable foes who would stop at nothing in their desire to conquer the world. Enemies who were causing so much misery and suffering wherever they had invaded and who were forcing their unfortunate victims into such degradation, humiliation, suffering, and death. How could he, Vice-Admiral Bernard St. John Lavering, serving member of the United States Navy, do any less than stand up for what he truly believed, irrespective of what would happen to him, personally?

But then, there was Jack to consider, he told himself. He did not deserve to be a part of this. He was a government employee, a civil servant, quietly going about his business, offending no one, just keeping to himself, and like his lover, only counting the days and the hours when they could be together and truly be themselves. His life, too, would be ruined. Unlike Lavering, Jack Rosen was unmarried, but still had his career to think of. Jack would never forgive him, no matter how hard he tried to explain. It would end their relationship, and this was something he was not prepared to contemplate. Not for Hedy Lamarr, not for George Antheil, not for the United States, not for the outcome of the war, not for anything!

"I am really sorry. We were unanimous," Lavering lied. "It was felt that your device would be just too unwieldy to put inside our torpedoes. The liabilities of the extra weight to distance ratio and the burden of accuracy reduction was just not balanced enough, I'm afraid."

"But the *National Inventors Council* and the O.S.R.D... Charles Kettering himself said we..."

"Miss Lamarr, with all due respect, neither the N.I.C. nor the O.S.R.D. have to take the decisions we have to daily. We must ensure that any equipment we install in our ships has to be safe for our servicemen to use. Your device just did not meet that criterion."

"But this is insanity. Everyone else we've shown these plans to has been so supportive and enthusiastic. And the organization that will benefit from it the most has rejected it. This just doesn't make any sense. There has to be more to it than you're telling us, Vice-Admiral. What are you keeping back from us?"

"I can assure you, Miss Lamarr, Mr. Antheil, there is no hidden agenda here." He looked at their forlorn faces, two people so full of hope and expectation, which he had dashed mercilessly. He wondered if he would ever have a peaceful night's sleep again.

As they were leaving, Commander Lansing approached them. "I'm sorry for you both, I really am. It wasn't my place to reveal our decision to you, but please believe me, had it been up to me and one or two others, the decision would have been different."

"Please don't lie to me, Commander. Lavering already told us it was a unanimous decision." Hedy cried.

"Miss Lamarr, as God is my judge, and on the lives of my wife and children, I swear to you I am telling the truth. It was far from a unanimous decision. I have no idea why Lavering told you it was."

"Maybe he thought it would be easier for us to hear if we believed no one in the room voted for it."

"No, I don't think that's it. I don't think that's it at all. He was acting strange all the way through the meeting. Very strange, indeed."

Antheil was already making his way down the hall. As Hedy was about to withdraw her hand, Lansing held on to it. Biting his lip with his upper teeth he whispered quietly, almost on impulse. "Miss Lamarr, I need to speak with you. May I call you again?"

"Why, yes," Hedy replied, taken slightly aback by his impromptu request. "I don't give out my home number but you can contact me through M.G.M. I'll tell the telephonists to expect your call and you can leave a number if I can't answer."

Lansing smiled his thanks as he released her hand. Lavering came out of the office they had been in, in time to see Hedy and Lansing ending their conversation. It may have been his guilty conscience, but he was sure Lansing was giving him a curious look. Was it his imagination, or was it something much more serious...?

* * *

Erben answered on Lavering's first attempt. He had tried to be as near to the telephone as he could for the past forty-eight hours, knowing the Vice-Admiral's call was imminent. "It's over. They're abandoning the project. I've done your dirty work, you bastard."

"You have done well, my friend. And to show my good faith, you have my word that I will not reveal your little indiscretions – for the time being."

"You'll forgive me if I don't take the word of a Nazi, but we may have another problem," and Lavering told Erben what he had witnessed just as he exited his office.

"You have fulfilled your part of the bargain. Now go back to work and leave Commander Lansing to me."

"What do you intend to do?"

"That is for me to know. It does not concern you. Just do as I say. Do not go into work tomorrow. You will call in sick and tell them you are taking the day off. Do you understand?"

"Yes, but..."

"That is all you have to do. Even Vice-Admirals take ill occasionally, do they not? Just make sure your wife is with you for the entire time." And with those last few words, Erben ended the call. This was a complication he was not prepared for, but he was a resourceful man and the one thing he could do, was think on his feet. If Lansing voiced his suspicions, this could change things. He would have to take action.

The following morning, after making a few purchases, Erben called the Navy Department offices again, and asked to be put through to the Commander. "Hello, Commander Lansing, my name is Doctor Herbert Fischer. I am Vice-Admiral Lavering's physician. The Vice-Admiral has told me something about a meeting he had with you yesterday afternoon. He did not go into detail, of course, but intimated that you and he had words over some project or other."

"He shouldn't even have told you that much, the idiot, but yes, we did have an argument. What of it? What's it got to do with you?"

"This argument, whatever it was about, has affected him very badly. He thinks he may have made a grave error of judgement, and now a lot of trouble might ensue. This situation has made him suicidal, and he called me to calm him down, but he keeps asking for you, ranting might be a better word. He wants to go over things with you and ask your forgiveness for what he did."

Lansing shook his head. He knew something was up. "O.K. Put him on. I'll speak to him." Lansing waited for a few seconds while he heard 'Fischer' speaking on the other end of the line. He could not hear Lavering, who must have been too far away. Finally, Erben came back on. "It's no use, Commander. He feels the only way he can ask for your forgiveness is if you meet with him personally. Right now."

"Sweet Mother of God. Can't this wait? He must know how busy we all are here."

"Commander, the Vice-Admiral is suicidal with torment at the way he treated you yesterday. I can only sedate him for so long. He has to show his contrition in person, if we are to have any hope of gaining any sort of recovery. Please, he needs your help now!" Erben begged.

"Very well," an ill-tempered Lansing responded. "Give me his home address and I'll come right over."

"He's not at home, Commander. He did not want his wife to see him in the state he was in, so he booked himself into a motor hotel just out of town. That's where I am now, calling from the receptionist's phone."

"Oh, for God's sake. That man is not fit for this job. Give me the address, then."

Erben gave Lansing the name and address of Lavering's trysting place, as well as the chalet number before adding, "Oh, and Commander, I would take it as a great personal favor if you would be as discrete as possible about this. The fewer personnel who know about the Vice-Admiral's condition, the better. For the time being, anyway."

"Very well, Doctor, I'll do as you say for the moment, but you must realize that I will have to report this incident eventually. We are at war, and we can't have men like Lavering in such a position of authority if he can't cope. If his mental state is so fragile, he ought not to be doing this job. Surely you must understand that."

"Yes, yes, of course. All I ask is that you come here right away. We can take care of the rest later, once the Vice-Admiral is in better shape."

"Fine. I'm on my way."

* * *

Erben watched as Lansing arrived, his car driving up to the chalet door. The Commander strode through the entrance, wanting to make this visit as brief as possible. He had important work to be getting on with, even if that fool Lavering hadn't. Let him voice his apologies, Lansing would accept them, shake his hand and leave. The whole business shouldn't take any more than two or three minutes.

As he entered the room, he was curious not to see Lavering or his doctor. He did not have time to register his surprise. Before he knew what was happening, Erben stepped out from behind the door, clamping his hand tightly over the Commander's mouth and nose, pulling his head back as he sliced his knife across the Commander's throat. Blood instantly spurted out in all directions as the Nazi severed his jugular veins and carotid arteries. The Commander was dead before the Nazi dropped him to the floor. Erben had come well prepared, and was sporting a lightweight full-length overcoat, which covered most of his body. He had taken off his shoes, and his legs and feet were covered by a pair of knee-length black rubber galoshes into which he had tucked his pants. His lower face was covered with a woolen scarf and he had even replaced his eyeglasses for swimming goggles with a ladies' bathing cap covering his head. A pair of rubber gloves completed this bizarre ensemble.

After releasing the Commander's lifeless body, he stripped off all the garments he had brought, now covered with Lansing's blood, and scooped them all into a large canvas hold-all with his blood-soaked knife. He checked himself in the bathroom mirror for any traces of Lansing's body fluids before he calmly left the chalet, softly closing the door behind him.

* * *

"Something isn't right," declared Hedy on a phone call to Antheil a couple of days later. "You heard what Commander Lansing said. Why would the Vice-Admiral tell us it was a unanimous decision, when it wasn't? Why did he lie to us?"

"Maybe he wasn't lying. Maybe it was Lansing."

"No, I don't think so. Lansing sounded sincere and so... so bitter, as if he really wanted to authorize our invention. Lavering just came over, oh, I don't know, evasive, somehow. As if he wasn't telling us the whole story, even though he said otherwise."

"Well, whatever the issue is, I'm afraid it's now out of our hands. The Navy has brushed us off, and quite frankly, Hedy, I don't have any more time to waste on this. I've been neglecting my other work, and I still have to earn a living."

"Wasting our time? Is that what you think we've been doing?" Hedy stormed. "The Nazis have all but overrun Europe, they've invaded Russia, they're sinking Allied shipping faster than they can replace it, and you think all we've been doing for the past eight months is wasting our time? George, how can you even say such a thing?"

"No, you're right Hedy, I'm sorry. I'm just a bit demoralized that the Navy didn't take up our submission. But I don't see what more we can do."

"There has to be something, surely?" Hedy had her radio playing in the background, when the program host announced a piece of breaking news. She stopped talking when she heard the word 'Lansing.' After a few seconds, Hedy came back on the line. "Oh my God, George, It's Commander Lansing..." she spoke into the mouthpiece.

"What about him?"

"He's dead, George! Commander Lansing has been murdered!"

CHAPTER 26

Washington, D.C., and Los Angeles, California
October 1942

Lavering had also heard the news about his colleague's death. What had he become involved in? Had his artifice caused Lansing's murder? And who had killed him? The Nazi, obviously. Who else could it have been after his phone call? And the location, too, was not lost on the Navy man. To make matters even worse, Lansing had been done away with, not only in the same motor hotel but the very same room he used with Jack. The message was unambiguous. But this was now as serious as it could get. Not only had he facilitated in treacherous deception, but he was also now implicated in the murder of a senior naval officer by an enemy agent. A murder he had precipitated.

It did not take long for the team from the Office of Naval Intelligence to learn of his spat with Lansing. They would wish to question, of course, and interrogate all the other members of the committee. He had a watertight alibi. He had done as the Nazi had instructed him and had hardly been out of Felicia's sight all day. She would swear to it.

Lavering was so distracted he did not hear his name being called by Lieutenant Jeffrey Waller as he sat outside the office that the O.N.I. had commandeered for their investigation. "Vice-Admiral Lavering," Waller repeated. Lavering looked up, for the minute seemingly unaware of his surroundings. He stood up as Waller invited him to enter the interrogation room. The office was sparsely furnished with just a desk behind which sat two O.N.I. officers. Facing them, there was one empty chair to which they directed Lavering.

"Good morning, Vice-Admiral. My name is Commander Keith Strawbridge," and turning to his left, he added, "and my colleague, Lieutenant Commander Jonathan Crawford. We all know why we're here, so let's get right down to it. We understand you, and Commander Lansing had some kind of argument yesterday. Would you mind telling us what that was about?"

"I'm not sure what I'm allowed to tell you, gentlemen, not that I don't wish to comply, of course. It's just that what we discussed, argued over, if you like, is classified."

Strawbridge was red-haired. With his hair shorn so close to his skull, he almost appeared to be bald, and it was only through his thin, pencil-like mustache, that Lavering could see what his hair coloring was. He had a penetrating stare, that seemed to know what you would say before you had uttered the words. Strawbridge spoke in an even, monotone timbre, but there was no disguising the authority behind his voice.

"We would not ask you to compromise security, but it would be helpful if you could give us some idea."

He's toying with me, testing me, Lavering thought. He must know already what we fought over. "I'll be happy to oblige once I get clearance from my commanding officer. Until then..."

Crawford produced a Navy letterhead with a typed missive signed by Admiral Mackenzie-Walker, which he passed silently across the table. It gave Lavering full authority to disclose all facts discussed at the earlier meeting. "Very well. I am still reluctant to talk about this, but as the Admiral has given his permission, I am prepared to tell you."

"Go on," urged Strawbridge. Lavering gave the officers a summation of what happened. There was no point in trying to be dishonest. All the other officers would give near-identical accounts, and it would look odd if his version varied in any substantive way.

"I'm still not clear why you were so opposed to introducing this anti-jamming device. Surely it would have been of immense benefit to you, the Navy, that is. Why did you try so hard to reject it?"

"It's not that I... that is, I wasn't convinced about its ability to do what it was supposed to do. That's all."

"No, Vice-Admiral, that's not all, is it?"

"I don't know what you mean."

"Didn't you also raise some doubts about the patriotism of the two inventors...?" Strawbridge glanced at his notes, although he knew very well who the people were, "George Antheil and Hedy Lamarr. Didn't you also question their loyalty to this country, Vice-Admiral?"

"I... I may have done. I really can't remember," Lavering replied, flustered.

"And a few minutes later, did you not also cast aspersions on Commander Lansing's allegiance to the United States? A Navy officer with over twenty-five years of unblemished service to his country?"

"I... I didn't mean that. Some things were said in the heat of the moment, which I now regret. I was certainly not trying to portray Commander Lansing as some sort of traitor. That's not what I...." His voice trailed off as he tried to regain control.

"I still don't understand why you were so dogmatic about turning down this invention. It had already passed muster by the N.I.C. and the O.S.R.D. What makes you think you know better than them? Do you have any science degrees, Vice-Admiral?"

"No," said Lavering, his voice rising an octave, "but I wasn't the only one who raised doubts about its use. Even the Admiral himself decided not to go ahead with it, and he made the final decision. Why don't you ask him?" Lavering almost shouted.

"Oh, don't worry, Vice-Admiral, we'll get around to him eventually, but it's you we're interested in right now. After all, you seem to have been the chief instigator in refusing the equipment. I'm just curious to know why."

Changing tack, Crawford said, "I believe you were off sick the day after the meeting, the day Commander Lansing was murdered." Crawford was six inches shorter than Strawbridge's six feet two. His slight, slim build belied a sinewy, tensile body that had fought and beaten men much his physical superior. He still retained a slight east coast of Scotland burr, his parents having emigrated to the United States from Kirkcaldy, Fife when Crawford was eight years old.

"Yes, I was. Even Vice-Admirals take ill sometimes," Lavering answered, echoing Erben's observation.

"What was the trouble?" asked Strawbridge.

"I just didn't feel well. I had a headache, and I felt ill. There were a few times I felt sick and thought I was going to throw up."

"And did you?"

"Did I what?"

"Did you throw up?"

"No, not exactly. I could feel some bile in my throat, some reflux acid, but it never amounted to an actual bout of sickness."

"And you thought those symptoms were harsh enough to stop you going into your office, even though we are at war?"

"I did not want to infect my fellow officers if it was contagious or infectious. It was the right thing to do."

"Did you send for a doctor?"

"No, it wasn't that serious. Doctors are busy enough treating patients who are really ill. I was just..."

"You were just...?"

"I wasn't feeling up to the mark, that's all."

Strawbridge rose from his chair and, excusing himself, walked out of the room. Once outside, he found the young lieutenant. The investigating officer gave his subordinate some instructions, ending with, "As quickly as possible. I want a report back within the hour. No later."

"So let's go back to the meeting," continued Strawbridge once he had resumed his place. "You were adamant that this machine was not suitable, yes?"

"I said as much. How can you possibly put a Pianola inside a torpedo? The idea is ridiculous, no matter what anyone else says."

"But didn't the Commander correct you? Didn't he say that it was only the roll that needed to be inserted, not the instrument itself?"

So they even knew about that part of the argument. "He... he may have done. I don't recall."

"It seems there's a lot you don't remember about this meeting, considering it only took place a few days ago. Is your memory that bad, Vice-Admiral?"

"A lot was said. We discussed various things. There was more than one item on the agenda."

"Quite so. And you've no idea why Commander Lansing was murdered, Vice-Admiral?" Crawford asked.

Lavering shook his head slowly, avoiding eye contact with either man. "No. No, I haven't."

They allowed Lavering to leave, warning him that they might need to question him again. After he had left the room, Crawford asked Strawbridge, "What do you think?"

"He was lying through his teeth. Plain as day. He's hiding something, I'm sure of it."

"But you don't think he killed the Commander?"

"It's unlikely. He doesn't look as if he's got it in him, but I could be wrong. Let's wait and see. This inquiry is far from finished. There are still a lot of bugs under stones waiting to be turned over."

* * *

It took Erben a few days to track down Errol Flynn. It was almost as if the actor was deliberately trying to avoid, if not evade him. No one did that to Hermann Erben, no one. But Flynn did have an excuse for not being available. Before the Austrian could explain the reason for his call, Flynn said, "They've just released me from prison, Hermann."

"Not being drunk and disorderly again? When will you learn, my good friend?"

"No, this was much more serious, I'm afraid."

"What was it?" asked Erben solicitously.

"Rape," Flynn said simply.

"Rape? My God. Whatever next?"

"It gets worse," the actor went on.

"Worse? How can it get any worse?"

"Rape of a minor. Two, actually. They're accusing me of statutory rape."

"*Gott im Himmel*!" exclaimed Erben, unconsciously reverting to his native tongue.

"Yes, quite," replied Flynn. There wasn't any more to be said.

* * *

Hedy knew she had to do something, but what that was, she wasn't quite sure. Finally, she telephoned her local police precinct, explaining who she was and why she had called. After being connected to the detectives' office, she was told that as the victim had been a naval officer, the case was being handled by the Office of Naval Intelligence in Washington D.C. Her contact spent a couple of minutes trying to find a number for her to call, and then he came back on the line.

"O.K., Miss Lamarr, do you have a pen and paper to hand?"

It took Hedy another hour to locate the officer in charge of the Lansing case, but finally, she was put through. After introducing herself, she said, "Mr. Strawbridge, I may have some information about the death of that navy officer."

Strawbridge's ears picked up. "It's Commander. I'm sorry, Miss Lamarr. Did you just say that you have information concerning the murder of Commander Lansing?"

"Yes. It may be nothing, but it's been troubling me and I..."

"Why don't you let me be the judge of that, Miss Lamarr?"

"Hedy; please call me Hedy."

"Very well, Hedy. Why don't you tell me why you called me and we'll see if it's important or not?"

Hedy told Strawbridge about her and George Antheil's trip to the Navy Department and what happened after she left Lavering's office.

"So he asked if he could see you again, is that correct?"

"Yes, just as I said."

"Forgive me for asking Hedy, but are you sure his request was not one of a more romantic nature?"

The actress smiled, unabashed. "No. The Commander seemed, well, agitated. I suppose that's the best way to describe it." She stared up at the ceiling in contemplation. Returning her gaze to the telephone, she insisted, "No, it was nothing to do with me, if you see what I mean. He was troubled about something; something that happened at the meeting. I'm sure of it."

"But he didn't say why he wanted to meet with you again?"

"No, unfortunately he didn't. He might have done so, but Vice-Admiral Lavering re-appeared and I think that stopped him from saying any more."

"Lavering saw you together?"

"He must have done. He was only a few yards down the hallway."

"Could Lavering have overheard this conversation?"

Hedy considered his question for a few seconds before replying. "No, I don't think so. Is it important?"

"I'm not sure; probably not," he responded, but inside, his adrenalin was racing. If Lavering had been aware of their discussion, that changed everything. And if he had heard the Commander's request to Hedy, why had he not mentioned it at their interview? He would need to speak to the Vice-Admiral again, and soon.

Strawbridge thanked Hedy for her help and her hospitality before quickly hanging up. He was getting a bad feeling about Vice-Admiral Lavering; a very bad feeling, indeed.

* * *

Loder arrived later in the day, to find a distraught Hedy crying into her handkerchief. He couldn't remember doing anything to upset her, and wondered why she was so unhappy. Hedy told him all that happened within the past couple of days and that how she felt partly responsible for Lansing's death.

"He wanted to confide in me, John. He wanted to meet me to tell me something. Oh, John, what was it? What did he want to say to me that he couldn't tell me in the corridor? What do you think it was?"

"I don't know, darling. I don't suppose we'll ever know now. Whatever his secret was, he's taken it with him to his grave. War's a terrible thing, Hedy. I should know. I saw enough of it the last time, and I never thought I'd be living through it again in my lifetime. I was saying as much to Errol the other day."

"Saying what?" Hedy's mind was distracted, and she was barely listening to Loder.

"Why, that we would be involved in another conflict which spanned almost the whole globe. I was telling him about your wonderful invention and he..." Hedy cut him off. "You told Errol Flynn about George's and my creation?" Hedy fired at him. "Errol Flynn; you told Errol Flynn?" she gasped incredulously.

"Yes. Why? It wasn't a secret, was it? You told me."

"Yes, John, I told you, but you're you! Errol Flynn. I can't believe you betrayed me, John. Please tell me you're joking, please! I'll forgive you for the prank if you tell me that's all it was, honestly, I will."

Loder grabbed her elbows, drawing her to him. "Calm down, Hedy. No, it's true. I believe I did tell him. I didn't think it mattered."

"Didn't think it mattered?" she echoed. "Do you know what they call him around the film studios? Hitler's ambassador to Hollywood, that's what!"

"Oh, come on, Hedy, you're over..."

"If you say I'm overreacting you can please leave my house right now. He's an out-and-out Nazi. You're working with him. You must have heard some of the things he's been saying. Don't trust him, John. Please don't trust him."

"But even if what you say is true, how could it possibly have anything to do with the murder of that navy officer? It doesn't make sense."

"No, it doesn't. But it's quite a coincidence, don't you think?"

"No, Hedy, I don't think. I don't think anything like that at all." Loder said angrily. "Errol's a good man. Yes, it's true he has some strange outlooks, and there's a lot I don't altogether approve of, but deep down, he's as loyal to this country as you and I are. Now leave it alone." A disgruntled Loder slumped into an armchair, reaching into his inside pocket for his pipe and matches.

Loder might have thought this conversation was over. It was anything but. Hedy now had some more information for Keith Strawbridge, and this time she had a witness to back her up, albeit a reluctant one.

* * *

Strawbridge and Crawford were keen to confront the Vice-Admiral. What did he know that he wasn't letting on? Whatever it was, they would sweat it out of him. The time for pussy-footing was over. This damn war was taking its toll on everyone, and Lavering would tell them what he knew. Strawbridge had asked the young lieutenant to get other agents to speak to the wife. She had told them her husband had been in the house the whole time. The neighbors also confirmed that the Vice-Admiral's car had been parked up all day, giving credence to his story. Although there was one inconsistency. His wife did not remember her husband claiming to feel sick or nauseous. It was more as if he were 'absent.' He was certainly there in body but his mind was elsewhere.

They tried calling his office and then his home. He was not in either place. His wife gave them a list of friends and family who were all contacted. His fellow naval officers, too, were in the dark as to his whereabouts. No one seemed to know where he had gone. The naval officers had come to the same conclusion. Lavering had disappeared. This was not the action of an innocent man; not when he had just been questioned about the brutal slaying of one of his colleagues; not when he had seemed so evasive to their inquiries. And not when he was not as sick as he had claimed to be. They doubted he would be foolish enough to try and leave the country, but put out a watch alert at ports and airports anyway. The authorities at the Mexican and Canadian borders were also contacted. Lavering would not get far.

* * *

Erben did not go into detail about why he would have to lie low for a while. The less the actor knew, the better; especially with his own immediate troubles. "I am going away for a short while, Errol. The reasons do not concern you, but you will be unable to contact me. I will get back in touch when I can."

"You're being very mysterious again, Erben? What have you done now? Tried to blow up the White House?"

"There would be no point in doing such a thing."

"Why ever not? Think of the kudos you would earn if you killed the President. They might make you the next Führer," Flynn suggested humorously despite his personal worries.

"All we would be doing is hastening the inevitable. Roosevelt is a sick man. He will soon die anyway, and I have done enough killing for the time being." Erben regretted his words as soon as he had spoken them.

"Oh, come on, Hermann. The next thing you'll be trying to tell me is that you were responsible for that naval officer's murder." Erben's silence was deafening. "It was you?" Flynn gasped. "I don't believe it. You don't have the stomach to do such a thing."

"Believe what you like, my friend, but I will have to disappear for a short while. That much is true."

"Where are you going? Back to Mexico?"

"Maybe, maybe not. I shall go where the winds take me."

"The only wind that blows you is the one that comes out of your arse, Erben. Out of your arse."

Erben had said too much. Did the actor believe him? Hopefully not. If he did, Flynn, too, would need to be dealt with.

CHAPTER 27

Los Angeles, California, and Washington, D.C.
October 1942

Loder refused to be with Hedy when she called Strawbridge. He wanted nothing to do with her suspicions about Flynn and would not be seen to have made a fool of himself when her fears were proved groundless.

"Hello, Hedy, it's nice to hear from you again," Strawbridge began when both had made themselves comfortable. "Now, what can I do for you? I should warn you that I'm married, and my wife is an extremely jealous woman," he quipped.

"I wish it was something as trivial as wanting to have an affair with you, Commander. Unfortunately, this is something far more serious." Her face took on a grave expression as she continued, "My, er, friend, told someone about our invention."

"So George Antheil said something to someone, and that's made you anxious because...."

"It wasn't George. It is someone I've been seeing romantically," Hedy confessed. "I don't want to get him into trouble, as he didn't know that I wanted it to stay between us. I won't give you his name. I can only tell you that he is a fellow actor, but it's not him I've called you about. It's who he divulged my invention to that's made me concerned."

"Go on," Strawbridge urged her.

She said, "He said... he told Errol Flynn."

201

"And why has that made you fearful?"

"It's not well-known outside of the studios. Flynn is a Nazi. He's a supporter of Adolf Hitler. You should hear some of the things he says, especially when he's drunk. It would sicken you."

"And you think Mr. Flynn has passed on this secret to someone else; a German agent, perhaps. And this could all be linked to Commander Lansing's murder?"

"Yes... no... I don't know," she stammered. "I just thought you should know, that's all. As much as I detest his views, I don't want to get him into trouble if he's innocent. It could be just a coincidence."

"Well, it certainly gives us another avenue to explore, but I doubt there's anything in it. Errol Flynn is an actor, not a Nazi spy; I'd bet my life on it."

After conversing for a few more minutes, Strawbridge looked at his watch. "I'm sorry, Hedy, as much as I'd love nothing more than to continue our chat, I have another appointment in a few minutes."

"No, it's fine. I need to ring off, anyway. Things to do... you know..."

As he ended the call, the receptionist rang his office. "Commander, there's a call just come in for you, sir. I think you'll want to take it in your office."

"Who is it, Genevieve?"

"It's the F.B.I., Clyde Tolson. He's on the line right now!"

* * *

Flynn was in big trouble, without the added complication of being implicated in Erben's crime if, indeed, he had murdered the navy man. He had been accused of raping two minors, one at a party and one on his yacht. It was all nonsense, of course. The girls were as keen as he was, maybe even more so. How often did girls like them get to meet famous movie stars, never mind sleep with them? But these charges, however false and trumped-up, could end his career. Where was Erben when you needed him? If he could kill a high-ranking U.S. naval officer, surely it would be no trouble to...? No, he was daydreaming, of course. It would never happen, and if anything, it would seal his fate. Coincidence was one thing, but the murder or disappearance of not just one but two teenage girls involved in a serious court case with him was one misfortune too many. The actor had no choice. He would have to go to court and plead his case, but he would need a good attorney; hell, not just a good lawyer. He would need the best.

Around the studios, one name stood out; Jerry Giesler. With a surname like 'Giesler,' he might be a Jew, but this was no time to be picky. He had already got off that theater owner Pantages from a similar charge back in the twenties. All the evidence said he was guilty as sin, but Giesler somehow managed to pull off a 'not guilty' verdict. He'd also been successful in many other celebrity cases. This was the very man for him, Jew or not.

At their initial meeting, Giesler had a few questions for his newest client. "So, you don't deny having intercourse with the young lady?"

"I... I can't remember. I was pretty drunk. I may have... but if I did, I... look at her, for God's sake. She could easily be taken for a twenty-year-old. What do you think, Mr. Giesler? Am I supposed to ask every girl I screw for her birth certificate?"

"Hardly, Mr. Flynn. The problem is, it is not up to the girl to prove how old she is; it is up to the man to use his judgment and common sense. It's not me you have to convince; it will be the jury. And, unfortunately, you do have a certain reputation with women, if I may say so. I want you to write down as much as you can remember about that night. Dates, times, anything you can. The reason I'm asking you to commit it to paper is that, as you write, it will jog your memory, and more will come back to you, maybe something we can use in court. Obviously, I won't mention anything that might incriminate you as long as you don't tell me that you knowingly had sex with a minor. That will change things entirely. Are we clear?"

"Crystal," Mr. Giesler.

* * *

Strawbridge raced back to his office to take the call from the deputy head of the F.B.I. As he ran up the stairs, he reasoned out the purpose of Tolson's call. His men were not up to the task. Better to move aside and let the professionals handle it. They would soon get the perpetrators, and the case could be closed. There was a war to win, and it would not be won while good men like Strawbridge were sitting on his ass nursing an investigation that was above his ability.

Tamping down his irritation, Strawbridge lifted the handset. "Good afternoon, Mr. Deputy Director. It's a pleasure to speak to you. What can I do for you, sir?"

"It's about this case you're investigating...."

I knew it, thought the O.N.I. investigator. Tolson's going to pull the case out from under us. He heard the Deputy Director continue, "I am very wary of cross-agency involvement. It tends to muddy the waters and can lead to the right hand, *etcetera, etcetera*. So I like clear lines of demarcation. Do you understand?" Tolson asked.

"Yes, sir. I do." Here it comes, he mouthed.

"But this is a damn serious case. We can't have high-ranking navy men being bumped off left, right, and center now, can we?"

Left, right, and center? How many other navy officer murders did I miss? "No, Mr. Tolson, we can't."

"So, I'm going to give you a bit of help. It won't surprise you to know that I'm already aware of what you've done in this case. Nothing much gets past this office, as I'm sure you know. The description you got from the desk clerk at the hotel where the Commander was found. Of the man who booked the rooms, yes?"

"Yes, Mr. Deputy Director?" How the hell Tolson knew what he knew was a mystery. He probably had one of the N.I.S. team on his payroll. When Strawbridge found out who it was, there would be hell to pay.

"His description matches that of someone we've been monitoring. It may be the same person; it may not be, but I thought I'd let you know anyway."

"And this person is...?"

There was a pause at the other end of the line. Surely Tolson wouldn't call him with this information, then not follow through, would he? Was he dangling a carrot, wanting some sort of quid pro quo? Tolson's next words assuaged Strawbridge's doubts. "His name is Erben; Hermann Erben. An Austrian Nazi currently in the employ of Hitler's *Abwehr*. A nasty little fellow; does a lot of dirty jobs for them. He had American citizenship, but we revoked it last year because, officially, he had been out of the country for five years. Off the record, we took away his U.S. privileges because of his anti-American activities. We couldn't tell him that; otherwise, he would know we were on to him. But we believe he's been traveling back and forth from Mexico during this time. The OSS has been tracking him down south. He could be your man. This is your case, and I don't want my men to get involved. But I would consider it a professional courtesy if you could let me know how you get on."

"Yes, of course, Mr. Deputy Director. I'll advise you one way or the other. Do you have any idea where Erben is right now?"

"No, he seems to have gone to ground. That's what makes my antennae twitch even more."

"Don't worry, sir, we'll find him."

"Good. That's the spirit. Oh, there's one more thing you should know. Might help to uncover his whereabouts."

"Any intelligence you can give us would be much appreciated, Mr. Deputy Director." This call had turned out very different from the one he had expected. Very different, indeed.

"He seems to be friendly with one of those Hollywood types."

"Oh? Who, sir ?"

"Errol Flynn. That's another character we've got a file on, although I'd be grateful if you'd keep that to yourself. You might want to have a word with him. He might know where your man is." Tolson ended the call before Strawbridge could thank him. Tolson was a good man. Would his boss, J. Edgar Hoover, have revealed such classified information, even under an important criminal investigation? Strawbridge didn't think so. Hoover tended to play his cards much closer to his chest.

Errol Flynn! Jesus Christ, this case was coming together faster than he could think. Errol Flynn. Fuck. Hadn't Hedy mentioned his name not thirty minutes ago? He picked up the phone handset and dialed downstairs. "Genevieve, I need you to book me on the first available aircraft that will get me to California, preferably Los Angeles. I'll need a car when I get there. I'll find my own accommodation. Oh, make that two flights. Jonathan Crawford is coming with me. And Genevieve..."

"Yes, Commander?"

"As quickly as you can. This is an emergency!"

CHAPTER 28

Los Angeles, California
October–November 1942

For one of the few times in his life, Flynn had followed directions; the orders of his attorney, to be precise. Taking a notepad and a pen, he began to chronicle all he could remember about that afternoon. He had had a lot to drink, so many of the circumstances were hazy, but as he marshaled his thoughts, events began to come back to him. Giesler was right. Jotting down what he could remember did engender more facts. He could recall the girl, Betty or Betsy, Someone-or-other had arrived at the party he was attending. It was at the Bel Air home of his sportsman friend, a fellow Australian called Freddie McEvoy. He had had his eye on another woman there, Lydia or Marion he believed her name was and was talking to her. She seemed not to be paying him too much attention. He admitted to himself this could have been because he had spent the entire evening staring down the top of her low-cut frock. Some women liked that kind of attention; others didn't. Flynn figured she must have been in the latter category.

That was when Betty/Betsy arrived. She had come in with someone, a young boy, maybe around eighteen or nineteen, and Flynn's gaze was instantly drawn to her, as it was to any new female in the room. She was staring at Flynn as if unable to believe that she was in the same room as him. At least, that was how it seemed to the actor in his less-than-sober state. As memories began to resurface, it started to come back to him. She walked toward him, 'weaved' might express it better. It did not seem to bother her that he was already engaged in another conversation or, rather, was trying to be.

She approached him, saying a few words he couldn't recall as his eyes had returned to stare at Lydia/Marion's ample bosom. Her boyfriend appeared to be trying to drag her away with little success. He was no competition to the great Errol Flynn. Her speech was slurred, and she was about to say something else when her body convulsed forward as if she was going to throw up. At this point, Flynn stopped writing. He was amazed at how much had come back to him, despite his precarious situation. Continuing his reverie, he remembered that he took her around the waist, guiding her upstairs to the restroom. If she were going to be sick, it would be better if she vomited over the toilet bowl rather than on McEvoy's expensive Axminster carpet. As they reached the landing, her eyes were drawn to an open bedroom door, inviting her inside. She did not want to be sick anymore. She wanted him, the man with his arm still encircling her.

Coyly biting her bottom lip, she demurely took his hand, leading him into the room with the large bed, enticingly calling them over. She wanted to be a movie star and heard rumors that the fast route to success was to sleep with someone famous in Hollywood, just like the man she was beside. Flynn allowed himself to be pulled onto the bed as she straddled him lustfully.

He chuckled as he wrote, remembering the old saying about mouths and gift horses. They got to grips, and within a couple of minutes, they were enjoying each other's bodies. It was over quickly for both of them, their breaths and sighs coming in rapid spurts as they lay together half-naked, smiling, and satisfied. They hastily got dressed, and Flynn escorted her back down the stairs. If anyone had missed either of them, it didn't show. Lydia/Marion was nowhere to be seen, and Betty/Betsy—Betty. It was Betty, he suddenly remembered. Betty — oh, damn, he couldn't think, but it was definitely Betty. She was standing peacefully, hands behind her back, casually observing her escort, who was blithely chatting away to another young woman. This young lady looked as if she would rather have been anywhere but where she was, almost as if she was seeking an escape route.

For Flynn, it had been no more than a pleasant afternoon's diversion, as he was sure it was for the girl. Both sought out others at the gathering, and as far as Flynn was concerned, that had been that. It had all come back to him. He would swear that was how it had been. He had been the seduced, not the seducer. This account was how he had truly remembered it, but it would not be the version he would jot down for Giesler. His 'recollection' would be much more sanitized and acceptable. It would be the girl's word against his. Who was the jury, or Giesler, more likely to believe?

It seemed that for Betty, however, it meant much more than some harmless fun. The following day, she confided in her sister, but realizing that she would land in trouble if she told the truth, she suggested that Flynn had enticed her into the bedroom. Her sister was horrified. Betty was only seventeen, and she was already doing it. She had heard that it was illegal for a man to have sex with a girl under eighteen in the state of California. It did not take long for her parents to become involved, believing that this terrible man had ruined their pure, innocent young daughter; a minor in the eyes of the law. From there, it was a short step to Flynn being arrested before being charged with statutory rape by District Attorney Thomas Cochran.

Flynn wrote his amended account, then signed and dated it before placing it inside an envelope. Now he would have to turn his memory to the night of his encounter with his second accuser, Peggy Satterlee. For some reason, he had no difficulty remembering her name. This situation was going to be a bit more problematic. This time, it was he who instigated the rendezvous. He could not think where he had met her but had found her easy to beguile with his offer of an evening on board his sailing boat, *Sirocco*.

As the actor sat in his favorite chair, reliving the events in his mind and putting his thoughts on paper, his front door sounded. It was late in the afternoon, and he wasn't expecting anyone. Fearing it might be fans or a newspaperman after a story – Flynn knew he always made good copy, especially now – he sat quietly waiting for whoever it was to go away. His substantial home was located within eleven acres of property, but his security was lax. It would be easy for prowlers to lurk in the trees and bushes before assaulting his front entrance. The banging became more strident, and this time, he could hear a voice, maybe more than one. Then the voice became more coherent and persistent, and the Tasmanian heard Strawbridge. "Mr. Flynn, this is the Office of Naval Intelligence. We need to speak with you now, please. Would you mind opening the door?"

Flynn slowly rose from his chair and sauntered to the front door. The Office of Naval Intelligence? What the hell did they want? He had applied to join the forces at the outbreak of hostilities, but they had turned him down due to a bout of malaria in his younger days and a string of other ailments. If they had changed their minds and now considered him fit for active duty, they could go to hell. He wasn't interested in playing soldiers or sailors anymore. At least, not for real. Opening his front door, Flynn asked Strawbridge truculently, "Yes? What is it? What do you want?"

"May we come in, Mr. Flynn?" Crawford asked.

"Why? What's going on?"

"Mr. Flynn, we've traveled a long way to be here, from Washington, D.C. to be exact. It would be better if we did this inside, believe me."

Shrugging his shoulders, Flynn stood aside, allowing the two Naval Intelligence men to enter. As they stepped into his front living room, the actor made a point of not inviting them to take a seat. With all three men standing close together, Flynn demanded, "What's this all about?"

Strawbridge decided to interrogate Flynn as if he was already aware that the actor knew the Austrian Nazi. There was no time to waste for Flynn to assert he was ignorant of their subject. "How well do you know a man called Hermann Erben, Mr. Flynn?"

They must be the officers investigating the death of that naval officer. If they were asking after Erben, then he had been telling the truth. He had been responsible.

"Who says I know anyone called Hermann Erben?"

"Mr. Flynn, I don't have time to play these stupid games. Now, we can do this here the civilized way or go to our office in Los Angeles. It's entirely up to you, but I'm sure your studio will be very interested as to why you're obstructing an investigation by the Office of Naval Intelligence. I'm going to ask you once more; how well do you...?"

"Alright, alright," said Flynn testily. "Yes, I know Hermann. We used to work together many years ago."

"Oh? And what did you do with Mr. Erben?"

"We were involved in the tobacco trade in the far east back in the early thirties. Thirty-one or thirty-two. We also went gold prospecting, but never made very much at either profession."

"Do you still see him?" Strawbridge asked. Flynn hesitated just a heartbeat too long, and he knew it. They would have seen his reaction. There was no point in trying to be clever. "Yes. We keep in touch from time to time, mainly by phone. The last time I heard from him, I think he was in Mexico." Strawbridge and Crawford exchanged glances. The F.B.I. file that Tolson had sent them revealed that the Austrian had spent time in that country.

"When was this?"

Flynn thought for a few seconds. "Hmm. Must have been about three or four months ago," he lied. "Do you mind if I ask why you want to know about my relationship with this man?"

"It's just a matter we're investigating. His name came up, and it was mentioned that he and you were acquainted with each other. Nothing for you to be concerned about."

"Is it about the murder of that naval officer?"

"Why would you think that, Mr. Flynn?" Crawford asked.

"You don't have to be a brain surgeon to work it out. A navy man gets killed, and the next thing, two naval intelligence officers are knocking at my door. I might not be the smartest kangaroo in the bush, but I'm not stupid either." Both men smiled together. No, indeed. Flynn was anything but stupid.

"As we said, Mr. Flynn, just following up on our inquiries. As a matter of interest, where were you on the afternoon of...?" and Crawford consulted his notes, although he already knew exactly when Lansing was murdered.

"I can tell you exactly where I was, gentlemen. I was at a party. You can check if you want to. There must be at least twenty people who can vouch for me. And there's one other thing you should know."

"Oh, and what's that?" this question came from Crawford.

"Well, you'll soon read about it in the papers, no doubt. You see, I have been accused of having sex with a minor on the day of that party. Now, I can be a rapist, or I can be a murderer. I can't be both."

CHAPTER 29

Los Angeles, California, and Washington, D.C.
November 1942

Although he was unlikely to be lying about something so serious, Jonathan Crawford checked out Flynn's story. It was exactly as he had said, so it appeared that he, at least, had a rock-solid alibi for the time of Lansing's murder. On his second interview with Strawbridge and his team, Flynn once again denied knowing Erben's current whereabouts despite being asked several times. Was Erben in Mexico as the actor had believed, or was he much closer to Hollywood?

Flynn was much more circumspect when questioned on his conversation with Loder. "Do you remember a discussion you had with John Loder about a device Hedy Lamarr and George Antheil had invented?" Crawford asked.

"Should I? John and I see each other occasionally. I don't remember everything we talk about. My memory isn't what it was, what with the alcohol and everything."

"Everything?"

"Oh, come on. This is Hollywood. Do you think we're all good little boys and girls and are safely tucked up in bed by nine o'clock every night? You must know what goes on once the studios close for the day."

"We have a fair idea, Mr. Flynn, but that's not why we're here. I'll ask you again. Did Loder tell you about Miss Lamarr's anti-torpedo device?"

"He may have done. If he did, I don't recall."

"Well, let's assume he did. Would you have mentioned it to anyone else, perhaps?"

"Now why would I do that?"

"That's what we would like to know. Why would you do that? Could you possibly have mentioned it to anyone else? Someone like Hermann Erben, perhaps?"

"I told you, I haven't seen Hermann in a few months."

"Doesn't mean you haven't spoken to him though, does it?" Strawbridge asked, pointing at Flynn's telephone.

"Oh, for God's sake," Flynn spluttered. "I haven't seen him or spoken to him for months. O.K.?"

Had he mentioned the device to anyone else he could remember speaking with? Flynn made a moue with his lips. No, he didn't believe so. Both Intelligence men had seen this gambit all too often. Someone with something to hide appearing as if he was co-operating to the best of his best ability. But he wasn't. They were sure of it. A close but covert watch would be kept on the Australian. Flynn wasn't as good an actor as he thought he was.

The Naval Intelligence officers also interviewed John Loder. He confirmed that he had divulged Hedy's secret to Flynn, but insisted he had told no one else. The Australian was a man you could trust, he asserted confidently. You had to be careful who you spoke to and certainly what you said these days, Loder accepted, but Flynn was one of us, a member of the British Empire, for goodness' sake. He wouldn't betray them. They were all on the same side, fighting the Hun, the Eyetie, and the Nip.

Strawbridge decided to go against protocol. Either Flynn or Erben might deduce that Hedy had given the Navy men Flynn's name. This information might not augur well for the actress, and he, Strawbridge, couldn't be around to protect her all the time. One man had already been brutally murdered, and the Navy official did not want to have the actress's death on his conscience. He found Hedy at home. She had given him her address on his last phone call, and he invited himself over. He tried to keep his call light, but Hedy could not help noticing the edge in his voice.

Something was wrong, and, whatever it was, it could not be discussed on the telephone. Hedy had had her fill of clandestine activity when she worked for the Haganah, not to mention her dramatic escape from the clutches of her first husband. She wanted to start afresh away from all of that and had succeeded for a while. But now it was happening all over again; whatever it was.

"I'll come straight to the point, Hedy. You must not repeat what I'm about to tell you to a living soul. I could lose my job, but you could lose something far more important. Am I making myself clear?" were Strawbridge's opening remarks after Hedy let him in. Hedy felt her stomach churn over. What was he going to tell her? She nodded her head slowly in assent, signaling him to continue. "We interviewed Errol Flynn, and there's something he's not telling us. Has he ever mentioned a man named Hermann Erben?"

"To be honest, Commander, I've very rarely spoken to the man. We've met at the odd party but never really chatted."

Strawbridge seemed surprised. "I hope you don't mind me saying so, Hedy, but I find that hard to believe. His reputation with women is not a secret, and you... ah..." He did not seem sure how to continue, but the actress knew exactly what he was trying to imply.

"Mr. Flynn is not my type, Keith. He has tried to, you know, get to know me, but I've always been very cold towards him. I suppose he finally got the message. His boyish charm doesn't work with me, I'm afraid."

"You need to be very careful around Mr. Flynn. You must never be alone with him if you can help it. And I don't mean just in a romantic or sexual way. I don't trust him, and, yes, I do believe that he is involved in the murder of Commander Lansing. I'm not suggesting that he killed the Commander, but I'm sure he had a hand in it somewhere."

"Do you suspect this... this Erben to...?"

"I don't know what I suspect, but if Flynn connects you to Lansing, things might get a bit sticky. Flynn told us that he thinks Erben is in Mexico, but that might just be a blind. I'll do my best to protect you, but I..."

"Yes, I understand, of course. You have your duties, and so on. Do you think I should hire some personal protection? A bodyguard, perhaps?"

"That might not be a bad idea, but it would have to be done very discretely. If Flynn or this Erben character sees you have someone watching over you, it will signal that you were aware of a threat. That would certainly give the game away, and I'm sure they would try to get to you at the first opportunity. Even the best-trained man lets his guard down sometimes. And these guys don't come cheap."

"I understand, Commander, but I can't spend my money if I'm dead, can I?"

After leaving Hedy, Strawbridge and his team returned to Washington. As soon as he arrived, he briefed his commanding officer about their time on the west coast. As he was returning to his own office, he noticed a greater degree of activity than he would have expected, even despite the current situation. Before he got to his door, Jonathan Crawford came running up to him. "Thank Christ I found you. All hell's going on here."

"Yes, I noticed. What's up?"

"They've found Lavering."

"Yes, I knew we'd catch up with him eventually. Where was he?"

"They found him in his car, behind an old disused soap factory."

"Right, Let's bring him in. I've got a few more questions for our Vice-Admiral."

"I'm afraid that won't be possible," said Crawford.

"Why not?"

"He's dead. Lavering's dead. Suicide by all accounts. The signs are consistent with him taking his own life. Gun to the head; single bullet. Blood and brains all over the car's interior and windows. His gun was lying in the well of the drivers' side."

"Oh, Christ. We're too late."

"I'm not finished. There's more."

"More?"

"There was a note lying on the front passenger seat."

"To the wife, presumably."

"I don't think so. It was very short; only four words."

"What were they?"

"'Tell Jack I'm sorry.'"

"Jack? Jack? Who the hell's Jack?"

"We don't know. They only found his body a short while ago. We haven't yet started to get to grips with this one. I was just about to go to Naval Command to see if anyone could enlighten us."

"It was suicide, do you think? I mean, it couldn't have been...?"

"Foul play dressed up? Listen, we've got enough to be going on with as it is. Don't go looking for conspiracies where there are none."

"You don't think Lavering murdered the Commander, then killed himself out of remorse, do you?"

"No. He's got a solid alibi, remember. His wife doesn't know yet. Poor woman. A couple of men are on their way there right now."

"Well, see if she knows who this Jack is."

"Somehow, I don't think she will. In my opinion, she'll be as much in the dark as we are." Crawford offered dolefully.

***

After Strawbridge and Crawford left, Flynn had returned in his mind to his tryst with Peggy Satterlee. They would sail down the coast to Catalina, he had promised her. Drop in for a drink in a little out-of-the-way place he knew; then they could spend the rest of the time just moon watching on his yacht. How could some girls be so willingly gullible? What did she honestly think he had in mind? Moon watching? Really? Eventually, she told him she was tired. He led her to her cabin, then gave her a little time to get comfortable before undressing and joining her in bed. She feigned surprise but did not struggle when he began to caress her, slowly edging his nimble fingers down her lithe body, fondling her breasts, then working his way lower until they found her soft, velvet mound. It only took her a couple of minutes to get into the spirit of the thing, then she, too, was licking his lips with her tongue before indulging in more intense foreplay. The lovemaking was slow and languid, neither of them in a hurry to climax. They had all night, and Flynn was determined to make the most of it. It turned out that she was as keen as he was. The second time they entwined, it was at her urging. Then a final engagement, just as the sun was coming up over the horizon. She was certainly no novice; that was for sure.

But once again, he would concoct a version which would show him in a much less troublesome light. He would finish writing it up and put it in the envelope with his first fake memoir. Then he would call Giesler to make an appointment. He hoped the lawyer could do something. He was certainly paying him enough.

* * *

"I knew it. I knew something wasn't right. He hadn't been himself for a few days," Felicia Lavering sobbed.

"Did he say why he was so upset?" asked Lieutenant Commander Ronald Fleming.

"No. I asked him, of course, but he just said he couldn't talk about it. I assumed it was navy business, so I didn't press him. I wish to God I had. He might have... he might still..." she could not finish her sentence.

Fleming drew a deep breath before asking his next query. He was a lawyer, and he was well versed with the old legal adage, 'never ask a question to which you don't already know the answer.' He did not know the answer to this one. "Mrs. Lavering, did your husband ever mention anyone called Jack? Does that name mean anything to you?"

Felicia Lavering cocked her head to the side, screwing her eyes in concentration as she struggled to consider his inquiry. Above-average height for a woman, she was tall and willowy with strawberry blonde hair framing her long narrow face. In normal circumstances, she would have been considered pretty, but now, with red-rimmed eyes and her nose dripping mucus, her features were strained and haggard. She shook her head slowly. "No, I don't think so? Jack? Jack who?"

"It doesn't matter, Mrs. Lansing. It's probably not important." Fleming was not going to tell Lansing's wife that the last words her husband wrote were not to her, but to some strange man she had never heard of. He and his colleague, Lieutenant Commander Derek Swan, asked her a few more questions. As desperate as she was to find the answers why her husband had done what he did, she could not help them. He was a good man and a devoted husband; she would swear to it. She had no idea why he would take his own life.

On their return to the Naval Intelligence building, the four officers, Strawbridge, Crawford, Fleming, and Swan, decided to have a thoughts and ideas session. They were missing something, but they could not deduce what it was or where this elusive intelligence would take them. Maybe by huddling together, they might solve at least one part of the puzzle. "There's something that's troubling me," said Crawford after a few minutes of discussion. "I'm going back to Lansing's murder for a moment if you gentlemen don't mind." The other investigators shook their heads. Crawford continued, "What was Lansing doing at that hotel? We know he took a call just before leaving the office, presumably from his killer, who we believe may be this Nazi agent called Erben. But how did Erben entice him away in the first place? And why that particular motor hotel? Was Lansing also in cahoots with Erben? It makes sense, I suppose." he postulated.

"I doubt it, Jonathan. Don't forget, according to Hedy…"

"So, it's 'Hedy' now, is it?" Crawford winked suggestively. Strawbridge ignored Crawford's jibe and continued, "Lansing was fuming with Lavering. He wanted to use their device and couldn't understand Lavering's truculence. It's more likely he was killed because of that. It's my betting that for some reason, Lavering and Erben were working together, and Lavering told Erben about Lansing's insistence on approving their project. We're still not clear why Lavering was so against it, but that's my theory."

"I still can't believe Lavering was working for the Nazis." His elbows on the table, Fleming nursed his chin with the heel of his hand, his fingers beating a tattoo on his cheek. He knew it was an irritating habit, but it helped him to focus. "Okay, so Erben somehow lures Lansing to the hotel, where he kills him. Judging by the medical report, Erben, if it was him, took Lansing from the back. Presumably, he was behind the door, awaiting the Commander's arrival. The autopsy says the wound to the throat was left to right, meaning the assailant was right-handed. It damn well near took Lansing's head off, so whoever did it was pretty strong and knew what they were doing. That suggests some kind of training. All the signs point to Erben. I'm sure of it."

"Why that particular hotel? There are other places nearer than Gaithersburg. If Erben and Lavering were working together, maybe we can tie Lavering to the hotel, too. Turning to his fellow officer, Strawbridge instructed Swan to go back to the hotel and show the manager Lavering's photograph.

"Could 'Jack' be short for Jaqueline? Was Lavering having an affair with a woman of that name?" mused Fleming. "Maybe that was his pet name for her or perhaps he used the masculine form to throw us off the track."

"Then why mention her at all, if we're not supposed to know who she is?"

"Or maybe the answer is so blindingly obvious we don't see it," suggested Crawford.

"Which is?"

"Maybe it wasn't a woman at all. Maybe he was having a thing with a guy; a guy called Jack."

"You mean...?" Strawbridge asked unbelieving.

"For goodness' sake, Keith. Do I have to spell it out?"

"I think it's time I was going," said Swan, who was uncomfortable about the subject. His younger brother, Martin, had confided in him two years ago, swearing him to secrecy. He, also, preferred the company of men.

It would have been hurtful enough if they had to tell Felicia Lavering that her husband was cheating on her. To have to disclose that his lover was a man would leave the poor woman devastated. It then occurred to Keith Strawbridge that as the senior investigating officer, it would fall on him to have to be the one to break the news. This was a prospect he was not happy with; not happy at all.

CHAPTER 30

Los Angeles, California, Washington, D.C., Gaithersburg, MD
December 1942

A slight mist had descended as Flynn arrived at his lawyers' office. It felt cold and damp, reminding the actor of his Tasmanian youth. Giesler's secretary asked him to wait, and her boss would see him shortly. What is it with these professional types, he asked himself? Doctors, lawyers, producers, no matter how often you had to see them, and even when you were prompt and punctual, they always kept you waiting. It must be a power thing, he felt. The reason they kept you waiting was simply that they could. He just wished that for once, he would be seen on time.

Eventually, Giesler buzzed his assistant. He was ready. Indicating the chair in front of him, Giesler asked Flynn to sit. He was smiling. The actor hoped this was a good omen. "Well, Mr. Flynn, I've been doing some work on your case, rather I should say, my investigators, have. Beavering away on your behalf, and I'm pleased to say, there is a glimmer of light at the end of the tunnel."

"Well, Mr. Giesler, you know what they say, the light at the end of the tunnel is sometimes the beam from the oncoming train!"

Giesler laughed heartily. "Not this time, Mr. Flynn. Definitely not this time. Not with the information my men have found on your accusers. We're not out of the woods yet, but I don't think you've got too much to concern yourself over."

It's not your fucking career on the line, Flynn thought. It was easy for Giesler to be so complacent. He was going to get paid no matter what the outcome was. Fucking lawyers.

* * *

The Navy officers had reconvened after Swan's trip to the motor hotel. His visit had not been very fruitful, but it was not an entirely wasted effort. "I'm sorry I took so long, but the clerk on duty wasn't any use, so I had to wait until his replacement came on. He was a bit more helpful, and he did remember seeing Lavering." He paused, letting this information take hold with his fellow officers. "Anyway, he never saw Lavering arrive or leave with anyone, but the clerk always suspected that there was someone else there, waiting outside. It was just in his manner, but as he said, when you've been doing the job as long as he had, you get a feeling, you know, and that's all it was—just a feeling. He assumed it was a dame, but, as we now suspect, it may have been, and probably was, 'the mysterious Jack.' As far as he was concerned, it was nobody's business but his guest's. He was only paid to take their money and make sure they didn't frighten the horses. Other than that, he didn't need or want to know."

Crawford took over. "Well, at least we now understand why Lavering chose such an obscure place for his intimacies with Jack. Had it been with another woman, he might not have been so cautious. It's likely Erben followed him there on one of his dalliances. It was no coincidence that Lansing was murdered in the same place. Erben was sending a message to Lavering. Okay. So it's now slotting into place. Hedy Lamarr tells Loder what she's done. Loder innocently tells the one person, the last person on earth he should have told—Flynn. Being the good little Nazi that he is, Flynn relates what he knows to Erben. Erben somehow finds out about Lavering and coerces, blackmails him, if you like, into rejecting the anti-torpedo device. Lansing is unhappy at this and suspects Lavering is up to no good. Lavering sees Lamarr and Lansing in hush-hush talks outside Lansing's office. He might not have heard what the Vice-Admiral said to her, but in his mind, the fact that they were whispering is all the proof he needs. They're on to him, so what does he do? He panics and phones Erben. We know the rest."

"And Lavering committed suicide because...?" asked Fleming.

"I reckon all the deception, all the duplicity, became too much for him. He was probably terrified that Erben was going to spill the beans, even though he had been compliant. Not only was he unfaithful to his wife, but he was betraying his country in a time of war. Probably against his will. Apart from what he did with this device, Lavering seemed to be a true-blue American and loyal to his country. At least, that's what's going down on my report."

"Yeah, I'd go along with that," agreed Strawbridge. " His poor wife will have enough to contend with without also thinking her husband was a traitor as well."

Swan said, "The key to all this has to be Erben. Flynn denied knowing where he was, but we all know he's lying. Maybe Erben is in Mexico, as Flynn implied. One way to find out is to wiretap the actor. We could..."

"No, we can't," countered Strawbridge. "Flynn's just been indicted on two counts of statutory rape. Can you imagine how it would play out with the judge if they discovered we were listening in on his conversations? It would be a gift to the defense team. They would argue for instant dismissal of all charges; and they'd get it."

"But this is an entirely different and unrelated matter," Swan shot back. "What we're dealing with here is a matter of national security. No judge in his right mind would..."

Strawbridge cut Swan off abruptly. "I know several judges whose sanity could be called into question. No, Derek, as much as I would like to do as you suggest, I'm afraid bugging Flynn's phone is out of the question. And there's something else."

"Christ on a crutch. What now?" swore Fleming.

"I've been looking into the charges that have been laid against Flynn. I thought, you never know, something might crop up; and it did."

"What was it?" from Swan.

"The party where one of the girls claim that Flynn seduced her. It was at the home of Freddie McEvoy. He's a friend of Flynn's."

"And...?" prompted Fleming.

"He's on the F.B.I.'s watch list. They think he's also a Nazi agent."

"Good Christ! How many more are there?"

Strawbridge shook his head. "Your guess... but now you see why we can't eavesdrop on Flynn. We might compromise any case the Feds bring on Flynn or McEvoy. It's just too complicated."

"Maybe there's another way we can get Flynn to open up," suggested Swan thoughtfully. "The penalty for what he's charged with is several years. Now..."

"Way ahead of you, Derek, my boy. Wait until he's convicted, then before sentencing, make him an offer he won't be able to refuse."

"Something like that, yes."

"No, Derek, not something like that. I would say exactly like that."

* * *

Strawbridge had called one of his contacts in the OSS. It would be unlikely for them not to know about Erben if he was as high profile as Tolson had claimed and been as prolific as described in his F.B.I. file.

"Yes, Commander. We know all about Erben, and believe me, we've been keeping him under observation. He spends a considerable amount of time in Mexico, where he consorts with other Nazi agents. We believe he may be organizing some sort of armed group to cause trouble on the Mexico and U.S. border. He regularly commutes clandestinely between there and here. Funny thing, though. He seems to have disappeared over the past few weeks. It would be a dreadful shame if his past caught up with him," Bill Loughlin, the OSS agent, said ironically. "It would be one less piece of Nazi scum to worry about."

"I'm sorry to burst your bubble, Bill, but I'm afraid it's unlikely anyone has murdered him. Quite the opposite, in fact," and Strawbridge explained to the security man what they believed the Austrian had done.

"He killed a United States Navy officer in cold blood? The dirty bastard. I'll get our men to pick him up the minute he comes back into circulation."

Good idea, thought Strawbridge. With Erben in their hands, they could play him and Flynn off against each other. Then we'd see who was the most devoted Nazi when their liberty, if not their lives, were at stake. Erben had been, and Flynn was a United States citizen. The act of treason and betrayal of the country came at a high price. Strawbridge would see that both men paid that price in full.

CHAPTER 31

Los Angeles, California
January-February 1943

The trial started on January 11th. 1943 with the selection of the jury. Giesler had chosen the panel with great care and deliberation. Nine women and three men. He had gambled that the preponderance of females would benefit him. Which woman could not fail to be attracted to Flynn's easy charm and his handsome features?

After the selection had been agreed upon between the two sides and the other preliminary formalities addressed, it was time to start the trial in earnest. The courtroom was packed and noisy as newspaper journalists jostled with interested onlookers and the downright nosy. The hubbub decreased to a low murmur as the judge, Leslie E. Still, entered the chamber and took his seat. He allowed a few more moments for the room to quieten before banging his gavel, bringing the proceedings to order. Even the low mumbling ceased, and a total silence descended. The circus was about to begin.

After the judge made his opening remarks and the formalities had been dispensed with, the trial got underway. Giesler and his colleague Robert Neeb sat smugly and confidently while the prosecutor, Thomas Cochran, outlined his case. The defendant, Errol Flynn, had sexual relations with two girls below the age of consent under Californian law, and Cochran emphasized the words. Whether he knew how old they were was immaterial to the case, Cochran asserted. Ignorance was no excuse. Even if he did not know their ages, the fact was that Flynn had committed the crime of which he had been charged and should be punished accordingly. Flynn had seduced Betty Hansen at the home of his friend, Frederick McEvoy. Testimony would show that not only had he taken advantage of her, but he had done so when she was in a state of intoxication and not in a fit condition to defend herself from his unwarranted advances. Cochran did not condone the girl's behavior, and neither should the jury. But it was not her morals that were on trial. It was Flynn's.

As to the second girl, Peggy Satterlee, he had had his way with her aboard his yacht. Enticing an impressionable young girl to go moon watching when his intentions were anything but to stare at the celestial body. There was only one body Flynn was keen to stare at, and that young body belonged to his other victim, who was sitting in this very courtroom.

Strawbridge and Crawford sat in civilian clothes in the public gallery. This was one trial they were determined not to miss. The Naval officers exchanged glances. There was no chance Flynn was going to walk away from these accusations. He was guilty as charged, and they would soon have him in the palms of their hands. Erben had not yet been found, but that would soon change once they had Flynn's unwilling co-operation. He would still go to prison, but his sentence would be reduced for helping the authorities in such a sensitive and important case. They might even allow him more privileges than he would otherwise be granted. They had all sorts of inducements with which to tempt him.

It was now Giesler's turn to present his client's case. Despite the prosecution's allegations, Giesler began, the girls were old enough to decline Flynn's alleged advances had they chosen to do so. And his evidence would show that the women – two could play at that game – were not as innocent as the prosecution would like everyone to believe. According to the testimony he would produce, Hansen was not as drunk as she claimed. Yes, she was unsteady, and she did lurch forward, but she did not actually bring up any vomit. And when Flynn had guided her away from the crowd of guests, the woman could easily have screamed out from the top of the stairs. She had not lost her voice. Someone would have come to her aid. Did anyone hear her cry out in fear and alarm? Yes? No? So, either she did not shout out at all, or she did so, but did it very quietly. The room tittered obligingly at this glib remark. All except Cochran, who remained stony-faced. There was no corroborating statement to prove this woman's allegation one way or the other. Mr. Flynn was just as adamant in his statement that no intercourse took place. The jury would have to make up its mind who was telling the truth.

He then turned his attention to the co-litigant. She did not deny being on Flynn's yacht, neither did Flynn dispute she was there. Again, there was no one else involved. Flynn could easily refute the whole charge, but chose not to do so. Why? Because in his mind, he had done nothing wrong. He admitted there had been a certain degree of lovemaking, but it stopped well short of sex. They had spent most of the evening just fondling and caressing while they stared dreamily at the moon. Eventually, Miss Satterlee said she felt tired, and Mr. Flynn showed her to her cabin. Everything else was just fabricated nonsense, and the defense would later provide evidence to back up his client's version of events.

* * *

During a break in the trial, Fleming managed to track down his superior. "It may be nothing," the captain ventured, "but we've just come across a coastguard report sighting Flynn's yacht off the coast of Mexico. It's the date that's puzzling me."

"You wouldn't have come all this way on a hunch, so what's on your mind?"

"Flynn was about to begin shooting his movie, *Edge of Darkness* at the time. They delayed the start of production because Flynn cried off sick. Everyone knows he does have health issues, so no one bothered to check. It was when he was supposed to be poorly that his yacht was sighted. Now, why would Flynn pretend to be sick but still manage to sail his boat down past Ensenada? That's as far as our vessel tracked him. No one knows how much further south he sailed."

"That's another question to add to the portfolio. After Giesler's opening remarks, let's hope we get a chance to ask it. I'm having some doubts."

***

After some other witnesses had given their evidence, Betty Hansen was the first litigant to take the stand. Cochran gently guided her through her sworn testimony, re-iterating her accusations against Flynn. Giesler did not interrupt or object to any of Cochran's prompting. There would be no point. He was not actually 'leading' Hansen. He was too smart a prosecutor to allow himself to fall into that trap. He was just edging on the careful side of suggestion without putting any words into her mouth.

Both girls had met with Cochran and his partner, John Hopkins, several times and had become familiar with their questioning methods. Hansen smiled softly when being questioned by Cochran, eager to tell her side of the story. After he had finished, he asked her to stay where she was, as Mr. Giesler wanted to ask her some further questions. Unseen by anyone, Cochran winked at Hansen. It was the signal of a universal language. Everything was fine. It was all going to be O.K.

Giesler resisted the strong temptation to jump right into his attack. After all, she was only a young girl, and this approach would only alienate the jury. He took her back through the events of the evening and was merely seeming to confirm what she had already told the prosecutor. Betty refuted any suggestion that it was she who instigated the alleged encounter. Giesler asked her what her ambitions were. She wanted to be in movies, she answered him honestly. Had she taken any acting lessons, Giesler quizzed her. She had not. Did she understand how hard it was to get even a small part in a production, never mind becoming rich and famous? She confessed it had not crossed her mind. Did she know how many other women were as keen and ambitious as she was? Again, she did not. Giesler breathed a sigh of relief. Neither did he, but he knew it had to be in the hundreds or even thousands. Hollywood was a Mecca for budding starlets like Betty Hansen. Keen and eager, yes, but a dime a dozen. And with little talent, apart from their looks. There were plenty of those waiting tables at the town's restaurants as well as doing other menial jobs. And they were the respectable ones. Many others had lost their integrity a long time ago.

And this girl, with average looks and no acting experience, hoped to hit the big time? How exactly did she plan to do that? The last few questions were not aimed at his witness; they were directed to the jury. They were full of suggestion and innuendo. He did not need to spell it out. All twelve knew what he was driving at. Now he was getting into his stride. Did she know any other women or girls who were struggling to make it, just as she was? For the first time, she looked flustered and did not know how to answer. Cochran rose to object on grounds and relevance. Giesler explained that it was a relevant question as he would soon show. Still overruled Cochran and instructed Hansen to answer. She cautiously admitted she did know a few girls. When pressed how many made up a 'few,' Hansen offered, about seven or eight. Giesler pushed her further. Did these girls never mention the 'fast way?' By being 'nice' to actors, producers, directors, and so on. Again, he did not need to explain what 'nice' meant. This was Hollywood, for goodness' sake. Everyone knew what it meant. Hansen shook her head vehemently, denying ever having such a conversation with anyone.

Giesler then asked her if she knew what perjury was. The girl nodded her head. Giesler said he was going to ask her the same question again. She should know that some of those friends that Betty had alluded to would testify that they had spoken about what it would take to get the big break they were all hoping for. Seeing she now had no choice, the witness changed her testimony. Yes, she suddenly remembered, the subject had been raised occasionally.

Cochran again rose to object, but Still merely shook his head. Giesler had done nothing wrong. The girl's reputation was fair game. She was not the one on trial, yet, in a way, she was. As was Peggy Satterlee. So wasn't it more likely, he quizzed her, that it was she who had come on to his client, hoping that by willing to have sex with him, he might help her to get her start in the movie industry? That when he declined her advances, she made up these false charges in a fit of pique? To get her own back on him?

Hansen shook her head. No, that was not it at all. He had seduced her. She swore on the Bible. Something she would not do unless it was true.

Giesler wasn't finished. His investigators had done a bloody good job. He asked her if she had a boyfriend. She admitted she had. The attorney asked her if they were having sex. Cochran immediately got to his feet. Glowering at Giesler, he asked what the relevance was, and the judge agreed. Objection sustained. Giesler then asked her to confirm that he was the one who had accompanied her to McEvoy's party the day she met Flynn. Again, she admitted that it was. His next question seemed to come like a snowstorm in July. Had she ever been in any trouble with the police? Again, Cochran sprung up. Before he could voice his objection, Giesler hinted that it went to the girl's probity and integrity. The judge allowed Hansen to answer. She reluctantly admitted that she and her boyfriend, the studio messenger, were currently the subjects of a police investigation. A felony charge, to be precise. She started to cry.

Cochran had assured her it would all be fine. He had even winked at her as he returned to his seat. How could it all have gone so wrong? How could this man have found out about these charges? Cochran scribbled quickly on his legal notepad. If any of these girls were to be called to give evidence, the prosecutor would ask them if they had been offered any financial inducements to appear as witnesses for the defense. After all, the girls were all supposed to be friends. Were this to happen, the girls could answer truthfully that no, they never discussed money. Giesler knew better than to offer anything so obvious as cash. What he got his investigator to mention was an inducement far more valuable to aspiring young actresses. He knew some folks in Tinseltown who could give these young ladies a leg up in their careers. They were not being asked to lie; they were only being required to tell the complete truth. Nothing more, nothing less. Where could the harm be in that? After all, it was their obligation to do their civic duty. If Cochran did not have the wit or intellect to consider any other inducements that might have been discussed, he, Giesler, was not going to disclose them. And if the girls should find some quiet benefit from complying with the law, where was the harm in that? The girls had not actually been promised anything. It was all 'maybe's' and 'perhaps's and 'possibly's.' And, besides, by trashing Hansen's reputation, it would be unlikely she would ever make it any further, thus narrowing the field, even by just a little.

Still asked Giesler if he had any more questions. If so, maybe they could give the witness a few moments to compose herself. Giesler had inflicted all the damage he had wanted to do. It was now time to get to work on Satterlee. He could hardly wait, but he would have to let Cochran go first. That was the protocol.

But Cochran was rattled. Why was he not aware of the information Giesler had dug up? Had he known about Hansen's police involvement, he could have dealt with it beforehand. He could have also addressed her acting ambitions. He would have coached her not to have been so ambitious about her answer. That was down to him, he realized. But not knowing about the possible felony charge? Earl Warren, the Attorney General, would hand his balls to him on a silver plate for missing that one.

"That was brutal," Crawford whispered.

"Yes. Cochran looked like a rabbit caught in the headlights of an oncoming car. He obviously didn't do his homework. I wonder what surprises his next witness will come up with."

"We'll not have long to wait. Here she comes now."

Once again, the District Attorney took Peggy Satterlee through her earlier evidence. Flynn had offered to take her on a moonlight sail on board his yacht. It sounded quite romantic, especially with such a famous actor as her captain. It was as Flynn had stated. They had sailed along the coast sheltering in a little cove where they stopped for a drink before sailing off again. Yes, she expected there would be a certain amount of romancing. Maybe kissing and some petting, perhaps, but that was where it would stop. She had no intention of having sex with him. She admitted to Cochran that she was not a virgin, but it should be up to her who she slept with. If she did not want to do it, then that should be that. The man should respect the woman's wishes.

When Cochran asked her why she had succumbed not once, but three times, she said that, well, he was Errol Flynn, after all, and after the first time, it did not seem so important anymore. And, no, she did not instigate any of their liaisons. They were all at Flynn's behest. Did she not get even a bit suspicious when Flynn asked her, a young girl, to go on his yacht by herself, without a chaperone? She had always looked up to Hollywood stars, she replied. They always seemed so upright, honest and trustworthy. At least, that was how they appeared on the screen, and she had no reason to think they might behave any different in real life. Especially someone like Errol Flynn who always seemed so polite and chivalrous towards his lady co-stars. She never thought for a minute he would take advantage of her, and so saying, she dabbed a handkerchief and piped her eye. No, they never had sex on the return journey. Maybe he realized he had overstepped the mark, but he did not molest her on the way back.

Flynn whispered frantically to his attorney. That was an out-and-out lie. Giesler motioned his client to relax. He had this situation well under control. Cochran then asked Satterlee if she had ever heard the expressions, 'J.B.' and 'S.Q.Q.?' Abbreviations for 'Jailbait' and 'San Quentin Quail.' She responded by telling him that she had heard Flynn use these initials as he was stroking her hair. Flynn again spoke quietly into Giesler's ear, the attorney brushing off his unheard remarks as if they were of no importance. Turning to the jury, Cochran them emphasized that this must surely have meant that Flynn did, indeed, know how old Miss Satterlee was, or at least, that she was under age. Cochran ended his questioning in triumph. He might have got it wrong with Hansen, but surely, the twelve people sitting in front of him would now see right through Flynn's tissue of lies.

Giesler sat for a minute, as if gathering his thoughts. It was an old lawyers' trick. Let your opponent think you're hesitant, as if you're not sure how you're going to proceed. Lull the witness into a false sense of security. Slowly rising to his feet, he walked over to the witness stand. He was going to ask her to jog her memory. Her attitude towards Giesler was diametrically different than it had been with Cochrane. She adopted a sullen pose, preparing herself for whatever unwelcome questions he was going to fire at her.

He asked her if she could remember when this alleged incident with his client had happened. If this was the hardest thing he was going to put to her, she had nothing to worry about and her attitude softened a little. It had been just over a year earlier. And yet, it was only now that she had come forward to accuse Mr. Flynn of improper conduct? The girl did not seem to know whether Giesler's question had been rhetorical, or if she was required to answer. Giesler continued without pausing. Had it not been the case that her father had tried to extort money from his client at that time by threatening to falsely claim that Flynn had had sex with his daughter? Cochrane started to rise, but then sat down. By objecting to this line of questioning, it would look as if, indeed, Satterlee had something to hide, and this was another issue of which he was unaware. Dear God, how many more were there?

The girl denied any knowledge of such actions by her father, and stuck to this denial, even when Giesler said he could produce a witness, Flynn's stand-in, Buster Wiles, who had been witness to this conversation. Those charges had subsequently been dropped, Giesler reminded her and the court.

Strawbridge and Crawford were both dumbfounded. How could the prosecution not know about these allegations? A conviction was now looking less likely by the minute. Giesler was not finished; not by a long way. He asked Satterlee if she had known her co-litigant prior to the trial. No, Satterlee responded, she did not. Giesler then turned his gaze towards Cochran as he asked her why, if this was the case, both girls had filed similar complaints within just a few days of each other, despite Satterlee's encounter happening many months earlier and those charges already having been dismissed. Was this just another 'coincidence' or had there been some collusion with the girls' families and the District Attorney? Cochran banged his hand on the table, spluttering in outraged indignation. Giesler withdrew his remark, but the damage was done. The jury might not be able to discuss this possibility, but it would not be too far from their minds.

Flynn was right about one thing. This girl could easily pass for someone five years older. Giesler asked her if she had ever lied about her age, before or since her alleged night with his client. This was now getting difficult. He could already produce a witness who would testify about her father's attempted extortion. Were there others who would confirm that she had, indeed, been less than truthful about how old she was? She, too, knew what perjury was, and what the penalty was if convicted. Yes, she responded angrily, she had sometimes not been honest about how old she was. Had she lied to Flynn? Had she told him she was over eighteen? She denied it, but the looks from the jury told Giesler they were less than convinced by her response.

He was now about to drop his bombshell, if Still did not consider it inadmissible. He held his breath for a second before approaching Satterlee, coming right up to within a few inches from her face. Not quite enough to be considered as intimidating, but near enough for her to know that he meant business. Was it true, he asked her, that she had had an abortion? Cochran immediately got to his feet. What was the relevance, he asked, even if this was true? He reminded the court that it was Flynn who was on trial, not Satterlee or her dubious morals.

Giesler retorted that if she had had an abortion, this would mean that she had already had sexual intercourse prior to being eighteen. Did she tell whoever the potential father was that she was under age? Probably not. This went to the girl's character and her integrity. Was the jury going to believe that a girl who had previously engaged in sexual intercourse and omitted to tell the man her true age, would suddenly admit to her current alleged lover, Flynn, that she was not old enough legally to sleep with him? Was this possible, or even likely? She had lied by omission, if not in fact.

Still did not answer right away. He had to weigh up in his mind whether this information was relevant to the case in hand. It was a difficult decision to make, but eventually he declared that Cochran's interjection was invalid and it was overruled. She must answer the question, no matter how painful it was. The defense lawyer turned to her and asked her again if she had had an illegal termination. She was now sobbing as she nodded silently. Still pressed her to answer vocally. There had to be an audible response for the court record. Giesler also reminded the jury that having an abortion was a criminal offence in the state of California. Not only had she lied about disclosing her age to his client, and sleeping with him on board his sail boat, she had committed a felony into the bargain. He had saved the best until last. He knew she would not be in a state to answer any more questions so made sure he ended with what he wanted the jury to remember the most.

Flynn had to cover his mouth to hide his trademark lopsided grin. It would not be seemly for the jury to see how pleased he was. It could not have gone better. In the gallery, Strawbridge and Crawford were two minds with the same thought. They would never get Flynn now. Not with the evidence Giesler had produced and the skillful way he had played his hand. And the actor was still to give evidence in his own defense.

Giesler led Flynn through the events of both evenings. He coached the actor how to frame his answers. Not to be glib, cocky or arrogant. Just answer quietly and confidently. Imagine he was on the set of his latest movie, Giesler advised him. The best actors were those who made it look as if they were not acting. That was how he should behave. Act without appearing to do so. Be himself; be natural. And that was what he did. He had nothing to hide. The girls had already come over as unreliable and selective in their narrative. They had also been shown to be dishonest. All he had to do was hold his nerve.

Yes, he had been at the party that Betty Hansen claimed to have seen him. Yes, he helped her up the stairs so she could recover her decorum. He had helped her sponge her face and hands, then helped her to dry off. She had been fully dressed the whole time. Once she felt better, he escorted her back down the stairs to rejoin the party. That was it. Why she had laid these false allegations against him was for the jury to consider.

As for Peggy Satterlee, yes, she had sailed with him as she had stated, but all they did was talk and moon watch. Although not aware of her age, Flynn was wary of getting 'romantic' with any girl who might have been under age, so did not do anything inappropriate. No, he did not know of the expressions, 'Jailbait' or 'San Quentin Quail.' He had never heard of them before today. Flynn suggested that it could have been Satterlee's father who had used them. After all, he had tried to extort money from him.

This proved he was a dishonest man, who had probably spent time in prison. Wasn't that a more likely place to have heard these phrases?

Cochran tried his best to throw Flynn off, by asking him to admit that he had been heard saying frequently that he liked his whiskey old but his girls young. Flynn agreed that he had said this, but people should not believe all they heard about him. He was merely playing up to his image, but would never knowingly have sex with any girl who was under the legal age limit. Yes, he could be immoral at times, but even he had his standards. For whatever reason, whether financial or for reasons of ambition, the girls were not being truthful. He remembered Giesler's injunction to smile at the jury as he said these words. No, he was not perfect, nor did he claim to be. But he was not a man who would ever take advantage of girls who did not know any better.

In his closing statement, Cochran reminded the jury that the only charges they were there to consider were the ones laid against the defendant. Nothing else was relevant, no matter how sordid the girls' private lives seemed to be. Flynn's preference for young girls was well-known in Hollywood, as was his hard drinking. It was obvious that the girls found giving evidence very traumatic. Why would they go through such an ordeal unless it was all true? Cochran had even produced an astronomer to confirm that the moon would have been visible that night from where Miss Satterlee claimed to have seen it. And were the jury to believe that a known womanizer like Flynn would persuade a young girl like Peggy Satterlee to go on a moonlight jaunt and not do anything except talk with her? Was that likely? With all the evidence stacked up against him, the jury had no option but to find Errol Flynn guilty.

It was then Giesler's turn to conclude his case for the defense. Almost everything the jury heard was circumstantial at best, he told them. Even the astronomer the prosecution got to testify had to admit under cross-examination that although the moon was out that night, it would not have been visible from where Peggy Satterlee claimed she and Flynn saw it. The prosecution's own witness contradicted her assertion. This whole trial boiled down to one simple fact. Who was more believable? Two girls who had lied or had been evasive under oath, and had only changed their testimony when confronted by the possibility of other witnesses who would challenge their statements? Or the defendant, Errol Flynn? Yes, it was true he was a drinker and a womanizer. He did not deny these facts. But would he seduce underage girls? Why should he, when he had the pick of Hollywood's most beautiful, available and much more experienced women to choose from? Why would he take the risk? It did not make sense, and that was what the jury had to consider. The very logic of the prosecution's case was flawed.

Still summed up very simply. There was little else to add to what the counselors had already stated. They must weigh up all the evidence which had been presented to them. The burden of proof lay, as it always did, with the prosecution. It was up to the District Attorney to present a strong enough case that would render the jury no option but to deliver a guilty verdict. If they had any doubt at all, then they must apply the adage about a person being presumed innocent until proven to the contrary. If they had any reservations at all, they had to move for an acquittal.

The jury then retired to consider their verdict. It was not as open and shut as Giesler or Flynn had hoped. Even Cochran began to believe he could win this case. They would not be influenced by Giesler's trickery and his attempt to misdirect them. After all was said and done, Flynn did have sex with these two girls. He could deny it all he liked. The jury would see through his lies and false charm.

In the gallery, Strawbridge and Crawford shared the same thought. This was not going to be as cut and dried as they would have preferred. Flynn had come over as a likeable guy, a reflection of his on-screen persona. If the jury knew what he was really like, they might well come to a different opinion. But it was not his political or ideological views that were on trial. And the girls had not exactly covered themselves in glory. Giesler had exposed a side to them that they would rather have kept hidden. The decision could go either way.

After six hours, the jury had still not returned. The longer they were out, the more likely, Cochran believed, they would come down for him. Judge Still decided to send the jury out for the day. They would continue with their deliberations tomorrow.

* * *

Finally, on the following day, after thirteen hours, the jury had come to a decision. It was time to deliver its verdict.

CHAPTER 32

Los Angeles, California, and Washington, D.C.
February-May 1943

"Not fucking Guilty!" swore Fleming once Crawford and Strawbridge had returned to their hotel and phoned the news to the others. "I don't believe it. How could the jury have been so blind? Of course, he was guilty." All four men were shocked. This shouldn't have happened.

The OSS had confirmed Erben was still in Mexico and had even furnished an address for him. This discovery was a good step forward, but unless they caught Erben on U.S. soil, there was nothing the Navy men or the F.B.I. could do. With Flynn's unexpected acquittal on all charges, the O.N.I. men had lost any hold they may have been able to exert over the actor who was now a free man.

"Where do we go from here?" asked Swan.

"Maybe still have another crack at Flynn, perhaps?"

"No. Flynn's out of bounds, at least for the time being. If we go and see him again, he could accuse us of harassing him. He's under no obligation to talk to us, and his lawyer could start cutting up nasty. He might even throw charges of malicious persecution at us. Before you know it, all sorts of unwanted lawsuits could go flying around. And once the newspapers get a hold of the story...."

"And that's another thing. As much as we need to resolve this case, we also have to be sensitive to the innocent parties here. I'm thinking specifically of Felicia Lavering. I would hate to see her name brought into all of this, even though she was unaware of her husband's infidelities."

"I'm sorry, Derek, but we've got a job to do. Sometimes the innocent have to suffer to prosecute the guilty. Let's put our heads together and see what we can come up with…"

* * *

Having done all they could, and after failing to convict Flynn, Strawbridge and Crawford returned to the nation's capital. For the next few weeks, the Navy officers liaised with their counterparts in the F.B.I. and the OSS to try and find a way to bring Erben to justice. Then, in early May, his counterparts on the east coast sent Strawbridge an article gleaned from the Los Angeles Examiner. It gave him the germ of an idea. He notated his thoughts lest he should forget them, collating them into a coherent manner to relate to his Navy colleagues. Gathering them together around his desk, he produced his written plans, saying, "If we can't get to Erben, maybe we can get him to come to us."

"And how exactly are we going to do that? Send him a dinner invitation?"

"No, Jonathan, something a little more subtle." and he outlined the plan he had thought of. Crawford, Swan, and Fleming looked at each other. Was this even possible? The logistics alone would be enormous, but, as Strawbridge said, it was the only plan they had. It was one hell of a gamble. If it came off, it would be the success of the decade, but if it failed, they could all be looking for new careers, especially Strawbridge.

The Naval Intelligence men spent the rest of the afternoon ironing out how they would execute their strategy. Everything had to go like clockwork. There could be no margin of error. Erben was a skilled agent and would be on the alert for any suspicious activity. Strawbridge divided up the assignments for his men, and when each officer was sure of what he had to do, all went their separate ways. It all had to be done very quickly. The opportunity that had become available to them would not be there for long.

* * *

Flynn was about to start making his current movie, *Northern Pursuit*, for Warner Brothers. Crawford phoned the studios, asking to be connected to the head of the studio, Jack L. Warner. Warner was a busy man with several films currently in production. He had no time for anyone outside the studios, and whoever it was would just have to wait. Crawford was nothing if not persistent and told Warner's secretary, Bill Schaeffer, that his call was to do with defense and national security matters. His studio could be implicated in a major scandal if he did not listen to what the Navy man had to say. Schaeffer knew the very word 'scandal' was an anathema to the movie maker. There had been far too many of those around the studios already. His boss needed another one like a *loch in Kopf*, a hole in the head, as Warner's mother often said in her native Yiddish.

Schaeffer connected Crawford to Warner's private line. After introducing himself, Crawford said he would not discuss the matter over the phone. The subject was too delicate to be heard by the wrong ears. The Navy man impressed the urgency, and Warner told him to come right over. To 'come right over' would mean returning to Los Angeles, but there was no alternative. Crawford hoped they would have the budget to allow him to make the trip. After ending his call with the movie mogul, Crawford instructed their secretary, Genevieve, to make the necessary arrangements. The sooner the Naval Intelligence officer could get over to Hollywood, the sooner they could put that part of their strategy into effect, the better.

As for Jack Warner, his only thought was how he could apply this situation to his studio's advantage. Who knows, Warner thought, maybe he could even turn whatever it was into a feature after the war was over.

* * *

Strawbridge arranged to meet his ultimate superior, the Chief of Naval Operations, Ernest King. Another part of his strategy would mean asking someone within high government office to bend the rules. He did not have the necessary authority to approach this person himself. King was reluctant to agree to his Commander's request. His men were 'Soldiers of the Sea,' not 'Cloak and Dagger' merchants. It was only when Strawbridge impressed the necessity and the urgency that King stopped to listen. This was their one chance to apprehend the person they believed was guilty of brutally murdering a senior U.S. naval officer. Surely any strategy, no matter how fragile, should be considered. He, Strawbridge, would take full responsibility if things were to go wrong. King finally agreed. He would call the President. The final decision would be up to him.

* * *

Fleming and Swan also returned to Los Angeles and were detailed to keep covert watch on their target, each taking twelve-hour shifts. They had to know where their subject was at all times. Any unusual activity or behavior out of the normal was to be reported to Strawbridge as soon as possible.

* * *

Crawford arrived at Warner's studios wearing smart, casual attire. For all anyone knew, he might be an actor there to audition for a part. Once the Naval Intelligence man was ensconced in Warner's office, and the introductions were over, he came straight to the point. "Mr. Warner, sir, we believe that one of your movie actors may well be a German agent working for the Nazis."

"But that's... that's impossible. No one here would ever...I mean...who? Who do you think it is? And what evidence do you have?" Warner had been anti-Communist and anti-Nazi ever since the rise of Hitler and Stalin. He was especially disgusted with Hitler for his treatment of Jews. He had been outraged by the murder of one of his salesmen in Berlin in 1936, a Jew called Joe Kaufman, who was beaten to death in an alleyway, simply because of his religion. The thought of anything like this happening on his own doorstep was more than he could stomach. Hadn't his own parents fled Poland because of the pogroms? "Just tell me who the bastard is, and I'll make sure he never gets another job in Hollywood or anywhere else for that matter."

"No, that's just it, Mr. Warner. This person must not know that you and I have had this conversation. Unfortunately, I can't tell you too much about the operation we're conducting, but it's imperative to its success that you keep *shtum.*"

"I see you have a bit of Yiddish, Lieutenant Commander. I'm just about to cast a role for a rabbi for a movie. You wouldn't be interested, would you?" he laughed.

"Please call me Jonathan. Thank you, sir, but no. This is a full-time job as it is." Crawford smiled. "You need someone with a bit more knowledge of *Yiddishkeit* than I have."

"My, my, Jonathan. You surprise me. Are you sure there's no Jewish blood in you?"

"Perfectly sure, sir. Scots, Irish, and a bit of Scandinavian thrown in for luck. But I was brought up in Crown Heights. One of the few places where Jews outnumber Gentiles."

"Quite so. Now, tell me, who is this person who is acting against the interests of our country? You must understand, I consider myself a United States citizen, despite being born in Canada."

"I didn't know that, sir. But thank you for your loyalty and patriotism. It means a lot."

"We can't have Nazi thugs and Blackshirts running through the streets of New York and Chicago now, can we? Who is this *beitz*, this low-life, you're interested in?"

"The individual we're looking at is Errol Flynn. I..."

"Flynn! I might have known," spat Warner. "Yes, I've heard some of the awful things he's said about Jews, including me, I might add. I shouldn't be surprised that you've got your eye on him. What do you want me to do?"

And Fleming revealed what his team required of Jack Warner and his studio.

"Consider it done. I'll supervise it myself. The fewer people who know about our little secret, the better. Even *mamzers* like Flynn have friends around the place. Is there anything else you need from me, Captain?"

"No," Fleming replied, then stopped. "Actually, as a matter of fact, there is. Just make as many movies as you can, showing what Nazi-ism is really all about. The more people who think like you and me, the more chance we have of winning this war."

Warner was outraged by what he had heard. But he should have known. Flynn had not hidden his dislike of Jews. Although he agreed to take charge of Fleming's project, Warner knew he would not be able to do it by himself. He buzzed his secretary. "Ask Bert Simmons to come up and see me, Bill. As soon as he can, please."

* * *

After getting Admiral King to agree to contact the President, Strawbridge made another call. This time, it was to Clyde Tolson. For his strategy to work, Strawbridge would need to employ the services of someone he did not know how to contact, but the Deputy Director of the F.B.I. certainly would. Tolson laughed when the Navy man explained what he wanted. Yes, he said, he knew the very man Strawbridge was looking for. He would be ideal for the job at hand, and also, he knew how to keep his mouth shut. His career depended on it.

* * *

"President Roosevelt, sir, thank you for taking my call. If you have a couple of minutes, there's something I'd like to discuss with you. It's a matter of national security."

"If it's a matter of national security, Admiral, why am I not hearing about it from Henry Stimson, Cordell Hull, or John Hoover? Surely the protocol would be for one of them, depending on the situation, to advise me of any breach of defense?"

"Yes, Mr. President, in normal circumstances, that would indeed be the case. But this matter is rather unique. May I continue?"

"Yes, Admiral King. What exactly do you want me to do for you?"

"Well,' Mr. President, it's not actually you that I want. It's someone in your administration."

"That makes a pleasant change, Admiral. So tell me, who is this person in my cabinet who is more important than I am?"

And Admiral Ernest Joseph King, U.S. Chief of Naval Operations, explained the reason for his unusual proposal.

* * *

Fleming and Swan had begun their round-the-clock surveillance of Errol Flynn while the President would have a private discussion with one of his cabinet members. It would not be long now before they could proceed with the next phase of their plan. Erben would pay for what he did. One way or another.

CHAPTER 33

Washington, D.C., and Los Angeles, California
May 1943

Frank Comerford Walker sat in a red velvet chair outside one of the many isolated offices located within the White House. Roosevelt had summoned him to a private meeting but would not reveal why over the phone. The President would only say that it was not personal and that his portfolio was not in danger. He rose as he saw Roosevelt amble toward him, hobbling on his metal canes, resisting the urge to help his leader. Roosevelt was a proud man and only acknowledged his frailty when absolutely necessary.

Bidding his aide to wait outside, the White House incumbent indicated that Walker should follow him into the private room. Once both men were informally seated on either side of an unlit grate, Roosevelt explained why he had asked his Postmaster General to the meeting. "You will see, Frank, that there are no aides or secretaries to take minutes of this engagement. As far as anyone is concerned, this meeting never took place."

Walker merely nodded in compliance. He wondered where this was going. Roosevelt was just about to enlighten him. "It has come to my attention that a well-known personality, someone who would be instantly recognized all over these United States, is secretly working for our enemies. Whether he is actually spying for them remains to be determined, but he was quite likely involved in Commander Fred Lansing's recent slaying. I'm sure you've read about it in the newspapers or heard about it on the radio.

I'm not suggesting that he killed the Navy man himself, but we have good cause to believe he was certainly complicit."

"Who, Mr. President? I can't imagine any American being involved in such a heinous crime. It staggers the imagination, but I'm sure you have the proof to back up your allegations."

"Well, the evidence we have is mainly circumstantial, but when you put it all together, it certainly adds up to something more than mere suspicion."

"Where do I fit into this, Mr. President?"

And Roosevelt explained to Frank Walker what he would require of his Postmaster General.

* * *

Crawford had returned from Warner Studios with the documents that Strawbridge had requested. Tolson had kept his word and introduced the Navy man to Enrico Schiaparelli, one of the best forgers the F.B.I. man had ever met. Schiaparelli occasionally did some work for the Bureau. In return, they turned a blind eye to some of his more nefarious activities. It was an amicable arrangement with benefits to both parties. Schiaparelli had been an avid supporter of Benito Mussolini and his Fascisti back in Rome, but became disillusioned when *Il Duce* formed his alliance with the German dictator. Had his people and his leader lost their minds in collaborating with these monsters?

In the mid-nineteen-thirties, he fled to the United States, bringing his disreputable talents with him. He had soon come to the notice of the law enforcement agencies recognizing someone who, although operating outside the norm, was driven by his hatred of the Nazis and mainly targeted German enterprises and individuals for his illegal activities. Strawbridge emptied the packet Crawford had brought back. The papers contained, among other things, a facsimile of Flynn's signature, as well as his penmanship. The Navy Intelligence man's plan had many strands. If even one of these strands were to fray, it could see his whole strategy becoming unraveled, and his part in the operation was the one most likely to fail.

* * *

As was reported in the Los Angeles newspapers, Flynn had been admitted to hospital with suspected tuberculosis. It was this article that had given Strawbridge his idea. They would build a false narrative around the true circumstances of his admission. Flynn was known to be a drunk and was also rumored to take drugs. Anyone in this state was sure to become paranoid, so why not have the actor contact his friend Erben? According to his F.B.I. file, Erben was a physician who specialized in tropical diseases. Who else would Flynn turn to in his agitated state?

Was it merely tuberculosis, or was it something worse, something they were not telling him? He needed someone he could trust, someone who would not lie to him. He needed Erben to come to Los Angeles. He knew it would be risky, but he depended on him. It would only take a few minutes to confirm the doctors' diagnosis; then, he could return to Mexico. It would all go well. Erben could slip in and out of the United States easily. He had done it several times already. Please, would he come?

Not only would the penmanship have to resemble Flynn's. The style and tone would also have to reflect the way Flynn would write such a letter. Crawford knew a psychologist, doctor Seamus Fitzpatrick. They would recruit him to give the message an air of authenticity.

There was always the unlikely possibility that Erben might try to phone his friend, and calls to the hospital were monitored. The hospital telephonists were instructed to tell any caller that Mr. Flynn was unavailable at the moment and would return their call as soon as he could. Crawford had instructed Jack Warner to hold all of Flynn's mail and send it by secure courier to the Naval Intelligence offices. Likewise, Walker had given authority for all posts sent to Flynn's home to be secretly redirected to Strawbridge's unit. Each letter would be examined rigorously for any trace of a coded message. If Erben were coming, they would know. And they would be ready.

CHAPTER 34

Los Angeles, California, and Mexico City, Mexico
May 1943

"'*Dear Hermann, I hope you are well* (the perfunctory and obligatory greeting Flynn would need to apply before writing about himself). *If you get the Californian newspapers where you are, you will see that I am currently in hospital.*(this would validate Flynn's reason for writing and could be confirmed if Erben wished to do so). *They say it's tuberculosis* (not 'I have been admitted with.' It would need to sound as if 'Flynn' was wary at least of the diagnosis he had been given. 'They say' sounds more like it is some anonymous decision that has been taken without his approval). *I'm not sure if this is the case or something worse that they're not telling me about. I wonder if my malaria has returned.* (in his state of alarm, Flynn would exhibit signs of insecurity and maybe even hypochondria). *They all appear shifty and don't look me straight in the eye when they attempt to answer my questions.* (underlining 'Flynn's' paranoia about his condition. He is suspicious of those who wish to treat him. Are they telling him the truth? He thinks not). *I would be so grateful if you could come and see me for yourself. Give me the 'once over.'* ('Flynn' does not overtly mention Erben's specialty. This assertion might be a bit too obvious. 'He' would not need to remind his friend of his own abilities). *I know it would be a bit of a risk* (acknowledging the danger his friend might encounter, not taking Erben's acquiescence for granted), *but it would mean so much if you could get here, even just for a little while* (giving Erben the confidence that he would not have to spend much time with Flynn). *You could be in and out within the hour, just as you have done before* (the F.B.I. knew of Erben's short, infrequent forays across the border). *It should not be too much of a problem for someone with your uncanny abilities.* (play to Erben's well-known sense of self-importance and arrogance). *Please say you will come.* (a final plea from a sick and worried friend). *Best regards, Errol.*"

Erben read 'Flynn's' letter three times. It certainly appeared to be in Flynn's handwriting. The wording, the way it was crafted, had just the right mix of pathos, self-pity, and insecurity that Erben would expect to find in such a message from his friend. But the Austrian was sure about one thing. Whoever wrote this message, it was definitely not Errol Flynn.

* * *

Strawbridge wanted to arrest Erben the minute he set foot on American soil. They would get the OSS to monitor his movements and alert the F.B.I. The Bureau would pounce as soon as he was over the border. Tolson had other ideas. Follow the Nazi and wait until he was at Flynn's bedside. Then they would capture them together. Flynn was sure as hell guilty by association, if nothing else, and the F.B.I. wanted to get their hands on him almost as much as they did on the Austrian. Imagine the sheer horror on Flynn's face when the Bureau burst in on both men.

Strawbridge reminded Tolson that this was a Naval Intelligence operation; hadn't Tolson himself said as much? His men were just as capable of making an arrest as the Deputy Director's. Was Tolson about to renege on the discussion he and Strawbridge had had earlier on? For a moment, it seemed like it, then Tolson agreed to give precedence to the Navy men, with his agents acting in a support capacity only. They needed to catch Erben too much to squabble over who would put the handcuffs on him.

Crawford and Swan had rotated their duties in surveilling Flynn. It was amazing how easy it was to pretend you were a doctor. All you had to do was wear a white coat, wrap a stethoscope around your neck, and look knowledgeable. But their plan had come unstuck early on when a nurse asked Crawford for some medical advice. He managed to fudge her off, but they realized this disguise was not going to work. They decided to play it safe and took on the role of maintenance men and cleaners. It was just a coincidence that Flynn's area needed a lot of upkeep. The floors also needed swept and mopped more than usual. It was a tiresome and weary charade, but vital to their strategy. Every avenue, both literal and figurative, had to be covered. If Erben made it as far as Flynn's bedside, it would be one of them who took him down.

***

Erben was troubled. Flynn had not written this letter; of that, he was sure. At least, not of his own free will. He could not have done. Erben had moved his base since the last time he had spoken to the actor. Flynn could not possibly know where he was. But this meant that someone else did. Probably one of the American security agencies, most likely the OSS. How they managed to find him was of no concern for the moment. The authorities had either coerced Flynn into framing his message to him or had someone forge his handwriting. Either way, it was troubling. This meant that he was being watched. He had been compromised, a situation not conducive to his trade.

The Nazi agent had a dilemma. If he did not go, they would suspect he had found out about their surveillance. To travel to California meant certain capture. They could try him for high treason, the penalty for which was death. But then another thought struck him. If the OSS knew where he was, why had they not come for him? Of course. They would learn far more from covertly following him. Why arrest one spy when you could arrest the whole network?

Another thought occurred to him. Did Flynn write the letter himself, or had it, indeed, been nothing more than a forgery? If it was from his own hand, it meant that he had been found out, and the authorities had struck a deal with the actor. Co-operate with us for a lighter sentence, or face the death penalty. Flynn had taken out U.S. citizenship so they could try him as an American. A death sentence for him, too, was not out of the question. It would not be a hard decision to take.

On the other hand, what if the message was a forgery, after all? What if he really did not send it, and they were trying to play him without Flynn's knowledge? He was in hospital; that much was true. This position would make it easier for them to entrap him. He would arrive at Flynn's bedside, and the actor would not even be aware that he, Erben, had been summoned. How delightful such an arrest would be to the F.B.I. Well, it was not going to happen. Whether or not Flynn was working with them, he was not going to fall for their trap. All of their plans and strategies would be for nothing. Erben would not leave Mexico, but one thing was for sure. He could no longer stay where he was. He would have to disappear—again.

CHAPTER 35

Mexico City, Mexico, and Los Angeles, California
July 1943

Word from the OSS in Mexico was that Erben had dropped out of sight. He had used the time-honored ruse of employing a look-alike, a Mexican who bore a resemblance to him, wearing the Austrian's attire and carrying a suitcase. They would allow this 'fugitive' to escape, then wait and follow the real Erben as he left his apartment. He would be tailed all the way right to the hospital ward. An arrest was imminent; except that it wasn't. The 'double' who slunk away without apparently being noticed was not an accomplice. Erben double-bluffed his erstwhile pursuers by using skin coloring makeup to appear Hispanic and merely an impersonation of his actual self. When the fake spy left the building sometime after, looking far more like their quarry than Erben did himself, it was him the OSS men followed. They shadowed him to the Mexicali border before they became suspicious, and it was only then that they realized their real target had outwitted them.

Erben was not going to Los Angeles. He was not going to California. He was not going to the United States. He was going to ground somewhere deep inside Mexico. They would never find him now. Erben had gone.

* * *

It was a couple of hours before Strawbridge and his men knew that their prey had outsmarted them. To make matters worse, it was they, themselves, who had caused their own downfall. They did not yet know how Erben had cottoned on to them, only that Los Angeles was now the last place he would go. It was over. Erben had eluded them once again. No blame or retribution would be laid at Strawbridge's door. It had been a good plan, perfectly reasoned and executed, yet something had gone wrong. Whatever they had missed had cost them dear. Him most of all. Finding Erben had now become more than just a job; it was an obsession. He owed it to the families of Fred Lansing and Bernard Lavering, and he had let them down.

Other cases were now beckoning for his attention. There was a war on, after all. But this one gnawed at him, like no other. Erben was no longer in the picture, but Flynn was; very much so. They had tried once and failed to get at Erben through the Australian actor. His team would not be permitted to try that tactic again. Not officially. He would work the other cases he was given in the Navy's time. It was what they paid him to do, but what he did in his own time was his affair, not his employers'.

He would start again, from scratch. Go back over what they knew, what they believed, and what they suspected. Maybe they missed something, anything that would put him on Erben's trail once more. He would begin with Flynn. If he were going to get anywhere with this case, it would have to start with him. There was one other person he had forgotten about. The one individual who had inadvertently put them on to Flynn in the first place – Hedy Lamarr. She had proven herself to be a clever, capable, and resourceful woman, far smarter than him in many ways.

Wasn't it Flynn who had helped Erben stop her wonderful invention from being adopted by the U.S. Navy and its allies? He could not, would not put her life in danger, but maybe she could help him nonetheless. She was a Hollywood celebrity, just like Flynn. They mixed in the same rarefied circles. Maybe there was something she could do to help him, to get some sort of retribution for Lavering's blunder. There was only one way to find out.

* * *

It was now July 1943. Hedy Lamarr was filming *The Heavenly Body* with William Powell. She was enjoying making the movie, but the plotline was weak and did not allow her to explore her range of acting abilities to the full. It was almost with a sense of relief during a break that an assistant told her that she had a visitor. At first, she thought it was John Loder. They had got married two months earlier, in May. Loder was currently acting as Preston Drake in the movie adaptation of *Old Acquaintance*. He must have had a bit of spare time, she thought. How romantic of him to want to see her, even though it would mean a brief sojourn only before heading back to the Warner studios.

Hedy was stunned when she saw Strawbridge. She had never expected to meet with him again. Her and George Antheil's association with the U.S. Navy was over. Lavering was dead; Lansing, who may have been able to shed light on the subject, had been brutally murdered. It had been almost a year since they had presented their invention for scrutiny. She had done her best to help her adopted country, and they had spurned her. Whether by subterfuge, misogyny or mistrust was no longer relevant. Like Antheil, she had a living to earn. It was time to get back into harness.

She was every bit as lovely as Strawbridge had remembered her. Even if she lived to a ripe old age, he thought, her beauty would never fade. Hedy automatically held her hand to her bosom as she caught sight of him. He was the last person she expected to see. What could he want now, after such a long time? The Navy had surely not considered their proposal and had had a change of mind. That possibility would be too much to hope for. She slowed her step as she walked toward him, hesitant about how their conversation would go.

The Navy man was unsure how to greet the movie star. Should he shake her hand (that would be too formal), should he salute her (that would be even more improper and inappropriate. She was not a fellow mariner, and Strawbridge was in plainclothes, anyway), or should he bend forward slightly to offer her a peck on the side of her face (like two old friends)? His decision was taken from him when Hedy herself raised her face to kiss him lightly on the cheek. He could never tell Alice about this. She would not believe him; even worse, she just might.

"Hello, Hedy. It's so nice to see you again after all this time. You look…" Strawbridge did not know how to tell her how she looked. She was in costume, but even the stage clothes she was wearing made her look good. He settled for "…lovely."

She took his compliment demurely before asking him, "You've come a long way just to say hello. To what do I owe the pleasure of your visit, Commander?"

"Keith. Please, call me Keith."

"Very well, Keith. So why are you here?"

Strawbridge took Hedy's hands in his, imploring her not to repeat to anyone, especially her husband, what he was about to impart to her. He took her nod for acceptance and then told her what they had done to try to capture Hermann Erben, using Errol Flynn as the sprat to catch their mackerel. They had failed in their exercise, but Strawbridge was determined to catch their man; one way or another. He could not forget the lives of all those American and Allied sailors that the U.S. Navy had lost, his navy, in not implementing her invention. Would she help him right the wrong, the wrong of all those families who would not see their husbands, sons, brothers, and fathers again? All because of the actions of two men.

Hedy did not have to think twice. She, too, had been brooding over the whole affair, frustrated that she had not been able to do more than travel the country, in between movie commitments, selling War Bonds, and kissing servicemen. Those who were responsible would need to face justice, no matter what it took. Yes, she would help him. All she needed was for him to tell her what he wanted her to do.

Strawbridge asked her to keep her eyes and ears open for any loose talk or actions that Flynn exhibited. She doubted he would come outright with his part in Lansing's murder. That would be too much to hope for, but any careless word he displayed that could be used against him, whatever it was, no matter how small, it would be a start. Needless to say, anything she heard or saw would be treated in the strictest of confidence. She should report to him, and him only. The fewer people who knew what she was doing, the better for all concerned, especially her. He doubted her husband would approve of her new role, especially as he and Flynn appeared to be such close friends.

Here we go again, thought Hedy. Am I never to be rid of this cloak of duplicity being draped around my shoulders?

"There is one thing I can tell you right now. I don't know how well known this is, but quite a few women will not go to any parties at his home. It is rumored that he had secret mirrors installed in some of the bedrooms. The kind of mirrors that a person can see through from behind, without the woman knowing she is being watched."

A transparent mirror, better known as a two-way mirror. Most security agencies employed them these days. Strawbridge smiled. He hadn't known this fact about the actor, but wasn't surprised where Flynn was concerned. Well, it wasn't much, but it was a start. She had agreed, reluctantly, to attend any parties where he might be, ensuring that she would not need to get undressed under any circumstances. Hedy was an excellent swimmer but would refrain from using the pool.

At this point, the director's assistant approached them. She was wanted back on set. Break time was over.

"Who was that handsome young man you were talking to?" asked her fellow actress, Spring Byington.

"Oh, just an admirer," she answered blithely. "Someone I knew a long time ago. Do me a favor, Spring. Please don't tell John. You know how jealous he gets." Spring Byington put her forefinger to her lips. "Your secret is safe with me, Hedy. We all have 'admirers,' don't we?"

Yes, we do, thought Hedy. Some more welcome than others. Her mind had to be on her role as Mrs. Vicky Whitley, but somewhere, in that remote part of her soul that only she knew, she was thinking about how she could help Keith in his quest to find justice for all the people Flynn betrayed.

* * *

Via dead letter drops and through dependable intermediaries, Erben had contacted Flynn on his release from hospital. No, Flynn had not written to him and knew nothing about the F.B.I.'s attempt to ensnare him at Flynn's hospital bedside. This revelation had come as unwelcome news to the Tasmanian. It was getting too much. All Flynn wanted to do was make movies, drink, and get laid, not necessarily in that order. If the Bureau were keeping tabs on him, as well as the Austrian, this would inhibit his opportunities to get into mischief. Remembering his recent court case, he acknowledged this might not be a bad thing. Nonetheless, the greater the distance, both literally and actually, that he could maintain between himself and Erben, so much the better. With Erben skulking somewhere in Mexico, no doubt attempting to foment his own brand of mischief for the good of the Reich, at least he was unlikely to turn up on Flynn's doorstep anytime soon.

This realization got Flynn thinking. How did the authorities discover their association? Was it by watching him or by surveillance on Erben, and just how far back did their vigilance stretch? What might they have uncovered about him that he would have preferred to have been kept hidden? Of course, there was also the satisfying notion that Erben had all but admitted to him his murder of the naval officer. The fact that Navy officers had come to his door during their investigations and mentioned Erben's name solidified Erben's claim. It was something he certainly had over his erstwhile friend. Then he was struck by a chilling thought. The only way Erben could have known anything about Lansing was through him. He had heard about Hedy Lamarr's device from her then-boyfriend, now husband, John Loder. Loder was a pretty face, but not very bright. However, even he might eventually put two and two together. Especially if the actress had already thought that one out.

The actor would need to protect himself from any consequences that might arise from his rash revelation to Erben about the actress's invention. He needed to know how much Hedy Lamarr knew and how much she suspected. The question was how to do it. He would hold a party; that's what he would do. A party with a special guest.

CHAPTER 36

Los Angeles, California
July-August 1943

"He's invited you to a party?" Strawbridge was incredulous. There were coincidences, and then there were coincidences. This was no happenstance invitation. The timing was just too obvious. Flynn wanted something from her, likely how much she knew about his involvement with the Austrian Nazi. The party was just a cover. There was only one guest Flynn would be interested in: Hedy Lamarr. She could always cry off, of course, and claim illness or just plain and simple fatigue. Making a movie was an exhausting business with early morning starts and late evening finishes. There was also her young baby to consider. She would want to spend some free time with him, wouldn't she? No, this was too important. It might give them the break they had been looking for, and Flynn would not do anything foolish, not with a houseful of people.

The Navy man sighed resignedly. She was right. They would perform a figurative pavane around each other, slowly dancing toe to toe, each with a wary eye on their partner, neither quite sure what steps the other party might employ next, neither quite aware of what the other knew or believed. It would all make for an interesting evening.

* * *

John Loder was not the party-going type, preferring to stay home and read or listen to the radio or gramophone when he was not on-set. Hedy normally had to drag him kicking and screaming to any affairs to the point where she gave up trying. He was his own man. Let him be that way. The last thing she could divulge was that she was as reluctant to go to this party as he was. Besides, it would be nice for him to spend some alone time with their adopted baby son. At least, that was what she told herself.

Hedy arrived fashionably late, not wishing to be one of the first party guests. She saw a few familiar faces, mostly actors and actresses that she had worked with over the last four or five years. The small talk was all about the movie business, who was doing what to who, making a particular movie, or up for an Oscar. The bitchiness was there, bubbling just beneath the surface. It would only take a small ripple in the calm waters to start the whole thing off. And where was her host? It was rather rude and inconsiderate of him not to welcome her himself. Probably trying his luck with one of the many female stars he had invited or who had tagged along with others.

Eventually, Flynn made an appearance, going to embrace Hedy, but settling for taking her hands in his when he saw her stance stiffen. "Hedy, thank you so much for coming," he gushed. "It's been a while."

Not long enough, Hedy thought. "Thank you for inviting me, Errol. What a beautiful place you have," she said, looking around her. They were by the pool, and several people were already splashing about. "Maybe you'd care for a dip," Flynn suggested.

"Sorry, Errol, I never thought to bring a costume."

"Oh, I'm sure I could fix you up with something. Why don't I see what I can find, eh?" He insisted.

"Perhaps later."

"Very well, later it is."

But Hedy had no intention of changing into a bathing suit in Flynn's home. Everybody seemed to have a drink in their hand, and Hedy stopped a passing waiter carrying a salver with champagne glasses. Holding her glass by the stem, she raised it in salute to her host. Flynn smiled at her. "It's amazing, isn't it?" he asked. "Look around you. No one would ever think we were at war. Our boys are fighting so hard in the far east, braving God-knows-what, and here we are, on a lovely moon-lit evening, completely safe, sipping champagne." He shook his head. "It's so unfair," he lamented almost to himself.

"What is?" she asked.

"Life, Hedy. Life is so bloody unfair. If they hadn't rejected me because of my illnesses, I might be overseas myself right now, fighting those damn little yellow menaces. Covered in muck and mud with Japanese bullets whizzing overhead."

They were strolling away from the pool area towards the back of his house, where a pair of French doors lay open. Several folks were milling around, paying neither their host nor his attractive guest any attention. "And you're complaining that you're not up to your neck in blood and gore? Most men would be glad to be out of that, don't you think?"

"I don't know if you've heard, Hedy, but the bloody Japs bombed Darwin. Darwin, for God's sake! The arse-end of nowhere! It's the capital city of the Northern Territory, the other end of the country where I come from, but all the same, they've bombed Australian territory. Right now, Hedy, I would like to kill every single one of those slitty-eyed fiends, starting with their emperor, Hirohito. I would dearly love it if the last thing he saw was my smiling face looking down on him before I wrung the fucking life out of that pitiless bastard's scrawny little neck." His voice had risen to where a few of his invitees stopped their own muted conversations to overhear what he was saying. Realizing he had spoken rather more loudly than he meant, he smiled lamely at those nearby before leading Hedy to a quieter part of his home.

That was quite a performance, the actress thought. Did he mean what he said, or was it all just for show? Japanese warplanes had certainly attacked Darwin, and Flynn would have every right to feel the way he did. Were his sympathies really with the Axis powers, which now included Japan, or only with the Nazis? There was only one way to find out. Choosing her words carefully, she responded, "I understand what you mean. Hitler invaded and raped my country back in nineteen thirty-eight. Most of the freedoms we enjoyed are now gone. It was even better under Dollfuss and Schuschnigg. God help us all if the Nazis win this war."

"Indeed," Flynn replied noncommittally. "Still, I'd rather be fighting the Japanese. Despite Hitler and his gang of thugs, the Germans are basically sophisticated and cultured. You only have to look at all the great thinkers and writers they've produced, not to mention scientists and academicians. I agree that the country is in the grip of a bunch of criminals and lunatics right now, but if we could get rid of them, things could only get better. The Japanese, on the other hand, well, they are just barbarians, always looking to pick fights with their neighbors, aren't they?"

"Are they? I didn't think they were until now. Still, I'm sure you're more familiar with all that than a simple actress like me."

Flynn smiled. "I think you are anything but a simple actress, Hedy. From what I hear, you've got brains as well as looks. Tell me I'm wrong."

"I've got no wish to flatter myself in front of you or anyone else. Besides, I'm not the only actress who is more than just a pretty face." Pointing aimlessly with her finger, she concluded, "I'm sure half of your female company out there could acquit themselves very adequately in other areas if they had to."

"Maybe, but not with such aplomb."

They were now alone. Flynn had navigated them both to one of his private areas. It suddenly occurred to Hedy that she could no longer hear the hubbub of background chatter and made to return the way they had come. "Your friends will think I have commandeered you for the evening, Errol. Perhaps we should rejoin the crowd, eh?"

"Yes, in a moment or two. Just before we do, there's someone I'd like you to meet. He's a great fan of yours, and when I told him you were coming tonight, I took the liberty of offering him a quiet word with you on your own."

Before Hedy had the chance to agree to Flynn's unannounced request, they both heard a sudden clatter coming from the main assembly. It seemed that one of the waiting staff had stumbled, sending a full tray of drinks over one of the guests, a bald man of average height wearing rimless spectacles and a middle-aged paunch. The waiter was stammering his apologies while trying to pad the excess champagne from the guest's jacket and pants. The male casualty was pushing him away, unable to hide his annoyance at this display of errant clumsiness. It seemed the attendant was only making matters worse, attempting to atone for his accidental encounter by studiously wiping his victim down. A small crowd had now gathered around this trivial scene, thanking whatever God they believed in that something had happened which would brighten up, even for a short while, this bland, eventless evening.

No one saw the glance of futile frustration that passed between Flynn and his hapless guest.

"So, where is this person who is so keen to meet with me?"

"At this moment, he's heading toward one of the restrooms to sponge himself off."

"Oh," said Hedy without emotion. "What a pity. Maybe another time."

"Yes, maybe," Flynn agreed unhappily.

Meanwhile, the waiter who had caused the melee was being upbraided none too discretely by his overseer. "You stupid prick. Can't you do anything right? This is the second, no, the third time you've caused trouble. You've had all the chances you're going to get. You're fired."

"You can't dismiss me now. I... I at least let me apologize to Mr. Flynn. It's the least I...."

"Didn't you just hear me? Are you deaf as well as stupid? I'll apologize to Mr. Flynn. Now gather your things and get out."

The waiter bowed his head, crestfallen. He trekked slowly to the wait staff area, disappearing from the assembly's view. Once out of sight, the 'waiter' quickly removed his white tuxedo before reaching into its inside pocket, carefully extracting a syringe filled with a clear liquid. Carefully wrapping it in a heavy cloth, he bundled it inside his jacket before leaving Flynn's home from a side exit. None of the guests saw him get into a waiting black sedan, its engine idling at the end of the driveway.

* * *

Strawbridge was taking no chances. The party might be legitimate; then again, it might not. It was unlikely Flynn or his cohorts would do anything foolhardy, assuming it was an actual party and not a ruse to get the actress there on her own. Just the same, this could get dicey. He had called Clyde Tolson to tell him everything that had happened and voice his concerns about Hedy's proposed visit to Flynn's home. Tolson agreed that the actor might have something in mind not very party-like for his Austrian guest. He would get his men to pose as waiting staff, keeping Hedy in line of sight at all times. It would be better if she did not know about their plan just in case a careless mannerism or look might cause their scheme to go south.

Erwin Bixby, one of Tolson's men, spotted Flynn's party guest almost as soon as he entered the room. This was another person the Bureau was watching. Like Erben, he, too, was a physician who was suspected of having Nazi sympathies. The chances of him being here at this time when Hedy Lamarr was a fellow guest were too astronomical to calculate. Doctor Abel Verstanden, or 'Dr. Abe' as he was more popularly known, would also be observed carefully. When Bixby saw Verstanden slowly but purposefully stride in Flynn and Hedy's direction, they put their hastily contrived operation into effect.

It was unlikely that they would harm her in any way. The possibility was that they would drug her with some barbiturate to tell them what she and the security services knew about Flynn and Erben, assuming she knew anything at all. This assumption was proved correct when the F.B.I. chemists analyzed the contents of Verstanden's syringe. It was a compound they had not seen before, likely one of the doctor's own creations; a combination of chlormethiazole, chloral hydrate, and some unknown barbiturate. The chances were they would quickly drug her, extract what she knew, then wake her. It would take no longer than a few minutes. She might be a little woozy, but that could be put down to excessive alcohol consumption. One thing was certain. She must not attend any more parties thrown by Flynn. They were lucky that time. Next time, she might not be so fortunate.

The pavane had almost turned into an apache. There could be no more dancing around. Next time, Flynn might just have a knife in his hand as he dragged Hedy away to a fate unknown.

CHAPTER 37

Los Angeles, California
October-December 1943

The months had rolled on. It was now October 1943, and finally, the end looked to be in sight for the Nazi regime. They had lost the Battle for Stalingrad back in February, and the Soviets had captured or killed much of the German 6th. Army. It marked the beginning of the end as the Nazis realized they were not as invincible as their party leaders had led them to believe. Similar reversals followed in North Africa. The Allies were finally victorious in the Atlantic, driving the German warships and U-boats out of this arena, ensuring American supplies reached British and Allied troops stationed in the United Kingdom.

Despite these victories, Hedy was still angered that her invention had not been used when it was most needed. As welcome as the war news was, with most of the Axis troops in retreat, she still railed at the thought of those lives that were needlessly lost. Strawbridge, too, had not lost sight of his quarries. Flynn was still making films, behaving like a true patriot in his war movies, fighting the Nazis and the other enemies of his adopted country. He was currently making *Uncertain Glory*, playing a patriotic French criminal who the Nazis eventually execute. It was not a Parisienne guillotine Flynn deserved, thought Strawbridge; it was an American firing squad.

Erben was still lurking somewhere in Mexico, they believed. He seemed to be keeping his head down after Lansing's murder, and the OSS had not seen him for some time. He might not have been in the country at all, for all they knew. All attempts to track him down had failed. If anyone knew where he was, they were not saying. Flynn's phone calls and mail were monitored, but there did not seem to be any communication between them. Either Flynn had severed all links to the Austrian, or the reverse was true. It did not seem to occur to the security forces that they might still be in contact but by more covert means.

Hedy took a break from film-making to spend time with her young son while her husband was shooting *Passage to Marseilles*. It troubled her that she could not confide her innermost thoughts to the one person she should have been able to. His friendship with Flynn forbade that and would only have imbued Loder with a conflict of interest.

Strawbridge had requested and was granted a transfer to the west coast. He spent as much of his free time as he could watching Flynn. It appeared that all of his vigilance was going to be a waste of time. Then an unusual occurrence happened which might not have registered with anyone else. It even almost slipped the Navy man's scrutiny. Almost, but not quite.

The mailman delivered Flynn's post one day. Nothing unusual in that. People got letters every day, bills, bank statements, personal correspondence, and so on. So why did a different mailman come to Flynn's door an hour after his regular mail deliverer had been? Did the actor merit special treatment from the postal service? Strawbridge didn't think so. A quick check with his local sorting office would confirm he only got one delivery a day, the same provision as everybody else. So, who was this mysterious 'ghost' postman, arriving after his regular one had departed? It was definitely not the same man: different height and build, different gait. This person was taller and more muscular, heavier. So it was not some conscientious worker who had forgotten to deliver an earlier packet.

But wait a minute. This 'mailman' was suddenly no longer in view. He was certainly not at Flynn's letterbox. Whoever it was had ducked out of sight. Where the hell was he, and more to the point, what was he doing? Strawbridge took out his service issue binoculars, scanning for signs of whoever this figure was. It took a further five minutes before he caught sight of his quarry. The man appeared to wave to the house as he crept away. So, Flynn knew he had been there. It was all beginning to come together. This was now a job for the F.B.I., but Strawbridge couldn't leave it like this. It would be better if he followed the fake postman to see where he went. If this was all part of a Nazi contact group, he might be able to corral the lot of them.

Strawbridge watched as the 'mailman' opened the driver's door to a green Buick sedan before slipping onto the seat. He quickly made a note of the car's number plate before hurrying back to his own vehicle. It wouldn't matter if he lost him now. Tolson could find the driver within a couple of hours, even less at a push.

* * *

"Are you absolutely sure?" the Naval Intelligence agent asked Tolson. "This doesn't make any sense. Are you telling me that this man, Ivan Daniels, is a confederate of Flynn's? You must be mistaken. If you're right, these Nazis have penetrated us even deeper than we thought."

"It's no mistake, Keith. The Buick is definitely registered to Daniels. Going by the rough description you gave us, it certainly looks like him. You've done a great job, and the Bureau owes you big time. Thank you. Leave this to us. He's one of ours, and I will take great pleasure in seeing the bastard strung up by his thumbs. I still can't believe it. How the fuck did he get past all of our security checks?"

"I don't know, but the worrying thing is, if the Nazis have got men in the Bureau, could they even have them inside the Office of Naval Intelligence?"

"Worrying times, Keith; worrying times, indeed."

* * *

It took Tolson a week to get back to Strawbridge, following their interrogation of Daniels, and getting corroboration of his story. Daniels was no more a Nazi agent than they were. "It was your actress friend, Hedy Lamarr. She got Daniels' name from Charles Kettering, no less. You know, the guy she first took her invention to. She somehow managed to coax Daniels to investigate Flynn in his own time, much the same as you've been doing."

"I guess that explains how he got his hands on a postman's uniform, but there's one thing it doesn't explain."

"Which is...?"

"I saw him waving goodbye to Flynn. How did he explain that away?"

"Yeah, I asked him about that. He wasn't waving at Flynn; he wasn't waving at anyone. He was shielding his eyes to try to see inside Flynn's home. You just misread what he was doing."

"Hm. Yes, maybe I did at that. Did Hedy, um, Miss Lamarr confirm his story?"

"One hundred percent. Daniels is in the clear. It takes the heat off, don't you think? I mean, thinking we had a traitor inside our ranks."

"It doesn't mean you haven't, Mr. Tolson. Maybe they're just better hidden than we thought Daniels was."

A thoughtful Tolson did not reply before he ended the call.

* * *

Strawbridge would need to speak with Hedy again. He could not have her going off on her own, trying to find evidence against Flynn. What he had asked her to do was one thing, although that, too, almost ended badly, not least for her. But, when all was said and done, she was a civilian. She did not have the training or the knowledge to catch Flynn, even by employing a more skilled third party like Daniels. She would need to leave this to the professionals like himself or Tolson's F.B.I.

"To the professionals?" Hedy scoffed after being confronted by Strawbridge. "It's been well over a year since Lavering rejected our device and committed suicide because of it. And you're equally no further forward in capturing whoever killed the other navy man. Errol Flynn is still making movies as if nothing has happened, dancing rings around you, and you have the nerve to tell me to leave the investigation to the professionals?" She shook her head determinedly. "No, Commander, I can't do that."

"Please, Hedy," Strawbridge implored her. "I know you mean well, but there's something you've got to understand. If we ever do build a solid case against Flynn, your meddling could undermine the whole thing. A not-so-friendly judge might dismiss the case because of your unauthorized involvement. Can't you see?"

"And tell me, just how close are you to building a 'solid' case against him, hm?"

Strawbridge bowed his head. "At the moment, not very close, I admit that, but...."

"I don't know if you are aware of what's going on in Europe right now. Jews are being murdered simply for being Jews...."

"I know. I've heard the stories, the rumors..."

"They're not stories or rumors. It's all true, believe me, and it's worse than anyone knows about. Jews are being killed in special camps designed for the sole purpose of extermination. They're hiding it, but it is happening. If we don't stop them, there soon won't be a single Jew left alive in the whole of Europe."

"But why is this of such...?" and then he stopped as a sudden realization struck him. Pointing at her, he breathed, "Oh my God, you... you're Jewish. You're Jewish, aren't you?"

Hedy was crying. "I've lost touch with all my family. Most Jews have. They've just disappeared. Word has got out, Keith. The Nazis are engaging in the wholesale, mass slaughter of Jews. Thousands, hundreds of thousands, are gone as if they never existed. Now perhaps you will understand why I have been so anxious to get to Flynn. He's one of them, I'm sure of it.

"So are we, Hedy; so are we. But believing isn't proving. And that's why you must leave him to us. All the accusations in the world will be no good unless we can find something, anything, that will positively tie him to Commander Lansing's murder."

"But will you ever find anything substantial? It's been so long now, and the more time goes on, the less chance you'll have."

"There's no statute of limitation on murder, Hedy. Even if it takes ten years, we'll get him."

"I'm sure that will be a great comfort to Commander Lansing's widow."

"That remark was beneath you, Hedy. We, I, am doing all I can legally. I promise you, Flynn is never far from my waking thoughts; my dreams, either, come to that."

"I'm sorry, Keith. I shouldn't have said that. I know you're doing your best, despite the workload you must have. I just didn't know what else to do. That's why I approached Daniels. I had to do something."

Strawbridge loosened his tie and scratched his neck. Hedy saw it for what it was; a sign of nerves. He was about to say or do something he was unsure she would agree with or approve of. "Tell you what, Hedy. Why don't we work in tandem? I know far more about the case than Ivan Daniels and certainly a darn sight more about Flynn. Let's work together and pool our resources. We'll work out some kind of rota system, taking into account your day job and mine. I can use my background and expertise, and you can, well, you can just be you." He held out his hand. "What do you say?"

She did not accept his grasp. Instead, she kissed him on the cheek. Far better than a handshake any time, he thought warmly.

CHAPTER 38

Los Angeles, California
August 1945

The War in Europe was over, and it looked like the Japanese were about finished in the far east. The United States had dropped the first atomic bomb on Hiroshima. With a weapon like that at America's disposal, how much longer could they hold out? There would soon be peace again, at least until some other megalomaniac with lots of firepower and a grudge against humanity decided to start the whole thing all over again. In the eyes of many, Stalin was a good bet for this mantle. He had not withdrawn his troops from the Eastern European countries that his forces had liberated from the Nazis. It seemed as if these people had merely replaced one type of tyranny for another. Some in the U.S. military were all for continuing the war, with the Soviet leader as the new bogeyman. Despite being an ally in the conflict just past, everyone knew that it was only a matter of time before the Georgian's salacious appetite for expanding his Communist ideology would lead to a confrontation between east and west. Better it was now, while his country was still in a weakened state. Truman was not so sure. The philosophy of 'keep your friends close, but your enemies closer' seemed to prevail. Besides, the American public had no stomach for another war, not when so many of them had lost their loved ones so recently.

Hedy was in between movies. She had finished making *Her Highness and the Bellboy*, her last movie for M.G.M., in February. Filming on her next vehicle, *The Strange Woman*, was not due to start until December. This break in her schedule gave her time to be with her new baby daughter, whom she and Loder had named Denise.

Although the war was all but over, it was not so in the mind of the actress. There were still too many scores to settle. Germany had finally been beaten, but no victory could ever compensate for what the Nazis had done to her country and its people, as well as the carnage they had caused across Europe. Despite her busy calendar, Hedy had not forgotten her focus. Flynn might have been only a small part of the Nazi war machine, but without the small parts, the larger components could not function. She had kept watch on him from a distance and occasionally even employed private inquiry agents despite Strawbridge's earlier admonition. Some declined to help her, refusing to believe that Flynn was anything other than a loyal adopted American citizen. The agencies who did agree to take her money could find no evidence of Flynn's alleged duplicity. Likewise, the Naval Intelligence officer's best efforts and security services contacts did not discover anything that could incriminate the Australian actor.

Erben had still not resurfaced and would certainly be as invisible as he could in the light of Germany's defeat. Courts were about to start in Nuremberg to indict those responsible for the devastation and mass murder of civilians, Jews, and many others. A new phrase, '*crimes against humanity*,' had been coined to reflect the gravity of the charges laid against the accused. Erben would certainly have been among those who would have stood trial had he been caught.

Hedy had never revealed to John Loder her continuing one-woman campaign against his friend. Her husband would not comprehend her sense of outrage at what people like Flynn had done. How could he? He was not Jewish.

It was on one of her infrequent meetings with Strawbridge that he dropped his bombshell. "I'm leaving, Hedy. I'm leaving the Service. It's time I looked around for another line of work. Besides, I'm getting too old now. This is a younger man's game."

"But... but you can't!" Hedy stammered. "Not after all we've been through together. Please, just give it another few months, a year at the most. We..."

The Navy man held up his hand to silence her. "It's no use, Hedy. I've made up my mind. It's time to go. You've got two young children, one still a baby. The dead are dead. It's time to make way for the living, for those kids who I pray to God will never have to go through what we did. Maybe we'll get Flynn one day; maybe we won't. But it's time to stop now. The trials will be a start, I suppose. At least it will let the whole world see what humanity can do if it is left to go unbridled. Those who perpetrated these horrible things will be held accountable for their actions and will be punished accordingly. Not enough of them, it's true, but at least some of them will get their just desserts. And it might also make some others think twice before committing similar crimes in the future, God forbid."

"Those were very fine words, Keith, and all that you said is true, but it does not deflect me from my purpose. With or without you, I will get to Flynn and even his counterpart, Hermann Erben. It shames me to my core that this man is an Austrian." She smiled before continuing, "But on reflection, so was Hitler, wasn't he?" Hedy shook her head sadly. "This will only end when one of us is dead. I don't know if you can understand that, but it is like a fire burning inside me, a fire that I can only quench once I unmask Flynn."

"No, Hedy, I do understand you. It's not that long since I felt the same as you do, but for me, the war is over. I have to move on with my life, and you should, too. I know it's a big ask, but please try. If you don't, that fire you spoke about will consume you, and then Flynn and his kind will have won."

"I suppose you're right. Maybe I will try to put it all behind me. It'll be a struggle, but I'll do my best."

But both Hedy and Strawbridge knew she would not do this. Not while Flynn still drew breath.

CHAPTER 39

Los Angeles, California, and Acapulco, Mexico
June 1950-April 1952

Flynn was no longer the matinee idol he had been in his heyday. His court case some years earlier had soured his reputation, and film parts were becoming harder to find. His heavy drinking was another reason why some major film studios were reluctant to offer him parts. He had just finished filming *Kim* in India, where he was concerned that his malaria might strike again, and was about to start work on his next project, *The Adventures of Captain Fabian*, with his movie associate, William Marshall. The script was written by Flynn himself and was originally titled, *The Bargain*. They had decided to film in France, which was no issue for the actor who spoke the language fluently.

Although the war had been over for more than five years, there was always a nagging suspicion in Flynn's mind that the authorities were still watching him. There was nothing concrete for him to confirm his fears, merely a healthy misgiving that a few of those people around him were not all they seemed. Relocating to France might help to assuage him. They, whoever they were, surely wouldn't follow him across the Atlantic, would they? Would they?

Meanwhile, Hedy Lamarr had spent some time in Mexico. Her career had seen something of a resurgence since starring as Delilah opposite Victor Mature's Samson in the epic movie directed by Cecil B. DeMille a year or two earlier. Sadly, her following movies did not receive such critical acclaim, which sent her into a depression. Her marriage to John Loder was long over. One of the few 'souvenirs' of that relationship was her third and last child, a boy they had called Anthony, a brother to Denise, and James, the child they had conceived while Hedy was still wed to Gene Markey.

Acapulco was no longer just a sleepy little Mexican coastal fishing town. Thanks to people like Teddy Stauffer, an expatriate Swiss and former bandleader in pre-war Berlin, it had been transposed into a thriving mecca for wealthy Californians who enjoyed its burgeoning nightlife. Stauffer, the former manager of the Casablanca Hotel, had opened La Perla, his first nightclub there, in 1949. Since then, it had attracted Hollywood stars such as Orson Welles, Rita Hayworth, and many others.

Hedy decided to spend some time down there. It would give her a chance to consider her future in the movie industry. Like Flynn, she was not the screen draw she had been, despite the success of *Samson and Delilah*. She had tried her hand at producing her own movies, a rare thing for an actor to do, and even more uncommon for a female to take on such a role. The two films she made with her own production company, Mars Film Corporation, did reasonably well at the box office but were not overly successful. Once more, this was a woman who was ahead of her time.

Hedy had heard through the Hollywood grapevine that her nemesis, Errol Flynn, was shooting a movie in France. When she reached Acapulco, she made straight for La Perla. The actress had briefly met Teddy Stauffer in Mexico City back in 1946 and thought it might be a pleasant diversion to renew their acquaintanceship. She might also discretely ask if he had heard of someone called Hermann Erben. In his line of work, it would be necessary for him to keep his ear very close to the ground. Hedy knew that Stauffer was almost as anti-Nazi as she was, having returned to his native Switzerland just before the outbreak of war. Although the Nazis had been tolerant of his music, they had been getting more aggressive in their anti-Jewish stance, and 'swing' music by the likes of Benny Goodman was no longer permitted. Stauffer, too, was eventually put on the Nazis' 'blacklist' for playing the forbidden refrains by Jewish composers.

His first remark shocked Hedy. His English was good but not as well-articulated as Hedy's. Preferring to converse in German, he told her that he did not know Erben personally, but his friend was a crony. "Oh," remarked Hedy, unconsciously lapsing into English, "who is this crony? Maybe I know him."

"I'm sure you do, Hedy, my dear. I would be surprised if you didn't. He's a fellow actor, Errol Flynn."

Hedy tried hard not to show her surprise. "You know Flynn, I mean, Errol?" she asked.

Stauffer laughed. Replying in very heavily accentuated English, he said, "Know him? I haff lost count ov de number off times ve haff tried to shteal each odders' fraulines! Ja, ve are ferry close buddies. I t'ink he's in France at ze moment."

"Does he... does he come down here sometimes?" she asked.

"Oh, ja, he sails down in hiss yacht, *Zaca*. I expect he vill come down vonce he iss back from France. I vould like to t'ink ziss iss hiss second home."

Hedy had married once before, not for love, but because she was persuaded to 'for the common good.' The stakes were high then, and in the end, they had not achieved much. Was she prepared to wed again, not out of affection, but to achieve her ambition? To finally get close enough to Errol Flynn to garner the evidence she needed of his complicity with Erben to sabotage the Allied war effort? She had three children to consider now, three lives that depended on her. What sort of mother would she be if she risked their welfare to embark on a selfish crusade of her own? One which might, once again, end in failure? But then again, what of all those mothers who had perished with their own children in the death camps? Who was to avenge them? Who was to cry out for justice in their name and bring the guilty into the light?

The trials had found many perpetrators guilty, but too many had not received their due punishment. Some suffered no penalty at all. What would the ghosts of all those poor souls be thinking? We had failed them. The world had failed them. No! It was not good enough. Not while one Nazi still survived. They had to know that the world would never forget, would never forgive. Even if she were only responsible for bringing one or two more monsters to trial, it would be one or two more who would finally get their reckoning. She had a bit of money. She could afford to take some time off, could afford nannies to care for her children, even just for a little while.

Her mother, Gertrude, was now living in California. Hedy was sure she would love to spend time with her grandchildren. Things would work out just fine. She would marry Stauffer, not because she loved him, but as the means to an end. To get Flynn and Erben into court, where their crimes could finally be laid bare for all to see.

* * *

Hedy and Teddy Stauffer married on June 11th. 1951. She knew from the start that Stauffer would be unfaithful, but hadn't she also betrayed Gene Markey? And that liaison had produced a child, a son. There was no point in being hypocritical. Besides, she did not marry Stauffer out of love. Hedy had assumed they would tie the knot at one of Stauffer's hotels in his beloved Acapulco. Instead, they were wed at the home of Superior Judge Stanley Mosk, in Santa Monica. They spent their honeymoon in Carmel before heading to San Francisco, where Hedy disposed of her previous wedding rings and other personal effects, claiming she 'wanted to make a clean break' with her past.

If Flynn was at their wedding, she did not see him. By this time, he was married to actress Patrice Wymore, having divorced his second wife, Nora Eddington, in 1949. She had borne him two daughters, Deirdre and Rory. That divorce appeared to be amicable, with both sides admitting fault.

She had wanted to see Flynn at her wedding, hoping that, perhaps, he might let something slip while intoxicated, toasting the new bride and groom in his own, inimitable way. After their trip to San Francisco, the couple returned to Acapulco, where, for a while, Hedy took on the role of 'hostess' in La Perla. Flynn did not appear, as Stauffer thought he might. He was obviously tied up with his other commitments, not the least of which were his two small daughters and his son Sean who he had sired with his first wife, Lili Damita.

It did not take Stauffer long to tire of his marriage to Hedy. A few weeks after their return, they were visited by actress Gene Tierney, with whom Stauffer immediately became infatuated. Hedy knew it would not be long before she became the next 'ex Mrs. Stauffer.'

Things had not worked out how she had planned. Neither Flynn nor Erben was anywhere in sight, and Hedy became more frustrated as the weeks passed. Even an impromptu romantic visit from Ava Gardner and Frank Sinatra did nothing to quell her mounting sense of impotence. She all but snubbed the couple, much to Stauffer's exasperation.

It would take a few more months before Hedy filed for divorce in Los Angeles Superior Court, citing Stauffer's cruelty as the reason for her complaint. He did not deny her allegations of violence when she asserted that although he was pleasant to his guests, his attitude to his wife was somewhat less agreeable. She claimed he had struck her across the face the previous November in the Beverly Hills Hotel. He did not think it would be appropriate to defend his actions by stating that the reason he lashed out at her was that she seemed 'distracted.' She was not paying him the attention he felt he deserved. This allegation would have been true, too. Hedy was engrossed in thinking of ways she could get to Flynn, either directly or through his wife, Patrice.

She revealed to the Hollywood gossip columns that her marriage to Stauffer had 'been a mistake.' The Hedda Hoppers and the Louella Parsons' all assumed she meant a romantic blunder. If that was what they wished to believe, good luck to them. It was April 1952, and time to move on.

Her desire for retribution had not dimmed. Everything she had tried so far had failed. There had to be some way she could get vengeance. And she would find it one day.

CHAPTER 40

Los Angeles, California, and Rome, Italy
May 1953-December 1954

A year later, Hedy had still not achieved her objective. According to the rumors circulating Tinseltown, Flynn was still as debauched and drunk as ever, despite being on his third marriage and recovering from an earlier bout of hepatitis. Then, she heard that he had gone to Italy to film his next movie, a 'swashbuckler' called '*Crossed Swords.*' She had also been toying with making a film there with Moravian-born director, Edgar Ulmer. Their relationship had not been an easy one. Ulmer had directed Hedy in her own company's production of '*The Strange Woman*' but found her attitude too demanding. Despite this, they decided to collaborate again to produce a movie, which was born out of a television series that never materialized. Hedy would star, and Ulmer would direct her. It was proposed to film the drama, entitled '*Loves of Three Queens*' in Europe, and where better to film than Italy? Much of the movie's funding came from Hedy herself. When she showed the first draft to John Loder, he scratched his head, troubled by what he had read. "Hedy, do you know how much this will all cost? I think it'll be far more expensive to produce than you imagine. Please be careful."

"Oh, I'm not doing this on my own. I'm co-producing it with Victor Pahlen, and I've hired Edgar Ulmer to direct," she replied airily. "Don't worry; everything will turn out Okay. It usually does."

This remark made Loder even more concerned. Ulmer had a prodigious output and was reckoned to be a safe pair of hands. It was not Ulmer's direction that concerned Loder. He knew of Pahlen, but his Hollywood output had been almost non-existent. And judging by the script Hedy had given him, this would take an enormous amount of capital. The sets alone would run into the hundreds of thousands of dollars, if not more. Did she know what she was doing? Loder fervently hoped so. "Have you secured U.S. distribution yet, at least?"

"No, but I'm sure there will be no problem. I want to get the film in the can, then I can worry about distribution."

Oh, Hedy, Loder thought. How can someone so smart and intellectual be so dumb?

* * *

Hedy's choice of location was not as arbitrary as Loder believed. Flynn had finished shooting 'Crossed Swords' and was about to start work on his next project, a movie about the life of William Tell, which was also to be shot in Italy. Like her, he, too, would produce his vanity project, with half the budget of eight hundred and sixty thousand dollars coming from his own wallet and the rest being met by a consortium of Italian businessmen. Unlike Hedy, he had already secured distribution of his yet-to-be-made movie with United Artists. Flynn's co-producer was his manager, Barry Mahon, whom the actor had worked on with his just finished movie, 'Crossed Swords.'

* * *

Ulmer soon regretted his decision to work again with Hedy. Her headstrong and demanding attitude did not sit well with the Moravian director. She may have been a reasonably good actress, and, yes, she had already produced a couple of movies that had not done too badly at the box office. But he had been hired to direct, and she had brought him in for that very reason—his directorial experience. If he said that particular shots had to be done a certain way, it was for a very sound reason, not on some capricious whim.

Eventually, their two personalities clashed into almost open warfare, and Ulmer finally had enough. After completing the section 'Genevieve de Brabant,' he walked off the set, leaving Hedy without a director. For a short while, she considered directing the movie herself but then thought the better of it. She eventually chose the Swiss screenwriter and director, Marc Allegret, to complete the direction. As much as she hated to admit it to herself, Loder had been right. This project was too big for her, and Pahlen also seemed to be out of his depth. It looked as if her attitude, inexperience, and poor choice of co-producer were going to cost her dearly.

* * *

Meanwhile, Flynn's 'The Story of William Tell' was also in trouble. His Italian partners appeared to be backing out, and it looked as if Flynn was going to be sued for unpaid hotel bills and salaries, as well as other debts. Creditors were threatening to remove equipment, and Hedy heard that Flynn was desperately scrambling around, trying to find alternative funding sources to complete his movie. Despite her own production problems or, perhaps, because of them, Hedy took some delight at Flynn's headaches. But it was also a headache for her. With so many disputes going on with his production, he would hardly have time to think about or indulge in any behavior which might reveal his dark secrets.

* * *

With Allegret's capable guidance, their film was finally completed, and she and Pahlen were able to secure distribution in Italy. The film was released in December 1954. They were, however, finding it difficult to arrange distribution in the United States. Without screening there, it would be impossible to recoup the money they had spent on production. It looked like it was going to be a costly lesson for her. Had she been able to bring Flynn to book, the whole exercise might have been worth it, as financially draining as it was. But in the end, what had she accomplished? Sadly, the answer seemed to be—nothing.

CHAPTER 41

Port Antonio, Jamaica, and London, England
February 1955–August 1958

Flynn had become disillusioned with Hollywood, and with Patrice Wymore and their baby daughter, Arnella, relocated to Port Antonio in Jamaica. Despite his earlier optimism, Flynn never got the investment he needed to complete his project. Like Hedy, his aborted movie had drained him financially, and he was desperate to recoup even some of his losses. For these reasons, he accepted an offer to work in England to make movies for producer Herbert Wilcox. Although they planned for Flynn to appear in six features, this contract was canceled after the third movie, '*King's Rhapsody,*' due to poor box-office receipts. The Tasmanian also made a T.V. series, '*The Errol Flynn Theater,*' in which he introduced each half-hour show episode and appeared in several himself.

The following year, 1956, he received an offer from Universal Studios to star in their forthcoming offer, '*Istanbul,*' a remake of the 1948 movie, '*Singapore,*' also released by Universal. It seemed that despite everything, his career had secured something of a revival. Towards the end of filming '*Istanbul,*' he was offered the lead in '*The Big Boodle,*' a crime caper set and filmed in Cuba.

His biggest role in a long time was his next performance. He was offered the part of the drunken, self-pitying Mike Campbell in Daryl F. Zanuck's production of the Hemingway novel '*The Sun Also Rises.*' Although the

285

character was written as a Scotsman, Flynn's accent was anything but, and the only thing vaguely Scottish about him was his tartan waistcoat. He played so true to type that other similar roles followed. It did not seem to matter. By early 1958, he was almost penniless again. He had to do something to augment his dwindling finances.

An idea occurred to him. He had led an interesting life; well, he thought it was interesting. Why not let the public have a glimpse into his personal affairs? All his affairs. He would not hold anything back. He would tell it all, the good as well as the totally indecent.

In the meantime, Hedy thought her luck had changed. Warner's had picked up the distribution rights to 'Loves of Three Queens,' and she believed it would not be long before her movie would be shown in theaters across the United States. However, she was disappointed when she discovered the company had purchased the rights so it would not be screened. They were about to release their own epic motion picture, *Helen of Troy*, and saw Hedy's movie as unwelcome competition. Although this helped her to mitigate some of her losses, it was nowhere near what she would have needed to earn just to break even.

By this time, Hedy was on husband number five, Texan oilman, W. Howard Lee, whom she had met at a horse show in Houston. They wed in December 1953 and spent the first few weeks of their marriage staying at the Shamrock Hotel in Houston, owned by fellow Texan oil executive, Glenn McCarthy. She then took her children and went to live with him in his palatial River Oaks home. Hedy had had enough of the Hollywood lifestyle and was content to live the life of an oil baron's wife.

The relationship was not without incident. A couple of years later, she noticed that some jewelry was missing from her bedroom, some of it very expensive. There did not appear to be any signs of a forced break-in, so the police believed the theft had been perpetrated by one of the staff, all of whom were given a polygraph test. They all passed except Hedy herself, who was, apparently, too upset for the officers to get an accurate reading. The gems mysteriously reappeared a few weeks later on a shelf in another room. No explanation was given, even though this room had also been thoroughly searched at the time. Neither Hedy, Lee, nor any of the staff ever commented again on this mysterious event.

Parts, too, were beginning to become scarce for her, and she did not film her next movie, playing Joan of Arc in *The Story of Mankind*, until the end of 1956.

Another occurrence as dramatic as the jewelry episode happened in the fall of 1957 when a fireplace in her home caught ablaze. Very little damage, however, structural or otherwise, was caused. A different fire still burned within her. It had not diminished with time, and she was still as determined as ever to see Flynn exposed for the crimes she believed he had committed during the war.

* * *

Flynn had settled into his Jamaican home and enlisted the writer, Earl Conrad, to help him ghost-write his memoirs. Conrad was well aware of Flynn's attitude towards Jews and wondered if the actor would have enlisted him had he known that his birth name was Cohen. The Tasmanian actor badly needed the book to succeed if he hoped to pay off his debts. Before leaving California, Conrad thought he might indulge in some pre-publicity for the work he was about to do. This effort resulted in an advance of $9,000 from Putnam Publishing. At least someone thought Flynn's life was interesting enough to put a price on it.

CHAPTER 42

Port Antonio, Jamaica, Los Angeles, CA, Vienna, Austria
August 1958–September 1959

The business of writing about Flynn's exploits took longer to get underway than the actor had imagined. Almost from the moment he arrived at Flynn's coconut plantation, Conrad seemed to apply himself more to see how much rum he could drink and how many Jamaican girls he could seduce, than start to get down to why he was there. Flynn almost saw in him a kindred spirit, a carefree soul who was only slightly older than Flynn himself. But Conrad was there to do a job, and Flynn made sure that he would do it.

Flynn had also authored a couple of books and was no stranger to the art of writing. He had penned an autobiography in 1938 titled *Beam Ends* detailing the purchase of his yacht *Sirocco* and his subsequent travels in New Guinea. The book was mired in controversy in April 1938 when a journalist, Frank Clune, pointed out several factual errors and disparaged much of what Flynn had claimed. The actor had also written a novel in 1946 titled *Showdown*, a romantic adventure yarn.

For his memoirs, he had decided to hold nothing back; after all, that was what the paying public would want to read; every salacious detail, warts and all. The two men collaborated on the work between August and October, not long after Flynn had finished filming *Roots of Heaven*, where his girlfriend, Beverly Aadland, had an uncredited part.

* * *

Hedy missed Hollywood. Despite having her children around her, she seemed unfulfilled; she had lost her creative instinct. Since shooting *The Female Animal* the year before, during May and June 1957, her only other acting performance was playing Connie Bowers in a Zane Grey Theater episode, *Proud Woman*. Movie parts had dried up. Although only forty-four years of age, she was considered too old to play the glamorous roles she was famous for not so many years earlier. To make matters worse, Hedy's marriage was in trouble again. Between her husband's drink problems and his long absences from home on business, Hedy felt alone and isolated. This situation was not a recipe for a lasting relationship and, inevitably, led to the divorce courts once more.

Some years before, she had persuaded Howard Lee to purchase some property in the mainly unspoiled snowy landscape of Aspen, Colorado. Homesick for her own country, Hedy built a lodge in the pristine white hillside, which she named Villa Lamarr, in the style of the Austrian dwellings of her homeland. She had hoped to acquire this as part of the divorce settlement, but was unsuccessful. She did not help her case by sending her body double, Sylvia Hollis, to stand in for her at the divorce proceedings. Her son, Anthony, had been seriously injured in an automobile accident the same day, December 11th.1958 and an unfocussed Hedy was not thinking clearly. Despite this traumatic incident, the divorce court judge was not sympathetic to her plight.

* * *

Flynn's forthcoming book also came to the attention of someone else; someone who had cause to be concerned about what Flynn might reveal in his tell-all autobiography. This person was his former friend and onetime fellow Nazi, Hermann Erben. Flynn could never reveal his part in Erben's crime without incriminating himself, but perhaps he had done a deal. The U.S. military had already interrogated Erben in the Far East in 1946 when he admitted to being in the *Abwehr* during the war. Of course, the Austrian Nazi did not confess to the murder of Fred Lansing, but imagine how many more copies of Flynn's memoirs the actor might sell if he admitted to being indirectly responsible for the murder of a serving U.S. Navy officer during the war. Erben was sure he had left no evidence of his murderous assault, and there could not possibly be any trace of anything that would link him to the crime, especially after so many years. It would be purely the word of a drunken, decadent actor against his. But even so, it would not look good for him.

He had rebuilt his life and was now a successful, practicing physician in Vienna and a pillar of the local community. What right did Flynn have to take that all away from him? What if he had even done a deal with the American authorities? Immunity from prosecution for handing over the real perpetrator, perhaps? No, this would not do; this would not do at all. Flynn would have to be dealt with.

CHAPTER 43

Los Angeles, California and Vancouver B.C., Canada
September-October 1959

Flynn's finances had gone from bad to broke, almost totally, stony broke. His hedonistic lifestyle had finally not just caught up with him, but had overtaken him. Practically everything had gone, and his book was yet to be published due to arguments Flynn had with his publishers who wanted certain sections 'toned down.' The advance royalties he received from Putnam had been long since spent, as had the fee he had earned from his semi-documentary movie, *Cuban Rebel Girls*. Financially, he was in a bind, and the only thing he had left of any value was his yacht, *Zaca*.

Not only was he in poor fiscal shape, but health-wise, also, he was not faring so well. Because of his lifelong addiction to tobacco and his hard-drinking habits, he suffered from liver cirrhosis and chronic back pain, as well as recurring bouts of malaria. He had also had two mild heart attacks, the first while filming *Gentleman Jim* some seventeen years earlier. He had recently undergone an ECG, and his doctor had warned him that if he did not cut down on both vices, his life would be in danger.

There was only one thing for it; his beloved *Zaca* would have to go. Flynn already had a buyer in mind. His friend and onetime financial adviser, George Caldough. Caldough had made no secret of his admiration for Flynn's sailboat and often said that if Flynn should ever think of selling it, he should keep Caldough in mind. So, with a heavy heart, the actor called his friend in Vancouver, British Columbia. An excited Caldough flew immediately to Hollywood to meet with his old friend. Once in Flynn's home, Caldough came straight to the point. "Errol, what would you say if I told you that you could have your cake and still scoff the bloody lot?"

Flynn cocked his head before answering. "Fine, but what cake exactly are we talking about?"

"The *Zaca*, you idiot! I'm talking about your yacht. How would you like to realize some capital on it but still sail it?"

"Well, sure, but I don't see how..."

"It's simple. I've been reading all about some U.S. company that intends to raise two million dollars to go treasure hunting off the coast of Spain. My God, Errol, with your yacht and your name at the helm, if you'll pardon the pun, they'll raise twice that amount. This couldn't have happened at a better time. It's fate, Errol. That's what it is, fate. You sell the yacht to me, and I'll do the rest. What do you say?"

Flynn did not want to tell Caldough it was the daftest idea he had heard in some time. He needed the money too much.

"You can't lose," Caldough continued. "Even if they don't find one doubloon, you still get your money. What do you say?"

What else could Flynn say but 'yes?' He would realize a tidy amount on the sailboat, which would keep him going until money started rolling in from the sale of his book. It would all work out just fine.

"Why don't you come to B.C.? Let's seal the deal in style. You can stay with us, and I'll contact the consortium who's planning the whole thing."

"Sounds like a plan," Flynn replied.

This conversation interested not only Caldough. Unbeknownst to Flynn, Erben had arranged to have listening devices installed in the actor's home, and his phone calls monitored. So Flynn was going to Canada, was he? Well, that was interesting. In fact, it fitted Erben's plans very nicely; very nicely, indeed.

Flynn arrived in Vancouver ten days later with his girlfriend, Beverly Aadland. Word had got out about Flynn's visit, and the press turned out in force. The Tasmanian regaled them with stories of his time in Hollywood before announcing his plans to film Vladimir Nabokov's exotic tale, *Lolita*, with Aadland in a starring role. They stayed with the Caldoughs in their rented two-level house at Eyremount Drive in The British Properties for several days while Caldough attempted to contact the treasure-seeking cartel.

It had been a long time since the Australian actor had been so happy and carefree. His money troubles were all but over. He was in no hurry to go back to Hollywood and enjoyed being the center of attention in the Caldough house. One endless party followed another, with the Caldoughs only half-heartedly trying to get Flynn to go back to The U.S., reminding him of his commitment to film a T.V. show in New York. They seemed to be enjoying his company as much as he loved staying with his guests.

By October 13th. Flynn finally decided that he really would have to return. He had not considered his obligation so urgent, not now that he had money in his pocket with more to come. To sweeten the deal, the Caldoughs would arrange a farewell party for the following day and invite all their friends to say goodbye to the actor and his girlfriend. It would see him go off in style. Midway through the affair, no one noticed a nondescript young man with short auburn hair, in a brown corduroy jacket and blue Levi denims slip some white powder into Flynn's drink. He came, and he went. Anyone who did see him assumed he had arrived with other guests.

Finally, when all the partygoers had gone, Flynn got ready to go to the airport. Bidding a last, sad farewell to the house, Flynn and Beverly Aadland climbed into Caldough's motor car. Not long after they had begun the drive to the airport, Flynn began to fidget in the back seat.

"Errol, what's wrong? Are you O.K.?" Caldough asked, glancing at his friend through the rear-view mirror. Even Beverly had noticed that Flynn was behaving oddly, but thought it was merely due to an overconsumption of alcohol.

"I'm sorry, George," he gasped. "I've had some pains in my back and legs since we left the house, and it's getting worse."

"What do the pains feel like?" asked a concerned Caldough.

"I don't know. I've never experienced anything like it. Ahh," he winced. "Christ, I don't know if I'll make it to the airport. How much longer before we get there?"

"Never mind the airport. Look, there's a doctor I know who works at the Sylvia Hotel. It's on Gilford Street, only a couple of minutes away. We can make a detour, and I'll get him to take a look at you. It's probably nothing, but you can never be too careful, eh? Besides," he smiled, "I've got to protect my investment, haven't I?"

"Thanks very fucking much," answered Flynn through his discomfort while Beverly tried to comfort him. By the time they arrived at the hotel, Flynn was in agony. He was drenched in his own perspiration and had begun shaking. Flynn was in no condition to get out of the back seat. "Wait here," Caldough said as he exited the car. "I'll get the doctor to come down to have a look at you. I'll be back in a minute." Caldough was a friend of Arthur Cameron, the manager of the Sylvia. He would make sure the doctor left whatever he was doing to attend to Flynn.

A minute later, Caldough came running out of the hotel like a man who had seen Armageddon. "He's not there!" he screamed. "The doctor's not there. He's at his practice. Hang on, Errol, I'm going there now."

It was almost three forty-five in the afternoon, and the chances of Errol Flynn and his girlfriend catching their flight were growing ever more unlikely. It took less than five minutes before Caldough arrived at the Burnaby Street block where the doctor, Grant Gould, practiced. With Beverly's help, they maneuvered Flynn up the stairs to Gould's waiting room. Gould immediately recognized two things. Who his new patient was, and the extreme distress he was in.

After a quick cursory examination, the doctor injected Flynn with a dose of morphine to lessen the pain. Whether it was the excitement of the moment or something else entirely, Gould immediately picked up the phone and called his friends. "You'll never guess who I've got in my office," he crowed. "None other than Errol Flynn. he's here right now." After convincing his buddies that he was serious, he returned to administer to the actor.

The morphine was beginning to take effect, and Flynn's pain was lessening. It did not take long for Gould's friends to arrive, and another party ensued, much to Caldough and Beverly's disgust. Couldn't they see how ill he was? Didn't they care about anything but their own selfish pleasure?

Despite his physical suffering, the actor did not seem to mind the attention. He recounted stories of his glory days in Hollywood through his pain, standing against the waiting room wall. "I tell you, friends, if you think I'm a hard-partying man, you should have seen W. C. Fields and John Barrymore in their day. They made me look like a member of the Temperance League," he grimaced. After a few more minutes of joking with his impromptu audience, Flynn said, "Listen, since you've all been kind enough to come and see me, I'll tell you what I'm going to do. I'm going to go for a lie down for a while to shake off this bloody pain; then we'll all go out to dinner on me. What do you say?"

A concerned look passed between Beverly Aadland and George Caldough. He was due on a flight to the United States, which he would not now make because of his condition, and he was offering to take a small crowd out to dinner at his own expense? This would never happen, and shame on them, these freeloaders who thought that was all their idol had to do; buy them all a meal. How dare they? They should all have been ashamed of themselves, especially the doctor who instigated this circus. The sad thing was—none of them were.

As he hobbled into a spare bedroom, he turned around and, waving a salute, said to them, "I'll be back."

One of the people who were in the room did not think he would. No one in the crowd noticed a young man in a corduroy jacket as he popped a stick of gum into his mouth. It was almost over.

After twenty minutes, a concerned Beverly stood up. "I'm going to look in on him. Don't worry; I won't make a sound," she said as she quietly opened the bedroom door. The mood outside had become much more somber, with some of the crowd now realizing, perhaps for the first time, how ill the actor was. He was lying very still, too still for her liking, and she gently shook him. It was only then that she noticed his skin pallor had turned a worrying shade of blue. She ran out of the room, unable to control herself. "He's turned blue," she screamed hysterically. "He's turned blue. Help him, someone, help him!"

Gould immediately ran into the room, took one look at the ailing actor, and hurried out, returning almost instantly with a hypodermic. He injected Flynn with a shot of amyl nitrate. Seeing no improvement after a few seconds, he left the room, coming back seconds later with another syringe, this one filled with adrenaline, which he administered straight into Flynn's heart. Gould then tried compressions and mouth to mouth, but it was too late. The Australian actor had gone.

A short time later, Erben, who had returned to Los Angeles for a little while, received a cable. It said two words; 'it's done.' The Austrian physician was secure. With all the narcotics already in Flynn's bloodstream, this drug, if it were ever analyzed, would be assumed to have been merely another in the long line of barbiturates with which the actor had taken. So, Flynn was dead. How sad, but how safe for him. No matter what was in Flynn's memoirs, it was now the word of a dissolute dead man against the reputation of an illustrious Viennese doctor. Who would the world believe? He was not even in the United States (he would claim – let anyone disprove him) when Lansing's murder occurred.

Hedy took the news with equanimity. She was glad it was finally over. She was still going through her acrimonious divorce with W. Lee Howard and had enough to contend with without thinking about his demise. Yes, she was sorry that she would never get him into a court of law, but he would now be judged by a much higher tribunal. Perhaps it was for the best. Let the world remember him how it wished. She knew the truth. In the end, that was all that mattered.

EPILOGUE

Hedy Lamarr died at the age of eighty-five on January 19th. 2000. After her death, a document was discovered among her papers, which was never made public. The article was hand-written and dated a short while before her demise. The handwriting was said to be that of the actress, but it was signed by the initials 'H.K.' The person who found it was confused by the letters, as they were not aware that her birth name was Hedwig Kiesler. The document was written in the form of a declaration and might even be construed as a 'deathbed' confession. It was not addressed to any specific person or agency and read, without preamble:

'*For over sixteen years spanning two decades in the 1940s and 1950s, I devoted much of my life and my wealth in trying to unmask someone I believe was an enemy of this country and caused untold damage during the Second World War. I also believe he was indirectly but knowingly responsible for the deaths of two high-ranking United States naval officers. This individual, a well-known personality and a U.S. citizen, made and spent a great deal of money, which he had earned in the largest part from American companies. Despite this, I believe that when this country needed him the most, he conspired secretly with our adversaries to try to bring the United States to its knees. I know for sure that it was he, among others, who prevented my anti-torpedo invention from being utilized by the U.S. military. This action caused the lives of many American servicemen and other Allied soldiers to be needlessly lost.*

It is also my understanding that this person was, in part, responsible for the attack on Pearl Harbor by giving the Japanese military confidential knowledge of American naval bases in San Diego and Hawaii.

This individual was known to have highly questionable and odious convictions regarding those people of a particular religion, of which I was one.

Once again, I hold this person to account in a small but significant way for the suffering and horrific deaths of so many of these people, my own family and friends included, in wartime Europe.

Had the device I developed with George Antheil been allowed to be put into service, it might have shortened the war by many months, if not years. By his actions, he lengthened the conflict by a considerable amount of time.

It is my sincere belief that had his political affiliations and hostile actions been known at the end of the war, he would have and should have stood trial with the other monsters at Nuremberg.

I ceased my crusade when this person died in the late 1950s. I regret bitterly that despite my best efforts and the efforts of others, I was never able to bring the crimes of this man into the open or this individual to justice. I pray that the judgment he evaded in this life will be meted out to him in the next.'

Despite being read by several people, no one knows where this document is now. It may have been destroyed, or it may be languishing in a desk, a filing cabinet, or a bank vault. Why Miss Lamarr does not mention by name, the person she tried so hard to bring to justice is unclear. However, one does not have to have much of an imagination to understand about whom she is writing. '*Well-known personality.*' '*U.S. citizen*' (Flynn was born in Tasmania but took out U.S. citizenship in 1942). '*Known to have highly questionable and odious convictions*' (Mr. Flynn's anti-Semitism was not a secret in Hollywood). '*Died in the late 1950s*' (The actor died in October 1959). It has also been suggested that he deliberately had his 1941 movie, '*Dive Bomber*,' made on location at the actual Naval Base in San Diego to give the Japanese military close-up information of the facility.

So only one question now remains. If Hedy Lamarr was not writing about Errol Flynn, who was the unnamed person she had been pursuing so doggedly for so many years?

THE END

AUTHOR'S NOTE

Although this work is based on real incidents and the lives of actual historical personalities, it does not claim to be an exact portrayal of any event or series of events connected to these characters. It should not be used as a reference source for anyone wishing to research any real-life person portrayed in this novel.

I have used some literary license to dramatize various actual episodes, while other incidents are wholly works of fiction and rely on a good deal of conjecture, speculation, and supposition. The central protagonists, of course, did exist; other characters such as Isidor Pralgovitch, Vice-Admiral Bernard Lavering, Commander Fred Lansing, and the O.N.I. agents are figments of the author's imagination. No suggestion of any impropriety should be implied or inferred by anyone in or connected to the Department of the Navy or any branch of the U.S. armed services in the era when this novel is set.

The radio broadcast that Errol Flynn listened to shortly before his departure for the United States is probably the same speech Churchill gave on Armistice day 1934, part of which I have reproduced in a later chapter. Churchill really did give this speech, which can be found on a YouTube audio recording, *https://www.youtube.com/watch?v=ReAkzTw8RHE*.

It is highly unlikely that Hedwig Kiesler/Hedy Lamarr ever came into contact with the Haganah. This plot device comes purely and solely from the mind of the author. Also, no such paper as the torn page from The Treaty of Versailles purporting to show Hitler's militaristic ambitions ever existed. Neither did the letter mentioned in the epilogue supposedly written by Miss Lamarr suggesting Errol Flynn's alleged treason during World War Two. This device was created purely as a singular way to end the story, and no reference to any individual, alive or dead, should be inferred or implied by this fictitious document.

Hermann Erben was an active Nazi agent who worked for the *Abwehr* during World War Two and was considered a dangerous spy by the American authorities. He was interrogated in the Far East in 1946 but was spared prison for incriminating his fellow Nazi agents. He went back into medical practice and passed away in Vienna, Austria, in 1985.

Finally, there has never been any suggestion that Errol Flynn died by means other than his dissolute lifestyle. To the best of the author's knowledge, there is no evidence to support the fictitious claim in this novel that he died by anyone's hand other than his own hedonistic excesses.

ABOUT THE AUTHOR

David Broadway Photography

David Philips was born in Glasgow, Scotland in 1953 and emigrated to Perth, West Australia with his wife Adele in 2009. He has two adult children who still live in Glasgow. David has had several careers including being the anonymous half of a comedy double act with an irreverent, mischievous keyboard playing robot called Mr. Hairy and it was always a matter of some chagrin that the robot continually stole all his best lines and got more laughs than he did. In his spare time, David plays folk harmonica, swears at the T.V. and reads. His favorite authors are Scottish crime fiction writers Ian Rankin and Craig Robertson. He is also a big fan of the books of Robert Harris and the late Robert Ludlum, from whom he draws inspiration for his own novels. David also writes short horror fiction and is a regular contributor to Schlock, an on-line e-magazine. His anthology of 13 horror stories, *The Finest Thread*, is available as an e-book from Smashwords.com. He has also written a comedy novella called *'The McBrides'* set in his home city of Glasgow in 1972. David's first novel, *The Judas Conspiracy*, a semi-autobiographical tale about the JFK assassination was published by Black Rose Writing in September 2022. *The Errol Flynn Conspiracy* is his second novel to be published by Black Rose Writing.

NOTE FROM THE AUTHOR

Word-of-mouth is crucial for any author to succeed. If you enjoyed *The Errol Flynn Conspiracy*, please leave a review online—anywhere you are able. Even if it's just a sentence or two. It would make all the difference and would be very much appreciated.

Thanks!
David Philips

REFERENCES

- https://en.wikipedia.org/wiki/Haganah
- https://en.wikipedia.org/wiki/History_of_Israel
- https://en.wikipedia.org/wiki/Jewish_Agency_for_Israel
- https://en.wikipedia.org/wiki/Irgun
- https://en.wikipedia.org/wiki/Lehi_(militant_group)
- https://en.wikipedia.org/wiki/Hedy_Lamarr
- https://www.britannica.com/biography/Hedy-Lamarr
- https://www.biography.com/actor/hedy-lamarr
- https://www.womenshistory.org/education-resources/biographies/hedy-lamarr
- https://www.smithsonianmag.com/smithsonian-institution/thank-world-war-ii-era-film-star-your-wi-fi-180971584/
- https://www.britannica.com/topic/Haganah
- https://www.jewishvirtuallibrary.org/the-haganah-museum
- https://en.wikipedia.org/wiki/George_Antheil
- https://www.thevintagenews.com/2018/06/09/bra-designer/
- https://cometoverhollywood.com/2011/11/09/the-most-beautiful-woman-in-hollywood-hedy-lamarr-book-review/
- https://thelifeandtimesofhollywood.com/old-rumor-resurfaces-errol-flynn-anti-semitic-star-is-a-reputed-nazi-spy/
- https://en.wikipedia.org/wiki/Errol_Flynn
- https://en.wikipedia.org/wiki/Canadian_Security_Intelligence_Service
- https://en.wikipedia.org/wiki/RCMP_Security_Service
- https://en.wikipedia.org/wiki/1929_Palestine_riots
- https://en.wikipedia.org/wiki/Friedrich_Mandl
- https://en.wikipedia.org/wiki/Otto_Eberhardt_Patronenfabrik
- https://en.wikipedia.org/wiki/Category:Fish_of_the_Mediterranean_Sea
- https://biblehub.com/isaiah/2-4.htm

- https://www.google.com/search?client=firefox-b-d&q=gangster+movies+of+the+1930%27s
- https://www.militaryfactory.com/smallarms/guns-1930-1939.asp
- https://en.wikipedia.org/wiki/Treaty_of_Versailles#Military_restrictions
- https://net.lib.byu.edu/~rdh7/wwi/versa/chart1.gif
- https://en.wikipedia.org/wiki/Torpedo#Invention_of_the_modern_torpedo
- https://www.youtube.com/watch?v=ReAkzTw8RHE
- https://winstonchurchill.org/publications/finest-hour/finest-hour-170/churchill-and-the-jews/
- http://marcuse.faculty.history.ucsb.edu/classes/33d/projects/1920s/CarlosTreaty.htm
- https://en.wikipedia.org/wiki/Adolf_Hitler_and_vegetarianism
- https://forum.axishistory.com/viewtopic.php?t=93063
- https://en.wikipedia.org/wiki/Herbert_Samuel,_1st_Viscount_Samuel   https://en.wikipedia.org/wiki/Julian_Goldsmid
- https://en.wikipedia.org/wiki/Winston_Churchill
- https://www.jstor.org/stable/j.ctt2jcvm4?turn_away=true
- https://www.austria.org/girl-in-the-whit-dress
- https://translate.google.com/translate?hl=en&sl=de&u=https://de.wikipedia.org/wiki/Hirtenberger&prev=search
- https://www.history.com/news/treaty-of-versailles-provision s
- https://www.loc.gov/law/help/us-treaties/bevans/m-ust000002-0043.pdf
- https://en.wikipedia.org/wiki/Austrian_Civil_War
- https://schoolhistory.co.uk/notes/hitler-and-mussolini/
- https://www.britannica.com/place/Italy/Foreign-policy#ref319058
- https://en.wikipedia.org/wiki/Vehicle_audio
- https://www.wien.gv.at/english/history/commemoration/february-1934.html
- https://www.cambridge.org/core/services/aop-cambridge-core/content/view/9C2F509D140980B3DB46B36D61041DA2/

S0147547900001526a.pdf/div-class-title-the-austrian-civil-war-of-1934-harvard-and-vienna-conferences-div.pdf

- https://en.wikipedia.org/wiki/Emil_Fey
- https://www.jta.org/1934/02/01/archive/pick-major-fey-to-press-war-on-nazis-in-austria
- http://pdfs.jta.org/1934/1934-02-01_2757.pdf?_ga=2.176988453.140457176.1582191154-1025070855.1582191152
- https://api.parliament.uk/historic-hansard/commons/1934/feb/07/inadequate-defences-of-great-britain-and#S5CV0285P0_19340207_HOC_264
- https://en.wikipedia.org/wiki/World_Zionist_Congress
- https://www.globalsecurity.org/military/world/europe/uk-pm3.htm
- https://en.wikipedia.org/wiki/National_Government(1931%E2%80%931935)
- https://en.wikipedia.org/wiki/Winston_Churchill#Warnings_about_Germany_and_the_Abdication_Crisis:_1933%E2%80%931936
- https://en.wikipedia.org/wiki/Ramsay_MacDonald
- http://www.bbc.co.uk/history/historic_figures/macdonald_ramsay.shtml
- https://en.wikipedia.org/wiki/Hermann_Erben
- https://thelifeandtimesofhollywood.com/did-errol-flynns-nazi-pal-convert-him-the-swashbuckling-actor-called-nazi-hermann-erben-the-greatest-influence-on-my-life-but-did-that-mean-that-flynn-too-was-a-nazi-th/
- http://ontheworldmap.com/uk/england/large-detailed-map-of-england.jpg
- https://en.wikipedia.org/wiki/Irving_Asher
- https://en.wikipedia.org/wiki/Chaim_Weizmann#Zionist_activism
- https://en.wikipedia.org/wiki/World_Zionist_Organization
- https://www.britannica.com/biography/Herbert-Louis-Samuel-

1st-Viscount-Samuel

- https://www.jewishvirtuallibrary.org/when-churchill-nearly-met-hitler
- https://www.palmbeachpost.com/article/20110408/ENTERTAINMENT/812034892
- http://adb.anu.edu.au/biography/flynn-errol-leslie-6364
- https://www.christies.com/lotfinder/Lot/flynn-errol-1909-1959-1916720-details.aspx
- https://www.vanityfair.com/news/2010/03/hollywood-wasnt-always-this-boring
- https://nationalpost.com/news/canada/errol-flynn-warts-and-all-how-the-broke-hollywood-film-star-met-his-end-in-vancouver
- https://www.oxfordchabad.org/templates/articlecco_cdo/aid/457389/jewish/Oxford-Jewish-Personalities.htm
- https://www.oxfordchabad.org/search/results.asp?searchWord=Frederick+Lindemann
- https://www.google.com/search?q=how+tall+was+james+cagney+in+feet+and+inches&rlz=1C1GGGE_enAU610AU617&oq=How+tall+was+james+Cagney&aqs=chrome.1.0l7.9904j1j15&sourceid=chrome&ie=UTF-8
- https://www.youtube.com/watch?v=fvZBNSxuSuo&t=729s
- https://www.google.com/search?q=when+was+czechoslovakia+invaded+by+germany&rlz=1C1GGGE_enAU610AU617&oq=When+was+Czechoslovakia&aqs=chrome.4.69i57j0l7.11675j0j15&sourceid=chrome&ie=UTF-8
- https://upload.wikimedia.org/wikipedia/commons/c/c5/Ssnormandie_sideelevation_NYC.png
- https://www.thesaurus.com/
- https://www.uboat.net/ops/convoys/convoys.php
- https://www.famechain.com/family-tree/19477/howard-hughes/hedy-lamarr
- https://play.stan.com.au/programs/1763843/play
- https://content.production.cdn.art19.com/validation=1606128648,4523f32c-62e6-5ce8-8197-496cc931b70d,duU_5xkj-

BJLc5CYkPQu9LDNMlY/episodes/fda62900-2cdc-403d-8b36-79043f216964/0bc1f1744014c71a1c3109f0911134bf8c9579926c77aa41b0c9bd8

- https://www.youtube.com/watch?v=0TqBoua3Rng6dc2510d3af3f26a56024f01556a8fb97057880ebbbbfd0cae6769b6f954e74cd6c772d9a/AI.Smithsonian.Ep04.AD_MASTER.mp3
- https://www.notablebiographies.com/supp/Supplement-Ka-M/Lamarr-Hedy.html
- https://www.imdb.com/name/nm0001443/bio
- https://en.wikipedia.org/wiki/Charles_F._Kettering
- https://en.wikipedia.org/wiki/John_Loder_(actor)
- https://en.wikipedia.org/wiki/Barbara_La_Marr#Health_problems
- https://en.wikipedia.org/wiki/Hughes_Aircraft_Company
- https://en.wikipedia.org/wiki/Howard_Hughes
- Women in tech history: Hedy Lamarr — Hitler, Hollywood, and Wi-Fi | by Jennifer Harrison | Medium
- https://content.production.cdn.art19.com/validation=1606128648,4523f32c-62e6-5ce8-8197-496cc931b70d,duU_5xkj-BJLc5CYkPQu9LDNMlY/episodes/fda62900-2cdc-403d-8b36-79043f216964/0bc1f1744014c71a1c3109f0911134bf8c9579926c77aa41b0c9bd86dc2510d3af3f26a56024f01556a8fb97057880ebbbbfd0cae6769b6f954e74cd6c772d9a/AI.Smithsonian.Ep04.AD_MASTER.mp3
- THE NATIONAL INVENTORS COUNCIL | Science (sciencemag.org)
- Harold G. Bowen Sr. - Wikipedia
- https://en.wikipedia.org/wiki/Glenn_Odekirk#:~:text=Glenn%20Odekirk%20(born%20Waseca%2C%20Minnesota,the%20work%20of%20Hughes%20Aircraft.
- https://en.wikipedia.org/wiki/Clarence_Brown
- https://www.tcm.com/tcmdb/title/92/come-live-with-me#articles-reviews?articleId=62618
- https://en.wikipedia.org/wiki/Adrian_(costume_designer)#Sexual

ity_and_marriage
https://en.wikipedia.org/wiki/Office_of_Scientific_Research_and_Development

- https://www.britannica.com/topic/Office-of-Scientific-Research-and-Development
- https://www.okhistory.org/publications/enc/entry.php?entry=WA021#:~:text=During%20World%20War%20II%20the,the%20Office%20of%20Production%20Management.
- https://www.loc.gov/rr/scitech/trs/trsosrd.html
- https://www.pbs.org/wnet/americanmasters/blog/bombshell-hedy-lamarr-story-pianola-played-part-hedy-lamarrs-invention/
- https://open.spotify.com/album/3QUsZ0RrtZJQVwEzOHgVYe?highlight=spotify:track:3XSVnUd6FyJiA74lfwlJVX
- George Antheil - New World Encyclopedia
- https://www.endocrineweb.com/endocrinology/overview-pituitary-gland
- https://en.wikipedia.org/wiki/Posterior_pituitary#:~:text=The%20posterior%20pituitary%20is%20not,vasopressin)%20directly%20into%20the%20blood.
- https://encyclopedia.ushmm.org/content/en/article/invasion-of-the-soviet-union-june-1941
- https://www.aenigma-images.com/2019/01/hedy-lamarr-beauty-brains-and-bad-judgment/hedy-lamarr-and-sylvia-hollis/
- https://aip.scitation.org/doi/abs/10.1063/1.1715004?journalCode=jap
- Errol Flynn, warts and all: How the broke Hollywood film star met his end in Vancouver | National Post
- https://www.theerrolflynnblog.com/2020/01/12/mail-bag-errol-flynn-in-spain-fighting-for-justice-and-freedom/ Facts and
- Falsehoods: Errol Flynn, The Commie Nazi.
- www.archive.org/details/ErrolFlynnFbiFileVolume4
- Women in tech history: Hedy Lamarr — Hitler, Hollywood, and Wi-Fi | by Jennifer Harrison | Medium
- https://kayfrancisfilms.com/another-dawn-

1937/#:~:text=Production%20began%20September%2026%2C%201936,the%20set%20of%20Another%20Dawn.

- https://en.wikipedia.org/wiki/The_Perfect_Specimen#:~:text=Bl ondell%20was%20cast%20and%20filming%20started%20in%20M ay%201937https://www.pbs.org/wnet/americanmasters/blog/bo mbshell-hedy-lamarr-story-pianola-played-part-hedy-lamarrs-invention/
- https://patents.google.com/patent/US2292387A/en
- https://patentimages.storage.googleapis.com/e0/dd/4e/0e04d56d 1d7604/US2292387.pdf
- https://interferencetechnology.com/spread-spectrum-clock-generation-theory-and-debate
- http://mpegmedia.abc.net.au/rn/podcast/2014/07/ssw_2014070 5_1218.mp3#t=420
- https://www.theguardian.com/culture/1999/jul/29/artsfeatures2 mentions silver matchbox, patent granted 11th. August 1942
- https://en.wikipedia.org/wiki/John_Loder_(actor)
- Hedy Lamarr: An Unknown Genius - Girl Spring
- https://en.wikipedia.org/wiki/Spanish_Civil_War
- Aug. 11, 1942: Actress + Piano Player = New Torpedo | WIRED
- https://drivemag.com/red-calipers/the-most-beautiful-cars-of-the-1940s   https://intelity.com/blog/a-brief-look-at-the-history-of-hotel-technology/#:~:text=1986%20%E2%80%93%20Teledex%20Corp., offer%20HBO%20in%20guest%20rooms.
- https://www.history.navy.mil/research/library/online-reading-room/title-list-alphabetically/b/budget-of-the-us-navy-1794-to-2004.html
- https://en.wikipedia.org/wiki/Donald_Nelson
- https://www.twoway-radio.co.uk/history-of-walkie-talkies#:~:text=The%20walkie%2Dtalkie%20was%20first,system% 20when%20working%20for%20CM%26S.
- https://www.military.com/military-life/heres-what-happened-navys-commodore-

rank.html#:~:text=The%20rank%20of%20commodore%20is,ships%2C%20often%20called%20a%20squadron.

- https://en.wikipedia.org/wiki/Naval_Criminal_Investigative_Service
- https://en.wikipedia.org/wiki/Commander_(United_States)
- https://www.youtube.com/watch?v=NS1Hx_7m7nM
- Errol Flynn Trial: 1943 | Encyclopedia.com
- https://en.wikipedia.org/wiki/Alexander_Pantages
- https://en.wikipedia.org/wiki/Clyde_Tolson
- https://en.wikipedia.org/wiki/Frederick_McEvoy   Was
- Hollywood Actor Errol Flynn a Nazi Spy? | Mysterious Universe
- https://law.jrank.org/pages/2974/Errol-Flynn-Trial-1943.html
- https://oag.ca.gov/history/20warren
- https://en.wikipedia.org/wiki/Jack_L._Warner
- https://en.wikipedia.org/wiki/Ernest_King#:~:text=After%20a%20period%20on%20the,as%20Chief%20of%20Naval%20Operations.
- https://www.latimes.com/archives/la-xpm-1991-04-24-me-495-story.html#:~:text=Email-,William%20L.,He%20was%2081.
- http://benscience1.weebly.com/history.html#:~:text=The%20first%20two%20way%20mirror%2C%20called%20the%20'transparent%20mirror','%20on%20February%2017th%2C%201903.
- https://ntl.nt.gov.au/story/bombing-darwin#:~:text=Often%20called%20'Australia's%20Pearl%20Harbour,destroying%20ships%2C%20buildings%20and%20infrastructure.
- https://en.wikipedia.org/wiki/Clomethiazole#:~:text=Clomethiazole%20(also%20called%20chlormethiazole)%20is,symptoms%20of%20acute%20alcohol%20withdrawal.
- https://www.ncbi.nlm.nih.gov/pmc/articles/PMC2424120/
- https://en.wikipedia.org/wiki/Chloral_hydrate
- https://www.encyclopedia.com/history/educational-magazines/turning-points-allies-begin-win-war

- https://www.bajajdefense.com/statute-of-limitations-for-murder-cases-in california/#:~:text=There%20is%20no%20statute%20of,has%20no%20statute%20of%20limitations.
- https://www.history.com/topics/world-war-ii/nuremberg-trials
- http://www.glamourgirlsofthesilverscreen.com/show/632/Teddy+Stauffer/index.html
- http://www.elantiquario.com/article.cfm?story=3b
- https://www.imdb.com/name/nm0550777/bio?ref_=nm_ov_bio_sm   bio of William Marshall
- https://www.youtube.com/watch?v=uD-xlM_vWwk
- https://peoplepill.com/people/teddy-stauffer/
- https://www.youtube.com/watch?v=ee91Z_JlqpI
- https://www.filmink.com.au/films-errol-flynn-5/
- https://www.imdb.com/title/tt0045499/
- https://pro.imdb.com/name/nm0656627/about Victor Pahlen
- Loves of Three Queens (1954) - Loves of Three Queens (1954) - User Reviews – IMDb
- https://www.sparknotes.com/lit/sun/characters/
- https://www.youtube.com/watch?v=DufU6vvregY
- The Sun Also Rises movie
- https://www.vanityfair.com/news/2008/10/oil_excerpt200810
- When Hedy Lamarr called Houston home - Bayou City History (chron.com)
- https://en.wikipedia.org/wiki/Earl_Conrad
- https://en.wikipedia.org/wiki/My_Wicked,_Wicked_Ways
- https://nla.gov.au/nla.obj-572881794/view?sectionId=nla.obj-576289643&searchTerm=%22beam+ends%22+flynn&partId=nla.obj-572906195#page/n49/mode/1up/search/%22beam+ends%22+flynn
- Too Much, Too Soon - Production & Contact Info | IMDbPro
- The Female Animal - Companies | IMDbPro
- Proud Woman - Production & Contact Info | IMDbPro

- William Howard Lee b. Sep 12, 1908 Texas, USA d. Feb 16, 1981 Houston, Harris county, Texas, USA: MyKindred.com
- Family Histories William Howard Lee & Hedy Lamarr Divorced, Joint Family Tree & History - FameChain
- http://tx.findacase.com/research/wfrmDocViewer.aspx/xq/fac.19620614_0040801.TX.htm/qx
- Hedy Lamarr receives $500,000 in divorce settlement — Calisphere
- https://www.theguardian.com/theguardian/2013/oct/16/errol-flynn-death-obituary-actor
- https://montecristomagazine.com/highlights/errol-flynn-death-vancouver
- http://www.vancouverhistory.ca/archives_flynn.htm#:~:text=The%20actor%20wanted%20to%20know,in%20Hollywood%20the%20following%20week.
- https://www.history.com/news/chamberlain-declares-peace-for-our-time-75-years-ago#:~:text=On%20September%2030%2C%201938%2C%20British,peace%20pact%20with%20Nazi%20Germany.
- https://www.theholocaustexplained.org/life-in-nazi-occupied-europe/foreign-policy-and-the-road-to-war/occupation-of-the-sudetenland/
- Assassination of Julius Caesar – Wikipedia
- United States Naval Research Laboratory
- Wikipediahttps://www.newyorker.com/magazine/2013/09/16/hitler-in-hollywood
- https://en.wikipedia.org/wiki/Joseph_Breen
- https://www.newyorker.com/magazine/2013/09/16/hitler-in-hollywood   https://en.wikipedia.org/wiki/Georg_Gyssling
- https://mppda.flinders.edu.au/people/67
- https://humanities.exeter.ac.uk/media/universityofexeter/collegeofhumanities/history/researchcentres/centreforthestudyofwarstateandsociety/bombing/THE_BOMBING_OF_BRITAIN.pdf

- https://www.newyorker.com/magazine/2013/09/16/hitler-in-hollywood
- https://www.google.com/search?q=when+was+loves+of+three+queens+released+in+italy&rlz=1C1CHZO_enAU900AU903&oq=when+was+loves+of+three+queens+released+in+italy&aqs=chrome..69i57.11404j0j15&sourceid=chrome&ie=UTF-8
- BFI | Film & TV Database | ERROL FLYNN THEATRE (archive.org)

We hope you enjoyed reading this title from:

BLACK ROSE
writing™

Subscribe to our mailing list – *The Rosevine* – and receive **FREE** books, daily deals, and stay current with news about upcoming releases and our hottest authors.
Scan the QR code below to sign up.

Already a subscriber? Please accept a sincere thank you for being a fan of Black Rose Writing authors.

9 781685 131661